The Kuiper Belt Job

THE KUIPER BELT JOB

Book One of the
Cannibal Club Chronicles

David D. Levine

CAEZIK
SF & FANTASY
ARC MANOR
ROCKVILLE, MARYLAND

✳

SHAHID MAHMUD
PUBLISHER

www.caeziksf.com

ISBN: 978-1-64710-090-2

First Edition. First Printing November 2023
1 2 3 4 5 6 7 8 9 10

An imprint of Arc Manor LLC

www.CaezikSF.com

This book is dedicated to Alisa, Amy, Lee, and Cynthia, who were there when I needed them.

CONTENTS

ONE

The Orca Job, Part One

The Cannibal Club—Ten Years Ago

We were seven then, at the end.

There was no "I" in the Cannibal Club, only "us." We were basically one person in seven bodies—Strange, Shweta, Max, Kane, Tai, Alicia, and Damien—and we knew each other like the palms of our own hands. We finished each other's sentences, or more often, didn't even bother speaking ... we just *knew*. After more than two years living in each other's pockets—job after escalating job making us richer and cockier and more certain of what we could pull off with our unique combination of criminal skills—we were at the top of our game and knew it. And the sex was *amazing*.

We didn't think that feeling would ever stop until we were ready to give it up. And the Orca job was supposed to make that possible.

But it didn't work out that way, of course.

Damien's fingers were light and gentle on the thrusters as we approached the station. Our pilot had brush-cut black hair, warm brown folded eyes, and the loudest rainbow batik shirt in the System.

His beloved Alicia, our thief, was right at his shoulder, long red hair tucked under a black watch cap for the job. Both peered ahead at the shifting shadows on Orca's rotating hull, her breath warm on his cheek. He tilted his head to touch her chin with his temple, a gentle skin-to-skin contact standing in for the kiss neither of them had the time or attention for right now, but his eyes never wavered from the target.

Tai, our hacker, was all business, their hands flicking across the controls of their gear—half stolen, half hand-built, mostly illegal, and all their own. Their hair, fashionably cut in an asymmetrical swing, was a shade of purple that perfectly complimented their Vietnamese complexion. "We haven't been spotted yet," they said, "but I can't promise more than another five minutes."

Damien grunted in acknowledgment. Alicia, her concentration fixed on the station ahead, didn't even do that. But Kane, the newest, youngest, and twitchiest member of the Club, glanced to his mentor Max for reassurance. Max gave a little nod to say everything would be okay, then slapped a magnetized card down on the bulkhead between them, not allowing the announcement to interrupt their game of two-handed skat. Max was our muscle, with a wrestler's build; his smooth round face bore long mustachios. Kane was his assistant—long, lean, and sinewy, with a broad nose and tight black curls.

Hiroshi, the accountant who had set this in motion, was not so easily reassured. "Hurry! Hurry!" he whispered under his breath. Though not a member of the Club, he was a good enough guest not to interrupt the professionals at work ... but not so good that he could keep completely quiet. His daughter Miyuki flinched. Clearly, in his tension, he was gripping her shoulders unreasonably hard. But her expression didn't change, and she didn't make a sound.

Hiroshi was a salaryman in a gray suit, indistinguishable from any other member of the species. If he didn't have information useful to us, he'd be beneath notice. Miyuki was a good kid, we thought, smart and well-behaved, but there was something a little ... off about her. Some of us thought she shouldn't even be here, but Hiroshi had insisted. And, to be fair, at nineteen, she was only two years younger than Kane. Her skin was porcelain-smooth, with slick black hair to match.

Shweta, floating beside Hiroshi, laid a reassuring hand on his shoulder, giving him her best warm, motherly look to tell him the situation was well under control, and he visibly relaxed. Inside, she was as terrified as he was—of all of us, she had the worst stage fright before a job and was the most unflappable during one—and with good reason, as she understood the situation better than he did. But effortlessly convincing people of things that weren't true was her special talent. Some of us sometimes wondered if she ever used it on us. Soft and round and smooth, with black hair and eyes, she looked like everyone's favorite auntie.

And behind everyone else, hanging near the aft bulkhead with arms folded across his narrow chest, floated Strange—The Man With The Plan. His gaze took in everything from the station a hundred meters ahead to the readouts on Damien's and Tai's instruments to the cards in Kane's hand. Every bit of information immediately found its place in his memory palace—a fortress built of facts, probabilities, and conjectures floating in the blackness of his mind like the biggest, most complex station ever conceived—and every other piece immediately adjusted itself to accommodate the new input. He had a sallow complexion, a long jaw and nose, and intense blue folded eyes.

Hiroshi's nervousness was no surprise to Strange, nor was Shweta's ease in tamping it down. Even the limited time remaining on the scrambler, which had Tai so concerned, had already been factored into Strange's plan, and in fact, the hatch that they sought was just now rotating into view. If nothing untoward happened in the next three minutes, they would dock there and sync *Contessa's* systems to the station with time to spare. But Kane's cards, and even more importantly Max's—which Strange couldn't see but could deduce from his play—were of concern. Kane was playing badly, his nervousness affecting his judgment, and rather than calling him on it, Max was letting him win. Kane, Strange knew, needed discipline, not indulgence.

But now was not the time to call Max on that. Strange filed the information away in his memory palace for later use. "There's the hatch," he said, his voice laconic and unruffled.

Damien, who hadn't noticed the hatch until Strange pointed it out—Strange noted that slip in his memory palace as well—triggered thrusters to nudge the ship toward it. "Docking in three," he said, and as the thrusters fired, everyone twitched in the air like fish in a sudden current. Alicia gave him a quick kiss on the cheek before moving away; she would be in the first group through the hatch once they docked. Damien smiled but kept his hands on the controls and his eyes ahead.

"What if they see us?" Hiroshi asked Shweta. "I mean, visually?"

"Do you see any windows?" she replied, gesturing. And, indeed, there were none on the outer hull, which was the floor of the lowest level of the rotating station's lifesystem. Who puts windows in a floor? Orca was a station on the "Thor's hammer" plan. The lifesystem formed the curved head, with the fusion plant and other mechanical systems a knob on the other end of the handle. The whole thing rotated around its center of mass, providing Inner Belt standard one-third gee to the inhabitants, and we were approaching the outer surface of the hammer's head.

And even if someone should happen to glance out a window or at a monitor screen, the chance of them spotting us was small. Planet-born people had little appreciation for just how big and empty space is, and how small ships and stations and even asteroids are by comparison. Right up to the last minute of our approach, anyone looking at us with the naked eye could cover the whole ship with their thumb. And as this was such a small station, it operated on a single shift, Ceres Standard Time. So the crew would likely all be asleep, or at their least attentive anyway at this hour.

No, the big danger was not visual but electronic detection, and *Contessa* was well-equipped to evade that. In addition to the scrambler Tai had programmed to evade Orca's systems—based on information provided by Hiroshi—she had countermeasures for the usual passive navigational probes, counterfeit tags to label her as space junk to any active pings, and a signal-deadening conductive-foam outer layer on her hull ... which was, incidentally, flat dead black, further reducing her visibility in the optical frequencies.

When we'd applied that black foam layer—which, for all its advantages, basically meant we would never again be able to dock at any legitimate port—Damien had said we should paint a big skull and crossbones on the ship's belly, and Kane and Tai had enthusiastically concurred. But Strange, Alicia, and Shweta had been opposed, and then Max had thrown in his lot with them, quashing the plan. This had surprised us since Kane and Max were so close, but Max told Kane that sometimes it was better to hide your intentions. We didn't think Kane had taken the lesson to heart.

Thumps of thruster fire echoed through the compartment as Damien brought *Contessa* in contact with the hatch, and with a gentle shudder, the ship's systems mated to the station's. Hiroshi cursed as he fell to the floor, the ship joining in with the station's rotational gravity, but everyone else—including Miyuki, we noted with approval—was either already seated or had positioned themselves appropriately for the change.

Tai's fingers flew across their instruments, caressing the connection to convince the station we were an automated cargo delivery. "Locked on," they said after a tense thirty seconds, and everyone relaxed, especially Hiroshi. But Strange relaxed only fractionally because he knew it was only the first step of twenty-seven.

Alicia and Kane were the first through the airlock. They were wearing Aquila uniforms, not vac suits, which carried some risk but would make moving, manipulating, and evading easier. Shweta, waiting with Tai and Max in the airlock, reported their progress to the rest of us in the cabin. We would have been happier to get a direct report, but everyone on the station had to maintain comm silence to avoid electronic detection.

Kane stuck his head up from the floor hatch into a dark, cold, and smelly loading bay. Also silent, except for the constant whir and rumble of the station's systems and a few creaks as its structure adjusted to *Contessa*'s added mass. After listening for half a minute, he switched on a dim red light. The walls were filthy and scarred; a cargo crane and some hoses and cables swung gently above. Nothing else moved. "Clear," he whispered to Alicia, and gave her a hand up.

The personnel hatch to the rest of the station was secured. This was not completely unheard of, but it was unusual, and corroborated

Hiroshi's information about the station's true purpose. Some of us had been skeptical about his story—Alicia for one extremely so—but an ordinary cargo warehouse wouldn't likely lock its back door, while a clandestine transshipment station for valuable and illegal pharmaceuticals would almost certainly do so. But though the door was locked, it wasn't Alicia-proof. Very, very few locks were.

Alicia edged the hatch open, peering through the crack. Beyond it lay a broad hallway, dimly illuminated, its floor scuffed with tracks leading to several large cargo doors on either side. From a pouch on her belt, she drew a faceted glass sphere the size of a walnut, squeezed it between her fingers, then rolled it down the hall. Five seconds later, it flared white, a flash of optical and other frequencies that would temporarily blind any tech monitoring the space.

Silently, she eased the hatch open just wide enough for her to pass, slipping through and slinking across the floor to a junction box on the wall. As she worked, prying the box open and working with cutters and clips to insinuate Tai's little leech into the station's systems, Kane kept watch from the hatch. "There you go," she whispered as the last connection was made. She checked a small screen at her belt—it showed the hall from four viewpoints, in visual and infrared, with all traces of herself and Kane digitally removed—and nodded. "We have our beachhead."

Kane remained in the hall, warily standing guard, while Alicia returned to the loading bay for Shweta, Tai, and Max. She moved swiftly and quietly because there was no telling who might notice a stray sound from the deck below. But so far, everything seemed to be going according to plan.

We had no idea how wrong we were.

TWO

The Thunderbolt Job

Kane—Present Day

"I'm putting the gang back together," the kid said.

"Right," I said. "Who are you again?"

It wasn't a place or a time I had expected to find a skinny teenage boy wearing faded Ganymede blues, but there he was—floating in the tiny space between my bed and my sink. My quarters were so small that I had had to back into the bed alcove to let him in. I don't do much entertaining.

"I'm Strange's son," he repeated. "Cayce." He pronounced it like "case" but the message he had sent just before he'd arrived spelled it C-A-Y-C-E. Which was, admittedly, exactly the sort of punk-ass name I would have expected Strange to saddle an offspring of his with. Score one point for plausibility, I guess.

"That's nice." Even as we spoke, I was sizing him up. He certainly did look like Strange—the same lean, sinewy frame, the same long jaw and nose—but the kid's black hair had a loose curl, where Strange's had been slick and straight, and the voice was softer, higher. And the eyes were brown, unlike Strange's piercing blue.

Even from the little I'd seen of him so far, I could tell he *moved* like Strange too. Another point. If he'd had any training at all ... well, I hoped it wouldn't come to a fight, not in these tight quarters. Nonetheless, I loosened my shoulders and did a quick mental inventory of the weaponry stashed about my person. And the Jeroboam, of course, was racked on the wall to my right, though I doubted there would be space to use it.

"How old are you?" I continued. "And why have I never heard of you before?"

"Sixteen," the kid—Cayce—said. "I was born on Io. Strange left my mom before I was born, and she didn't tell him about me until much later." He paused, hesitating slightly. "I didn't actually meet him in person until three years ago."

So Cayce had been born five years before I met Strange and didn't meet up with him until after the last time I'd seen him? Score another point for plausibility. "Who's your mom?"

"Her name's Lee. She works in security for one of the big corps."

My eyebrows went up at that. "She and Strange must have gotten along *great*."

"It was ... complicated," he acknowledged. "They didn't know each other well when they first got together and broke up pretty quickly thereafter."

"Is she okay with you being out on your own like this?"

He paused, his mind going elsewhere for a moment, then shook his head. "No. There was ... a big fight. I ran away. She doesn't know where I am."

I nodded, stroking my chin. I could relate. "Why didn't you go to your dad, then?"

"I can't." He took a deep breath, let it out, and looked me straight in the eye ... and those brown eyes were a lot more than sixteen years deep. "He is in serious, serious shit. I have to get him out. I can't do it by myself." He gestured to his own skinny body, raggedy outfit, and empty pockets. "And you and the rest of the Cannibal Club are the only ones I would trust to do it."

"There is no Cannibal Club, kid. Not anymore. That dream died on Orca Station."

"Dreams don't die, Kane. Even when you wake up, the dream is still there."

His sincerity and intensity, not to mention his eloquence, took me aback. "Damn, you really *are* Strange's kid. Did you get that line from him?"

He smirked, the little bastard. "Maybe it's genetic." His taut, skinny frame relaxed in the air, and he folded his arms in a way that was oh, so familiar. "So … are you going to help me, or not?"

"Have you eaten?" I said, matching some of his evasions with one of my own.

"Starving."

Over an early dinner—he wolfed his food like a skinny teenage boy who hadn't eaten in days—Cayce explained how he'd found me. No one else was in the restaurant at that hour, which was good because it cut down on questions.

"By asking around, I found out you were involved in that little altercation on Tardive Station. Chip and Davy—you remember them?—had contacts on Tardive who knew the Rat. And once I knew you were working for the Rat, it wasn't hard to track you here."

Here was a lumpy little Inner Belt rock called Blue Iguana. Once upon a time, it had been a cobalt mine, but that had played out long ago. Now, it was a transshipment point for cargo of variable legality. And Justin Rattner, aka the Rat, was a big wheel in the machine that ran the place. I wasn't exactly part of his inner circle, but when he needed someone to bust a few heads or put pressure on a debtor, he knew he could count on me. "Pretty impressive work for a teenager."

He shrugged. "Dad taught me well."

I tapped my empty beer bulb back and forth between my palms. Back and forth. Back and forth. "So you first met him three years ago, you said. You've been together since then?"

"Not the whole time. It's complicated." He pressed his lips together, shaking his head with a slight, strange smile. "I can tell you this—we spent more than enough time together for me to pick up some of his tricks and tics. More time than *he* would have liked."

"More time than Strange would have liked to spend with a thirteen-year-old boy? As in, more than zero?"

He inclined his head in acknowledgment of the truth. "But even though my existence was a surprise—an unpleasant surprise, to be blunt—he acknowledged his responsibility for bringing me into the world and gave me the support I needed."

I stared at him over my beer bulb as it popped back and forth between my palms. "So what's the job?"

"Prison break." I blinked, but he kept talking. "Dad is being held prisoner by a private concern on a station called Cronos. They can't kill him yet. But when they learn what he knows and what he has done—and they might, just might, be able to get that info out of him if they hang onto him long enough—they surely will kill him, and a lot of other people will suffer as well. Including *you* and all the other Cannibal Club survivors. So we have to act as fast as we can."

"Who's holding him? I can think of a lot of people who might want revenge on the Cannibal Club."

"Company called Turvallis." I didn't know the name. "But they're just managing the station."

I nodded. "What kind of opposition are we likely to face?"

"Heavy. Smart, ruthless, well-funded, determined. That's why I need to get the gang back together. No one else has the chops."

The bulb went back. Forth. Back. Forth. Like my thoughts.

The Cannibal Club *was* dead. The best anyone could do at this point—and even that would be a very tall order—was to reassemble a subset, four out of seven. Five out of seven, if you counted Cayce as a replacement for his dad, which I didn't. That subset *might* have all the necessary skills and motivation … *if* you could get all of us.

There might be other gangs who could do the same job, but it would almost certainly take a while to find and recruit them, and even if you found one, no one else would take on a job this hairy for nothing upfront.

Something about the kid's story felt fishy to me. All my instincts were telling me that the correct response to a take-it-or-leave-it offer is always to leave it.

But I owed Strange my life, many times over. All of us did. And doing odd jobs for the Rat wasn't exactly a shining path to career advancement … more like a filthy dead-end corridor.

I caught the tea bulb with my left hand and stuck out my right. "I'm in," I said.

"Great." The kid's grip was surprisingly strong. "So who do we go after next?"

I didn't hesitate a moment. "Alicia. If we can't get her, the whole thing collapses."

He nodded, but his expression was rueful—matching my own misgivings. "I had been thinking the same. How soon can you go?"

I shrugged. "Just let me get my toothbrush."

"There's just one problem," he said, and he looked abashed. "I … I kind of used up the last of my means getting here. Do you have access to a ship?" The way he said *means* told me that he'd spent something other than cash money, and furthermore that even that well was completely tapped out.

"Not one of my own, no. But I might be able to get the use of one if I ask nicely." By *ask nicely* I meant *call in a substantial favor*, but I did have a few of those in the right places.

I wondered how deep into favor-hock I would get before this operation played itself out completely.

It took me two days to track down my old friend Ellen Marks, who ran a mostly legitimate ship delivery service, and another couple of days after that for her to find a vehicle in her inventory that was heading our way. "It's a rental relocation," she explained to me. "The ship will make the whole run on autopilot. If you keep it immaculate, and resupply the consumables when you get there, no one will care that you were along for the ride."

While we waited for the ship to arrive, the kid pretty much stayed out of my way while I wrapped up my life at Blue Iguana. It was kind of depressing how easy that was.

The ship was a four-place asteroid hopper with a class seven drive and a nominal eight-week range. Her lifesystem consisted of a single not-very-large compartment combining wardroom, kitchen, and cabin, plus four sleeping alcoves and a head. It was clean enough, but to be completely frank, it did have a certain odor. It wasn't easy to maintain a viable lifesystem in a ship that small.

We were headed for Amalthea, Jupiter's third moon. The kid had been pretty insistent that we would find Alicia there, but I couldn't see why a smooth operator like her would pick such a pointless little mining moon. Cayce had finally won me over with the argument that if she wasn't there, she was, at least, very likely to be somewhere in Jupiter space, that being her home territory; Amalthea would provide a good jumping-off point for a search there.

After we'd stowed our stuff, I told the ship we were ready to depart. It undocked itself without further ado and, once it had cleared the bay, headed out at its maximum skip. Our estimated transit time was eight days and ten hours.

The kid winced at that, but I shrugged—no autopilot could navigate the skip like a well-trained human brain. Damien could have done it in less than half the time, but Damien …

Well, Damien wasn't coming back.

Strange was being held on a station called Cronos, run by the private security firm Turvallis. Turvallis was headquartered on Saturn's moon Rhea, and of the couple dozen stations called Cronos in the ship's database, one of them was in polar orbit around Saturn. It was listed as a science station but might actually be Turvallis's private prison.

Turvallis had a Saturn League charter, but the money trail went underground and vanished soon thereafter. My gut told me it led to Earth, but which of that rotting skull of a planet's billions of corps, govs, sects, and clans was responsible was anyone's guess. Not that it really mattered. The Inner Belt had been independent and self-sustaining for over a century, with the Outer Belt and Jupiter Union not much younger; only Martians and Moonies cared about Earth. Earth might be where we all came from, originally, but Earth's economy and politics have as much bearing on most spacers' day-to-day lives as my grandparents' sex lives do on mine. But, like my grandparents, sometimes they do send money.

But Turvallis, secretive as it was, was only performing a service. Who had snagged Strange, who was paying for him to be held on Cronos, and why? All Cayce could say was that the snag had been pretty sophisticated. Strange had been lured to a casino on Enceladus to participate in a long con on a mark from one of the Mars terraforming corps. The offer had seemed legit, and if I knew Strange—and I had thought I did until his never-mentioned-before kid turned up on my doorstep—he would have investigated thoroughly before even approaching. It might even *be* legit. Given the amount of money I was catching the scent of, if they really wanted Strange, I wouldn't put it past the perpetrators of the scheme to set up an actual con for the express purpose of luring him in.

In any case, just as Strange was about to spring the trap, the con had turned inside out. Strange's allies had turned on him, drugged him, and spirited him away, and the next he'd known, he was waking up on a Turvallis shuttle to Cronos.

"How is it that you know all this?" I'd asked the kid, who was speaking without notes.

"Dad managed to smuggle out a message. Private family code."

"And you learned this code … when?"

"After he came back into my and my mom's life, the three of us spent a couple of years together. It was good for a while, but … well, he's not exactly a people person, and I was a pretty rebellious kid. Eventually, the tensions escalated to the point that there was … there was a big blowup." He shook his head with a wry smirk. "I found myself on my own then and discovered he'd already taught me everything I needed to survive. Maybe even more than he'd intended to."

"When was that?"

"Last July."

I kept quiet, considering this assertion. For a sixteen-year-old kid to kick around the deep black solo for more than a year was quite a stretch. I mean, yes, I'd only been nineteen myself when I hooked up with the Cannibal Club. But I hadn't been solo before that. Even after my folks threw me out, I hadn't been completely alone … my uncles and aunties had kept an eye on me.

But he certainly did carry himself like someone who'd waded through a pile of shit already in his short life. And being

Strange's kid would certainly have prepared him for it, in several different ways.

Damn, he did remind me of his dad. It was almost eerie.

Could he be … a clone?

No. Get real.

Cloning isn't that hard—everyone knows where steaks come from, right?—and while cloning humans is illegal in most places, so was just about everything else Strange had ever done. But he didn't look exactly like Strange, and even if he were a clone, he'd still have his own mind and not some creepy duplicate of his clone-parent's. It takes years and years to grow a newborn into a self-sufficient human being—there's no rushing that process—and unless you managed to exactly re-create the circumstances of Strange's childhood, most of which were obscure or in dispute, the result would not be the same person.

But when we were sparring together or playing skat, filling up the long idle hours on the way to Amalthea, I was sometimes surprised to look up and see brown eyes instead of Strange's blue.

I admit it, I was kind of a messed-up kid when I met Strange. A life on the docks, drifting from situation to situation, dodging the law, sleeping in corners sometimes, had made me … not a nice person. Suspicious. Judgmental. Quick to anger. And more than a little violent. But when you were as big and as mean-looking as I was, people were going to think the worst of you no matter what you did. So I used my size, my sneer, and my reputation to intimidate my way out of the situations my temper and inexperience got me into. Even people who didn't know me took one look at my Angry Face and backed down rather than pushed back. And when intimidation didn't work, I used my fists.

I was good at hitting people. I had a lot of experience, had even fought professionally. I was fast—lord, I wish I'd appreciated that while I had it—and strong, and I had a long reach that was even longer than it looked. So there were people who would pay me to hit other people for them. Or to keep other people from hitting them. Or to keep me from hitting them. Sometimes it got kind of complicated, with everyone paying someone else to hit or not hit, but I didn't care about the details … whoever had paid me the most, or the most recently, would tell me what to do and I would do it. It covered my bunk, food, and oxygen with a little left over for booze and ammo, and, to be frank, I enjoyed it. To go up against another person, meat and bone and skin slamming against each other with nothing held back, was a challenge and a thrill beyond words. Even the pain after was worth it because it showed I was still alive.

But although I was alive, I was … I don't know, not really a *person* back then. I had no loyalty to anyone or anything. I didn't care who I hurt; in fact, I got a thrill out of hurting people, and not just with my fists. I could be a real asshole to people who trusted me. Usually, I didn't realize just how much trouble I was creating for myself, but even when I did, I just didn't care. I acted in the moment, just for the joy of breaking things and stirring up shit.

And so I broke a lot of things and stirred up a lot of shit. And it kept biting me in the ass. I got thrown out of more than a few bars, and more than once, came damn close to getting thrown out of an airlock. I accumulated scars and enemies and grudges even faster than I collected knives. And when I figured out I'd made the air in my vicinity too foul to breathe, again, I'd just hop a freight to another dock or another station and start over.

It was Strange who stopped the cycle.

I met up with him in a bar on Titan. The barkeep there owed me a favor, so I came to her when I'd gotten pretty badly cut in a fight. I stumbled in the front door with my hand pressed to a bloody gash over my left eye, and she hustled me into the back room and left me there with a clean rag, a disinfectant patch, a bandage, and a shot of whisky. After I'd patched the cut and downed the whisky, while I was cleaning myself up, I realized I was being watched. A skinny guy with long black hair was leaning nonchalantly against the kitchen door frame. I hadn't heard him come in.

"That's a pretty nasty cut," the man said. He had an Outer Belt accent and showed the typical Outer Belt mixed heritage: his eyes had those Asian folds but the irises were a startling light blue. Mid-thirties? I figured I could take him if I had to, but even then, I was beginning to catch on that just because a guy was older didn't mean he'd be a pushover in a fight … far from it. In fact, the way this guy moved told me that his experience might make him a very dangerous opponent.

"I've had worse," I muttered in a leave-me-alone tone, continuing to swab the blood away. It was *everywhere*.

"You missed a spot." He stepped closer and held out a hand toward the rag, making it a request with a tilt of his head. Under any other circumstances, I would have taken that as a threat—being approached by a stranger when I was already injured—but this guy moved so calmly and was so clear in his intentions that he wasn't threatening. It was a skill I wouldn't learn until *much* later.

I tossed him the rag with a grunt, then turned my head at his gesture. He wiped behind my ear with a surprisingly gentle touch. I barely even flinched.

"Lotta scars here," he observed in a tone somewhere between sympathy and admiration.

"Yeah," I admitted, "but I won this fight, and most of those other ones too."

"Hard to call it a 'win' when you lose this much blood."

"I walked away. He didn't."

He paused and looked me right in the eye. "Sometimes the one who doesn't walk away is the winner in the long run. Did he have friends?"

"I don't know and I don't care. He got in my way."

He crossed his arms on his narrow chest and regarded me very seriously. "You knocked a man down so hard he couldn't get up *because he got in your way?*"

I glared back. "Are *you* getting in my way?"

"I don't know. Am I?" His balance shifted. It was a very subtle movement and a lot of guys wouldn't even have noticed, but I knew—and he knew I knew—that he was readying himself for action, if action became necessary. I didn't know his moves, and he was standing above me, fresh and uninjured.

I consciously relaxed my Angry Face. It wasn't easy. "All I want is to be left alone."

"Are you sure about that? Because alone kind of sucks."

I snorted. "What do you know about it?"

"I know you washed out of the refinery trainee program. I know you're sleeping under dock four and dodging the oxy tax. I know you have a bad rep and you don't have many friends here."

I felt the Angry Face come back, and my shoulders tensed. My fresh cut throbbed under its bandage. "You been watching me?"

He stepped back, shrugged nonchalantly. "Not personally, no. But I have friends … friends who like to know things. It's good to have friends."

"Easy for you to say." I meant it as a dismissal but it came out kind of plaintive.

Without taking his gaze off me, he pulled a box away from the wall and sat down on it, putting himself at my eye level. "It *is* good to have friends," he repeated. "I'm part of a … well, we call it a club. It's a pretty exclusive club. Mostly we're in it for ourselves, but sometimes we do odd jobs for people. And we have a job coming up that needs an extra person. A person with your particular skill set. We asked around, and your name kept coming up."

"I guess I do have a few friends after all, then."

He grinned sardonically. "I didn't say what else they said when they mentioned your name. But, all in all, you seem to be the person we need."

I looked him up and down. He was almost twice my age, but now that I knew him a little better, I *really* didn't want to go up against him in a fight. "I don't think I have anything you need."

He leaned in just a bit, lowered his head, and showed his teeth. "I'm too *gentle* for this job." He handed me the rag.

"Oh." I cleaned my hands, working the dried blood out from under my fingernails. Not all of it was mine. "I … I see." I lowered the rag and looked him in the eye. "How much?"

"Five thousand Titan dollars, plus one-sixth of the take if there is any."

I wasn't good with fractions, but that seemed like a pretty damn big cut for a nineteen-year-old kid with big fists and a short temper. "How many in this … club?"

"Five, at the moment. We split everything even-steven."

"Even-steven." I rolled that around my mouth. I liked the taste of it, even mixed with a little blood. What did I have to lose? I stuck out my hand. "I'm in."

17

He took it, and his grip communicated both the considerable strength of his hands and how much control he had over it. "My name's Strange. Welcome to the Cannibal Club."

On the fifth day out of Blue Iguana, I was cleaning myself up and ran out of wet wipes. I put a towel around myself, entered the wardroom for some more, and found Cayce in deep concentration at the nav scanner. He immediately blanked the display and turned away from it, but it was clear he hadn't been expecting the interruption. "Since when are you a navigator?" I said.

"I know a lot of things," he said, carefully neutral.

Before he blanked the screen, I had seen a bright dot on the midrange display. "What do you know about *that*?" I said, gesturing at the black screen where the dot had been.

"It's …" He blew out a breath. "Someone's following us."

I folded my arms across my chest. "How long have you known this? And why didn't the ship tell us about it?"

"I muted the notifications." His gaze was an accusation, as if *I* were the one who had been holding things back.

"Now why the fuck would you do a thing like that?" The air in the little space suddenly felt cold, and it wasn't just because I was only wearing a towel.

"I didn't want to worry you. I was hoping it was just a coincidence. But I shifted course yesterday and they just changed heading to match."

"You changed our *course*!?"

"Just a little. Just to check."

So many questions. But the one that came out first was "Who are they?"

Again he blew out a breath, and his narrow shoulders slumped. "Turvallis, I think."

I tightened the towel around my waist. "You think."

"I've been keeping one step ahead of them for a while."

My first impulse was to throttle him, but he was only a kid. Ten years ago, that wouldn't have even slowed me down, but I'm a lot more mellow now than I was then, and besides, he was *Strange's* kid.

"For a while," I said after I'd calmed myself down a bit. "How long is 'a while,' and when were you planning on telling me?"

"I think they've been tracking me since I left Cronos. I was going to tell you all the details after we got the whole gang together."

This was getting surreal. "You were at *Cronos?*" I shouted.

"I ... I left my dad there." His expression was unreadable. "I'm not proud of how it went."

Which wasn't an answer, but there wasn't time to go into details. I took in a deep, calming breath, then let it out slowly. "Okay. So what are we going to do about it? This rental isn't exactly a battle cruiser."

"Well, I'm pretty certain *you* aren't unarmed. From what Dad told me."

"That's true, but I didn't anticipate we'd have to fight off a boarding party." I looked at the control board, then back to Cayce. "You didn't lock me out of any command functions, did you?"

"That would have been foolish."

Which, again, wasn't exactly an answer, but it would have to do for now.

There was only one vessel in our vicinity, a light hauler registered to Delirium Salvage out of Ceres—which meant nothing. An outfit like Turvallis wouldn't announce themselves. It would intercept us in nineteen hours if no one changed course. Class ten drive, overpowered for its registered dry mass of eighteen tonnes. And its radiation signatures and mass profile suggested that it was armed with cannon firing depleted uranium slugs.

"We can't outrun them or outfight them," I told Cayce, though it was clear from his expression that he already knew that.

"So we'll have to outsmart them," he said in a matter-of-fact, just-like-his-dad tone.

Two of them came over from the Turvallis ship, bringing with them the chill and the vague metallic smell of vacuum. They didn't remove their helmets, which didn't surprise me.

"You shouldn't be storing gear in the airlock," the first one said, his voice made even harsher and more inhuman by the cheap speaker in his helmet. He kicked a floating duffel bag aside.

"Shit, I forgot about that. It's some dockside clothing." I gestured around the tiny space. "Not a lot of room to spare in here."

"If we were the law," said the other one, "we'd have to write you up for a safety violation." The distorted voice sounded female.

"But you aren't the law, are you?" Despite my pounding heart, I kept my tone neutral, almost pleasant. I wouldn't have been able to do that before I met Strange.

"No, we are not." But though her tone too was neutral, she kept her suit's right forearm, with its twin muzzles, pointed nonchalantly but unwaveringly in my direction. Standard load for this type of suit would be an aluminum crosspoint slug, lethal but offering limited risk of holing the hull. Outside the forward window, her ship, with an unknown number of other crew on board, hung in a matched orbit with its own projectile muzzles showing round and black and aimed directly at us.

The silence went on. She didn't say who she was, if not the law. I let that slide; pressing the issue would get me nothing except possibly shot. "So … what's the occasion for this lovely visit?" Over comm, they had been brusque and uninformative: prepare for boarding or be destroyed.

"We are looking for a fugitive," the male boarder said. Cayce's picture appeared in the air between us. "Sixteen-year-old boy, black hair, brown eyes, slim build." He held up a hand at Cayce's height, relative to his own feet, which floated a half-meter above the deck. "About yea high."

"Haven't seen any such."

"We know he left Steeljack Station headed for Blue Iguana," the boarder continued, "and you departed Blue Iguana about a week after he would have arrived. Not many others did. You're *sure* you don't recognize him?"

I made a show of considering the image, sucking on my teeth and clucking my tongue to cover my nervousness. I've never been a very good liar—it was usually easier to just punch my way out of any situation where lying might otherwise help. "Nope," I said. "Sorry."

"You don't mind if we look around, I hope?" said the female boarder. Her tone was cordial on the outside, solid ice on the inside, like some kind of poisonous frozen dessert.

"Be my guest." I gestured around the wardroom, where the two suited figures and I made a decent crowd. "Won't take long."

It wouldn't have taken nearly as long as it did if they hadn't been so thorough. They made me open the deck plates, the storage bins, and the access panels under the control console, and even the clean-out port behind the head, which was just as nasty as you'd expect. They looked everywhere within the pressure hull that might have accommodated a skinny sixteen-year-old who was desperate not to be found, and several places even smaller than that. They even opened up each of the emergency vac suits—all four were fully provisioned and stowed in the proper places—to check that no one was hiding inside and that no one had taken one to hide on the outside of the ship.

They didn't say anything about the guns, or the knives, or the other things. Further proof, if any were needed, that they were not the law.

"Well," the female finally admitted, "I guess you're clean." She sounded disappointed.

"Told you."

The two of them looked at each other, conversing via comm. I could hear their voices through their helmets but couldn't make out the words. Finally, the male turned to me. "All right, we'll let you go. But if you see that kid … we are prepared to be extremely generous. And no questions asked." He flicked a finger at me and my pocket comm vibrated, indicating it had accepted his contact info.

"Aren't you going to help me put this stuff away?" I gestured to the large amount of gear they'd left floating around. At least they hadn't damaged the rental.

"No." And with that they turned and left.

Before the inner airlock door closed, the female pointed to the duffel still floating within and said, "You seriously shouldn't store stuff in the lock, you know. It really is a safety issue."

I didn't turn from where I was trying to cram a box of crackers back into the galley. "Yeah, yeah, whatever." I waved at her over my shoulder to scram. "Once I get everything else put away."

They closed and cycled the lock, exposing the duffel to vacuum for the second time. I waited a count of sixty before moving to the lock—being careful to note what could and could not be seen from outside through the forward window—and refilling the lock with air.

I unzipped the duffel to find Cayce trembling with cold but still breathing. He was folded up tight, his skinny limbs belted into a package smaller than I'd imagined a living human body could make, wrapped in two layers of airtight storage bag with more belts on the outside to keep it from ballooning, and with an oxygen mask and tank from the medical kit strapped to his face. It was an insane plan—there were at least eight ways he could have died, and it must have been mighty uncomfortable, not to mention terrifying—but it was his idea, and when the time had come, he'd gotten into the bag without hesitation.

I gave him a squeeze bulb of hot tea. "You'll have to stay in the lock until they're beyond visual range," I said.

He nodded, still shivering. The whites of his eyes had gone almost entirely red from the pressure drop, and the tip of his nose was white from cold, maybe even frostbitten. But he didn't say a word. He just gave a weak smile and raised the bulb to me in salute.

"You are one tough cookie," I said, and returned to packing the scattered equipment away.

It would be several more hours, at least, before we could be sure they weren't still watching us, and blanking the windows would be suspicious.

Once we were in the clear, the Turvallis ship arcing away under full skip and Cayce's limbs chafed into something resembling a normal range of motion, I let him have what I'd been holding back. "What the *hell* were you thinking? Why didn't you tell me you were being followed?"

"You wouldn't have helped me," he said, doing his teenage best to feign nonchalance.

"Damn right I wouldn't have!" I turned away, struggling to get myself under control.

Cayce *was* just like his dad. Strange had always held his cards close to his chest, but—damn him—it had almost always worked out in the end.

But Cayce wasn't Strange. He was just a kid.

I turned back to Cayce. "Why should I trust you? You've brought danger literally to my airlock."

His brown eyes were steady on mine. "Because Strange is in trouble, and we are the only ones who can, or would, help him."

And damn if he wasn't right.

Amalthea was one of those little moons that might as well be a station or an asteroid, for all the mass it had. Gravity was much less than one percent, amounting to little more than a slight downward drift that was just enough to trip up people accustomed to zero gee—who were used to being able to release objects in midair and have them stay there—but not enough to avoid the health effects of microgravity. And it was deep in Jupiter's radiation belts, which made it a poor prospect for a long-term stay. I could practically feel the high-energy particles sleeting through my body, doing God knows what kind of damage.

But the view was spectacular. Jupiter more than filled the forward window, a swirling, hypnotic maelstrom of golds and browns that seemed to move *almost* fast enough for you to catch the motion with the naked eye. Even if you moved up close to the plex, it nearly filled your field of view. If you looked right at the center of the planet, there was just a thin ring of black at the edges of your peripheral vision.

After we docked at Amalthea and restocked the ship's consumables, it was with great reluctance that I released it to the rental company. I didn't like not having a getaway vehicle, but there was no help for it. When the time came to depart, we'd just have to find another way.

The dock area was slick and carpeted, all white and soothing pale shades—though the slight smell of sulfur from the moon's surface could not be completely eradicated—but after we passed through inspection, Amalthea showed its true colors. As we exited the last inspection station, a few people in fashionable business attire peeled off to the left, following signs for the dock level's hotels and meeting facilities, but the majority of the arriving travelers were wearing work clothes, like us, and continued down a broad corridor to the elevator banks.

A rock with as little gravity as Amalthea usually doesn't bother with elevators; you can jump up or down levels just as easily as you can traverse a corridor. But Amalthea was a mining moon and most of the action was near the core, both because that was where the interesting metals like nickel and molybdenum were and because that was where you could be comparatively safe from Jupiter's radiation without spending a fortune on active shielding.

We followed the green Number Six guideline to an enormous circular room with walls and ceiling and floor of scarred filthy plastic, lit by flickering ancient light bars. It was already seemingly packed with people and equipment when we arrived, but the attendants kept shuffling folks in, and those already inside, left with little other choice, shifted to accommodate them. Cayce and I wound up crammed in between a couple of battered shipping crates and a gang of roustabouts who chattered among themselves in some language I didn't recognize.

As the doors closed, an automated voice requested in three languages that we orient ourselves with our heads *down*, which didn't make sense to me until the horn sounded and the elevator started down, gradually building up speed until the upward acceleration was five or ten times greater than the moon's tiny gravity pull. Small objects clattered gently on the ceiling, and most folks settled themselves on that surface or atop something secured to it.

The descent to the core—which felt like an ascent for the first half—took an hour and a half. There wasn't a magnetic surface to play skat, and after eight days together in the rental ship, we were pretty well talked out. I dozed, mostly. Cayce read something on his pocket comm. At the halfway point of the trip, the horn sounded again, and everyone flipped head-to-feet for the remaining forty-five minutes, at the end of which the doors opened and everyone tried to exit the car at once. Cayce sussed out the situation and just stayed where he was, still reading, until the crowds cleared and the cargo handlers came in for the big crates.

We drifted out at the tail end of the crowd, which quickly scattered down the corridors and tunnels leading off in every direction from the elevator station. Here, at the moonlet's core, there was even less gravity than there had been near the surface, and people followed guidelines, caromed off the walls, or floundered around in midair, depending on their skill level and familiarity with the area. Unlike the surface-level dock facility, which was built with a pretty strong sense of up and down despite the microgravity, these working levels were all pragmatism—the directions of the tunnels followed the ore deposits, and there were hardly any right angles and no consistent "up." In fact, most of the directional signs painted on the walls were lettered to be easily read from two or more orientations.

"Where are we even going to start?" I asked Cayce, staring at the elevator station's orientation map. Even a holographic map was barely able to convey a sense of the moon's labyrinthine tunnel structure, which had evolved pretty much at random over the seventy-something years of its history as an inhabited world.

"There," Cayce said, poking a finger into a large yellow blob near the center of the map. I squinted and read the label: THUNDER-BOLT CASINO.

Of course.

It was a story told over and over again in human history: when miners struck it rich, suddenly finding themselves with a huge pile of cash and a long way from any place civilized to spend it, they started gambling. Amalthea had been a gambling hub nearly as long as it had been a mining facility. And the Thunderbolt, built in the cavity left behind by the old Big Moly molybdenum mine, was the largest, richest microgravity casino in the entire solar system. There were bigger and fancier casinos on planets and on the major stations with spin gravity, but if you wanted to play spherette— which had been invented here—or bet on zero-gee jai alai, there was no better place to go.

"If she's here for a job," I said, rubbing my chin, "she'll have made herself hard to find."

"It won't be easy," Cayce acknowledged. "But I have a few ideas. We'll take a room here." He pointed to an arc of hotels that nestled up close to the casino, places with names like MOLY MILLIONS and BIG STRIKE and JOVE'S PALACE. The curving corridor that connected them to the casino was labeled Golden Way.

"Those sound expensive."

"They are. But if she's here for a job, whether it's a con or a heist, she'll be where the money is."

I looked askance at him. We'd already established that he was pretty much completely tapped out. "You think working for the Rat comes with a retirement savings plan?" I snorted.

He stared back at me, those brown eyes somehow looking just as sharp as his dad's blue ones. "No, Dad told me all about your habits. But I think you've saved *some* of it."

"Ammo doesn't come cheap," I muttered, "but I do indeed have a little saved up."

"Takes money to make money," he said, and tugged the shoulder straps on his bag a little tighter. "Come on. The sooner we get started, the sooner we'll find her."

After dropping off our bags at the Cloud Tops Inn—the second-cheapest hotel on Golden Way—we made our way to the casino floor. It wasn't hard to find; in fact, it would have taken considerable effort to avoid it. Not only did all the rapid transit options and draglines lead directly to the casino, it seemed to me that even the air currents in the vicinity led inward. "You're not just being paranoid," Cayce said when I muttered this suspicion. "They really do arrange the air intake to draw people in. And did you notice that the incoming air is scented?"

I had not, which reminded me of other threats that I might have overlooked. I started to pat my pocket, to make sure my comm was still there, but the more rational part of my mind checked the action, which would be a sure signal to pickpockets. But far more vulnerable than anything physical on my person were my data and my money, which the casino itself was designed to extract as rapidly and efficiently as possible. The casino entrance wouldn't even open for us until we'd enabled location tracking on our comms and access to our public financial records. "We need this information to serve you better," the perky animated welcome host insisted.

Given what I knew about Cayce's parlous financial situation, I was actually a little surprised when he opened his records without hesitation, and even more surprised when the casino let him in. "You don't think I gave them my real info?" he said mildly when I asked him about it.

It didn't occur to me until later that he was not actually old enough to gamble.

Once we made it through the garishly lit, perfume-scented entrance and past the rows of little shops just inside it, the casino floor itself spread out before us like Ceres Main on Christmas Eve. A dark and enormous space, its walls invisible in the distance, it was filled with dozens of floating stations, each outlined with colored pinlights and spewing its particular sounds and scents into the air between. Each major station provided a different game—slots, cards, jai alai, spherette, you name it—with minor stations in between offering food, drinks, drugs, and sex. The air was crowded with yammering gamblers, many tumbling randomly and laughing in inebriated glee, and between the rattle of the spherette balls and the bells of the slot machines, you could barely hear yourself think.

When I was a kid on the docks, who had never seen anything farther away than the end of a corridor, this was what I imagined the Belt outside the station walls looked like. It turned out to be a lot bigger, a lot emptier, and a lot more deadly than I'd thought. But it did contain noisy, crowded, brightly lit spaces like this … and they were even deadlier, in their own ways.

"Where to?" I asked Cayce.

"Follow the money," he said, and grabbed onto a guideline leading to the spherette station.

Even though most gamblers at the Thunderbolt spend most of their time and money on pedestrian games identical to their planet-side equivalents, give or take a few magnetic cards and foot restraints, spherette was the emblematic game of microgravity gambling. It was a high-stakes game, which drew the kind of classy clientele who attracted publicity, so the spherette station was big, bright, and right in the middle of the action.

It also had its own bouncers, who stopped us as we approached. We weren't dressed like the other players, not even remotely, and I was legitimately afraid they wouldn't let us through. But though one of them looked from me to his handheld and frowned skeptically, the other examined Cayce's data and waved us both through with a polite microgravity bow. If you're going to lie about your finances, I guess you should lie big.

Each of the spherette tables was a flat ring, like Saturn's, around a two-meter transparent sphere studded with numbered magnets. Inside the sphere, a little railgun fired a steel marble, which whizzed and rattled around the inside surface, pulled this way and that by the magnets, until it slowed, orbited, and finally came to a trembling halt on the surface of one. I couldn't imagine how such a complicated system could possibly be truly random, but as we watched, Cayce explained that the unfairness of the mechanism was part of the game. "Of *course* the game is rigged," he said as though explaining that water is wet. "But everyone knows it, and they tweak the magnets every night so it's always rigged *differently*. The experienced players are watching the croupiers, not the ball. And the inexperienced players are funding the whole enterprise."

We accepted free drinks—nothing in a casino is ever truly free, of course, but we didn't have to pay cash for them right then—and settled in to watch the action. Cayce gave every indication of keeping his attention focused on our table's spherette ball, but I could tell that he was actually looking everywhere but. Was that something his dad had taught him, or was it genetic? As for myself, I didn't have that talent, but I did my job, which was to watch out for anyone who might be a threat to Cayce.

I wasn't the only one doing so. As I scoped out the space, I noticed many other bodyguard/client pairs or triads. Some of them were even doing a camouflage thing, where the muscle was better dressed and betting more flamboyantly, while the client faded into the background with quiet, sizable wagers. The croupiers knew who was who, of course—the clients got the top-drawer booze, while the bodyguards got colored water—but it was an effective strategy against run-of-the-mill thugs and swindlers.

One or two of the bodyguards noticed me checking them out, and acknowledged my attention with a nod of professional courtesy or a hostile glare. I factored those attitudes into my assessment of the situation, keeping in mind who would be more likely to lash out in attack, and who would just hustle their client away, if anything unexpected happened. And which ones were armed. I wondered how they'd managed that, what with the weapons scanners at the casino door and all.

Even with the big money wandering around, I noticed that the waitstaff were giving us more than our share of attention ... and the free drinks had stopped coming. Fooling a credit check was one thing, but betting required actual money, which we didn't have. Cayce had been doing a good job placing small bets, playing the role of an experienced gambler just scoping the game out, but that was a ruse that couldn't go on forever.

I leaned in close to Cayce. "They're getting impatient."

Cayce grimaced. "Yeah. We'll have to come back again tomorrow."

I assessed the expressions on the waitstaff. Some of them were armed too. "That may not be an option. They've sussed us out quicker than I'd hoped."

Cayce's frustration was evident. He had his dad's instincts but not his control. "Well, we'd best not wear out our welcome any more than necessary." He gathered up his few betting tokens and waved for an attendant to cash them out.

The staff kept a sharp eye on us until we were well away from the spherette station. "What have you learned so far?" I asked Cayce as we drifted along a guideline toward the exit.

"Damn little. I'm not seeing any signs of infiltration or any cons in progress, and I think I know Alicia well eno—" He fell silent, stopping himself dead with a hand on the line, looking off to one side.

I grabbed the line and reversed myself, all senses on high alert, wishing I had more than the little plastic belt knife I'd managed to sneak past the entrance detectors. But as I followed Cayce's glance, I didn't see the threat I'd expected but ...

Alicia. We'd come right past her on the way in an\\\\\\\\\\\d hadn't noticed her at all.

No surprise, really. She didn't much look like herself.

The years hadn't been kind. She was thin and wan, with hollow-looking eyes. Her long red hair had gone straw-colored and straw-textured and was pulled back in a severe ponytail. Frown lines were etched into her forehead, her eyes, and the corners of her mouth.

She was dealing blackjack, the magnetic cards flipping from her fingers with meticulous care.

"An inside job," I muttered. "Or some kind of long con. I should have expected."

"That was never her style," Cayce countered. "She was always more direct."

"It's been ten years. People change." But though Alicia had lost some of her looks, her situational awareness was just as sharp as ever, and she noticed us almost as soon as we'd noticed her. Her eyes snapped wide, looking straight at me, and the cards in her hands paused and trembled.

But only for a moment. She finished dealing and, as soon as her hand was empty, she sent a fast hard gesture toward us: *later*. Even though I hadn't seen one of the Cannibal Club's hand signs in ten years, I would never forget them.

"She says 'later,'" I told Cayce as I grabbed the line to resume our journey.

Cayce was already on the move. "Got it."

We made our way back to the entrance as nonchalantly as possible. I saw no sign that the staff had noticed our hesitation or its cause, but there were always cameras you couldn't see. We didn't pause or converse until we'd reclaimed our bags and were well outside the casino.

"So now what?" I asked as we took a trolley-cab down the broad commercial way that led to our lodgings.

"I'll open a blind box on the local net under the name Zephyr Sedgwick-Foxley."

I smiled to myself at the memories that name evoked. "Did your dad tell you who that was? Damien and Alicia's pet turtle."

Cayce looked sidewise at me. "Tortoise. And he was Strange's before he took up with Alicia. But she loved Zeph so much that Strange left him with her and Damien when he broke up with them. That was before you joined the Club."

"I see." But I didn't see, not really. "So what happens with this blind box?"

"If she's open to further contact, she'll see it and leave a message there."

"And if she's not?"

He blew out a breath. "Then we'll have to see if we can get along without her. But I'd rather not."

But she did respond, and the next day, we found ourselves waiting in a crowded, noisy diner in a low-rent district much closer to the surface than the casino. My skin itched at the thought of the radiation zipping through me, even though I knew there were still over fifty kilometers of ice and rock between us and Jupiter.

"Not like Alicia to pick such a third-rate joint for a rendezvous," I muttered, holding my drink bulb up to the light. The plastic was hazy from too many passes through the washer.

Cayce sat with his back to a wall, peering in all directions. "Well, if she doesn't want to be found ..."

I knew the rest of that quote. If you don't want to be found, move somewhere no one knows you and take a job you hate. But I couldn't imagine Alicia, who always landed on her feet, being reduced to that. Her presence at Amalthea had to be part of some scheme, con, or operation.

"There she is." Cayce did not point.

Alicia floated just inside the entrance, looking around while trying not to appear so. Her hair was hidden under a knit cap, and her eyes by dark glasses, which given the dive's uneven lighting, must have made it hard for her to see. Her clothing, too, had clearly been selected for anonymity, which was as much like Alicia's usual casual elegance as this hole was like her typical haunts.

Cayce put a hand on my wrist. I'd been about to wave. "Wait," he said.

We waited. Eventually, she took off the glasses and spotted us. Catching my eye, she acknowledged my presence with an upward jerk of her chin, then gestured. It was more Cannibal Club hand sign: *Outside. To the left. Fifty meters. Five minutes.*

I repeated the message back to verify I'd gotten it. She nodded and left the joint.

"She says to meet her outside in five minutes."

"Thanks, but I caught that. Dad taught me the code."

I blinked. "*How* long were you together?"

He seemed taken aback by the question. "I guess I'm a quick study?"

We finished our drinks, paid, and made our way out of the place. Fifty meters or so to the left was a derelict storefront, dark and densely grimed with graffiti. But a playing card had been jammed in the front door's lock—it was fresh and white, the ace of spades from a Thunderbolt blackjack deck—and, after checking for observers, we let ourselves inside.

Alicia floated within, her back to the counter and a small but efficient pistol aimed right at us. To my surprise, the muzzle shook slightly. I'd never before known her to display any nervousness whatsoever. "Come inside," she said in a neutral tone, "and close the door quietly behind you."

We slipped inside and raised our hands. "Nice to see you too," I said.

"Who's the kid? He looks ... familiar."

"I'm Strange's son," the kid replied. "The name's Cayce."

Alicia gave Cayce a long hard look, then slipped the weapon away. "All right." But she didn't take her eye off of him. "Where's Strange?"

"He's being held prisoner on a station called Cronos." He pulled himself to his full height—trying to look more adult. "I'm putting the gang back together to break him out."

The expression on her face was difficult to read, and probably would have been even if the light hadn't been so bad. I knew that she and Strange had been lovers once. The affair had ended amicably enough, and they'd continued to work together until Orca Station ... but what had happened there certainly did not presage a happy reunion. "I'm listening," she said.

Cayce gave her a quick summary of what he'd told me, and she asked the same sorts of questions I had, plus a few I hadn't. Including "So what made you think I'd go along with this harebrained scheme?"

"I was hoping you'd do it for Strange."

She snorted. "Your dad might have given you an unreasonably optimistic assessment of the state of our relationship."

Cayce's face fell at that, and I reached in to try to salvage the situation. "The kid's harebrained scheme is better than whatever you've got going here," I said, gesturing around the deserted shop. It had once been a jewelry store, I think. The signage was all in

Chinese, but the little display stands remaining in a few of the cracked and dusty display cases looked like they'd been intended for earrings and necklaces.

"I'm doing all right here," Alicia retorted defensively, but I could tell I'd struck a nerve.

"I don't think you are," I said. "Are you planning a heist? Running a con? Or are you just dealing cards?"

"I've ... I've got plans." Her gaze drifted to the floor. She wasn't the confident, self-assured thief I'd known ten years ago.

"You're just *hiding* here," Cayce said.

"What do *you* know?" she spat back, thrusting her chin forward. "You're just a kid!"

"Dad told me all about you. The Alicia he described wouldn't just crawl into a hole like Amalthea to die. What are you afraid of?"

She kept up the front for a moment longer before letting out a breath, allowing her spine to curve into the forward bend an unconscious body takes in free fall. "I'm afraid ... I'm afraid of being useless. I'm afraid you'll be disappointed in me."

"Nothing could make me disappointed in you," I said. And Cayce reached out to touch her shoulder with more tenderness than I would have thought possible from a teenage boy.

But that tenderness only seemed to enrage Alicia further. "Look at me!" she shouted suddenly, slapping Cayce's hand away and gesturing down at the length of her body. I saw a frame that had once been alluringly slim now uncomfortably close to gaunt. The hands that emerged from her threadbare cuffs had wrinkles, swollen knuckles, and prominent veins and tendons, and they trembled slightly. The back was bent, even more than the usual free-fall curve. And the feet in their Thunderbolt black and yellow socks were curled like claws.

"So you're sick," I said. "That's no fault of yours."

"I'm more than *sick*," she said in a disgusted, half-despairing tone. "I'm *broken*."

I waved at my own body, at the scars and contusions and broken bones that Alicia and I both knew were there. "I've been broken too. But what's broken can be fixed."

Her response to that was a derisive snort. "Not always."

"So what's the problem?" I asked.

"Early-onset Parkinson's," Alicia replied in a flat, diagnostic tone.

"Parkinson's is curable," Cayce replied, equally flat.

"It is. And the treatment is ninety-three percent effective. Which sucks if you're in the seven percent."

I didn't get it at first—math isn't my strong suit—but Cayce's eyes widened immediately. "Oh shit," he said. And then I got it too.

"So you got dealt a bad hand," I said. "That doesn't mean you just ... give up! Damien wouldn't have given up on you!"

That didn't turn out to be as reassuring as I had intended. "Damien's *dead*."

But Cayce's face showed he was thinking fast. "What are your symptoms?"

"Weakness and trembling, obviously." She held out her hands, fingers spread, and now that she'd pointed it out—or perhaps because she wasn't working to suppress it—I saw how severe the trembling I'd noted before was, and understood that it was not nervousness. "My hands aren't so bad I can't deal cards, not yet ... I've got a year or three to go, maybe five. But as for these ..." She waved to her legs and feet. "The last time I tried walking around in Inner Belt standard gee, I had to sit down after half an hour, and I was shot for the day. That was last year. By now, I probably couldn't stand up at all." She sighed, then looked up again. "I get these random twitches and jerks. I'm stiff and sore all the time. I have trouble sleeping, and I've got constipation like you wouldn't believe. Oh, and I'm depressed. Can you blame me?"

"But you can still run a con!" Cayce insisted. "Your condition might even help, for some cons, for some marks."

"You are *so* like your dad," Alicia replied with scorn. "He always insisted I could be a grifter like Shweta. But I am a *thief*. I climb, I squirm, I crack, I fiddle. Or I did." She looked down at her hands. "And you can't teach an old dog new tricks."

"Grifting is a skill like any other," Cayce said. "It can be learned. You've got an excellent mind, and it doesn't seem like the disease has affected it. The only thing that's keeping you from learning new tricks is *you*."

"Don't you *dare* tell me what I can and cannot do!"

I interposed myself between them. "Whoa, whoa, *whoa!*" I didn't think it would really come to blows but I didn't want the argument to get any closer to that than it already had. "We're all friends here."

"I don't even know you," Alicia growled, glaring at Cayce.

Cayce shook his head, raising his hands placatingly. "No need to be hostile. I'm here to help."

"Are you? *Are* you? Or are you here because you want something from me?"

That took Cayce aback for a moment. "Well ... yes, I do want something from you. I want your help getting my dad out of captivity. But I swear to you that if you help me, I'll help you."

"I don't need any help, and certainly not from a little shit like you. Dealing may be a crap job, but it covers my oxy, my cubic, my food, and my meds with a little left over. I'm independent and I don't owe anyone anything. And as long as I keep working, I'll *stay* independent."

Cayce's expression combined sympathy with pleading. "What happens when you can't? Casinos are not known for their magnanimity."

The flare of anger and raw hatred that blazed across Alicia's features took even me, Mister Angry Face, by surprise. And then it was gone. "No one knows that better than me. But what's done is done."

Plainly there was a story here. "Oh?" I said.

Alicia's mouth contorted and her eyes rolled upward in an expression that might have been anger, might have been shame, might have been both. She held that for a moment, then blew out a hard breath through her nose. "Okay," she said, "it's like this."

She sighed and gathered herself, then looked at the wall as she spoke. "I came here about two years ago, not long after my diagnosis. I was already having some trouble with my hands, and I knew it would get worse. I was looking for a place with low gravity where I could settle down with a legit job. I had some contacts at the Thunderbolt." She sighed again. "My old *friend* Maxon said he could set me up with a deal that was too good to be true. Well, he was right about that." Now she looked at Cayce. "Kid, if you ever get that feeling in the back of your head that something isn't right ... listen to it." She blinked, shook her head, then continued. "Maxon was a grifter I'd known in my earliest days, but he told me he'd gone legit, working in the insurance industry. The Thunderbolt has a lot of sick people on staff—it's the radiation, it gets everyone sooner or later—and so they have really good insurance. I mean *really* good, the kind that'll set you up for life if you get so sick you can't work."

She paused, looking down into her cupped hands. "The insurance is good all right ... but the casino takes a cut. A *big* cut. Like over ninety percent. It's all legal, but that might have something to do with the fact that Amalthea's lunar council is a wholly owned subsidiary of Thunderbolt Holdings Limited. And the contracts are ... complex. By the time I figured out how bad the deal was, I was too sick to go anywhere else. So I stay here, and I'll keep dealing until my hands can't take it anymore. It's not a bad life."

Cayce looked like he wanted to reach out and comfort her. But she was almost three times his age, and that would have been weird. "Don't give up," I repeated, not mentioning Damien this time.

"I haven't given up!" she spat. "I've just admitted that I can't fight City Hall, not at this scale. Not that I didn't try! But Maxon and his ilk have this whole moon locked up tighter than a drum, and I'm just one ex-safecracker. You'd need a whole team of crooked lawyers to unpick the net they've woven here." She shook her head. "Don't worry about me. I'll make do."

As she spoke, Cayce's gaze went away inside himself. I'd seen that look on his dad's face many times.

Strange had told me about this "memory palace" he had in his head, where every idea and fact he'd ever encountered was stored for quick access, but though he'd tried and tried to explain the concept to me, I'd never been able to manage even a memory shelf. Why bother anyway when everything you might want to know is on your pocket comm?

Cayce's attention came back to the conversation just as Alicia was saying not to worry about her. "What if ... what if I told you you didn't have to just make do?"

Alicia's gaze turned scalding. "The last time someone said something like that to me, the man I loved ended up dead and I wound up alone and on the run. Bake me no pies in the sky, kid."

Cayce winced visibly at that. "It's not going to be like that this time. What I have in mind is a straightforward con. Something that'll put Maxon in his place, set us up with more than enough cash to break Dad out, *and* leave you with a tidy nest egg. Low risk, high return."

"And how many times have you run this con ... *kid*?"

He looked down, abashed. "I, uh, I haven't." He looked up again. "But Dad taught me a lot, and I never forget anything he showed me."

"There's a difference between learning and doing."

"I know, but ... look, I am my father's son, and I know I can do this. All we need is an in and an out. With you already working there, we've got our in, and getting out after the job is done is just a matter of logistics."

"And in between?"

Cayce grinned and cracked his knuckles. "Leave that to me."

We adjourned to a café, a lot more comfortable than the abandoned storefront though not quite as private. But Cayce had a gizmo to keep people from overhearing us as we talked. It made my ears feel stuffy.

"Thunderbolt has Amalthea's lunar council in the bag," Alicia explained, shaking her head.

"What about Jupiter Union?" Cayce countered. "That's a government too big to be bought."

"Maxon is paying off the Union inspectors," Alicia said. "Thunderbolt has more than enough cash and knows where the bodies are buried."

Cayce's attention went away inside himself again. "What we need is an outsider," he mused aloud. "Someone not already in Maxon's pocket. With hard evidence of Thunderbolt's crimes, and a credible threat to share it with the Union unless properly compensated."

"There is no such person, and there is no such evidence!" Alicia said, spreading open hands on the table. "I've been looking for over a year and they're too good at covering their tracks."

Cayce grinned. "*I* can be that person."

The idea pulled a snort of laughter from me. "You're just a *kid*!"

Suddenly, Cayce straightened in his seat. He held his head completely still, and tilted it ever so slightly back so that he seemed to be looking down at me from a height. "I may be young, sir, but I have a master's in business forensics from Callisto University. With honors."

"Really?" I said, taken aback.

Just as quickly, Cayce was himself again, and winked. "Of course not. But Dad showed me how to be convincing."

Alicia smiled at my discomfiture at being so easily taken in, but then her gaze moved from me to Cayce, and it was filled with the beginnings of respect. "Being cocky can only get you so far," she pointed out.

Cayce had the grace to feign a blush, and shrug. "As for the evidence," Cayce continued, "we don't actually need evidence. We just need to convince Maxon that we have it."

"And how are 'we' going to do that?" Alicia said, folding her hands and leaning forward over them.

"That is where *you* come in."

Alicia raised her hands. The fingers trembled ever so slightly, each with its own separate fitful rhythm. "I told you, I'm not up for thieving anymore. And if you're expecting me to hack into Thunderbolt's systems, that was Tai's job."

"All we need is employee-level access."

She snorted. "I'm lucky if I can figure out how to update my payroll information."

"That'll do. Between what you know about yourself, what you can learn about your co-workers, and what I know about the insurance industry, I'm confident we can fake up something that'll fool your old friend Maxon."

"And what do *you* know about the insurance industry?"

"I have a master's in business forensics." He smiled ever so slightly.

Alicia's face screwed up into a grimace that showed her natural caution and world-weariness were warring with her desire to believe that someone, especially Strange's kid, might actually be willing and able to help her. "Okay," she said after sucking her teeth for a minute, "but I'm not going to take an active part in the job, and I'm not going to give you any personal info that can be traced back to me. If this falls through, it's on *you*. I can't risk my last best employment, not when I'm so close to not being able to work at all."

Cayce took in a long slow breath, then let it out. "I ... can see where you're coming from. That'll make my job harder, but okay." Then he looked at me, and those brown eyes were as serious and keen as his dad's blue ones had ever been. "How about you, Kane? Are you in?"

"I shouldn't be. A casino, especially one as big as the Thunderbolt, is a target even the Harker Gang wouldn't tackle."

Cayce conceded the point with a small shrug. "If we're going to break Dad out of Cronos, we're going to have to take some risks."

I nodded, not to say that I was in but to acknowledge the truth of what he'd said. To extract Strange from Turvallis's private prison—or whatever Cronos really was—we would need money. A lot of it. And casinos were a good place to find that. Also to find people who would happily kill you or worse if you tried and failed to get some of it.

Strange's kid or not, I should tell Cayce no thanks. I could just hitch a ride back to Blue Iguana and my safe, comfortable life there—well, as safe and comfortable as a hired thug's life can ever be.

But I owed Strange. He had taken a risk on me, picked me up from the docks and given me a full share of the Cannibal Club right from the start.

"Yeah," I said. "I'm in."

Eight days later, we were in Maxon's office. I couldn't believe how fast Cayce had made it come together.

He'd given Alicia a list of questions—he rattled them off like he was reading from a questionnaire, but as near as I could tell, he was coming up with them on the spot. Some of the questions were about her, some were about her supervisors and co-workers, and some seemed completely unmotivated, like a list of pet boarding centers near the casino.

While Alicia was finding those answers, Cayce and I went shopping. This had not been what I'd expected.

First, we bought clothes, very nice business outfits for me and him, custom tailored and with very specific fabrics. While those were being made up, we haunted the secondhand stores and came away with two sets of used but very high-end traveling cases, which we obtained for pennies on the dollar of their original extravagant cost. I had a feeling that the cases' original owners had found themselves in sudden need of funds—perhaps it had something to do with the proximity of the casino. A different, and somewhat less savory, set of secondhand stores netted us each a first-rate pocket comm, fully functional but somehow lacking the usual trace codes, and a few related accessories.

The tailors wouldn't find out Cayce's credit wasn't good until we were long gone, but the rest of the purchases required actual cash money. That came out of my pocket, as did the rent for our room at the Cloud Tops Inn. It added up to a pretty big chunk of my savings, but I'd said I was in, and when I was in on a job, I was all the way in. If this job came off as Cayce intended, I'd be paid back in full and then some; if it didn't, lack of money would be only one of my problems.

By the time the outfits were delivered—they fit beautifully and made both of us look extremely sharp—Cayce had set up an appointment with Maxon. We packed up our spiffy cases, took public transit to the elevator station, then hailed a private jitney from there to the Thunderbolt business office so we'd arrive in style.

In the jitney, we went over the plan one last time. It seemed solid to me, but I had to acknowledge I was not a planner. "Are you *sure* about this, kid?" I asked him. "We're waltzing right into the lion's den here, and we don't have backup."

At first, he seemed about to berate me for questioning him, but then he looked at his own hands. They were trembling. "I'm as sure as I can be, up here," he said, tapping his temple. "But I guess my body has other ideas."

"It's not too late to back out."

"No." He shook his head once, definitively. "It wasn't easy for me to set up this meeting with Maxon. All the pieces are in place." He balled his hands into fists, stifling the trembling. "This is the first step in a long process," he said, half to himself. "If we stop here, the whole plan collapses." He looked at me. "I'm in. I'm in up to my neck. Are you?"

"I'm in," I said.

By the time we arrived at Maxon's office, Cayce had conquered his nerves completely. He walked into the reception area not like he owned the place, but like he was considering it for purchase. He was calm, reserved, and attentive, with his head held high and very still—I'd have to try that myself. It made him look like a snot-nosed university grad rather than the secondary-school drop-out he actually was. When asked to wait, he inclined his head and waited … patiently, quietly, but without moving from in front of the desk. He acted like someone who expected to be paid attention to.

As for me, I tried to act like myself, only a little bit more refined. "The kind of person I'm supposed to be," Cayce had said, "needs someone like you for protection but doesn't like to acknowledge it. Officially, you are my administrative assistant, but in reality, you are my bodyguard and muscle. Everyone understands this. But I will act as though I expect you to handle paperwork, not security."

"I don't know the first thing about paperwork."

"Nobody expects you to. But appearances must be maintained. Yes, you are a threat—that is your job. But you must also be prepared to hand me a stylus if I request it."

Maxon drifted out from the office and drew to a halt in front of Cayce, ignoring me completely. This was what Cayce and I had expected, and indeed what everything about our clothing and accessories was intended to suggest. Maxon was exactly as Alicia had described him, a smear of grease in an expensive suit. "You must be Mr. Chang," he said, smiling carnivorously.

"It's just Chang," Cayce corrected, taking Maxon's proffered hand. Strange's habit of using a single name might have been an affectation, but it did serve to put people a little off balance and Cayce had adopted it as part of his persona. "This is my associate Mr. Davis." He indicated me with an offhand gesture. "I am a busy man, Mr. Maxon. May we speak privately?"

Maxon ushered us to a small conference room. Cayce peered into the room, then pulled back and looked Maxon right in the eye. "I said *privately*."

Maxon blinked. He was doing a good job of covering it, but his body language showed that he was both annoyed and impressed by this young man's presumption. Which was, again, exactly the intended effect. "Of course," he said, then spoke to the air: "Hold my calls for the next ninety minutes." Then he escorted us to what was obviously his personal office.

Maxon did not offer tea. He settled himself at his work station, fitting his feet into the straps with the ease of long habit, and offered Cayce a guest station on the other side of his work surface. I was left to float by the door. "I, too, am a busy man, Chang, so let us get right to the point. Your message referred to ... I believe the term you used was 'consequential' information?"

"I am an insurance adjuster, Mr. Maxon." Cayce held out a hand over his shoulder, not looking at me. I opened my case and brought out a data block, which Cayce took and held up like an auction paddle. Maxon did not reach for it, though his eyes showed he wanted to. "It has recently come to my attention that, in the past six years, approximately five point two billion Ceres dollars of payments to the disabled employees of Thunderbolt Holdings has not reached its intended recipients."

He set the data block on a sticky pad on Maxon's work surface, but held it down with one finger. Maxon still did not reach to pick it up. "Insurance contract number 2207-108271-G. Twenty-five thousand six hundred and eight covered employees." Cayce tapped the data block. "Five. Point. Two. Billion. Dollars." The insurance contract number was on Alicia's benefit checks; the number of covered employees and amount stolen were educated guesses, extrapolations from Alicia and her co-workers.

To my surprise, Maxon's tension eased at this statement. "Speaking frankly and privately, sir, that money *has* reached its *intended* recipients. I have the personal assurance of Mr. Chushingura"—that was the president of Thunderbolt's insurance company, I knew—"that all funds redirection is entirely legal and well within the bounds of generally accepted accounting principles. And Mr. Chushingura would not take kindly to any suggestion otherwise."

Funds redirection, he said. A term of art, I suppose, and much more polite than *theft*.

"I do not work for Mr. Chushingura, Mr. Maxon," Cayce said. "I work for Candela Limited." Candela was not Thunderbolt's insurance company, nor the accounting firm that issued Alicia's paychecks—that was Agrani Limited—but *Agrani*'s insurance company. Maxon's eyes widened at the name. "And *if* this information should become public knowledge, Candela would be compelled by Jupiter Union regulations to pursue legal action to recover its customer's—that is, Agrani's—'redirected' funds. Thunderbolt Holdings would have no standing, and no influence, in this action ... except possibly as a defendant in any ensuing criminal proceedings."

Maxon swallowed, his eyes fixed on the data block. "You said 'if.'"

Cayce allowed a very slight smile to creep onto his lips. "You are a perceptive man, Mr. Maxon."

"Under what circumstances might this release be avoided?"

"If, perhaps, a payment of one point two million Ceres dollars were made to a certain charity, which I will name later."

Maxon raised one eyebrow. "A properly registered charity?" Cayce nodded. "So we get a tax benefit as well. Clever."

Cayce acknowledged the compliment with a small zero-gravity bow.

"However, one point two million is excessive. I'll make you a counter: seven hundred thousand Amalthea dollars, in cash"—that was only about half a million Ceres, but a cash payment was always preferable—"payable upon inspection of your data." He gestured to the data block.

The data block was blank.

Cayce continued to hold it down with one finger. "You know I can't let you see my data," he said with utter calm and not a small degree of contempt. It was a very impressive performance for a sixteen-year-old kid. "You would simply reshuffle your finances to hide the crime, and probably retaliate against my sources as well, before the Jupiter Union can act."

Maxon held up his hands in a performative display of helplessness. "Surely you do not expect me to simply hand over a million dollars on your say-so."

"Of course not." He removed his finger from the data block. "So here is my proposal: I will leave you the data, in escrow as it were, as a demonstration of good faith. It is encrypted, of course, and any attempt to access the data without the key will cause the block to wipe itself immediately. After payment is received, I will provide you the key, and you may do with the data as you wish."

Maxon didn't reach for the block. "I have no reason to trust that you will actually do so, and several reasons to believe you will not. Once I have your data, I'll be able to use it to retaliate against you."

"But if I learn that you have begun to move against me—and, please do be assured, I have many sources within your organization—I will immediately reveal my data to the Union authorities, as well as your personal involvement in the cover-up. With this as my insurance policy, I will be free to provide the key to you."

Maxon reached for the data block and laid his fingers gently atop it. "I will need some time to consider your offer." By which he meant to begin trying to ferret out Cayce's sources and bury evidence of the crime.

Cayce waved negligently at the block. "By all means. Will twenty-four hours be sufficient?"

"Certainly."

"Very well." Cayce held out a hand. "We will be in touch tomorrow."

They shook hands. Neither of them acknowledged my presence in any way.

We left via the same circuitous route we'd taken.

Back at the Cloud Tops Inn, the three of us gathered around one of our just-purchased cases, staring at the small screen within. It showed a rotating series of displays—views of Maxon's office, data streams, and audio channels—flowing from the several bugs I had planted while Maxon and Cayce had been ignoring me.

"We probably have only a few hours before Thunderbolt security spots the bugs and destroys them," Cayce said, scrolling through the video streams. "But I think I rattled Maxon enough that he will take action quickly." His eyes widened. "Ah, there he goes." He zoomed in on Maxon's desktop screen. "Oh."

"That wasn't a happy noise," Alicia said.

Cayce didn't immediately respond, but his absolute stillness as he read whatever Maxon was typing was telling. "We need to clear out of here. Now."

We might have been a kid, a hired thug, and a middle-aged blackjack dealer, but we were still the Cannibal Club, or at least whatever was left of it. Fifteen minutes later, the room was clean and empty, and we were moving down Golden Way with our cases in tow. "I spooked him more than I intended," Cayce explained as we moved, staying in the thickest, noisiest, and most civilian-dense part of the crowd. "He moved immediately to track and destroy me. Us." I kept a sharp eye out in all directions, but there was as yet no sign of pursuit. "He's a money guy. I didn't expect him to be so ... belligerent."

The plan had been for Maxon to check that his actual data proving the crime was safe, thereby revealing it to our spying eyes, so that we could provide it back to him in exchange for the ransom. Instead, it looked like he was moving against us—fast and hard.

"So what's your plan now?" Alicia asked, exasperated. I couldn't help but notice that not only had she said *your*, but her body language was edging away from us. She, of course, had not been in Maxon's office.

Cayce's eyes unfocused, showing he was thinking fast and consulting his memory palace. He reached into his pocket and I felt the stuffy feeling in my ears that told me he'd activated his security gizmo—which was a bit of a giveaway in itself, but we weren't the only people in the crowd using one. "He'll have security watching the elevators. We'll have to go to ground, and fast."

Alicia's eyebrows shot up. "I'm not taking you in like a stray cat!"

Cayce looked to her with a pained expression. "We can't go to your place anyway. Cameras at our hotel will certainly have seen you with us. You're compromised."

"Shit." She glared an accusation at Cayce. "You said this would be a straightforward con."

"I'm sorry. I didn't think Maxon would move so fast or so hard. And there may be ... additional factors I haven't yet shared with you." Even as her face twisted into an expression of shock and disappointment, he pressed on. "Look, we'll have to deal with that later. Right now, we can stick together, or we can go our separate ways. Which is it going to be?"

"Damn it." She visibly tamped down her rage as she considered her options. "I think I'm stuck with you. I'm in no shape to run and hide on my own."

Cayce looked at me. I was pretty pissed at him myself, but from what I'd learned of him already, I knew that he'd be more likely to think his way out of this situation than I could punch my way out. "I'm with you," I said. "For now."

Cayce nodded, then looked to Alicia. "Do you have any hideouts prepared?"

She considered the question. "The old jewelry store is probably out. Same for everything else in that neighborhood." She thought a little more, then her face lit up with a wicked grin. "But I know just the hole for a filthy rat like you."

Alicia's "rat hole" was a literal sewer—a clammy, dank maintenance compartment crowded with pipes. Foul reeking droplets of water shimmered and wobbled in the air and on every stinking, filthy surface.

"I hate this," Cayce groused. It seemed that, like his dad, he was fastidious and disliked damp places.

"Thought you would." Alicia indulged herself in another evil grin, then turned serious. "But you can bet no one will come looking for us here. The cameras in this whole zone are dead and, as near as I can tell, no one's inspected the place for years."

Cayce waved a brownish miasma away from his face. "Well done," he said.

"So what are those 'additional factors' you haven't yet shared with us?" I demanded. I wasn't going to let that statement go.

Cayce took in a breath to reply ... and immediately inhaled something, falling into a gagging cough. I didn't help him, didn't pat him on the back. I just waited it out.

"Aquila," Cayce gasped out at last. "Maxon ... Maxon called Aquila. As soon as we left his office. Told them I'm here."

"Shit," I said. Aquila was a corporation with which I'd studiously avoided all contact since Orca Station. Alicia's face showed she was just as dismayed. "But wait ... what did *you* do to piss them off?"

He put his hands over his mouth and tried to catch his breath without actually inhaling any of the filthy air. "They're the ones holding my dad," he rasped. "Turvallis is just a contractor. I ... tried to break Dad out by myself. Didn't work. Knew I'd need help ... to try again." He gestured to Alicia and I. "They've been trying to track me down ever since. I guess Maxon got the all-points bulletin."

"He recognized you?" I snarled. "So the whole time we were talking … he was conning *us!*" I should have known better than to blindly trust the wisdom of a teenager. Despite all his smarts and Strange-taught techniques, he was still only sixteen.

Cayce grimaced. "Looks that way, yeah."

"I should have indulged my first impulse," Alicia said, "and kicked you in the nuts as soon as I saw you."

"Wouldn't have helped." Cayce shook his head. "Not in the long run. Aquila's looking for you too. Both of you. The whole surviving Cannibal Club. They're still pissed off about the Orca job. Dad's just the first one they caught."

Alicia seemed more disappointed—or maybe, exhausted—rather than angry. "Why didn't you just *tell* us?"

"You wouldn't have believed me. Or you would just have gone to ground as soon as you heard the name Aquila." He hesitated, showing his vulnerability for a second, before hardening his resolve. "I need to get the whole gang together—which means you all coming out of retirement, not deeper into hiding—because no one else can do what needs to be done."

"And you were gathering us up," I growled, "to run like a flock of good little chickens right into the fox's den?"

"Better that than to scatter like frightened hens and let the foxes pick us off one at a time!" Cayce's eyes were pleading, his hands held out in supplication. "We're better together than separately. Ten times … a hundred times better! Dad knew that. You know it. None of us can fight Aquila alone. But together … we can form a weapon that can break them for good and all."

"Tall order," I grunted.

"But he's not wrong," Alicia said, looking sidewise at me.

"Wait … you're *agreeing* with him?" I looked back and forth at the two of them.

"Well … not exactly, no." She shot him a glare. "I certainly don't agree with his tactics. But if Aquila is hunting us … we *are* better off together. I'm certainly in no shape to fight them myself." She looked down the length of her body to her curled and trembling feet. "Or

47

even to run." She closed her eyes. "Strange could be … difficult, at times. But he was very, very smart, and he always had a plan. I'm getting the impression his kid is just the same. And I'd rather have him on my side than not." She looked up then, looked me straight in the eye. "How about you?"

I ground my teeth. Right then, I just wanted to punch something. But the only targets at the moment were a teenage kid, a sick middle-aged woman, and a bunch of filthy and corroded pipes that would probably just burst, spewing sewage all over the place, if I did. "I'm in," I said again, "for now. *For now.* But if I see an advantage in throwing you to the wolves, or foxes or whatever they are, I'll do it."

"*There's* the Kane I remember," Alicia said. "I was worried old age had made you soft."

"I've never been harder," I growled.

"Good," Cayce said. "Because that's just what we'll need to get out of here." He folded his arms across his chest. "Now here's how we're going to do it."

After Cayce outlined his plan, we split up, then rendezvoused at a hostel where Alicia knew the owner and no questions would be asked. After I'd run my errand, I found her there but not Cayce. "I was planning to hold this prime hidey-hole back," she told me, "keeping it for myself in case the whole operation blew up, but finally relented when I saw how miserable Cayce was in the sewer." She went a little contemplative then. "He *is* a lot like his dad—for good or ill—but he's still just a lost puppy."

I snorted. "More like a feral weasel."

Cayce arrived then, bringing the two small traveling cases. Alicia and I had each taken one of the two large ones. "Did you get your pills?" he asked Alicia.

She patted the satchel at her hip. "Yep. We'll probably run out of places to hide before I run out of meds."

"If this works, that won't be an issue." Then, to me, "How'd your shopping trip go?"

"I got what you wanted," I said, handing over a small packet, "but I'm still not sure this is going to work out."

"I have confidence in both of you." Cayce opened the packet, revealing the three cheap in-ear comms I'd purchased at a back-alley vendor. He picked one up and inspected it, pronouncing it "good enough"—not exactly a ringing endorsement—before sticking it in his ear. He handed one to Alicia and one back to me.

I eyed the device dubiously. Cayce's whole plan depended on Alicia and I working as a seamless team, and in my experience, these little gizmos were clairvoyant. They always flaked out just when you needed them the most. I sighed and stuck it in my ear. "Check check," I said.

"Check check," came Alicia's voice in my ear. Her mouth barely moved. I was impressed.

"Check check," Cayce repeated, his voice echoing slightly as it reached me through the air and through radio waves. "Right. And here's the last piece of the puzzle." He opened one of his cases and pulled out another packet, which contained a tiny bead camera. He licked the back and stuck it to my forehead. A moment later, the screen in the case lit up, showing my view of Cayce.

"Does that little thing have enough resolution?" Alicia asked, dubiously inspecting the screen.

Cayce shrugged. "It'll have to do."

I waved a hand in front of my face, watching the screen echo my view. There was a little lag. "I'm more worried about the crawling-through-ducts part of the job."

"It's easy in microgravity," Alicia told me. "And you're pretty flexible for a big guy. You'll be fine." I wasn't entirely reassured. Then she drew a flat black leather case from her satchel but hesitated before handing it to me. "These are … some of them are the first burglar tools I ever owned. I kept them in my go-bag for sentimental reasons as much as anything. Now they're the only ones I have." She sighed. "But I guess I'm not using them anyway." She offered the case to me. "Don't lose 'em."

I was genuinely touched. "I'll try not to."

We spent the next few hours with Alicia giving me a crash course in lock picking and safe cracking, starting with the locks on the traveling cases. Everything was so small and finicky, and I kept pinching my fingers or having little springs fly off into the air. "Damn it!" I shouted, flinging the pick across the room.

"Don't be so hard on yourself," Alicia said. "I'll be right in your ear whenever you need me."

"Stick it in your ear," I muttered under my breath.

"We heard that," Cayce replied through the comm.

"Try again," Alicia said, returning the pick to me. "Gently."

I felt my jaw tense, but consciously relaxed it. It would be so much easier just to pull the damn case open with my hands—it was just a suitcase, after all—but that wasn't the point here. The point was for me to learn Alicia's way.

I tried again. Alicia's way.

And the latch popped open!

"There!" Alicia said. "I knew you could do it."

I glared at her. "Don't mollycoddle me."

Cayce cleared his throat and turned from the screen where he'd been researching something. He seemed to share his father's ability to give his full attention to a task while somehow remaining aware of everything around him. "Is he ready?" he asked Alicia.

She and I exchanged a look. "Ready enough, I guess," she said.

"Good. Because it's time to move." Cayce folded his screen, tucked it into his shoulder bag, and drifted toward the door.

We made our way by back routes to another maintenance compartment, this one drafty and dusty rather than foul and damp. Noise rattled down the air ducts that converged on this point from various parts of the Thunderbolt complex.

Cayce latched the hatch behind us, then pulled up an engineering diagram on his screen. "This is the duct to Maxon's office," he said, highlighting the route on the diagram, "and this is where the safe is." He tapped a tiny rectangle adjacent to the office.

It didn't look like much on the map, and when we'd been in the office, it hadn't looked like anything more than a blank wall. But on that visit, Cayce, with his unerring eye and memory, had noted that there was a gap between the visible walls, an unaccounted-for space, which the engineering charts showed did not contain air ducts, water pipes, or wiring. It was the perfect size, shape, and location for Maxon to have a secret, private safe.

That seemed to me to be a very thin thread upon which to hang our only chance at survival. But it was the only thread we had.

"Any questions?"

I didn't say "What if that isn't really a safe?" or "What if there's a silent alarm?" or "What do we do if the comms fail?" because, really, the unavoidable answer to all of those questions was "Then we get captured and/or killed." We all knew the risks and were prepared to face them, and to improvise our way out if anything went wrong. That was what being in the Cannibal Club meant.

And, God help us, we really were the Cannibal Club again. Or at least part of it.

"Okay," Cayce said after waiting a moment longer, "let's go."

While I smoothed down my clothes, watching out for any protruding straps or buckles, and checked that Alicia's burglar tools were safely stowed in my pocket, Cayce and Alicia unscrewed the grille to the duct leading to Maxon's office. Once the grille was removed, we nodded to each other, then I slipped inside. I don't know when we decided that wishing good luck was bad luck, but it's been the way we do things in the Cannibal Club since forever. Maybe we got it from theatre folks.

The duct—greasy-looking metal walls with trails of dust in the lee of each seam and rivet—was only a little bigger across than my shoulders, so I had a choice between holding my arms out in front of me or down at my sides. I chose to keep them out in front, pulling myself along with some help from my feet. This proved to be a good decision, because once I got a few meters in, the dimness faded to black. "Can't see a damn thing," I growled.

"Your camera has night vision," Cayce replied. "I'll guide you in." I heard his fingers tapping on his screen. "First intersection's coming up in about two meters. You'll go left."

"Got it," I said. I edged forward, feeling ahead with my left hand, then levered myself around the tight corner. "Made the turn."

"Good," said Cayce. "Now about five meters, then another left."

I continued pulling myself along, probing ahead in the darkness with my hands, making the best time I could. The smell was of metal and hot dust. Every once in a while, my fingers found a harsh metal edge, but nothing sharp enough to draw blood. Then I came to an opening on the left. "Left here?" I asked.

In response, I heard a harsh rattling sound through the comm. "What's that?" I said.

"We have company," Cayce subvocalized.

I stopped where I was, trying to listen hard for any sounds that might reach my ears directly as well as through the comm. There was more rattling, then voices I couldn't quite make out. Not Cayce's or Alicia's.

I moistened my suddenly dry lips. "You want me to come back there?"

A long uncomfortable pause, then Alicia subvocalized, "No. Keep going. Maxon's safe is still our best shot at getting off Amalthea in one piece."

"And if we get captured," Cayce said, "you'll still be free."

My fingers tightened on a seam in the metal as I considered my options. "I hope you know what you're doing," I said at last, and pulled myself through the opening to the left. "Where to next?"

"Eight meters," Cayce enunciated slowly and carefully, "then up."

"Got it."

As I made my way down the duct—I was getting better at maneuvering, but the dust was really starting to annoy my nose and eyes—I heard more noises and voices.

Then the comm went silent.

"Cayce!" I whispered loudly. "What the *fuck* is happening there?"

Cayce came back on. There was a lot of noise in the background. "We're clearing out. Keep going to Maxon's office. Five more meters forward, then up, then ten meters, then right. Ping me if you get lost." Then the comm went dead again.

"Son of a bitch," I breathed into the darkness. Then, lacking any better alternative, I started moving forward. I pulled myself along the greasy, dusty metal, trailing fingers against the wall to judge my progress. After what I estimated as five meters, I slowed down, feeling the ceiling … and damn if I didn't find a gap. I squirmed around the corner and kept going.

The next stretch of duct was straight and uncomplicated, and even seemed a little cleaner. But, by the same token, it was hard to measure my progress against the seamless wall. I started feeling on my right—he had said right, hadn't he?—after what I judged to be eight meters, but found nothing more than smooth wall for two ... three ... four meters more. I felt ahead and still found nothing but wall.

"Cayce," I said. "Alicia?"

No reply. Damn it.

I paused, panting from exertion. At least, in microgravity, I didn't have to hold myself in place. I could rest without worrying about falling down the duct to my doom in some enormous whirling fan. But the air around me *was* moving, and after a moment, I reached out to the wall and realized that I was moving silently along with it. Which meant I was even *less* sure about where I was.

Now what?

Perhaps I'd misremembered which way to turn, or gotten turned around and felt the wrong wall. I felt all four walls. Finding nothing, I started edging slowly back the way I'd come, feeling all four walls every half-meter or so. Nothing but smooth metal.

I was just beginning to consider panicking when Cayce came back on the comm. Thank fuck. "Where are you?" he asked.

"No goddamn idea," I admitted. "Where are *you*?"

"We found an alcove where we can hang out for a little while." He paused. "I'm not sure where you are. I need you to look around."

"I'm wedged in a fucking duct," I growled, but I swiveled my head around, trying to give the camera a view behind me—along the length of my body—as well as ahead.

"Okay, I think I've got you. Looks like you missed a turn. You're going to need to back up a little."

"How far is 'a little'?"

"About five meters."

"Shit." I took in a deep breath—and immediately choked on dust. After the coughing subsided, I started pushing myself backward with my hands. "Say when."

Eventually, Cayce managed to navigate me to a point where I was peering through a grate into Maxon's office. It was unoccupied, door closed, illuminated only by the light of the screen on the desk. Thank god. "Okay," I subvocalized, "here goes."

The grate popped off easily but tumbled away; I had to scramble to catch it before it hit something. I stowed it in the duct for a quick getaway, then moved in close to the stretch of wall behind which the safe supposedly lurked. It was covered with papers, held in place with decorative magnets. "You're *sure* about this?" I asked.

"The access has to be from Maxon's office. He's not the type to inconvenience himself. Look high, look low."

Even though Amalthea was nearly in free fall, the office was built by and for people who'd evolved in gravity; the surface where the desk was mounted was carpeted as a floor, and the lights were mounted to the opposite surface, making it a ceiling. I peered at the wall where it met the ceiling—Cayce gave me the go-ahead to pull out my comm and use it as a flashlight—but neither I nor he spotted anything resembling a catch, door, or opening. Then I moved to the carpeted end. "There!" Cayce said, so excited he spoke aloud. Alicia shushed him. "Look at the lower edge of those papers," he subvocalized, chastened.

"I see it," I said. The papers close to the carpet were yellowed and frayed along their bottom edges, as though they'd been handled many times. I poked at the frayed edge with a fingertip. "Glued in place."

"The heart magnet," Cayce prompted. I saw immediately what he meant. The paper around a red, heart-shaped magnet showed more wear than elsewhere.

As soon as I touched the magnet, I felt a little give. I pushed it like a button. It depressed into the surface with a click, and the wall section's lower edge popped open slightly. "Bingo," I whispered, and pulled at the opening. My fingers fell naturally on the frayed edge of the papers.

The wall section slid upward, revealing the door of a small safe. "Komatsu 400 series," Alicia breathed in my ear. "Economical, well-built, easy to install ... and it has a flaw that makes it easy to crack. You'll need the slim probe for this one."

"Don't they know about the flaw?" I asked as I dug the slim probe out of Alicia's tool case.

"Of course. But admitting it would be a public relations nightmare. Now slip the probe in right above the latch plate."

A job that probably would have taken Alicia under a minute took me ten nerve-wracking minutes, with her walking me through every step of the process. It was finicky, painstaking work. Ten years ago, I would have probably given up and started smashing at it with the butt of my pistol. But I had to get in and out without leaving evidence of my passage, so I bit my lip and kept trying, with Alicia's gentle voice in my ear. "Good job, kiddo," she said as the latch clicked and the door swung open.

I wanted to shout a giant "Got you, motherfucker!" at Maxon, the safe, and its manufacturer, but I kept my cool and just breathed out a sigh of relief.

In the safe, I found a box of antique baseball cards—probably worth tens of thousands, but of no interest to us—a jewelry case with a pair of his-and-hers engagement rings, a letter opener with a jewel-encrusted handle, and a data stick. "Grab the data stick and get out of there," Alicia said.

"Wait," Cayce interjected. "Those two guys could still be in the maintenance compartment."

"So what do you expect me to do?" I replied, clutching the data stick.

"Close the safe, get back in the duct, and hold tight there while we check out your exit options." He paused for a moment. "And while you're waiting, send me the data stick. It'll be encrypted; just upload it as a binary image."

"What?" That whole last sentence might as well have been Tai's favorite waka-waka music for all the sense it made.

I swore I could hear Cayce's eyes roll. "Plug the stick into your pocket comm. It'll appear as an icon. Just pick up the icon and place it into a message to me. Pick and place the stick itself ... don't try to open it."

That *almost* made sense. "Okay ..."

"I have confidence in you. Now hang tight. We'll find you a way out."

I stared into the silent darkness after the comm went dead, fuming, wondering exactly where I'd made the decision that got me into this mess. Then I set about closing everything up and making sure I'd left no trace of my presence.

I was floating in the duct and had just finished uploading the data stick—I hoped—when Cayce came back on the line. "Bad news, Kane. You're going to have to walk out the front door."

"What?" It was a triumph of self-control that I neither screamed it aloud nor smashed my fist into the duct wall hard enough to reverberate through every sports book and massage parlor in this whole radiation-riddled casino moon.

"I'm sorry. There are *five* workers where you went in, and the ducts in the other directions are too narrow for you to pass."

"You can do this, Kane," Alicia said. "The getaway is just part of the job." We had discussed this, though briefly. "Brush yourself down so you don't look like someone who just crawled out of a hole in the wall. Keep quiet, move fast, stay out of the light as much as possible. And if you meet anyone, remember that you can get away with anything if you just act like you own the place."

"Yeah, right." But I started removing the grate again. Then I paused. "Wait, what about security cameras?"

"If you move fast enough," Cayce replied, "you can be out the door before anyone gets to where you were."

"But there'll be recordings!"

"That could actually be to our advantage."

Before I could ask for a clarification, I heard loud voices through the comm. "Shit!" Alicia said, then her microphone went dead.

I hung there in the wind-rushing dark for a while, hoping they'd come back online. That I could at least know that they'd gotten away. But the comm stayed dead.

I slipped out of the duct again, fitted the grate back in place again, and took a moment to brush myself down as Alicia had suggested, smacking dust off my arms and legs with my hands, coughing into my elbow until the dust cleared.

I eased Maxon's office door open and found the corridor outside empty and dim. Though the casino itself ran twenty-four seven, the back office kept Jupiter Union business hours.

I'd been here once before, of course, but remembering things like routes was never my forte. However, I did seem to recognize the stretch of corridor to my left, while the one to my right seemed unfamiliar. I went left.

Drifting as nonchalantly as possible, keeping quiet, I moved down the hall with my eyes and ears wide open. When I came to an intersection, the sounds of the casino floor came distantly from the right, so I headed that way. There might be an employee entrance as well, but the main entrance was a known quantity. Better to get there and get out fast than to stumble around the back offices for who knows how long. And "heading out the front door" was what Cayce had suggested.

Of course, there were security guards on the casino floor who knew our names and faces and had probably been told to watch out for us.

I took a moment to crack my neck and stretch my joints. I'd punched my way out of tight spots before.

I was just approaching public space—I could tell by the increasing noise of slot machines and spherette tables—when my comm sputtered to life. "—an you h—"

It sounded like Cayce. I paused, stupidly holding my ear as though it would boost the signal somehow. "I can just barely hear you," I whispered as loud as I dared.

"—eaking up pretty ba—"

"You're breaking up too. Can you see where I am?"

"No." Crackling. "—ut of range—"

"Where are you?"

More crackling. "—avy bo—"

"You're at the Gravy Boat?" It was a greasy little eatery near the casino entrance where we'd had lunch the previous day.

"—es, at the Gr—" Then silence.

"Cayce?"

No response.

"I don't know if you can hear me," I said, "but I'm going to try to come out the main entrance and meet you at the Gravy Boat. Okay?"

Nothing.

"I'll meet you at the Gravy Boat," I repeated. "Okay?"

Still nothing.

I was on my own.

I was unarmed.

I took a deep breath, made sure Alicia's burglar tools and Maxon's data stick were well secured in my pocket, and moved out.

I came to a door with a small window in it. White light—brighter than anything on the casino floor—came through the window, along with chipper happy-to-serve-you voices. Back office space, but open for business. The incessant sounds of the casino floor were there too. This might be one of the teller cages, or some other customer service space.

I looked left. I looked right. No better option presented itself.

Act like you own the place, Alicia had said.

I opened the door and pulled myself confidently through it.

Half a dozen uniformed people were on the other side of it. Every single one of them turned to face me. "Can I help you?" said one.

I froze, jaw flapping pointlessly. Bluffing wasn't my strong suit. I really wished Shweta were here.

A long counter faced out into the noisy darkness of the casino floor, with a few customer faces on the other side of it. There weren't bars between the counter and the ceiling—it wasn't a teller cage—but there were no visible exits from the area except the door I'd just come through.

"Can I help you?" the employee repeated, a little more insistently.

I was wearing a dark coverall, and the bright office light revealed that I hadn't done nearly as good a job of getting the duct dust off of myself as I'd hoped. "M-maintenance?" I said. I congratulated myself on my brilliant improvisational skills.

One of the other employees spoke up. "Maybe he's here for the air thing." She turned to me. "Are you here for the air thing?"

"Air thing," I repeated stupidly, then, more confidently, "Yes. The air thing."

"Show him where it is," she said to one of the others.

The indicated person rolled their eyes in annoyance, pulled their feet from their workstation stirrups, and drifted over to me, ushering me back out the door I'd come in. They pointed down the corridor, back toward Maxon's office. "That way, two doors down. I hope you can fix it. It's been freezing in there for a week."

I smiled and nodded, then headed in the indicated direction. I would wait until I heard the door close behind me, then double back in search of a different route to the casino floor. At least now I knew which direction that was.

At least, that was the plan. But then a big crewcut guy in a security uniform came out of one of the doors right in front of me. His eyes flicked up and down, scoping me out, and his face immediately went hard. "You're out of uniform," he said. "Where's your badge?"

I made a show of patting myself down—sending dust poofing into the air—as I drifted closer to him. "I could have sworn I had it," I said, patting the backs of my legs … in the process of which I casually brought my knees up in front of myself.

"Hold it right there," the man said, holding up a hand. I was less than a meter from him.

Close enough. I drew in my knees to my chest, then shot my feet out at him, snapping my hands up behind me to increase the force of the blow. I caught him right in the chin with both heels. He grunted, tumbling back and away, as I drifted backward, rotating slowly heels-over-head. I doubled up, increasing the speed of my spin momentarily, then straightened out again to slow the spin when I was facing back the way I'd come. Grabbing a handrail, I pulled myself toward the door I'd just come out of.

"I told you where the—" said the annoyed employee as I entered.

"Sorry," I said, not meaning it. I pushed past them, planted my filthy feet rudely on the wall next to the door, and shoved off hard through the opening above the counter.

I sailed across the counter into the clamorous dimness of the casino floor, customers ducking out of my way. Shouts came from behind me, yammering "What the hell?" and "Call security!" Faces turned toward me, drawn by the noise and motion.

I had just emerged from an information desk on the back wall of the casino, as far from the entrance as possible. Naturally. But several guidelines converged here, and I snagged one and began hauling myself along it hand-over-hand. Customers floated along the line like lazily bobbing grapes; I pushed past them. Some of them shouted in panic as they floated away from the line. They might be a useful distraction.

I had already made myself conspicuous, and security was on its way. My best hope was to get out of the casino as quickly as possible and try to rendezvous with Cayce and Alicia at the Gravy Boat. If I didn't find them there, at least I'd have more options once I was outside.

Alicia had explained that casinos were carefully designed to draw people in and keep them gambling. So I shouldn't have been surprised that my route out from here wasn't obvious or easy. As I continued to haul myself along the line, batting clueless gamblers aside as I went, I scoped out the guidelines ahead and saw that I'd have to make at least two transfers before I reached the entrance. Each of those transfer points, where several guidelines converged, was a good place for an ambush. I could try leaping directly across toward the exit ... but that would leave me drifting, wide open and unable to maneuver, for way too long. Besides, there were inconspicuous safety nets to snag drifting customers.

So I stuck to the guideline, approaching the first transfer point. By now, the tourists had heard and seen me coming and were clearing out of my way voluntarily, except for a few—drunk or foolhardy or both—who were moving toward me. None of them posed a serious threat, but they could complicate the fight when it came.

And there was a fight coming, for sure. Four security guards were already converging on my position; several others, plus more casino employees, were working to shoo customers away. I doubled down on my hand-over-hand speed, hauling ass to reach the transfer point before they reached me.

In free-fall combat, you have to keep control of your anchors. The convergence of three guidelines at the transfer point, anchored by guy-wires attached to the distant walls, would provide things to hang onto or kick off from to keep station, maintain orientation, and put power behind my punches and kicks.

But I didn't make it. The four guards converged on me before I reached the intersection, coming in fast in a cross formation. The ones to my left and right were closer, approaching with hands out-stretched; the ones above and below were hanging back, readying their lassos. These were half-meter sticks with a loop of tough cord on the end, which would pull closed with the press of a button.

The one on my left, a beefy bald white woman, reached me first. Before she could mouth whatever comforting platitude she'd pre-pared to get me to go quietly, I reached cross-body with my right arm, grabbed her right shoulder, spun her around across my body, and grabbed both her shoulders, putting her directly in front of me. Then I planted my right foot on the guideline beside me and kicked her in the butt with the left, sending her tumbling feet-first into the guy on my right.

Zero-gee fighters have to be really good at the splits. I knew one guy who had tendon surgery so he could spread his legs wider.

The bald woman's flailing feet caught the second guard under the chin, sending him tumbling out of the fight. The woman herself remained near me, still a potential threat, but turning in the air with nothing to grab onto. I hooked my left foot around the guideline and flipped myself away backward and up.

I turned heels-over-head twice before arresting myself on an-other guideline. The first two guards were still flailing helplessly in the air; the other two were moving toward me fast with lassos drawn. No one else was nearby, but several more guards were converging on my position. And they now knew, as the first two had not, that I knew my stuff.

"Kane!" came a voice in my ear. Alicia. The signal was still muddy but much better than before.

"Kind of busy here," I said.

"Have you heard from Cayce?"

"What? No!"

"I left the Gravy Boat to scope out an escape. When I came back, he was gone. He's not answering his comms."

"Fuck." The nearer guard was about four meters away. I grabbed the guideline with both hands and bunched my feet under me, preparing to spring. "Captured?"

"I don't think so." A pause, while both of us considered what that probably meant. "I'm on my way in to help you."

"No!" I said. The guard was only two meters away and was reaching out with his lasso. "Stay out! Save yourself!"

"*I'm* not running out on you!" Her emphasis showed exactly what she thought had happened with Cayce's disappearance.

I wanted to argue further, but I'd run out of time. I launched myself off the guideline at the guard. That didn't surprise him, but my next maneuver did: I whipped out a hand at the last moment and grabbed the lasso by the stick, yanking hard to pull myself past him and send the two of us into a tumble. The lasso's loop *snick*ed shut on nothing.

Both of us were too experienced to be disoriented by our rotation. The guard pulled on the lasso, hauling me back toward himself while drawing the other hand back in preparation for a strike at my head. But I used that momentum against him, using my grip on the stick to bring up my feet for a good solid smack in the torso. I released the stick just as I connected, propelling me toward another guideline.

Unfortunately, I misjudged my strike, hitting him in the left chest rather than in the solar plexus. With the blow landing away from his center of gravity, it didn't hurt him seriously and didn't send him flying away from me, just set him spinning longitudinally. His remaining partner, holding onto a guy-wire nearby, reached out a hand to stabilize him.

Now I had two stable, anchored, aware, and uninjured opponents, with more coming in soon.

I reached the guideline and stopped myself on it, looking both directions. Left would take me back to the transfer point, a more defensible position; right would take me onward toward the casino entrance. I went right, expecting the two guards to launch themselves toward me. I hustled along the line hand-over-hand, preparing myself to strike at them with my feet as they approached.

But they didn't. To my surprise, they stayed where they were. I reached the next transfer point without being assaulted.

This wasn't good.

I held onto two lines and hung there, panting, looking in every direction for the attack I knew would be coming soon. Were the guards preparing to move on me en masse? No, there was no sign of that. They were just hanging back. Waiting for something.

Then I spotted one of them speaking to the air, with a finger to his ear. Talking on the radio.

And looking above and behind me.

I turned my head, following his gaze … and saw a black-uniformed security officer lurking in the shadows, aiming a rifle with a telescopic sight right at me.

I was a sitting duck.

THREE

The Orca Job, Part Two

The Cannibal Club—Ten Years Ago

Tai and Max were next to enter Orca Station. Tai and Alicia slipped swiftly into the broad cargo-handling hallway and to the first of the wide rolling doors on the left, while Max moved down to the far end of the hall to intercept anyone entering from that direction. Kane positioned himself near the airlock where we'd come in, ready to help the next group enter and pass along messages in either direction.

The cargo door, we saw, was old and scarred but the lock mechanism was new, and the lock itself a remarkably sophisticated model for a commonplace goods warehouse. Alicia pulled a set of lock picks from her belt while Tai ran a handheld scanner around the door's edge. A red light blinked on the device; Alicia stepped away slightly, giving Tai room to work.

Tai took out a small but powerful jammer. The door's alarm system, difficult though it might be to bypass, was both a confirmation that this job might actually be worth as much as Hiroshi had promised and an interesting technical challenge.

Tai's tongue tip stuck out unconsciously from the corner of their mouth as they worked—adorable, Alicia thought, even as she kept an eye out for any unexpected intruders—but their eyes and hands were all business as they tuned the jammer to the alarm system's frequencies. It was a matter of physical positioning as well as finding the right pulse width and modulation … *there!* The jammer's status light turned green, and Tai waved to Alicia to proceed.

The lock, likewise, was a little harder to crack than expected—much harder than the station's ostensible purpose would require—but well within Alicia's skills, and with a slight sigh of satisfaction, she finally unlatched the final tumbler.

Hand signals to Max and Kane confirmed that the coast was still clear. Alicia grasped the latch and gave it a cautious twist.

To our relief, the latch turned smoothly and without undue noise. But the door itself, as old and discolored as the outer lock, was not so cooperative. At first, it didn't budge at all. Then, when Alicia and Tai both pulled upward on the handle, it began to move … with an alarming shriek of metal on metal.

Immediately, hearts pounding, they froze, listening with all senses. We all did, even those of us back on *Contessa* who were getting the news by relay. But after a full two minutes had elapsed with no sign of any unwanted attention, we moved cautiously back into action.

Alicia found a tube of fullerene lubricant in her kit, which she squeezed into the door's track on both sides, working it deeply into the tightest areas with her fingernail. Then she and Tai both bent, gripped the handle, and pulled.

The door rolled upward with only a small scraping sound.

They stopped when it was open just thirty centimeters. No point risking any further unexpected sounds. Tai flashed a smile to Alicia and, swift as a sparrow, ducked underneath.

The cargo compartment revealed by Tai's probing flashlight was filthy, with scabrous discolored walls, and echoingly empty. Deep scratches on the floor showed where heavy pallets had been moved in and out, but there was no telling how recently that had occurred.

Disappointing, yes. But there were ten doors on this corridor.

The second door we tried—the middle one of the five on the right—was a duplicate of the first, with the same alarm system and lock ... and we were not completely surprised to find that compartment empty as well. After a little consideration, we tried the fourth door on the left, with the same result.

"Shit," Tai breathed.

Alicia and Tai returned to *Contessa*, where Strange and Hiroshi regarded each other coldly. "My information is solid," Hiroshi insisted, though his voice betrayed uncertainty.

"Not worth checking the other compartments," Strange said, an assertion based on his assessment of the time required versus the estimated chance of a different result. "Where else in the station might the drug be stored?" He asked the question of the room in general; Hiroshi had never claimed specific knowledge of station operations, which the current situation had reinforced.

Damien pulled up a map on the screen: a construction diagram of this station type. Utility stations like this were massproduced ... but there were always differences, and this station had already shown itself to have a unique personality. "Lower level is cargo and mechanical," he said, pointing. "If we're giving up on the cargo compartments ... life support systems take up most of the rest of that space. Middle level might be more cargo, might be living or working areas. Upper level, probably living space and administration."

"If this is a drug production facility," Shweta said, "the labs would be on the middle level, for easy access to water and air from the systems in the basement."

Strange frowned, one finger scratching his chin. "The locks on the doors show that this facility *has* been used for valuable cargo in the recent past. If they just sent out a big shipment—bad luck for us. But there might be recent production in the labs. Worth the risk?"

Shweta considered the question. "The staff would all be on the upper level at this hour."

Miyuki nodded. "Lower gravity for comfortable sleeping."

Hiroshi looked from the map to Shweta to Strange. "We've come this far! We have to risk it!"

"Sunk cost fallacy," Strange muttered. But his memory palace was shifting, fitting together different pieces in new configurations. This was Hiroshi's one big chance. He'd be more likely to advocate for a stupid risk. But the profits on our target—the illegal anti-aging stimulant called Blue Diamond—would be huge; the potential benefits of taking even a partial shipment would be enough to justify considerable additional exposure.

We discussed the question for a little while, but our course of action soon became clear: we would chance an incursion into the middle level. Alicia insisted that she should go in alone, but Damien refused to countenance this—he couldn't bear the thought of having to abandon her if the job went south—and Strange and Shweta backed him up.

"We have very limited time," Strange said, "and a whole level to examine. We may have to carry out a lot of cargo quickly. Or we may have to fight our way out."

Shweta finished his thought. "So we have to go in with force."

"Damien stays here," Strange continued, "watching for incoming ships and keeping the drive warm for a quick getaway. You"—he indicated Miyuki—"would just be an impediment." She ducked her head in embarrassment. "But you"—he pointed a rigid finger at Hiroshi—"come with us. You might, just possibly, have some useful information to contribute."

Hiroshi swallowed, but nodded his assent.

"I'll keep your father safe," Alicia said to Miyuki. "I promise." Strange shot her a glare, but said nothing.

We prepared for assault.

FOUR

The Emperor's Scroll Job

Alicia—Present Day

Even for me, an employee with two years and God knows how many shifts under my belt, the casino floor was disorienting—a dark, cavernous, noisy space busy with colored lights, music, chatter, and the various electronic sounds of slots, keno, spherette, and the sports book. It was *intended* to be confusing—to keep the clientele distracted and disoriented to the extent that staying where they were and continuing to lose money was less effort than finding their way out. I knew that the lights and sounds were not nearly as random as they seemed, that lasers and focused speakers made sure that each customer received the optimum dose of stimulation. And I knew that, despite the raucous babble of the place, there was also plenty of active and passive sound deadening going on, because too much noise could be as bad as too little when it came to keeping the customers properly confused.

Which was why I saw Kane before I heard him.

It wasn't Kane himself I saw, of course. It was a swirling knot of Thunderbolt security—not all of them were uniformed, but even when they were in plain clothes, you could tell—which looked more than anything else like a model of an atom, a tiny nucleus surrounded by a cloud of electrons swirling randomly about and occasionally fissioning off to collide with other nearby particles.

The nucleus couldn't be anything else but Kane. I'd seen plenty of security incidents in my time at Thunderbolt, but I'd never seen one that needed that many people to control a single miscreant. And Kane, I knew, would not be taken easily. I drifted closer to the scrum, looking for some way to help without getting caught up in the mess.

I wasn't sure what I could do. I'd left my gun back at the hostel—there was no way I could get it through the scanners at the employee entrance or on the casino floor—and I certainly wasn't in any shape to help Kane with the fight physically. But, I told myself, I knew things about this place Kane didn't, and as the officers weren't expecting me to take action, I might be able to engineer a surprise or a distraction.

Back in the day, Max once tried to educate me in free-fall combat. It hadn't taken, but I still remembered a few of the basic lessons. "You have to keep control of your anchors," he'd said. And I could see that Kane was doing so masterfully; he hovered near the intersection of three guidelines, which gave him something to hang onto or kick off from to keep station, maintain orientation, and put power behind his punches and kicks. Every time a security officer came at him, Kane launched himself off a guideline, struck the offender with a foot or elbow, and caromed back to another guideline where he could easily redirect himself against the next attack. Meanwhile, the officer went tumbling off in an unexpected direction, often colliding with other officers in a chain reaction of startled confusion.

But despite his strength and skill, Kane was still just one against a dozen or more. He was in no position to get away from the scrum, and they weren't stopping. I didn't know enough about combat to see his fatigue, but I felt certain he wouldn't be able to keep this up forever.

"Kane!" I subvocalized.

"Kind of busy here," he responded. His voice was a rasp in my ear.

I explained the situation with Cayce. "I'm coming to help you."

"No!" he replied. "Stay out! Save yourself!"

"*I'm* not running out on you!" I insisted.

He didn't respond to me. Instead, he launched himself at the nearest guard. I couldn't fault his priorities.

As the fight continued, I moved in closer. Some of the officers were trying to move civilians away from the fight, but there weren't enough of them to cover the whole three-dimensional perimeter and I had no difficulty moving through it, skimming along a guideline toward the scrum. I didn't really know what I could do, but I figured the closer I could get to Kane, the more likely I was to be able to help.

The next time I saw Kane, he was hanging at an intersection, panting, looking in every direction for the next attack. Then, suddenly, he turned and looked over his shoulder, his eyes widening.

Alarmed, I followed his gaze to the security post at the top of the spherette station. Of course the spherette tables had their own security detail, but that station also served as the central command post for the whole casino floor. It had a view in every direction—the sightlines were carefully kept clear—and would be the perfect place to stage a ...

Shit. I was right.

A black-uniformed security officer lurked in the shadows there, one foot hooked around a stanchion, carefully aiming a rifle at Kane. It was something with a telescopic sight, long barrel, and narrow bore, and probably fired something offering a comparatively low risk to bystanders or property. But even a small slug could kill if properly placed—and in expert hands, at that range, against a target that wasn't expecting it and with no place to hide, it almost certainly would be a kill shot.

It might be a tranq dart, too. But knowing Thunderbolt, it almost certainly wasn't.

I grabbed the nearest guideline, bunched up my legs between me and it, and pushed off as hard as I could.

I had time to think *that was a pretty bonehead maneuver* in the seconds it took me to sail through the empty air between my previous location and the sniper. But my aim was good, and in the casino's dim and intermittent lighting, coming in from an unexpected direction and at fairly high speed, I took the sniper by surprise.

Me too.

The big, bald, black-clad officer with the wicked-looking weapon grew in my vision with alarming speed, and I won't lie: at the last moment, I shrieked involuntarily and closed my eyes, throwing my hands up to protect my face. A moment later, I collided with the man, leather and metal and flesh striking my arms and head even as the gun went off with a startlingly loud bang.

A moment later my eyes snapped open to see the man's equally startled eyes looking right back at me. "Where the hell did *you* come from?" he shouted, and grabbed for me. But I was already caroming off of him after our impact, and I was able to bring my feet up between us and push off from his chest, sending us sailing in opposite directions.

But he had reflexes I didn't, and before he'd gone half a meter backward, he grabbed the stanchion he'd been using to position himself and flung himself after me. Floating free, backward, with nothing to grab to correct my course, I could do nothing to avoid him, and a moment later, we collided with a grunt that came from both of us.

I clawed at his face, but he caught my wrist in an iron grip and forced it behind my back, leaving the other hand to scrabble ineffectually at the rough fabric of his shoulder holster. He grabbed that hand too, and held both of my wrists behind my back in one enormous paw while he pulled out a sticky-strip and wrapped them together.

I did manage to kick him in the nuts before he got me completely restrained, but he was wearing a cup and I think I did more damage to my sock-clad toes than I did to him. Bastard.

"All right, Missy," the man growled, "who are you?"

"Ask my lawyer," I spat back. I didn't have a lawyer.

We tumbled together for a time, me struggling ineffectually, waiting for someone or something to come within reach to stop our random drift. The casino's lights spun dizzily around me and, as I began to catch my breath, I searched for Kane. The gun had gone off just as I'd impacted the sniper ... had the bullet found its mark?

And then I saw Kane ... in the middle of a knot of security officers. He wasn't going to get away, but he was still fighting back. Not dead, at least, and judging by his vigorous struggles, probably not seriously injured.

71

I'd accomplished that much, at least.

Both of us were going to live ... to be sentenced.

"You are in a *lot* of trouble," said the man on the other side of the desk.

My wrists were still sticky-stripped together behind me. They itched terribly, and my shoulders and elbows ached even more than usual. My ankles, too, were fastened together, leaving me completely helpless to maneuver even in free fall. I'd been none-too-gently manhandled from the casino floor to the security office and deposited in a holding cell. There I'd waited, bound hand and foot and deprived of all my possessions, for what seemed like hours. I'd heard a lot of yelling outside the door, but very little had been comprehensible. Finally, one of the officers had unlocked the door, hauled me out, and fastened me to a chair in what appeared to be someone's office. Posters on the walls reminded me of my rights as a casino employee under the Jupiter Union, but I suspected my employment had been terminated the moment I'd collided with the sniper.

I didn't say anything. I couldn't think of anything *to* say that might improve my situation. I was guilty of assaulting a Thunderbolt security officer, at the very least, and probably conspiracy to commit fraud and/or blackmail. Probably a lot more than that.

I'd had a good run here. And I'd probably saved Kane's life.

But I really wished I'd never met Cayce.

The man at the desk—he was slim, with a trim executive beard stylishly bleached to contrast with his dark skin—picked up a screen and scrolled through it, ostentatiously looking from it to me and back. "You've been a good employee up to now," he said. "Kept your nose clean. You could have kept going and retired with a nice pension."

I snorted at that.

He glanced up from his screen, waiting for me to say something. I didn't. "If you hadn't gotten involved with Mr. Kane," he continued, "we might never have known about your criminal past. But now we know all about your previous career with the Cannibal Club." He waved the screen. "It's actually quite an impressive resume. So what was the plan?"

We stared at each other in silence for a long time.

He blinked first. "I can't believe that someone with your background would be content with a life as a blackjack dealer," he said. He folded up the screen and tapped it on the desk. "There has to have been some kind of long-term plan."

I didn't respond, but he kept up the waiting game and, somewhat against my will, I found myself considering the question he'd raised. Would I *really* have been happy working at the Thunderbolt until I got too weak to continue?

Finally I spoke. "The plan *was* to keep going and retire with a nice pension. But Maxon made sure *that* wouldn't happen."

"Ah yes, Mr. Maxon. I'm aware that you hold a grudge against him."

"It's not a *grudge*." I would have made air quotes if my hands weren't bound behind me. "It's a *grievance*, and it's legitimate." Even as I spoke—and I knew at some level I was digging my own grave, and I knew at a deeper level that I really didn't care—I found myself growing angrier and angrier.

Angry at Maxon, certainly—him and all his spotless professional colleagues, for stealing my disability payments and the payments of thousands of others. But angry at myself as well, for rolling over and letting them do it.

I'd let them define me by my illness. Let them manipulate me and minimize me and put me in a little box, where I would move less and less until I stopped moving completely.

And then Cayce had come along and treated me as a partner. Yes, he did it because he wanted something from me. Why else does anyone do anything? But he'd treated me the way his dad had, and never let my limitations reduce me to a *thing*.

"Maxon *stole* that pension," I continued with cold, tight-jawed fury. "It might have been all clean and legal, but it was still theft, and I'm glad I finally at least *tried* to do something about it."

"Unlike yourself, Maxon didn't participate in a criminal conspiracy, associate with known felons, or assault anyone."

"I'll grant you that he's never physically assaulted anyone," I replied, "*that I know of.* The others are subject to debate."

He steepled his fingers and looked along his fingertips at me as though they were a gunsight. "Look, we hold all the cards here and you know it. If you agree to cooperate with the prosecution, I can definitely get you a reduced sentence. Maybe even avoid jail time completely."

I just glared at him.

He replied with an elaborate, performative shrug. "All right, it's your funeral. But, just so you know, we'll be making the same offer to Mr. Kane. And if he lacks your admirable sense of solidarity … well, it will go better for him than it will for you."

When I still said nothing, he straightened and tucked the folded tablet in a pocket. "I'll just leave you here to consider your options while I'm talking with Mr. Kane," he said, and left. The door closed with a complicated, definitive click that indicated he wasn't expecting me to be able to leave the room at the time of my choosing.

Between the Parkinson's, my lack of tools, and my hands being firmly trussed behind my back, he might even have been right. But I wasn't going to try it in any case, because I knew that we were deep in the Thunderbolt security offices and I wasn't going to just waltz out of there.

So I waited. And although I knew this was just a psychological ploy—"Prisoner's Dilemma" isn't just the name of a band, look it up—I didn't have anything else to do, so I did wind up considering my options as the man had suggested.

Kane and I had a lot of history together. But I knew he had limited smarts, anger issues, and a real tendency to go off half-cocked. If he took it into his head that I was somehow to blame for his situation, he might decide to hang me up to save his own neck.

And Cayce … well, he was a real unknown. Certainly he'd shown himself to have his father's brains, strategic sense, and cold-blooded bravado, and between that and his physical resemblance to his dad—a younger, slimmer, sexier version of his dad, no less—my heart wanted to mother him. But my head knew that Strange was poison, and suspected his kid might be the same.

I couldn't hold Damien's death, or any of Strange's other crimes, against Cayce. But the kid was *so* much like Strange that I'd be foolish to expect him to be any more altruistic, compassionate, or forthcoming than his dad had been. And I knew from bitter experience that although you could one hundred percent rely on Strange to keep his promises, you needed to be very careful that you understood exactly what he had promised and what he had not. He was a genie in a bottle, that one.

There was a time I'd trusted Strange with my life. And there was a time that trust had led to the death of my best beloved. It had taken me ten years to get past that betrayal. Maybe I still hadn't.

Had Strange betrayed us? He'd certainly denied it at the time. He'd been mistaken, he said, possibly misled, maybe even outsmarted—and that was a big admission for him—but he'd never, ever betrayed our trust.

He *did* bear some responsibility for Damien's death, though, no question, and he'd acknowledged that. But Damien himself certainly came in for a big share of the blame. Hell, all of us had played a part in the fiasco, even me.

I hadn't seen Strange in nearly ten years, and I would have said I never wanted to see him again. But then Cayce had come waltzing into my life, asking me to help his dad out, and I hadn't been able to say no.

And now … here I was. Locked in a security office with my hands bound, facing prison time.

Damn my soft heart.

And damn Cayce! Where the *hell* had he gone?

Had he been captured? Had he chickened out? Had he turned himself in?

He'd been cagey the whole time—always holding his cards close to his vest, never sharing any information he didn't really have to. Had he been hiding something? Had he always intended to sell us out? Or had he just seen an opportunity to scram and taken it?

The next time I saw that boy, he would have a *hell* of a lot of questions to answer.

I seethed for an hour or more. And then the lock clicked, and the man with the bleached blond hair came in, along with Maxon.

They were followed by Cayce.

He looked smug.

I screamed "You *fucker!*" and hurled myself at him.

I admit it was a futile gesture, as my wrists and ankles were still taped. But I had to do *something* with the pent-up anger and energy inside me, and seeing Cayce, the author of my most recent troubles, floating in free and easy just called on me to unleash it on him.

Cayce caught me by the shoulders, but my momentum carried us both onward until he struck the door frame with his shoulder, sending both of us into a tumble. "*Why*, you bastard?" I shouted in his face. "Why did you just run out on us? What did we ever do to you?"

"Good job," he replied with remarkable calm, neatly halting our spin with a foot hooked into one of the floor loops. "But you can stop the act now. I've told Maxon everything."

Despite my crying need to head-butt him into unconsciousness, I forced my anger down and took a moment to assess the situation.

Maxon was the type of slimy con man who was always on top of the world even when he wasn't. But his veneer of confidence was about as thin as I'd ever seen it. His smile was broad and toothy ... a little too much so. And there was a sheen of sweat on his brow.

The blond was withdrawn, deferential to Maxon, even cowed. And that attitude extended to Cayce as well.

And Cayce, though he was deep in the nest of vipers, was conspicuously *not* handcuffed. And though he wasn't grinning—his expression was serious, contemplative, even a little judgmental—the set of his shoulders and the way his attention was focused entirely on me, seemingly dismissive of Maxon and the threat he posed, told me that he was the one in command of the situation.

My mouth went dry. What was really happening here? "Everything?" I temporized.

"Everything. You, me, Kane, Candela, the security assessment." He turned to the blond. "Why is she still restrained?"

The question was delivered mildly, but the man jerked as though he'd been slapped. "Terribly sorry, sir," he said, and produced a pocket knife, which he used—with admirable delicacy—to remove the sticky-strips from my wrists and ankles.

"Where's Kane?" I asked, rubbing the glue off my wrists.

"In the clinic," Cayce replied. "He'll be all right." He turned to Maxon. "Your people will be getting full marks for diligence, but I'm going to have to take points off for unnecessary roughness."

Maxon's attitude was outwardly deferential, but he was clearly seething inside. "In their defense, sir," he said, glaring at Cayce, "the man resisted with considerable force."

"Exactly as he was instructed to do." This was a surprise to me, and I suspected would also be a surprise to Kane. "This was part of the test, and you failed. The Thunderbolt security manual specifies policies and procedures for restraining an uncooperative customer, and if those had been properly followed, no one would have been hurt."

"Uncooperative—!" Maxon snapped, then gritted his teeth, preventing himself from saying anything that would get him into any more trouble. He took a breath and let it out slowly. "I will … I will refresh their training, sir." He nodded to the blond, who shrank into himself as he made a note in his tablet.

"Good." Cayce looked around in a proprietary manner. "All in all … I'm reasonably impressed, and my report will reflect this."

"Thank you, *sir*," Maxon said, inclining his head but not letting his gaze leave Cayce's eyes. The emphasis he placed on the last word spoke volumes; this situation was even more complex than it looked.

"Now, if you don't mind, my associates and I will retire and debrief." He extended a hand to me—a free-fall courtesy—and we left the office together.

What's happening? I signed to him as we moved down the hall. The Thunderbolt employees all bowed and got out of his way like he was visiting royalty.

Everything is under control, he signed back. *More later.*

Two hours later, we were ensconced in a Golden Way suite ritzier than anything I'd ever seen the inside of in all my years working for Thunderbolt. The concierge bowed and exited, closing the door behind herself. Cayce fixed us a couple of margaritas and triggered his gizmo so we could speak privately.

It was just him and me. Kane was in one of the bedrooms, sleeping off the painkillers they'd given him in the clinic. If I knew him, he'd resisted treatment just about as hard as he had the security officers, but he'd probably been restrained at the time.

"What the *fuck*?" I said, without preamble. "You *abandoned* us!"

"You're welcome," he replied, still as smug as he'd been when he entered the office, "for the rescue."

"If you hadn't left us in the lurch, we wouldn't have *needed* rescue!"

Now he looked hurt. "I did not 'leave you in the lurch.' I explained everything before I left the Gravy Boat."

"What?"

"I sent you a message."

"Well, I didn't get it!" I pulled out my pocket comm to show him …

… and there was a message. From Cayce. *Got a handle on Maxon,* it said. *Going radio silent for a bit. Sit tight.* The timestamp was a little before the time I'd come back to the Gravy Boat and found him gone.

I stared at that message for a long time, my emotions roiling. I was still pissed at Cayce, but couldn't really justify it any longer. But I couldn't really forgive him either. "This isn't exactly 'explaining everything,'" I said at last.

"I was in a hurry."

"And I didn't get it until … well, now." It definitely hadn't arrived before Thunderbolt confiscated all my stuff. I tried to remember if I'd looked at my messages when I got the comm back. Maybe not. I'd been distracted.

"I sent it before I left the restaurant, I swear!" Cayce frowned. "I had to shut down completely so Maxon could maintain plausible deniability that he'd met with me. There is a … possibility that I might have turned off my screen before the message actually went out."

That very tentative admission of possible guilt made me a little more willing to forgive him. Just a little. "So," I said, changing the subject. "How did you manage to convince Maxon we were doing a security audit?"

"I didn't 'convince' him." A slow, satisfied smile spread itself across Cayce's face. "I blackmailed him."

"Oh?" I squeezed margarita into my mouth and waited. This was going to be good.

"The data stick in Maxon's safe didn't just have the info we needed to prove that Thunderbolt was embezzling your disability payments. It also showed that Maxon was skimming the proceeds for himself. When I showed him what I had, and explained that I was willing and able to share it with both the Jupiter Union authorities and his bosses, he agreed—quite reasonably—to not only release us but to provide us with transportation off Amalthea and a substantial payment to assure our continued silence. All paid from his personal slush fund."

I raised my squeeze bulb. "Very impressive. But wasn't that data stick encrypted?"

"It was. But you may recall I asked you for a list of the pet boarding centers near the casino?"

I immediately saw where this was going. "Son of a bitch!"

"Son of a *queen*, actually. In two ways. Maxon's password was based on the name of his cat, Akhenaten. His *late* cat Akhenaten. Very sad."

"It must have taken you a while to suss that out."

"Background process." He waved a hand dismissively. "The question now is, where do we go next?"

I gave the question serious consideration. "I'm done here," I said. "I need to find a new place to settle where I can get ongoing care for my condition." I raised my trembling hands. "How much was that 'substantial' payment?"

"Not enough for that," he admitted. "What I had in mind was more about where do we go next to put the rest of the Club back together so we can rescue Strange from Cronos Station?"

"What makes you think I would go along with that? I'm *done* with the life."

"Well, you risked your life for Kane."

I had. "That was … stupid. I acted in the moment."

"I think it was who you really are." He was holding my hand. Something about that felt so familiar, so *right*, that I didn't even realize I'd accepted the touch until now. But he hadn't asked.

I pulled my hand back. "Don't touch me without permission."

"I'm sorry. I won't do it again." He seemed genuinely contrite … though I wondered if I could trust Strange's kid to be genuine about anything.

But my hand hadn't trembled while he held it.

I rubbed my fingers. "What did you mean, 'who I really am'?"

"This isn't you." He gestured around, taking in the suite, the Thunderbolt, Amalthea, everything. "You don't belong in a nine-to-five life. You are the sort of person who lives life twenty-four seven, on your own terms."

Something in his words tugged at my heart. "I would *like* to be," I amended, which was true in a way I had tried to deny for the last two years. "But I can't. Not anymore." I held out my hands, supplicating.

"But you can. You're part of the Cannibal Club." He hesitated. "I know I wasn't there, but Dad talked about it constantly. It was more than a gang, more than a family. Practically one person. Look at how this job went down! Your skills, Kane's hands. You did it together. And you saved his life, when no one else could have or would have. You know he'd do the same for you."

I looked away, not wanting Cayce to see the tears that were beginning to blur my vision. "Have you *met* Kane?"

He snorted at that. "Yes, but just between you and me, I don't think he's as heartless as he makes himself out to be." He leaned in closer. "We can put it together again, Alicia. Maybe not the same, not without Max and Damien, but a new Cannibal Club, greater than the sum of its parts." He paused, swallowed. "A new family."

I realized that, with his dad in prison and his mom who knows where, we were all the family Cayce had. Kane had said he'd been solo in the deep black for more than a year. "You make it sound so nice."

I wiped my eyes on my sleeve and pushed myself away from the table, leaving my empty margarita bulb slowly spinning above it, and drifted to the panoramic window. It was a screen, of course, like all the windows in Amalthea, but it was huge and very high-res and showed a dramatic live view of Jupiter. I watched the clouds' slow, hypnotic flow for a while, and Cayce left me to my thoughts.

He was right. The Club *was* more than a family, and together we'd been capable of extraordinary things. We'd also gotten in extraordinary trouble, and in the end it had killed us. Could something like that ever be put back together?

I wasn't sure. But damn, it had felt good when I'd plowed into that sniper. It was the first time I'd felt *alive* in more than two years.

Two years of days all the same, uniforms and cafeterias and surly customers and a little tiny cubicle with a cracked screen and water that tasted tinny.

If I were smart, I'd tell Cayce to fuck off, take my share of Maxon's blackmail money, and find another job—a good steady *legal* job, with proper health insurance, in some populous asteroid where I could fade quietly away while being properly taken care of. I had smarts, I had skills, I was sure I could do it.

But I didn't *want* to.

I turned back to Cayce. "I'm in," I said. "Better to burn for the stars than to drift into a gravity well."

"Thank you." He smiled and nodded, and for the first time he also looked a little bashful. "Hug?"

We hugged. And lord, it felt good.

The next morning, after a long luxurious night in a bedchamber twice the size of my old cubicle, I counted my pills. Eighty-nine days' worth remained for most of them, after this morning's dose, but only fifty-seven Virtafimab. That was the most expensive one, and the one I could least afford to do without. Three days without Virtafimab, and my hands would be so weak and shaky I couldn't even deal cards. And a half dose was worse than nothing.

I was glad to have even that much, of course. It had taken a lot of work—careful filling of prescriptions at the earliest possible moment for months, swapping of favors with friendly pharmacists, and renting an anonymous storage locker in which to stash my go-bag—but that work had bought me the freedom to run away, at least for a bit. Most of the other people I knew with similar health issues were shackled to their employers without even fifty-seven days of wiggle room.

Whatever. Kane and I were both part of Cayce's scheme now, and I'd just have to keep my eyes, and my options, open.

After an incredibly decadent hot-water shower, the three of us rendezvoused in the suite's dining room to strategize over a lavish room service breakfast. All paid for out of Maxon's personal slush fund, which made the beignets even more delicious.

Kane ate like a famished wolf but seemed otherwise completely recovered from the previous day's adventures. I envied his youth and fitness.

"Short term," Cayce said, "we have to get my father out of Cronos as quickly as possible. The longer he's there, the more likely Aquila will be able to get what they want out of him, after which they will certainly dispose of him."

"And what they want is …?" I asked.

Cayce blew out a hard breath through his nose. "I don't know," he admitted. "But they must want something, not just retribution, or they would have killed him already."

Kane spread butter on a scone, popped it into his mouth. "Maybe they already have." Crumbs drifted out with his words.

"I got a message from him just a short time before I met you," Cayce insisted, batting crumbs away from his face. "If anything had changed since then I would have heard."

"If that's your *short* term plan," I asked, "what's the *long* term?"

"Once we have the whole Club back together, including Strange, we get back into business in a big way. I've picked up some leads, I've got some contacts." He looked at me. "Your share will be more than enough to pay for your medical care."

"Your short term isn't short enough," Kane said, wiping his mouth. "We aren't in any shape to break Strange out of anywhere. We don't even have a ship."

"Acquiring a ship is part of my plan. But to make that happen, we need technology and diplomacy, in addition to the skills we already have."

I shook my head. "Tai's happy where they are, and Shweta … well, in case you haven't heard, Shweta's got a day job. It's pretty cushy."

"I *do* read the news." The flatness of Cayce's reply was a suitable acknowledgment of my statement of the obvious. "But I have a way to get Tai, no matter how happy they are, and once we get Tai, we'll be able to get Shweta." I snorted derisively. "And we need you," he continued, talking right over my snort, "to get Tai."

I didn't like being considered as just a means to an end, but he was right: of the three of us, I was the only one Tai would listen to, because of our shared history. Tai had history with Kane too, but not in a good way, and Cayce was an unknown quantity to them. "Okay," I sighed. "Last I heard, they're on Ngo Quyen Ring in the Trailing Trojans."

"That matches my intelligence. I've already investigated our travel options and we can be there in about two weeks."

Kane scoffed. "That won't be a cheap ticket." Moving from Jupiter to the Trailing Trojans, a third of the way around the solar system in the same orbit, wasn't easy. A low-energy transfer ellipse would take years; to do it in two weeks implied a high-end skip drive with a crack pilot.

"Maxon will be happy to buy us that passage and get us well out of his hair," Cayce replied with confidence. "But once we get there, we'll be on our own."

"That's not a new situation for us." Kane cracked his knuckles. "When do we leave?"

Our passage to Ngo Quyen Ring was on the *Django*, a trader out of Vesta. Our quarters were sparse but clean, and the owner/pilot, a person called Najah, kept mostly to themselves. Just as well, really.

Najah was slim and wiry, with a huge puff of black curls contained in a spiral of smart wire. They spoke little, and when they did, their utterances could sometimes be baffling. Like when they said one day over dinner, completely out of nowhere, "There's another storm on Jupiter at the exact antipodes of the Great Red Spot, but you can't see it." None of us knew what to say to that, and after a long uncomfortable silence, we just went back to picking the bones out of our fish. But apparently that kind of … unconventional mind was well suited to being a skip pilot.

Damien had been a little on the weird side too, of course, but in his case, it had manifested in a wry, unpredictable sense of humor and a fashion sense that had once been memorably described as "an explosion in a paint factory." That quirkiness had been what had first attracted me to him—it was a perfect, if often aggravating, counterweight to my own caution and fastidiousness—and it was apparently part and parcel of his piloting skill.

Damien had tried and tried to explain how skip piloting worked, but it had never quite sunk in. This was perhaps because of my own logical mind. "The skip *isn't* logical," he'd explained. "It's a remnant of the Big Bang, when the universe was chaotic—or at least wasn't ordered the way it is now. Applying present-day logic to it just doesn't work. That's why no AI has ever gotten as good as a human pilot." And then he'd start waving his hands around, and no matter how many metaphors he used, it never got any clearer.

Damn, I still missed him.

The only thing that really mattered was that the skip permitted interplanetary travel without crushing acceleration or the need to carry massive volumes of fuel. The latest skip drives could do almost a tenth of one percent of the speed of light, which is enough to get you from Earth to Jupiter in five weeks but doesn't introduce any serious relativistic effects.

But at that speed it would still take over four thousand years to get to Alpha Centauri. Interstellar space is *really* big.

We all gathered at the forward windows to watch as Ngo Quyen Ring grew from a dot to an ellipse to a city-sized structure rotating in space. Unlike Amalthea, where the surface was home only to mining robots and antenna farms and Jupiter was the most interesting thing in view, Ngo Quyen sparkled with windows and docking-port beacons and huge illuminated signs advertising the businesses within. Most of those signs were in Chinese, of course, given that history and the facts of orbital mechanics tied the Trojan Asteroids much more closely to the Outer Belt than to Jupiter, but there was a fair sprinkling of Roman letters as well.

But almost all of those Roman letters sported Vietnamese accent marks, and I wondered how much English we'd find spoken inside. None of us had ever visited Ngo Quyen before. I had a translator on my pocket comm, of course, but those never worked as well as you'd hope.

"We'll be docking in about half an hour," Najah announced, and we left the windows to finish packing up our things.

"Are you ready for this?" Cayce asked.

He was floating just outside my cabin door. My two bags were packed and bungeed to the luggage rack. And the *thing* floated just beside them.

It had been remarkably easy to pack up and leave Amalthea with no intention of returning. I've never been one to accumulate stuff, and almost everything I might need for practical purposes could be purchased or fabbed at any decently equipped station or even ship, so I wasn't too surprised that when I'd finished the selection and packing process, I wound up with only two smallish bags. The surprise had been how little emotional baggage went along with it. I'd closed the door of the cubicle where I'd lived for two years and walked away without a single tear—a confirmation that, as Cayce had said, I'd never really belonged here.

No, leaving Amalthea hadn't been difficult. But arriving at Ngo Quyen was going to be hard.

The *thing*, as I thought of it, was a walker: a light, foldable three-sided frame about a meter high, with cushioned hand grips at the top and two wheels and two non-mar feet at the bottom, still smelling of fresh plastics. Cayce had downloaded the pattern, fabbed the parts, cleaned them up, and assembled them. He'd even fabbed it in purple, my favorite color. Even so, the thought of using the thing—of being dependent on a stupid rattle-ass plastic framework just to get around—was galling, and shameful, and frightening.

A powered exoskeleton would have been better, of course, but even if we'd had the pattern—and patterns for medical devices were regulated and didn't come cheap—*Django's* little fab unit didn't have the resolution or the high-strength materials to build it, and we didn't have anyone with the expertise to fit it. This rattletrap thing would have to do.

At least Ngo Quyen Ring spun at Outer Belt standard, only a quarter gee rather than a third. But it had been more than a year since I'd tried to stand up in any gravity at all. I'd been doing my exercises—well, most of them, most of the time ... *much* of the time anyway—but I still had very little confidence.

"As ready as I'm going to be, I guess," I said in response to Cayce's question.

"We'll be docking soon," he said. "There's a chair in the galley for you, with a seat belt and a nice soft cushion. You can stay seated through the docking procedure, and once we're docked and stable, we'll take it from there. All right?"

"All right," I said, but I felt foolish and weak and coddled, and when he held out a hand for me to help put myself in motion—an unexceptional free-fall courtesy under other circumstances—I pointedly rejected it and pushed myself off from my luggage. I might have limited mobility but I was damned if I'd consider myself a cripple.

We drifted down to the galley and got me settled. Kane, never comfortable with any sign of weakness, made himself scarce. Cayce was overly solicitous until I snapped at him, after which he tried to be purely practical, only helping when explicitly requested to.

I wasn't certain whether the pity I saw in his eyes was really there, or just a projection of my own feelings of inadequacy.

Django's thrusters boomed and I felt the seat press against my bones. I gripped the chair's arms, then berated myself for nerves. Cayce settled himself into the chair next to me, but I was certain this was for my comfort rather than his own. "All hands brace for docking," Najah announced, and with a reasonably gentle series of nudges, rattles, and bangs, *Django* nosed into the dock. Immediately there was a sense of rising fast in an elevator ... but it went on and on.

We were locked onto the ring. Outer Belt standard one-quarter gee.

I raised my arms and held them out in front of me. The hands seemed to be trembling more than usual, but that might just be anxiety.

I held my arms out straight for a count of ten. It felt like I was lifting a full jug of wine with each hand, but I managed the full ten-count before I let my hands drop to my lap with a sigh. "Okay," I said, "let's see how this goes."

Cayce brought over the walker—the hateful thing—while I un-buckled my seat belt. He unfolded it, clack clack, and placed it on the floor in front of me. I put my hands on the handgrips, leaned forward, and raised myself to a standing position.

Or tried to. I made it up only about halfway, and after a few seconds of trembling effort, I let myself drop back into the chair. "Are you all right?" Cayce asked.

I grunted and waved him away.

If you've lived your whole life in gravity, you might not believe that standing up is a skill. But it is, and it needs practice. I took a deep breath, grabbed the walker, and pushed myself up with every muscle in my arms, legs, back, and belly.

It wasn't easy, but this time I got up and stayed up.

Cayce moved in to steady me, but again I waved him away. "If you want to help, take my bags out to the dock. I'll make it there under my own power."

I pushed the thing forward on its wheels, remembering the instructions that had come with the pattern: keep your feet under you, stand up straight, don't drag your feet. I only pushed it ten centimeters before I stopped it, put my weight on the handles, and took a step forward.

It was work, bearing my whole weight on my hands and one foot, but I did it.

And then I did it again.

And again.

This isn't too bad, I thought and shuffled forward with increasing confidence.

But I found that when I reached the galley door, just three meters away, I was already feeling a little winded, with my heart pumping strongly. I paused to catch my breath. Twinges pinged almost audibly in my arms and legs.

I'd never visited Ngo Quyen before, but I'd spent some time on rings of comparable size ... and there was a *lot* of walking involved.

Well, there were accommodations. I'd have to find out what they were and use them.

Grimly, I resumed my progress through the ship and out onto the dock.

You can do this, I thought. *One foot in front of the other.*

I made it to the dock and sat heavily on one of Kane's cases, which rested in a tidy little pile with the rest of our stuff. Most of Kane's luggage was military-looking hard cases and I hoped we wouldn't have any difficulty bringing the contents onto the ring.

"How you doing?" Kane asked. Which was, if not completely unprecedented, at least an unusual degree of concern from him. I must really look like shit.

"Fine," I snapped, then caught myself and said it again in a more pleasant tone. "Fine. I'm ... it's an effort, I'll admit it. But I'll get there, okay? Just give me a moment to catch my breath."

"You sit tight. Cayce is dealing with customs now."

I nodded absently and closed my eyes, concentrating on moderating my breathing, feeling my leg muscles twitch randomly. It was always Shweta who'd dealt with customs, back in the Cannibal Club's heyday, and I was a little afraid that Cayce's do-you-know-who-you're-dealing-with attitude would get us all in trouble. But I guess he managed not to look *too* suspicious because he soon reappeared with a visa chip for each of us and a bundle of maps and documents on his comm, which he shared with us. They were in English, mostly, though in some cases, the grammar left something to be desired. "I don't suppose you speak Vietnamese?" I asked him, looking at a document that was printed in three languages, none of them European-descended.

"Alas, no. And my Mandarin is only so-so."

"Just find me a drink, a smoke, and a strip club and I'll be fine," Kane said.

"We're here for business," Cayce replied, a bit testy. "We need to find Tai and get out with them as quick as we can."

"Just joshing, boss," Kane said with a smirk, waving Cayce's attitude away. But I wasn't really sure how serious he'd been before ... or how sincere he was being now.

"Tai still hasn't answered my messages," Cayce said, pulling out his screen and calling up a map.

"That's not a good sign," I said. I hadn't heard from Tai myself in over a year.

"Well, I'm not certain the contact info I have is still good, so it might not mean anything. I expect they'll be somewhere in here." He pointed to a densely crowded section of the map labeled NIGHT MARKET in English.

"Sounds like Tai's sort of place," I agreed. "But where exactly? It looks like an easy place to get lost." I zoomed in the map and the area's complexity became bigger but no less confusing.

"Just go in there and listen for the screech and thump," Kane grumbled.

Cayce's eyes and mine met in an amused glance. Kane and Tai had never agreed on music, and Tai had been fond of sharing their favorites with the whole ship at top volume. "That's not a completely stupid idea, actually," I said. "Last I heard from Tai, they were working as a deejay. Maybe that was just a cover for their other work, but it'll be a public face we can find more easily."

Cayce nodded and tucked the screen away. "Okay. Let's shift our stuff to the apartment and head out. No time to lose."

"Shifting our stuff to the apartment" proved to be more of a chore than we'd expected. Although Cayce had located and booked us a place to stay while we'd been en route, figuring out how to get ourselves and our baggage there from the dock was a bit of a challenge.

For one thing, I couldn't navigate with the walker and carry even a single bag at the same time. I was used to traveling light, and hadn't dealt with luggage and gravity at the same time in years, so the idea that I'd need help with my pathetic little load was a terribly disheartening surprise. Cayce and Kane distributed my stuff between them, with only a little grumbling on Kane's part, but I was still disappointed in myself as I clumped and scraped along with just my shoulder bag. No way was I going to risk getting separated from my meds.

Then we discovered that the rapid transit line that ran along the station's outer rim was a nightmare of crowds—a noisy, jostling, chaotic mess, with low ceilings and hard surfaces that magnified the noise. The signage was impossible to see through the constantly shifting throng, even if we'd been able to read it, and we could barely even keep our group and luggage together. The walker was the only thing making it possible for me to remain vertical and move forward, but it was also a terrible impediment.

Somehow Cayce got all of us and our stuff onto the same jam-packed transit car, despite mutters and glares and a torrent of incomprehensible words that didn't sound friendly. But then, after traveling several stops, we realized we were going in the wrong direction.

We seriously considered just staying where we were until the car came all the way around the ring to our destination, but not only would that have taken hours, it wasn't actually an option—the system map projected in the air above our heads showed that only one line went all the way around and we weren't on it. So we had to get out and negotiate another station to get on a car going the other way.

And then the elevator at our station wasn't working. "There's no way I'm managing those stairs," I shouted to Kane over the ascending crowd's din. After what turned into a rather heated argument between the two of us, we boarded another car, traveled one stop, and took the elevator up to the main level, where Cayce and Kane parked me at a tea shop with the pile of luggage while they went out to reconnoiter a route to our apartment.

As soon as they had left, I wept. I bawled like a damn baby and just glared at the overly solicitous proprietor until he left me alone with a stack of paper napkins.

I wasn't feeling sorry for myself, or at least that was what I told myself. I was just tired and frustrated and *angry*—angry at Kane for being a shithead, at Cayce for getting me into this situation, at Ngo Quyen Ring for being such an uncooperative madhouse, at Tai for not answering their messages, at the stupid damn walker for rattling and squeaking and catching on everything, and most of all at that asshole Parkinson and his fucking disease.

Why did everything have to be so *hard*?

And then I remembered something Max had said once, when a job had gone badly and we were licking our wounds in some ratty back alley: "It only hurts because we're not dead yet."

"Not dead yet," I said aloud, and blew my nose with a stentorian honk. I dropped the sodden paper napkin in my teacup, rested my head on my folded arms, and tried to calm my breathing. "Not dead yet," I repeated.

Eventually, Cayce and Kane returned with a route to the apartment and, wonder of wonders, a luggage cart they'd scared up somewhere. That made transporting our stuff for a kilometer or so through the crowded streets on foot a lot more plausible, though I still had to stop and rest frequently. Electric jitneys zipped by on occasion, whipping through the dense crowd with jittery AI-driven efficiency, but we couldn't figure out how to hail one. And there were tricycle rickshaws, pedaled by wiry sweating humans, but they were all engaged. So we just kept walking.

We would figure this place out eventually, I told myself. Probably just about when it was time to leave.

Ngo Quyen was very different from Amalthea, I observed on one of my rest stops, and it wasn't just the gravity and the language that made it so. Despite the fact that Amalthea was a natural body and Ngo Quyen a built station, this place felt a lot more like a planet-bound city. Amalthea's corridors were generally fairly low-ceilinged and evenly lit, making the whole place feel like a single large building. But Ngo Quyen had *streets*, wide pathways supporting a dense mix of pedestrian and light vehicle traffic, walled with buildings going up four or five stories to a transparent ceiling giving a view of the other side of the ring and the rotating stars beyond it. Brightly illuminated signage in a half-dozen languages, with animated images and competing audio tracks, made the whole place feel like Thunderbolt's casino floor … and it went on and on and on. Forty kilometers in circumference, I thought I'd read.

Finally we arrived at our apartment. Which was on the second floor, reachable only by a narrow staircase.

Cayce was suitably apologetic. "I swear I specified 'no steps' when I booked the place!" he said. But we were here, and we'd already paid for the first week, and finding and booking another place, not to mention getting there, felt like more work than any of us were up for. So I patted Cayce's hand and told him it would be okay for now.

At least the stairs had a sturdy handrail, which I used to haul myself up one laborious step at a time. Kane kept watch on the luggage cart; I refused Cayce's offer of assistance. "I'm not dead yet," I told him.

I finally made it through the door, and collapsed on a couch with my arm across my eyes while Kane and Cayce hauled the luggage up the stairs. A moment later, or so it seemed, I awoke to find the walker leaning against my couch and the apartment quiet, except for the continuous low clamor coming in from the street below.

I was grateful to have been left to rest, but frustrated by being left out of … whatever was happening right now. I checked my comm and, finding nothing of immediate import, sent a remarkably restrained message to Cayce and Kane saying that I was awake and wondering what was going on.

I'd have to have a talk about that with the boys when they got back.

Ngo Quyen kept Outer Belt time, eight hours earlier than Jupiter Union's UTC. Najah had changed *Django*'s ship time by an hour every other day during the trip to sync us up, but Kane and I hadn't completely adapted and were still waking up midday and staying up well past midnight. The good news was that, knowing Tai, they were probably on the same schedule.

Cayce, of course, woke up whenever his alarm told him to and was perfectly chipper. Damn his teenage resilience.

We'd arrived in the early afternoon local time, which meant that after we got settled and ate something we were in good shape to hit the Night Market.

The Night Market, according to the tourist brochure, was open dusk till dawn every day except Tet. Tet was Vietnamese New Year, which was months away, but "dusk" and "dawn" were not quite as obvious as they might seem. It turned out that although the sky visible through the windows above the street was always space-black, the powerful lights at the structural intersections between panes went through a twenty-four-hour and three-hundred-sixty-five-day cycle matching sunrise, sunset, and seasons at Ho Chi Minh City back on Earth. Confusingly, this was an hour earlier than Beijing-based Outer Belt time, so at this point in the year-long seasonal cycle, the market opened at about 17:30, right around the time many office workers were quitting for the day. This was, according to the brochure, a "happy accident" which contributed to the market's popularity.

The Eastern Gate to the Night Market was a huge freestanding Chinese-style gateway surmounted by glowing holographic dragons, which writhed and blew cardamom-scented steam from their nostrils above the passing throng. Just within the gate, rank on rank of stalls, brightly painted in red and gold, offered roasted ducks, delectable-looking baked goods, and colorful fresh vegetables. Grinning shopkeepers offered samples to the passersby.

None of the locals paid any attention to these at all; better and cheaper foodstuffs were available elsewhere on the ring. Instead, they streamed past the gaudy stalls to the real heart of the market: more than a square kilometer of densely packed tiny storefronts, offering every good and service imaginable. We followed the throng, ignoring the tempting smells of barbecued pork and freshly baked pastries.

Although the simulated daylight above was long gone by the time we arrived, the narrow streets of the Night Market were as bright as day. Admittedly, that light was multicolored, flickering, and accompanied by cacophonous music and sales pitches in a half-dozen languages, but it was still bright enough to read by. But despite the fact that everything was fiercely illuminated, very little of the brightly glowing signage was in English and, even with the translators on our pocket comms, we found ourselves completely disoriented.

We worked our way through the crush of bodies, all trying to go in different directions at once, to a comparatively open space where Cayce could consult his screen without as much worry of it being knocked out of his hand. I took the opportunity to rest, leaning against the wall with my hands on my knees. I really needed to sit, but this was better than nothing. "This sector here is all entertainment software," Cayce said, looking around and trying to find the corresponding area on the map. "Do you see any live fish vendors?"

"For pets, or to eat?" Kane replied.

Cayce peered at the map. "I'm not sure."

"There's a tank of lobsters ..." Kane said, pointing.

We headed off in that direction.

After passing the odorous, bubbling fish tanks, we entered an area of small consumer devices, comms and screens and holo projectors and every kind of recording device. In this area, the shops were stacked on top of each other, with a second and, in some cases, a third level of tiny, brightly lit storefronts accessible by rickety stairs.

Accessible to people other than me, that is. I was really, really wishing I could just stop the ring's rotation for the duration of our visit and float wherever I needed to go. Of course, the lobsters might not like that, but then again their lives were going to be short anyway.

"Up there," Kane said, jerking his chin upward. I followed his gaze.

It was a second-story storefront, not as brightly lit as its neighbors but far louder. Thumping dance music from dozens of speakers overpowered the more numerous but less coordinated sounds from the many screens and projectors in the vicinity.

The music was exactly to Tai's taste. The sign above the storefront, below the Vietnamese and Chinese, read SKITTER in smaller English letters.

And Skitter was one of the aliases that Tai used for their non-criminal activities.

"Told you," Kane remarked smugly.

I looked at the stairs and sighed. We had agreed early on that I would be the one to meet with Tai and suss out what it would take to get them on board. Tai and Kane differed on a lot more than their taste in music, and though Tai had gotten along well enough with Strange, Tai was skeptical—justifiably so—of strangers and Cayce's story of being Strange's kid would probably raise more suspicions than it settled. It certainly had with me. But those stairs looked rickety, and steep, and there was no sign of an elevator. "All right," I said, folding up the walker and handing it to Kane. "Here I go."

I'd been walking for hours; my legs were weary, trembling, and full of random tics. As I made my way toward the stairs, leaning on the wall, I realized that I could barely get my right foot, the weaker one, off the ground; it dragged on every step despite my best efforts to lift it.

I just had to reach the top of the stairs, I told myself, and then I could rest. Tai would give me a cup of tea and we'd have a nice chat, while the boys waited and wondered on the crowded street below. The turnabout would be educational for them.

I made it to the bottom of the stairs and raised my left foot to the first step, clutching the handrail—it was just a narrow strip of metal—and leaning on the wall for support. But getting the right foot up to the second step was more than I could manage; even dragging my pants leg up with my hand, I could barely get it up one step. So it was one step with the left, drag the right up to meet it, one step with the left, drag the right up to meet it … all the way to the top.

I could feel Cayce's gaze burning between my shoulder blades. But I didn't turn back and ask for help, and—bless him—he didn't come over and offer it. Nor did Kane, to no one's surprise. I just kept lifting and dragging my protesting, trembling body up those stairs.

I paused at the landing, breathing heavily. It would be so easy to slip down to a sitting position and rest, just for a moment … but I suspected that if I did, I wouldn't have the strength to haul myself vertical again. So I only let myself pause for the space of three breaths before I forced myself up to the next step, and the next, and the next.

Finally, I reached the top, a narrow catwalk held to the building face by skinny little brackets which looked entirely inadequate to me. I had to remind myself that I was judging a one-quarter-gee structure by one-third-gee standards … but even so, the whole thing seemed way too cheap and flimsy. I leaned hard on the wall, as far as possible from the tiny wire that served as a railing, and shuffled along until I reached the storefront labeled SKITTER. I peered inside, feeling the throbbing dance music pulse against my whole face.

Tai wasn't there. No one was.

I took a breath and stepped inside, leaning heavily on a thumping speaker. I felt like I was inside a dark womb, with the music's pulsing drums pressing in on me from all sides. The space was tiny, crammed with audio equipment whose green and blue lights glimmered from ranks of shelving between enormous speakers. All of them were pushing out the same song, which I recognized as one of Tai's favorites, but the space behind the counter was vacant. Just a single chair, with a cushion flattened by a curvaceous butt, and a floor littered with discarded drink cups and drug vials.

"Shit," I said, leaning heavily on the counter. I could barely hear my own voice. *Now what?* I thought.

And then, impossibly, over the pounding beat, I heard a tiny click.

It must have been survival instinct that made that possible. At some deep visceral level, my body recognized the sound of a pistol being cocked.

I didn't move. "Are you the proprietor?" I said, loud enough to be heard over the music but not loud enough to be constituted as a threat. I hoped.

"Hands up," came a voice, ignoring my question. Tai? Maybe. It was hard to tell over the din. I complied as best I could, though I had to lean hard with my hip on the counter to keep from falling over.

"Turn around." I rolled myself around to face the voice.

It was Tai, all right. Diminutive, upright, still with the same slim waist and shapely hips, though their skin was no longer so clear and smooth as it had been. Their clothes, as always, displayed an amazing and unique sense of style I'd never been able to approach. At the moment they were wearing a long pirate-style coat in a dark-blue floral pattern, with broad cuffs, silver piping, and two rows of silver buttons on each side. A high-collared white shirt, blue and silver pinstripe vest with matching pants, and shining black boots completed the ensemble, and the hair, blue shading to purple at the tips, was no doubt styled in the very latest fashion. "Hey, sexy," I said. "Miss me?"

"Alicia?" they cried and slipped the pistol into a pocket. I couldn't help but notice that they snapped the safety on as they did so; Tai was always cautious and precise around all forms of technology, especially weapons.

Tai opened their arms. Unthinkingly I stepped toward their embrace … and collapsed on the floor.

Tai didn't have any tea. Not even water. "No plumbing above the first level," they said. "In fact, I was just coming back from the bathroom. What the *fuck* were you doing sneaking around like that? Like to scare me half to death!" They struggled to get an arm behind my shoulders and help me up, but the narrow space and my dead weight made that difficult.

"Sneaking? How could you possibly have missed me stumbling around out there?"

"My hearing's not as good as it used to be."

"Speaking of which … could you turn the music down?"

They did, and then somehow the two of us managed to get me levered up and into the one chair. It completely filled the available space; Tai sat on the counter to face me.

"That's no way to greet an old friend," I said after I'd caught my breath.

They shrugged. "I wasn't expecting you."

"The door was open." I wasn't even sure there *was* a door. Maybe the whole storefront closed with one of those big rolling steel doors.

"Quarters are tight here on the Ring. You do *not* enter another person's space without an explicit invite. Especially a person in my line of work."

"I'll keep that in mind." How many other faux pas had I already made, lurching from place to place as I was? Maybe that was why the guy on the transit car had been so upset. "Is this your line of work, then? Audio gear?"

"Part of it." They quirked a smile. "Okay, it's a front. But I really do know my stuff. If a legit customer somehow makes their way up here, I can give them solid advice and a pretty good deal."

"What else are you up to, then?"

"Oh, you know, the usual." They raised their right hand, ticked off fingers with the left. "Hacking, cracking, industrial espionage, digging up dirt on romantic partners, deejaying dance parties." That last was the thumb, which they waggled. "That one *isn't* a front. I do it for the love of music."

"I'm glad." I sighed. "Damn, I've missed you." We'd been intimate now and then over the years, though never for long and never emotionally involved. Still, they were a lot of fun in bed.

They smooched the air in my direction. "So what brings you to the Ring after all these years? I certainly never expected you to make your way here from Jupiter space, especially considering ..." They gestured to my lower legs, which I was unconsciously rubbing; after all my recent exertions, the twitching was fierce. I'd messaged Tai when I got my diagnosis, though we hadn't communicated very frequently since then.

"It's complicated." I let out a sigh. Where to begin? "First off, did you know that Strange has a kid?"

"No! Do tell." They crossed their legs and leaned forward in a conspicuous performance of rapt attention.

I summarized the situation as quickly as I could, ending with "and Cayce and Kane are downstairs now."

"Hm." They cupped their chin in one slim hand.

"I know you and Kane were never ... close."

"Kane isn't the problem. It's the child."

"His name's Cayce." I realized I had stopped thinking of him as a "child" some time ago.

They waved a hand dismissively. "What's his motivation?"

"He loves his father." But I realized that assessment wasn't quite accurate even as I said it. Cayce was certainly extremely committed to getting his father out of Cronos, but I'd never really sensed any filial affection from him.

"And if he's so very clever … why does he need us, specifically? He could hire a perfectly adequate crew to carry out his plan, whatever it is, in half the time and without running all over the System."

"I don't think he has the money. And he knows we're the only people he's certain he can count on to rescue Strange."

"Or is it the other way around?" They drummed fingers on the countertop. "Is rescuing Strange the only thing he can count on to recruit us?"

"Are you saying this is some kind of scam? That he's gathering us together to … what, turn us all over to Aquila for a reward, or something?"

"I didn't say that. But I *don't* know what's going on in his head, and neither do you, and that's what worries me."

I considered what they were suggesting … considered it hard. "I trust Cayce," I said, and even as the words came out of my mouth, I knew that I believed them at a very deep level. "He reminds me so much of his dad. And though Strange and I had our differences, lord knows, and even though he made some spectacular mistakes, he never, ever broke a promise."

"Strange was a grifter and a cheat. Professionally!"

"That was only for the marks. He never went back on his word with me or anyone else in the Club."

"Do lies by omission count?"

I paused, breathing hard. "Look, you took off right after Orca. You didn't see how losing Damien and Max affected him. It damn near killed him! But, despite that, he stuck around to make sure I was all right, even though I hated his guts and did everything I could to drive him away. I didn't realize until much later just how hard that must have been for him."

"So you feel you owe him," Tai said, "despite the fact that he got your best beloved killed. And you've transferred that debt to his son. To someone who *says* he's his son."

"Oh, Cayce is Strange's kid all right. No one else could be so insufferable in exactly that way."

"But what about Damien?"

That hurt. "Losing him was like a black hole in my heart," I said, "and that kind of pain doesn't ever heal. Not even after ten years. But I've learned a lot in those ten years, and one thing I've learned is that every single person in the Cannibal Club is more important to me than family. If I gave up on a chance to save Strange, I don't think Damien would ever forgive me."

Tai regarded me for a long contemplative moment. "You still love Strange," they said at last. "In spite of everything."

"Of course I do. In spite of everything. And so do you."

"I don't love Strange, never did. Though he *so* wished I had. If I'd told him I loved him at the right moment, there's nothing he wouldn't have done for me."

I snorted. "How many lovers do you have right now?"

They had to stop and think. "Three girls, one boy, and two other. Plus a couple of fuck-buddies. But I don't really *love* any of them."

"You only tell yourself that so it doesn't hurt so much when they leave you." Tai's face showed I'd scored a point there. "And even you have to admit that what we had in the Cannibal Club was special."

"It was." They didn't even hesitate. "But the Cannibal Club is dead, and I don't owe this *child* any favors."

"It's not about the kid, it's about Strange! We have to help him!"

Tai leaned back on the counter, hands behind hips, ankles in those gorgeous shiny boots crossed and swinging. "I'm sensing an opportunity."

Something had shifted. Suddenly I was on the other side of the negotiating table. "Oh?"

"There's a job here, a *potential* job rather, that I've had my eye on for quite some time. It is a unique opportunity with an amazing potential payoff, but I haven't felt able to tackle it by myself. Among other problems, even if I can pull it off, I'll have to leave the Ring."

"So you need help. To pull the job and get out."

"I've been here for more than five years. It's getting a little stale." They leaned forward, elbows on knees, and fixed me with those luscious deep brown eyes. "You and Kane are known quantities, and Cayce needs me for reasons of his own. Even if I don't trust him, and I don't, I know that I can count on his self-interest. I think that the four of us can do this job and get away, and after that's done I'll have the freedom and the money to do whatever I want. Which might—I stress that *might*—include working with Cayce to rescue Strange from whatever trap he's gotten himself caught in."

"I think Cayce is hoping for a little more of a commitment than that."

Tai shrugged. "It's the best he's going to get. Tell you what—to sweeten the pot, I'll offer to split the proceeds evenly with you three, even though I'm providing the target, the plan, and the client."

I couldn't help myself. "How much are we talking?"

"Twenty. Billion. Yuan. Tax free."

That was … tempting. Even though the Outer Belt yuan really took a beating in the last recession, five billion of them was still a life-changing amount of money. Even though Cayce was fixated on putting the Cannibal Club back together, I thought that he might accept that, plus a chance at Tai's continued participation, as a reasonable exchange for participation in Tai's job.

"Let's go somewhere we can all talk about this." I thought about the stairs. "I don't suppose there's an elevator somewhere?"

"Sorry. But I can help you down the steps."

My first instinct was to reject the offer. But I was *so* tired, and the thought of Tai's soft hands on my elbow and hip was rather attractive …

Once we got down to street level, the reunion was rather more strained than I'd hoped for. Kane got a smile but only a handshake; Cayce didn't even get a smile. Rather, he and Tai regarded each other as they shook hands like fencers preparing for a match.

I felt waves of disappointment coming off of Cayce as we made our way to a tea shop Tai knew. Which was understandable, but he shouldn't have gotten his hopes up so high. He was, after all, an unknown quantity to Tai; this was the first time they'd even met.

Hopefully, they would warm up to each other as we worked together on this job, whatever it was.

Tai poured the tea. The tea shop proprietor had greeted Tai like a beloved nibling and bowed us into a private room. The sliding door looked like paper but was laced with smart wire—we needn't fear eavesdropping.

"The job is the Scroll of Emperor Ly Nam De," Tai said. I blinked at that—even I had heard of it. It was a thousand-year-old illustrated poem, supposedly painted by the first emperor of Vietnam, and its discovery in some dusty archive twenty years ago had been System-wide news. "It's the single most valuable artifact in the Ring. The Vietnamese community would say that it's the most valuable object in the entire Outer Belt. When trillionaire Nguyen Van Thu bought it and brought it out to the Ring for display, it was a major cultural coup."

Kane snorted derisively. "No point in stealing something you can't fence."

Cayce nodded. "And if any private collector were discovered to have it in their possession, they would have a dozen contracts on their life within a day."

Tai raised their cup in acknowledgment of the issue. "That was actually the first piece of the puzzle—I would never in a million years have thought of stealing the thing myself, but someone approached me and asked if I would consider it. This is someone with serious money, obviously, and a very personal reason to want to remove the Scroll from the Ring. That's all I can say."

Cayce rubbed his chin. "Lots of people on Earth were upset to lose this piece of their heritage to the Belt. It might be worthwhile to some of them to return it to Earth ... even at considerable risk of retribution if they were ever found out."

"Could be one of the Earth governments too," I said. "They could put it on display in the main square in Ho Chi Minh City and just *dare* the Belt to try to take it back."

"Not saying," Tai said, spreading their hands. "And not our problem. If we can get away clean—and I think we can—we can take the money and leave any subsequent recriminations to the client. Their offer includes very substantial guarantees of protection for our identities, whether or not we're successful, even if we're found out years later."

Cayce looked skeptical about that. "Do you trust their intention and ability to follow through on those guarantees?"

"Yes. Unequivocally."

"Government," I said, nodding. "Gotta be."

Tai looked at me, impassive. "Not saying. The important thing to me is to tweak the nose of that asshole Nguyen Van Thu. And the money, of course."

But Cayce still wasn't convinced. "If you trust the client this much, why do you say you need to leave the Ring after the job?"

"I'm a known quantity here. I'd be an immediate suspect, no matter how plausible my denials. Easier to be gone before the news of the theft comes out."

Kane shook his head. "Guarantees or no," he said, "if we get caught during the job …" He drew a finger across his throat.

"Even if we're caught, I trust the client to keep our asses out of jail and our names out of the news. We should be fine, as long as we don't do something stupid and get killed before we're arrested." They looked around the table. "So, are you in?"

"How much was my share again?" Kane said.

"Five billion yuan."

"What's that in real money?"

Tai rolled their eyes. "About a million seven in Ceres dollars."

"A million seven? Hell yeah I'm in!"

I looked to Cayce. "It's a *huge* risk, in my estimation," he said to me, "but I'm in if you are. And *only* if you are."

I considered the question carefully. The job did seem awfully ambitious, but Tai was *so* cautious and precise that I couldn't imagine them getting involved without an ironclad guarantee of protection. And if we could pull it off … five billion yuan would mean I'd never have to worry about paying for my meds again. And we'd be sticking it to Nguyen Van Thu, everybody's least favorite trillionaire.

I took in a breath, let it out. "Okay. I'm in."

"Excellent!" Tai said and raised their cup. "To the Emperor's Scroll!"
"To the Emperor's Scroll," we chorused, and downed our tea.

It was a good thing my walker was made almost entirely of plastic, because if it had been metal, I would not have been allowed to bring it into the exhibit with me. As it was, I had to stand on my wobbly legs, hands in the air, and turn in a circle in a tiny booth while scanners examined me, top to toe. There were accommodations for those with more severe limitations, but the line for hand-inspection was long and moving slowly, so I elected to forego that privilege.

The Emperor's Scroll exhibit, the crown jewel of the Ngo Quyen Ring Museum of Vietnamese Cultural History, involved far more than the Scroll itself. It started with a huge and garish display thanking and aggrandizing Nguyen Van Thu, of course, but once you got past that it became really interesting. The series of small rooms leading up to the Scroll were filled with related artifacts, many of them precious treasures in their own right, and fascinating information about the period and personalities. Kane just fumed and tapped his foot at the glacial pace of the packed crowd, and Tai, who had seen it all a hundred times before, spent the time staring at their pocket comm. But I actually enjoyed the text and multimedia presentations as well as the objects themselves. To think that this inkwell was used by a scholar over two thousand years ago! Cayce wasn't quite as fascinated as I was, but I think he still enjoyed the exhibit in his own way.

Eventually, though, we reached the Scroll itself. Entry to the Scroll room was carefully controlled: the number of people inside at any one time was strictly limited, and only one person was permitted to pass through the armored airlock into the room on each cycle. Even after you reached the front of the substantial line, you had to wait by the door until a green light illuminated, indicating someone had left via the *other* armored airlock. And you had to watch a holo of Nguyen Van Thu personally welcoming you to the exhibit before you could enter.

But you know what? It was worth it.

The Scroll was displayed before an enormous window of bombproof glass, ten centimeters thick. As you entered, you saw it perfectly centered in your view, the only illuminated object in an otherwise darkened room, seemingly floating in space with the stars and the asteroids of the Outer Belt rotating silently behind it. It was an awe-inspiring sight.

The Scroll itself was not large, twelve by thirty-one centimeters. It was displayed under rather dim light in a glass box, sitting atop a waist-high square cabinet. This cabinet, Tai had explained, was actually a ten-tonne vault of molybdenum steel, into which the Scroll would retract in a fraction of a second if anything at all unexpected occurred in the vicinity.

Having read all the introductory materials, I felt I could really appreciate the Scroll, which consisted of a short poem in ancient Vietnamese calligraphy and an ink-wash painting of rushes and cattails. A tiny frog nestled at the base of one reed, barely a sketch of a frog really, but somehow it gave the whole thing life and meaning.

An Emperor, a person who had managed to unite and command an entire country in the days when the fastest means of transportation or communication was the horse, had taken the time to compose and execute this intricate, delectable artwork with his own hands. And the fact that he had chosen to include this tiny frog, a bit of whimsy and humor, made me like him and wish that I could meet him.

I sighed happily and turned my attention away from the Scroll. I was here on business.

I began by cautiously scoping out the room's security cameras, which betrayed their positions by the small amount of visible light leaked by their infrared illuminators. There was one in each of the room's four upper corners, one directly above the Scroll, and two just above the entry and exit doors.

The window behind the Scroll might be bombproof, but the frame around it ... not as much. Properly placed explosives would weaken it considerably. And although the vault was firmly secured to the floor, its designers had been more concerned with protecting the Scroll than keeping it in one place; its four thick legs were also vulnerable to explosives. Put it all together ... and the bombproof glass wasn't several-bombs-plus-one-ten-tonne-vault-proof. A series of timed explosions would send the vault, with the Scroll sealed safely inside, smashing through the window and into the vacuum outside.

Once outside the window, the inexorable forces of physics would do the next part of the job for us. The vault, still traveling at the Ring's rotational speed of about four meters per second, would be flung into the void by its momentum. From the perspective of a hypothetical observer standing in the just-blown-up exhibit hall, it would appear to drop downward under Outer Belt standard gravity; from the view of someone outside the Ring, it would travel in a straight line tangent to the Ring at the point of the explosion. From either perspective, it would take about six minutes to reach the edge of the Ring's navigational perimeter, where a ship belonging to the client would swoop in at full skip from outside detector range, snag the vault with a magnetic grapple without slowing down, and whisk away before it could be tracked. Timing would be critical: due to the rapid rotation of the Ring, one second early or late on the detonation would fling the vault to a spot a kilometer or more away from where it was expected.

But we would be gone before any of that happened. All we had to do was plant the explosives; everything after that would be handled by automatic timers. By the time everything went boom, we'd be halfway to Ceres, and no one would have any reason to suspect we'd ever been involved at all.

If we did our jobs right, that is.

Tai's plan was a little easier than the alternatives because it involved sneaking things *into* the museum rather than *out*, but it would still require all our skills, smarts, and abilities. The job needed Tai's hacking skills to disable the alarms and video surveillance, Kane's muscle to haul and place the explosives, and Cayce's brain to figure out a way to smuggle the bombs into the museum complex.

It also depended on my thievery skills, to get the team in and out of the museum and the Scroll room to plant the explosives. Tai and I had a long talk about that while Cayce and Kane were off picking up some equipment.

"I really appreciate your confidence," I said to them, "but I'm still not certain I can do this work." Even as I spoke, I inspected my hands. The tremors were not as bad as they had been on that first, stressful day on the Ring, but they were still there. They were always there.

"Kane told me how brilliant you are as a teacher," Tai reassured me. "And we have a lot more time and resources to prepare than you did on Amalthea. We can figure out exactly what we're going to encounter before we go in, and you can train Kane on those specific things. By the time we do the job, he'll be an expert."

"But I still need to go in with him—after what happened at the Thunderbolt, I don't want to depend on cameras or comms—and I'm afraid I'm going to fuck everything up with my walker."

Tai held out their hands palm up, and I put mine in them. They were so much softer than mine! All Tai's criminal activities were committed with keyboards and maybe a soldering iron or two. "Don't worry," they said, "there won't be any crawling through ducts on *this* job. I'll make sure the cameras and motion sensors don't see you; you just need to help Kane crack the physical locks. Once you get through the doors, you'll just be walking through the exhibit, the same as we did the other day. Only without the crowds." They grinned. "You'll have as much time as you want to read the signage while Kane and Cayce are dragging bombs around."

"Please don't patronize me."

"Sorry."

"But thank you for the reassurance. It's appreciated."

Tai squeezed my hands, then released them. "Any time, sister."

But first we had a chicken-and-egg situation to deal with: before we could break into the museum to plant the bombs, we had to plant the bombs in the museum.

The problem was that we needed a *lot* of explosives. Bombproof windows and ten-tonne vaults might not be completely impregnable but they were still pretty tough. We needed over a hundred twenty kilos of explosive clay, which would be pretty conspicuous and would take more time to haul into the museum from the street than we could spare. Even four people would be hard pressed to do it in time, never mind two: Tai would be busy hacking the security system, and I was in no position to help with heavy lifting.

It was Kane, believe it or not, who came up with the solution. "We should just hire a delivery service to bring it in for us," he'd said late one night. It was a joke, but as soon as the words were out of his mouth, Cayce's eyes lit up.

And so it was that we pulled up outside the museum's delivery entrance one morning in an electric truck loaded with cans of condensed milk for the museum café. Well, that was what the boxes were labeled as, anyway.

The electric truck hadn't been the hard part. Nor had the little powered forklift, which I would be driving to shift the boxes from the truck to the café's storage room. Nor had the coveralls or the paperwork. Tai had plenty of contacts in the Ring's service industries, who were happy to take a few yuan to look the other way while we borrowed those items for a few hours. No, amazingly, it had been the boxes. Of all the thousands and thousands of boxes of canned condensed milk that passed through the Ring's restaurants and cafés every single day, it seemed there wasn't a single one that wasn't either full of cans or already broken down for recycling. We had finally been reduced to stealing an entire pallet of canned condensed milk from the back of a grocery store, just so we could pull the cans out by hand, replace them with eight-kilo blocks of explosive clay, and seal the boxes up tight again.

"I can't believe this," Tai had muttered as we'd loaded the boxes of stolen milk into the back of the truck. "We are *professionals*. This is … this is just petty theft! It's embarrassing!"

"Shut up and keep stacking," Kane had replied.

Tai hopped out of the truck and went inside to speak to the museum staff. As the only fluent Vietnamese speaker in the group, they were our front person by necessity. I tapped my trembling fingers on the truck's steering wheel as we waited, but it wasn't very long before Tai came out, smiling and waving an electronic clipboard. "You can get away with anything as long as you carry a clipboard," they said.

Tai looked very strange wearing something as unfashionable as a shapeless coverall. But their hair was still fabulous.

I pulled the truck into the loading dock and made my wobbly way around back to where I could climb back into the driver's seat, this time of the forklift. Cayce and Kane loaded boxes onto the fork while Tai directed the work, without lifting a finger to actually help.

"You don't have to enjoy this so much," Kane growled.

"It's part of our camouflage," Tai replied. "No supervisor would be caught dead loading boxes when there are lower-level employees to do the work. It's a status thing. Trust me."

I don't think any of us really did trust Tai on this—I, for one, thought they were just doing it for the fun of lording it over Cayce and especially Kane—but even without their help, the forklift made short work of the task. The biggest problem we encountered was that the café didn't actually have a place to put such a large quantity of condensed milk, especially as we couldn't afford to have the boxes be opened before we got to them that evening. We eventually found a corridor on a lower level, fortunately not too far from the Emperor's Scroll exhibit, where several stacks of boxes were already sitting. It didn't look like any of them had been touched in a while.

"I'm sorry we won't have the forklift tonight," Cayce panted as we made our way back to the truck.

"Don't be such a baby," said Kane.

In theory, we spent the rest of the day packing, practicing, and resting. I, in particular, really intended to sleep once I'd packed up my stuff for the getaway. But sleep refused to come, and eventually I came back out to the apartment's common room, where Kane and Cayce were continuing their long-running skat tournament. While they played, slapping down cards with the occasional grunt, I watched a show on the video. It was all in Vietnamese, but the costumes were colorful and the dancing was pretty.

Outside the windows, the light faded to black.

The noise from the street outside rose, then fell away.

I've never been one to suffer stage fright before a job. I didn't have a chance to suffer it on that last night at Amalthea, either, because the whole thing blew up so quickly and unexpectedly. But tonight, with several days of preparations and a full day to rest before the job … I was scared.

You can do this, I told myself.

But I didn't believe it.

I didn't want to ask either Cayce or Kane for support, for fear they'd either condescend or freak out. Tai was unavailable, being off preparing their technological … stuff. And no one else on the Ring would possibly understand, even if I could trust anyone else on a job this big.

So I sat and stared at the screen without seeing anything more than colorful moving images, and I felt my whole body shiver. Only part of which, I think, was the Parkinson's.

Finally, a little after midnight, Tai came in. "Okay," they said, "I'm as ready as I'll ever be. Let's roll."

I rolled. Literally. My stupid walker's wheels squeaked as I made my laborious way to the door.

But by god, we were the Cannibal Club again, and I wasn't going to let the team down.

We split up a couple streets from the museum, Tai peeling off with the traditional lack of any formal send-off, just a little salute. In the Cannibal Club, wishing good luck was bad luck.

Tai's destination was a network maintenance closet on the lowest level beneath the museum. There, they could tap into the museum's systems to selectively blind its cameras, deafen its motion sensors, and fog its memory. No one who wasn't physically in the room with us would know that we were there, or had ever been there. Once the museum's security systems had been disabled, Tai would remain in the closet to monitor our progress and deal with any unexpected detections, then put everything back tidily after the job was done. We would keep in touch by in-ear comm, but after Amalthea, I didn't personally put too much faith in that.

Tai could also open some doors for us, but most of the museum's doors, especially those in the Scroll exhibit, were closed by physical locks. Those were my responsibility, with Kane as my hands. Kane was also responsible for my safety, and to a lesser extent Cayce's, but he was under strict orders from Cayce to immobilize or render unconscious, rather than kill, anyone who spotted us. We were counting on Tai's client to keep our identities secret.

We descended two levels by street elevator, then made our way to one of the museum's lower-level staff entrances. As we approached, Tai's voice sounded in our ears: "I can see you on the security cameras ... but no one else can. You're good to go."

The staff entrance door had a pitiful standard lock like you might find on a cheap apartment. Part of me wanted to crack it myself, because it was *so* stupidly simple that I might be able to do it even in my current state. But it would also be a good confidence-building exercise for Kane, so I left it to him. He satisfied both of us by cracking it in less than a minute without any help from me. "Good job, kiddo," I said.

He just grunted. There was much more work to be done tonight.

With Tai blocking the museum's security systems, and keeping an eye on us through those same systems, we could get away with exercising only minimal caution. We used infrared flashlights and goggles, of course, and moved as quietly as possible, but we wore street clothes, rather than those horrible sweaty stealth jumpsuits, and we didn't have to be as paranoid about the slightest sound as we had been on some jobs. And when human guards came around on their rounds, Tai would see them on the museum's cameras, and we could easily avoid them.

Once inside, we split up, with Kane and I going upstairs to the Scroll exhibit and Cayce going downstairs to begin hauling up the boxes of explosives. Tai had reassured us that we could use the elevator without substantially increasing our chances of detection.

The door to the Scroll exhibit, through which visitors passed after being scanned, was pretty formidable. When open, it resembled a bank vault, and when closed, as it was now, it presented a solid steel wall tessellated with sensors. This intimidating appearance was for public relations as much as anything, but it actually was a very secure door and would have presented a difficult challenge. But there was also a staff entrance around back: a heavy, although conventional, door, secured with a retina scanner and monitored by cameras and motion detectors.

Tai had already taken care of the scanner, cameras, and sensors. All we had to do was crack the physical lock.

We had already scoped it out, and the necessary tools were pocketed in order in the canvas tool roll that Kane now unrolled on the floor. First was the special screwdriver to remove the plate that covered the lock mechanism. This was supposedly impossible for non-specialists to obtain, but Tai already had three of them.

Kane made short work of the screws, and he and I peered into the mechanism revealed. It was covered with dust, as they always are, but Kane knew not to blow it away—dust left behind after the job could betray our intrusion. "Forceps here?" he asked, pointing, and I nodded.

This lock was tricky but straightforward, with three bolts designed to be retracted simultaneously by an electromagnet triggered by the retina scanner. Kane used a special three-tined tool, which Tai had fabbed to my specifications, to apply continuous pressure on the three bolts as he teased the latches behind each bolt open with a probe. The top one clicked open first. The middle one took a few tries. And then came the bottom one, which was under the most tension due to the slight angle introduced by the first two being open. Kane tried and tried, but the latch simply refused to click.

And then, in the middle of the seventh or eighth attempt, Kane momentarily relaxed the pressure on the three-tined tool and the first two latches clicked closed again. "Damn it!" he growled, and I saw his fingers tighten on the tool.

"Breathe," I said. "Relax. If you push too hard, you'll never get in."

"Like a woman," he muttered under his breath. Under the circumstances, I decided to let the remark pass, but I'd give him shit about it later.

Click. Click. And, finally, click again. The bolts retracted with a smooth, solid *snick* and the door eased open.

Cayce had brought up about half the explosives while we'd been managing the door, and Kane began shifting them to the Scroll room, making several trips with the heavy boxes while I shuffled my way to the airlock.

The entry and exit doors to the Scroll room itself were standard personnel airlocks reinforced with additional armor. Like all airlocks, each had an emergency release, which theoretically made getting in extremely straightforward. But the designers of the system had known this and equipped the release lever with a heavily alarmed and tamper-evident seal.

The alarm trigger was beyond Tai's power to defeat—it was a simple wire stretched taut across the lever. Pulling the lever would inevitably break the circuit, causing the attached klaxon to let out an ear-splitting wail, and it would keep wailing until it was turned off with a key or its battery ran down. And the wire had a secure, serial-numbered crimp which would be extremely difficult to replace in the field.

Which, given that our plan depended on getting in and out without leaving any sign of our passage, was a non-starter.

So we went around it.

Kane carefully pried the emergency release lever's surrounding bezel away from the wall in which it had been installed. This wasn't supposed to be possible, but I knew a guy who had done it on Titan and he'd been happy to share tips. Once the bezel was free, Kane was able to ease it out almost a full centimeter, which was just enough for us to see the cable that connected the lever to the actual release mechanism inside the airlock.

I held the infrared flashlight—there was some tremor in the beam but not enough to be a problem—while Kane reached in with a hook and teased the cable out. It took a couple of attempts, but he was able to bring it within reach of the opening and secure it there with a clamp.

Now came the tricky part. Kane had to cut the cable's woven metal sheath, exposing the working cable within, without cutting the cable itself. They were both made of mild steel, not particularly strong, and there was effectively zero clearance between them. Also, we were working through a one-centimeter gap.

We'd argued for a long time about how best to do this. Tai had said a small electric torch would be the quickest way through, but I'd worried that it might fuse the cable to the sheath and prevent it from moving. Eventually, I'd won out. Kane used long-nosed snips to carefully nibble away the sheath, one strand at a time.

Soon he'd exposed a couple centimeters of the underlying cable. Now he reached in with locking forceps, carefully grasped the cable, and eased it to the left.

The effect was dramatic. The airlock's emergency lights came on as the door slid open, spilling a spreading fan of bright white light onto the red and gold terrazzo floor. There should have been a choir of angels singing.

Kane, never a sentimentalist, immediately set to work carrying boxes of explosives through the airlock while I pulled all the clamps, tucked away the cable, and carefully re-seated the bezel. There was a little scratching of the paint where Kane had pried it loose; I used a brush to blur the edges of the scratches. Then I rolled up the tools, wiped up a few bits of metal and paint chips with a tack-cloth, and inspected the area. There was no sign whatsoever that we'd been there ... unless and until someone opened the emergency release lever's housing and saw the damaged cable. Which would probably happen during the investigation of the theft, but would most likely not be traceable to us.

I cycled myself and my walker through into the Scroll room and sat on one of the benches within, gazing at the Scroll itself while Cayce and Kane brought the last few boxes of explosives in. There was little for me to do from this point forward, so I just caught my breath and admired the Scroll.

What a beautiful little thing it was. It was kind of a shame that it was so unique, so historical, so caught up in controversy. It deserved to be appreciated for itself. But because of who had made it and where it had wound up, a lot of people wanted it and were willing to pay handsomely, even kill, to control it.

"I'm sorry, little frog," I whispered. I could only hope that the vault would work as designed and protect it from the violence that was coming.

It was Cayce's job to place the explosive clay. I had no idea when he'd managed to learn how to deal with explosives, but his hands seemed sure as he carefully shaped the clay around the feet of the vault and the edges of the window, pushed detonators into it in just the right places, and strung wires to the timers that would set them off. "Dad gave me a few pointers," he said in response to my query. The trickiest part was setting the detonator timing between the vault's front and back legs so the explosion would throw the vault toward the window. It was a matter of milliseconds, but Cayce was confident. "It's just physics," he said.

While Cayce worked, Kane brought him block after block of clay. For my part, I took a perverse pride in breaking down and folding up the boxes we'd worked so hard to procure.

Several hundred cans of condensed milk now sat unregarded in an anonymous rental storage room near the store we'd stolen them from. We weren't planning to take them with us when we left. They would, I supposed, provide a puzzle for the next renter.

Soon the work was done. Anyone who came into the Scroll room would immediately see the clay, the wires, and the control boxes, but Tai assured us that no one was allowed to enter the room between the time the cleaners finished their work—which had been right before we'd entered the museum—and the exhibit's opening time. Until then, Tai would keep anyone from seeing anything amiss on the security cameras, and just to make sure, they'd also jigger the exhibit locks to prevent any unexpected entrance before the planned detonation.

We exited through the entrance airlock, reset it to its normal state, and made our way back through the museum, making sure to eliminate all traces of our passage.

Tai met up with us back at the apartment, driving a small electric van. Cayce and Kane loaded our luggage into it, while I rested gratefully in the passenger seat. We made our way through the darkened, nearly empty streets to the interplanetary terminal where our commercial transport awaited, tickets already purchased by Tai's client through a secure intermediary.

We had just handed our luggage over to the baggage-handling machines and were heading to the terminal's passenger entrance when Tai swore under their breath and turned rapidly around, ducking their head and pulling up the high collar of their maroon velvet coat to hide their face.

Cayce immediately turned to face the same direction as Tai. "What's up?" he asked, *sotto voce.*

"I ... I said this place was getting a little stale?" Tai muttered in reply, still trying to hide their face. I resisted the urge to look in that direction to try to figure out what they were hiding from. "Well … it's actually a little worse than that. Not stale, exactly. More like too hot. Red hot."

"What kind of trouble are you in?" Kane growled. He did look around, even though Tai plainly winced at this action.

"I might have offended some people. Some very important people. I was hoping they had stopped looking for me, but apparently not. These aren't people you want to spend any face-to-face time with if you can help it."

Cayce leaned in close to Tai, all casual. "Where are they?"

"Either side of the entrance."

I tried to glance in that direction without being too obvious about it. There was no question who Tai was referring to: two women with long dark braids, both bulky with muscle, both pretty conspicuously armed. Between the two of them, they had full coverage of the terminal's whole entrance plaza. And they were looking right back at us.

"Do they have friends?" Cayce asked Tai.

"Probably."

A glance passed between the two muscular women and they started walking in our direction. Not fast, but determined.

Every muscle in my body went rigid. It might have been the Parkinson's. "I can't run," I said.

"Well then, let's walk," Cayce said.

We started heading back to where we'd left the van. It might still be in the same place, if no one else had hired it. "Give me one good reason not to clock you and hand you over to them," Kane growled.

"You've been seen with me," Tai responded. "And they're the shoot-first-and-walk-away-from-the-bodies-later type."

"And the Cannibal Club sticks together," Cayce cautioned Kane. "That's two good reasons."

Kane growled but didn't respond otherwise. We all kept walking, but with Tai, Kane, and Cayce keeping to my sluggardly pace, the two women were catching up quickly.

"What's the etiquette here?" Cayce asked Tai. "Are they likely to open fire in public?"

"This close to the terminal? Not likely. If we can make it to the van before they catch us, I think I can get us away."

I risked a glance behind. "They don't seem in any particular hurry to catch us." In fact, we might get to the van first … if it was still there. But if our pursuers decided to pick up the pace, I, for one, would get caught for sure.

"They don't need to do anything more than keep us in sight," Tai said. "They know my favorite hidey-holes. As long as we stay on the Ring, we're vulnerable."

"We have to get out of this tin can before the big boom," Kane snarled.

"Tell me something I don't know," Tai snapped. "And if they're watching this terminal, they'll be watching all of them."

"Well then," Cayce remarked with studied calm, "we'll have to take another way out."

"What?" Kane hissed, and I have to say I agreed with him.

"Keep quiet," Cayce replied. "I'm thinking." He turned his attention to me. "Can you walk just a little faster?"

"I can try." I pushed the walker as fast as I could. It'd cost me later … if there *was* a later.

Cayce glanced forward, back, from side to side. His eyes were theodolites, measuring every angle and distance. "Hire us the van," he remarked to Tai, "assuming it's still there. Then when we get fourteen and a half meters from it, I want you to run flat out, jump in the driver's seat, and open the doors. We should be able to get in before those two can catch up." His voice had the same preternatural, robotic calm I'd heard from Strange when he was deep in thought. It managed to be disquieting and reassuring at the same time.

Tai pulled out their pocket comm and began poking at it. "Fourteen and a half meters," they muttered as their fingers worked. "How far is fourteen and a half fucking meters?"

"I'll tell you," Cayce said. It might as well have been a remark on the weather.

"I've got the van," Tai said, slipping their comm back in their pocket.

"Good. Five meters to go." Cayce glanced my way. "Is it all right if Kane carries you?"

"At this point, I'll take any help I can get."

"Good. Kane, you carry Alicia. I'll grab the walker."

"Got it." He cracked his knuckles.

"Okay, everyone get ready to move on my mark, and I mean *move*." I wasn't sure how much *moving* I would be able to do. I was already getting tired. But the van was in sight ahead, at least. "Three. Two. One. Mark."

Kane wasn't gentle. He grabbed me up and flung me over one shoulder like a sack of potatoes, painfully wrenching my shoulder and neck. I gritted my teeth and did my best to brace myself against the pain and the shaking around I was getting—this was a life-or-death scenario. It would have been much worse in Earth gravity, I supposed.

I heard a Vietnamese shout of surprise and feet began pounding the pavement behind us. I couldn't see behind us, but it sounded like it was going to be close.

We reached the van, and Kane threw me unceremoniously into the back, jumping in on top of me. It hurt some more. Cayce and my walker clattered into the seat ahead. "Go!" he yelled to Tai.

The van surged into motion, rotors shrieking in protest, nearly throwing me out the open back hatch. But Kane held onto me and the seat and nobody fell out.

We careened down the empty street. Shouts diminished behind us and I ducked, expecting gunshots to follow, but I guess we were still too close to the terminal for that to be "etiquette." Kane managed to get the hatch closed. "Where to?" Tai shouted.

"Back to the museum," Cayce replied.

"What?" all three of us shouted at once. Although Tai kept driving.

"Think about it. We need a way off the Ring—one that Tai's friends won't anticipate and can't intercept. We already have one. Let's take it."

He quickly outlined his plan: we would break back into the museum we'd just left, don vacuum suits from one of the museum's emergency lockers, and wait in the Scroll room until the explosives went off. Then we'd be sucked into space along with the vault and get picked up by the client's ship six minutes later.

"Assuming we survive the explosion!" I yelled.

Cayce was undeterred. "I placed those explosives to direct all their force toward the window. The resulting decompression will prevent injuries from blast overpressure. And as for the flying fragments … Tai, can you get into the museum's security office?"

"I think so," they replied, not taking any attention from the street ahead. They were driving ridiculously fast and turning frequently to evade pursuit.

"They'll have blast blankets, in case of a bomb threat. We can protect ourselves with them."

"You are absolutely fucking insane," Kane said.

That clearly shook Cayce's confidence, and mine. If even Kane, the man who'd never seen an explosion he didn't like, thought this plan was too dangerous, what the hell were the rest of us doing risking our lives on it? "Yes," Cayce conceded. "But do you have a better plan?"

"Let me point out," Tai said, not waiting for Kane to admit that he didn't, "that it was my hacks that got us in before. I'm not going to sit in that maintenance closet while you three get blown up, or escape, or whatever it is you wind up doing!"

"You still have the cameras jimmied, right?"

"Only in the Scroll room. I rolled the rest of the hacks back before we cleared out."

Cayce wasn't happy about that. "We don't have time for subtlety. How long would it take you to just knock the whole museum offline? Lights, cameras, alarms, everything?"

"Uh … ten, fifteen minutes? But they'll notice right away."

Cayce's face showed he was thinking fast. He looked at his watch. "Right. There's just enough time. They'll call for backup as soon as the place goes black, but before they reach the Scroll room, we'll be gone."

"One way or another," I muttered darkly.

It actually took Tai only seven minutes. They came charging out of the maintenance closet and slammed the van into motion. "I probably set off all kinds of alarms," they said, "but we'll have the run of the place for a little while."

Cayce clapped them on the shoulder. "Perfect."

The van screeched to a halt right outside the same staff entrance we'd used before. All the lights in the area were out, but we still had the infrared flashlights and goggles. Kane opened the door with the tire iron from the van; we didn't have time for subtlety.

No audible alarms sounded as we made our way through the pitch-black museum to the Scroll exhibit. There were voices and occasional flashlight beams, but the museum's staff were treating this as a simple power failure, so far, and we managed to evade them. I silently cursed my rattling walker.

We made it to the Scroll exhibit's staff entrance. Kane and I settled in to crack the lock—fortunately, I had kept my burglar tools, including the special three-tined one, in the shielded compartment of my backpack, which also held my meds and vital documents—while Tai and Cayce ran off to the security office and emergency locker respectively.

But Kane kept flubbing the lock, and after the fifth failed attempt, he looked to be on the verge of throwing the tools down and trying to kick, punch or, I don't know, *gnaw* his way through. But this lock was stronger than that.

"Breathe," I told him. "Don't think, just do."

"I'm *not* thinking!" he hissed back. Which was, in a way, one of the more self-aware statements I'd ever heard from him. But he did pause, take a breath, and try again.

The three bolts snicked shut for the seventh time as Cayce appeared with four standard emergency vac suits. "You distracted me!" Kane snarled at him.

Cayce looked at Kane, then to me. "You can do this," he said to me. Kane shrugged and waved at the tool roll in a "go ahead, be my guest" gesture.

"I *can't!*" I replied, with perhaps more vehemence than I'd intended. I was maybe a little on edge myself, what with the guards prowling the darkness behind us and fiery death up next on the agenda.

"Just try," said Cayce. "Once. For me."

I looked at the tools, at the lock, at Kane, at Cayce. At my trembling hands. Back to Cayce. "All right," I said at last. "Just once."

"Just once," he agreed.

Kneeling down to put the lock at eye level was one of the hardest things I've ever done, but Cayce steadied me.

Kane had already done half the job. All I needed to do was put a little pressure on the three bolts and tease open the latches with the probe. But I wasn't sure I had the strength in my hands, never mind the steadiness.

Breathe, I told myself. *Don't think, just do.* Suddenly I had some sympathy for Kane's resistance to this advice.

Pushing against the three-tined tool helped to steady my left hand, and it honestly didn't need very much strength—just enough pressure to keep the latches from snapping shut after I'd pulled each one back. The probe trembled hard, an amplified version of my fingers' tremor, but I rested my wrist on the wall next to the lock and held my breath.

The trembling probe tip approached the latch … and then made contact, stilling its motion. A little pressure and the latch clicked open, sweet as you please. The second one wasn't quite as easy, but it, too, snapped open.

One more. I closed my eyes, took a deep breath, let it out, opened my eyes.

And … *click*. The three bolts slid open like this was what they'd wanted all along. My breath shuddered, almost a sob, as I let it out.

"Yes!" Kane said, pumping his fist.

Cayce smiled and offered his hand, in congratulations as well as to help me up. We moved into the exhibit.

This second time, the airlock emergency lever was something Kane could handle by himself. All he had to do was pull the already-loosened bezel away from the wall, hook out the cable, and pull the already exposed inner cable to the side with the forceps. Cayce and I cycled in, with the vac suits, while Kane was cleaning up. He would probably miss something, but it was dark and would only need to pass muster for another … twenty-six minutes.

Yikes.

It was the first time I'd donned a vac suit in over five years. You don't forget those childhood drills, but adjusting the suit to fit my frame was a pointed reminder of just how much muscle I'd lost, and pulling on the gloves was a struggle. "All okay?" Cayce asked as I fiddled with the wrist joints.

I checked myself over. Apart from the blinking red light indicating a malfunction in the suit's radio—Cayce had disabled the transmitters and tracking beacons to reduce the chance of us being picked up by Ring authorities before the client's ship arrived—everything seemed to be in order. "I'll be perfectly comfortable as we're blown to bits," I said. But my trembling voice turned the sarcastic remark into a revelation of my true feelings.

"*You* got us this far," he said, clapping me on the shoulder. "Trust me for the next bit. Okay?"

I took in a sharp breath through my nose, squeezed my eyes shut, swallowed hard. I would *not* cry in front of this child. "Okay," I managed at last.

Cayce nodded, squeezed my shoulder, then finished donning his own suit.

Tai arrived then, struggling under the weight of four large black duffels, which hit the floor with a thud. Each was clearly labeled BLAST SUPPRESSION BLANKET. "Jesus, those are heavy," they said, massaging their hands. Kane immediately began unzipping the bags.

"The better to shield you with, my dear," said Cayce. "Come on, we've got"—he checked his suit's wrist—"six minutes."

We distributed ourselves along the back wall, as far from the coming explosion as possible. I lay on my side, facing the wall, and Cayce gently placed the blast blanket over me. "Nighty night," he said as he tucked me in, as though he were the adult and I the child.

My feelings at that moment were … complex. "Shoo," I said, and closed my faceplate.

The heavy blanket was … actually kind of comforting, as I trembled in the dark with the display on my wrist counting down to zero. The packet of meds, documents, and tools I'd shoved into the suit with me pressed painfully against my ribs, but I wasn't going to try to rearrange anything with less than a minute to go.

Thirty seconds. I wished I could say something to my compatriots, but, honestly, I wasn't sure what I would say if I could. Wishing good luck was bad luck.

Ten seconds. Five. I covered my vulnerable faceplate with my folded arms.

And then there was an enormous *whump*, a feeling like a giant stepping on me hard, and a bright light that flashed under the edge of the blanket. A moment later, light and sound and, well, everything vanished with a *whoosh* that quickly diminished to silence, as I was pulled tumbling and screaming across the floor, across the shattered window's sill, and out into naked space.

It felt exactly like falling. Endlessly falling. Somehow my body, thoroughly habituated to free fall though it was, had grown reaccustomed to gravity in the past few days, and my barely evolved monkey brain made me scream and thrash in a way that probably wouldn't have helped even on a planet. Eventually, though, I got myself under control, calmed my breathing, and assessed my situation.

I was tumbling pretty fast, with no way to stop it, but again those childhood emergency drills came into play. I fixed my eyes on the Ring to reduce dizziness and used my peripheral vision to scope out my surroundings. The vault, the second biggest thing in sight, looked fairly intact, though the four squat legs were twisted, shattered, and blackened. The opposite surface, from which the Scroll in its glass box had until recently projected, was now a smooth flat plane with a seam in the middle where the two vault doors had slammed shut after it retracted. With any luck, the Scroll itself was safe within.

The vault was rotating in space, much more slowly than I, and as it turned, I saw a vac-suited figure clinging to it. From the figure's size, I could tell it was Kane, and even as I watched, he spooled out the attached tether from the suit's waist and began lashing himself to the vault. Two other figures tumbled nearby; I couldn't tell which was Cayce and which Tai, as they were of similar height and build, but neither suit showed visible damage. I breathed a preliminary sigh of relief.

Then I realized we had a problem. To be more precise, *I* had a problem.

The distances between Cayce and Tai and the vault were all less than ten meters. But I could easily see all of them at once, which meant I was considerably farther away—at least fifty meters, maybe a hundred. And the tether attached to the suit's waist was only ten meters.

These emergency suits didn't have maneuvering jets. They were designed to survive loss of pressure, not to be blown into open space without hope of rescue.

And we all had to be firmly fastened to the vault when the client's ship came swooping in. The grapple's magnetic field would snag the vault, but not a human in a plastic vac suit.

My mind went strangely calm, even as I felt my core contract in terror and my fingers and toes go cold. Everything was very clear and crisp, vacuum-bright in the light of the distant sun.

I was going to die.

FIVE

The Orca Job, Part Three

The Cannibal Club—Ten Years Ago

W e moved into Orca Station with Max taking point, Kane watching our tail, and the rest bunched up in between. Strange stayed close to Hiroshi, near the back of the pack, monitoring him for stupidities or missteps while simultaneously keeping an eye out for threats and opportunities ahead. Back aboard *Contessa*, Damien tried not to let his nervousness seep out to infect the already-anxious Miyuki.

Max stepped cautiously into the cargo-handling hallway, leading with his pistol and glancing left and right before waving the rest of us forward. Nothing had changed in the twenty minutes we'd been gone, but you never know. Silently we crept down the hallway, bunching up at the personnel door at the far end and doing a quick head count before proceeding into uncharted territory.

The door wasn't locked. A short hallway beyond led to two doors, one labeled MECHANICAL SYSTEMS—AUTHORIZED PERSONNEL ONLY and the other a stairwell leading up. Max eased the stairwell door open a crack, edging one eye and his gun hand through, then proceeded with the others following. The stairs were dark, illuminated only by a dim emergency light on each landing; this suited us just fine. The sound as we ascended was a gentle susurrus of soft-soled Aquila uniform shoes on metal stair treads, marred only by the thudding rhythm of Hiroshi's inexperienced feet. A whispered comment from Strange improved the sound, at the cost of a decrease in our speed.

Max reached the middle-level door—the stairs continued upward from here—and peered through the window in it, then nodded to Shweta. Shweta was our negotiator—the motherly deceiver who could sell you your own helmet and make you believe you got a good deal on it—and not a fighter. For her to take the lead in an unknown situation terrified her, but we all knew she was the best one to deal with any unexpected personal interactions. She took a breath, nodded to Max, then stepped through the door.

Darkness beyond, again illuminated by a few emergency lights. It was the middle of the station's night, as expected, but we hadn't been sure there might not be a few Aquila personnel burning the midnight oil. Shweta blew out a sigh and the rest of us slipped through into the long narrow corridor. The walls here were scuffed plastic, not scarred metal; still industrial but a bit more people-friendly than the cargo and mechanical areas below.

Kane stationed himself by the stairwell door, guarding the exit and watching for company coming from the level above; the rest of us divided into two groups, moving away from the stairwell in both directions along the upward-curving corridor floor. We acted by instinct and experience, coordinated by a few hand signals. Only a little light showed through the window in each door.

The convention on stations like this was that forward was the direction of rotation, with aft the opposite, up and down defined by spin gravity, and port and starboard being left and right while standing facing forward. Strange, Hiroshi, and Tai went forward; Alicia, Max, and Shweta went aft. The corridor was plainly closer to the starboard hull; the half-dozen doors on the starboard side led to bathrooms, closets, and small offices. But the door at each end of the corridor and the two doors on the port side led to larger rooms. If there were drugs being produced and stored here in quantity, that's where they'd be. Strange's group entered the first door on their left, while Alicia's kept going to the aft end of the corridor.

Strange edged the door open and slipped into a room that looked like a chemistry lab, which made his mouth tighten with anticipatory greed. But it soon became apparent that the workspace's appearance—slick plastic cabinets, hard surfaces everywhere, numerous sinks, and nozzles for water and gases at intervals above the work surfaces—belied its current purpose. Because none of those nozzles were in use, and instead of glassware and tubing, the work surfaces supported only data terminals, noteboards, and several unfamiliar pieces of equipment. Tai could tell from the brand names that they were some kind of digital measurement devices, but what they were intended to measure wasn't clear.

"Looks like a software lab," Hiroshi commented, and Strange pushed down a surge of annoyance at his waste of words to state the obvious. Instead, he moved to one of the noteboards to inspect the diagrams and notations scrawled upon its digital surface. But nothing was familiar—waveforms annotated with Greek letters and complex state diagrams that might have come from the realms of physics, astronomy, biology, or finance. Pulling a blank data stick from a pocket on his sleeve, he plugged it into the board and requested a copy of all its data.

Nobody ever bothered clearing the history in boards like these.

Tai, meanwhile, was looking over the hardware. It was a pretty sophisticated setup—new, high-end equipment, tightly networked with the latest high-speed protocols—but the really impressive part was the system's data capacity. Each of these nodes had a thousand times as much storage as a typical device of its class, stacks and stacks of data bricks connected by fat high-bandwidth cables. Tai had never even heard of any project that needed so much data, not even massive System-wide financial models. Their fingers itched to take one of the stacks away for analysis, but a slim red security thread connected each piece of hardware to the work surface on which it sat and that kind of security would take time to defeat.

Then, silently and without preamble, the door to the hall opened. Strange reacted instantly, ducking behind a worktable and leveling his pistol, but just as swiftly checked his action: the intruder was Kane. *We've got company*, he signed.

Alicia's team reached the aft end of the hall and slipped into the room they found there. This one, too, appeared to have once been a chemical production facility but had since been converted to other uses. But where the room that Strange and Tai were now searching resembled a software lab, this one looked more like a medical facility. There was a smell of disinfectant, and padded chairs sat surrounded by all sorts of electronic equipment. The whole thing, Shweta thought, looked as though it was set up to study the person in the chair rather than to support the occupant's work. The equipment looked crude to Alicia's eye—open racks of components, hand-lettered controls and inputs—but there was a lot of it, and the Earth-based brand names carried implications of precision, accuracy, and expense.

Shweta and Alicia's inspection of the space was interrupted by a swift, sharp hiss. It was Max, at the door, attracting their attention. He gestured through the door's frosted glass; the hallway lights had come on, and several moving figures were blurrily visible. Their body language wasn't familiar, nor were their voices—and though the words weren't clearly audible, they were chatting like people who belonged where they were and weren't expecting to encounter any intruders.

"Shit," Alicia whispered to herself. Her eyes met Shweta's. Hadn't Kane been guarding the stairway door?

Kane quickly whispered an explanation to Strange, Tai, and Hiroshi. A large group—a half-dozen people or so—had come down the stairs all at once and, rather than escalate immediately to gunfire, he'd elected to retreat. That wouldn't have been Strange's inclination, but he was prepared to cut the kid a little slack under the circumstances. Nonetheless, the Club was now divided and incommunicado, with an unknown number of possibly armed adversaries between them.

Still, they had the advantage of surprise, and as Strange's memory palace reconfigured itself to accommodate this new information, he considered that the divided Club could perhaps be turned into a tactical asset. "Check your badges," he whispered. "And act natural."

Tai saw Hiroshi's eyes go wide, looking about as natural as a megawatt distress beacon. But before they could say anything to him, chattering voices approached the door from outside. The door opened, the lights came on, and there was a sudden silence as the new arrivals confronted their unexpected visitors.

"*There* you are," said Strange.

"Who the fuck are you?" said the one in the lead, a tall, lean, bald Caucasian. Their bearing read as military but they wore an Aquila corporate uniform, the same as everyone else in the room.

Strange gave every impression of looking them straight in the eye. But his attention was focused behind them, through the open door and into the hallway beyond. A small crowd of five or six was bunched up behind the bald person; the brightly lit corridor behind them was empty. He could make use of this. "Bennett Wong," he said, flicking his Aquila name tag with a finger. "Corporate security. We're here for a snap audit."

"I'd have been warned about any audits," the bald person said, entering the room and crossing their arms on their chest. Kane noted that they carried a small-caliber antipersonnel pistol holstered on their left hip—a lefty, interesting—and their eyes took in the Cannibal Club members and everything else in the room in one devouring glance. Two of the other Aquila people came in with them, but the remaining two—Kane was now certain there were five all together—remained outside looking very uncertain of themselves. Techs or management, probably, likely unarmed and/or ineffective. The other two might be security and had to be treated as armed. Kane checked his pistols and began shifting, very slowly, into a position from which he could target the leader, their two more confident subordinates, and the door, all at the same time.

Tai, meanwhile, was keeping an eye on Hiroshi. His body language screamed *trapped rat*. Tai yawned and leaned with extravagant nonchalance on a nearby countertop, seeking to lower the emotional temperature of the situation and to take the new arrivals' attention off Hiroshi. One hand crept toward the security thread on the nearest workstation, which would probably trigger a loud and distracting alarm if snapped.

Strange gave the bald person an insolent eyeroll. "If we warned you, it wouldn't be a snap audit, would it? Why didn't you have anyone monitoring the lab?"

But the bald leader clearly hadn't ordered any bullshit and wasn't going to accept delivery. "Who authorized this audit?" they shot at Hiroshi, clearly the weak link in this chain.

Hiroshi gulped and pointed to Strange. Strange, accepting the gesture as the best he was likely to get, looked to the bald person and shrugged. "Boss's kid," he mouthed to them.

But the bald person lowered their head, and with a very slightly feral grin, asked Strange, "*Whose* kid, exactly? And what's your departmental billing code?" Kane saw that their hand had drifted to within centimeters of the pistol, whose holster snap was exceedingly well worn and probably wouldn't hamper the draw at all. Strange, on the other hand, had pocketed his pistol as the door had opened—his uniform lacked a holster—and wouldn't be able to retrieve it with anywhere near the same speed.

Kane shifted his balance and prepared to draw and fire.

"Ahem."

Everyone except Strange and the bald person looked toward the sound, which came from the back of the group in the hall. It was Shweta, with Max and Alicia behind her. "What seems to be the problem?" she asked, in the smooth motherly tone that had charmed a thousand marks.

"Ah, Lakshmi," Strange said to Shweta. It was the name on her badge. "I was just telling these nice people all about the security audit they're failing."

Now the bald leader's pistol did come out, and immediately the other two Aquila employees in the room followed suit. They were clearly professionals and divided the targets—us—among themselves without speaking. "Shut. Up," the bald person said to Strange, their pistol focused unwaveringly between his eyes.

Strange raised his hands. He did it smoothly and without visible fear, but it was a clear acknowledgement that he'd lost the initiative.

But Shweta stepped forward, politely but insistently pressing past the employees in the hall, until she stood near the bald person. "My name is Lakshmi Jagannathan," Shweta said. "I am a senior security analyst in the Special Projects Division, and Mr. Wong works for me. My superior is Lorelynn Mirage Cardo, who just happens to be the mother of Mr. Ryuchi there"—she nodded to the trembling Hiroshi—"and my departmental billing code is JYX-5040. Any further questions?"

Shweta had very good hearing, and she had done her research before the job. She *always* did her research.

Very slowly and deliberately, the bald person put their pistol up, nodding to their two armed subordinates to do the same. They favored Strange with one last withering glance before turning their attention to Shweta. "I can't say I'm exactly pleased to meet you, Ms. Jagannathan," they said, extending their right hand for a handshake even as their left slipped the pistol into its holster. They did not, Kane noted, snap it closed. "Robin Garrett, chief of operations."

Max and Alicia watched this exchange from behind the employees in the hall, who eyed them suspiciously. Max put on his best friendly face, which didn't help much. Alicia kept an eye out behind herself, wary of any further interruptions.

"I'm sorry for any misunderstanding, Mx. Garrett," Shweta replied, in a very convincingly regretful tone, as she released the leader's hand. "As I'm sure you understand, even the most sensitive projects—*especially* the most sensitive projects—must be subjected to surprise inspections from time to time."

"I do understand," said the bald person, though their understanding didn't extend so far as a smile. "But still, this is ... highly irregular. This station is *not* under the jurisdiction of Special Projects. We report directly to Mr. Terce."

Strange lowered his hands, but slowly. He knew when to not press his luck, and Shweta seemed to have the situation under control, but his mind was whirling. *Terce?* he thought, with surprise, admiration, and not a little fear. The patriarch of Aquila Corporation? Not the CEO, not at the moment anyway, but certainly one of the few people with hands on the very complex levers of Aquila's considerable power. And Orca Station was *his* personal fiefdom? Very interesting. Very interesting indeed.

"I am aware of this," Shweta said. "And, well, as you may know, there are ... some tensions, at the very highest levels." Shweta was making it up as she went along, of course, but she was so sincere that the rest of us just assumed this was something she'd researched.

Garrett nodded—their expression showed that this was news to them, but they could easily believe it—and their posture relaxed. "Yeah, working for Terce can be like shadowboxing barefoot on thumbtacks sometimes." Their immediate subordinates smiled at that, and Garrett turned their attention to Hiroshi. "I haven't seen your mom in a while," they remarked casually. "How's she doing?"

And then Hiroshi had to go and blow the gaff completely. "She's ... just fine," he said, but his pale trembling sweating face showed he had no fucking idea.

With one swift gesture, Garrett had their pistol out again, this time leveled directly at Hiroshi. "Apart from the terminal cancer, you mean?"

"Don't shoot!" Hiroshi cried, throwing his hands in the air and dropping to his knees.

A metallic fusillade of clicks and rattles sounded then, as the two other security people, Max, and Kane all drew simultaneously. Kane trained his two pistols on the subordinates, who targeted Strange and Shweta as the obvious leaders. Strange and Shweta both froze, hands out and visible. Tai ducked down behind a countertop and began creeping off to one side. They weren't armed but thought there might be an opportunity to create a distraction.

But it was Max who held the trump card. He threw one massive forearm around the nearest Aquila employee's throat and pressed his pistol's muzzle to the man's temple. "Everyone freeze," he stated calmly.

Everyone in the room heard it and everyone froze. The other Aquila tech looked fearfully at Alicia, who glared a threat at him to mask the fact that she too was unarmed.

Standoff.

Strange's mind raced. He trusted that Garrett wouldn't do anything too rash, but the two junior security types were unknown factors. They did clearly recognize, though, that Kane had the drop on them and Max had a hostage, which might make them hesitant to pull the trigger. They didn't know that Max, despite his size and appearance, was a kitten at heart. "Let's be reasonable here," Strange said to Garrett, and very slowly eased into a slouch against the countertop behind him. His posture appeared casual, and he kept both hands in sight, but his right hand was ten centimeters away from his own pocketed weapon. And Tai was still creeping around behind the counter, out of sight. "No one has to get hurt here. In fact, no one has to know we were even here. Just let us go and we'll leave quietly."

Garrett kept their eyes and gun trained on Hiroshi, but their response was directed to Strange. "Sorry," they said. "You don't scare me as much as Terce does."

There was a slight metallic creak as Garrett's finger tightened on their trigger.

And then Tai burst out from behind the counter, five meters from where they'd last been seen, screaming and grabbing up a stack of data bricks from the countertop. Security threads snapped and alarms wailed as the bricks hurtled toward Garrett's head.

And we acted as one.

Kane pulled both triggers simultaneously, drowning out the screaming and wailing with his pistols' thunderclap. Max literally threw the Aquila tech he'd been holding at Garrett. Alicia tackled her Aquila tech at the knees. And Strange ducked to one side, fumbling his pistol from its pocket.

One of the Aquila security people immediately collapsed, bleeding profusely from the neck. The other one got off a shot at Shweta before being knocked back by Kane's bullet, but Shweta did that evaporating thing she did, slipping to the floor before the bullet arrived where she'd been. Garrett, with a stack of data bricks flying at them from one side and one of their employees coming at them from the other, managed to dodge both, but it took all their attention and they didn't notice Max, coming in right behind the tech he'd thrown, swooping in to tackle them.

It probably would have worked if Hiroshi hadn't been such an idiot. He stood up, still holding his hands above his head and wailing incoherently, and blundered blindly into Max's path.

Max very nearly managed to avoid him. But Hiroshi, completely panicked and blinded by tears, hooked Max's foot with his own, taking both of them down in a heap.

Garrett, recovering, fired twice at the heap, then dropped, rolled, and came up with their pistol trained on Strange.

But Strange had his own pistol out by now, and dropped Garrett with a shot between the eyes before they could pull their own trigger. "Sorry," he said.

Ears ringing, we gasped for a moment in the acrid smoke and still-shrieking alarms. Garrett and their two security people were dead or dying. Both of the living Aquila techs whimpered incoherently on the floor, curled in postures of surrender.

And Max and Hiroshi, still entangled, lay unmoving in a spreading pool of blood.

Strange leveled his pistol at the nearer surviving tech. "How many more of you on this station?" he demanded. He didn't shout it, quite, but it was as close to shouting as any of us had ever heard from him.

"Eight!" the tech blubbered, hands up and eyes wide. "Eight, eight, eight! Please don't kill me!"

"Shit," said Strange, and put his pistol up. The alarms and gunfire would certainly bring them running, probably armed. "Let's move."

We moved, pounding out of the lab and down the stairs with Strange in the lead. But Kane, in the rear, held his position at the stairway door for a long moment. "We're missing Alicia," he called down.

We paused on the landing, looking at each other: Strange, Tai, and Shweta, quickly joined by Kane. Tai said they'd seen Alicia leaning over Max and Hiroshi, and we all remembered that she'd promised Miyuki to keep Hiroshi safe.

Tension. Hard stares. Hard choices.

And then we heard descending footsteps on the stairs above. A lot of them.

Strange summed it up. "We have to go," he said.
We went.

Back at *Contessa*, the four survivors quickly caught Damien and
Miyuki up on the situation. "We're outnumbered," Strange summarized, "six of us, ten of them. They know we're here. They're probably
armed. And they've certainly already raised the alarm with the home
office. We have to leave *now*."

"Not without Alicia," Damien insisted.

"And what about my dad?" Miyuki said, her voice astonishingly
unemotional.

"He's dead," Strange told her with matching chill.

"We don't know that for sure," said Shweta. "He was under Max."

Damien pulled his gun belt from under the console. "You all
can do what you want," he said, buckling it on, "but I'm going back
for Allie."

Strange shook his head. "You'll just get yourself killed," he said—
it was a cold statement of fact, devoid of judgment—"and you'll take
us all down with you. We'll need a top pilot to get away from the
Aquila ships that are already on their way here at full skip."

The rest of us weren't so certain. Shweta ached to go back and
save Alicia but knew that her particular skills would be of little use
against the armed and alarmed Aquila people on the station. Kane's
instinct for self-preservation and desire to follow Strange, who'd
rescued him from the docks on Titan, warred with the silent crush
he had on Alicia and the itch to wade in and break some corporate
heads. And Tai, still fizzing with adrenaline after the firefight, wanted nothing more than to run away and hide.

Damien, undeterred by Strange's words, continued toward
the hatch.

Strange pushed off the console and into his path, blocking the
hatch with his body.

"Let me go," Damien growled.

"Fly. The damn. Ship," Strange countered. "Or we'll *all* die."

We all stared at each other, breathing hard.

SIX

The Malakbel Job

Tai—Present Day

Holy fuck, I did it. That was my first thought after being blown into space. Against all odds, I'd managed to evade two goons, take down the museum's power, find and retrieve the blast blankets, and survive being blown into space, all in a matter of about two hours.

I luxuriated in that feeling of accomplishment for approximately one nanosecond before it was overwritten with wordless panic, as I realized I was tumbling free with no tether, no maneuvering jets, and no radio. But the panic was almost immediately overlaid with a rush of relief, as I realized that the vault was rotating slowly nearby, with Kane clinging to it, and he was reaching out a hand to me.

That might be the first time in my life I was actually glad to see the man.

Kane caught my wrist and hauled me roughly in until I could catch his suit tether, which he had already looped around the vault, with my other hand. But though my hand grabbed the tether, which was rotating *this* way along with the vault, my torso kept going *that* way, impelled by Kane's yank. My shoulder was the loser in the argument between those two, but I kept holding on through the pain and didn't let go. I pulled myself closer to the vault and looped my own tether around it, hooking it firmly so I wouldn't pull free when the pickup ship snagged the vault with its magnetic grapple. Then I just hung there for a moment, panting heavily from the exertion, the pain, and the panic.

Still alive. Hallelujah.

A sudden thud announced the arrival of Cayce, who docked with the rotating vault as neatly as a cruise ship at Ceres Main. With swift assurance, he tethered himself to the vault, then pressed his faceplate to mine so we could talk. "You okay?" he asked. His face showed that he was yelling, but his words were barely audible.

"For now!" I yelled back.

Cayce nodded and pulled away, looking outward. I followed his gaze, but saw nothing except the Ring, rotating unperturbed as though we had not just blown a huge hole in its hull, and beyond it, the still and silent stars.

No, wait. There was one other thing. A small suited figure, tumbling fast end over end, maybe a hundred meters off.

Oh shit. Alicia.

The way her arms and legs moved showed that she was alive … at least for the moment. But she was way beyond the reach of our tethers, even if we connected them all together, and drifting farther away every second. And anyone who wasn't firmly tethered to the vault when the pickup ship arrived—in about four minutes—would be left behind. She didn't have a chance.

No. Stop that. She still had a *chance*. Even if she was hyperventilating, and with her suit's tracking beacon disabled, a ship from the Ring might still pick her up before her air ran out.

After which, she would face trial for one of the biggest thefts in Outer Belt history.

Of course, if that sort of rescue seemed imminent, she could choose to open her faceplate. Death was *always* an option in space. But I didn't think she would choose that route.

There had to be another option. Using breathing air as a maneuvering jet? No, these emergency suits didn't have any oxy to spare. If only we had a longer line …

Then something passed between me and Alicia. Something black and oddly shaped, barely visible against the darkness of space.

It was one of the blast blankets.

And I remembered how damn heavy they were ...

Before I could lose my nerve, I hooked one foot under my looped tether and reached out, stretching my hand out as far as I could in the direction of the floating black blob. It was hard to judge its location. This far from the sun, it was almost invisible against the blackness of space. Then I caught a glint, and stretched out my hand even farther. My recently wrenched shoulder complained, but I kept reaching ...

And I caught it!

I hauled the massive thing back toward the vault—my shoulder aching hard—and bunched it up into a ball, clutching it to my chest. Then I scrunched myself up into a ball as well, drawing my center of gravity back toward the vault with my legs bunched beneath me, and unhooked my tether. The vault's rotation would bring me around to face Alicia in just a few seconds.

What the *fuck* was I doing?

The primary rule of space rescue is *save yourself first*. Jumping away from an anchor point with no safety line, no jets, and no fixed target was insane. Doing it from a spinning vault, with no possibility of a second chance, was suicide.

I breathed hard through my nose, clenching my hands into fists and biting my lips hard enough to hurt.

I didn't want to do this.

But we were the Cannibal Club, damn it.

I've never been athletic, but I've always been good at trajectories. In secondary school, I made the varsity free-fall volleyball team every year, despite being the smallest and skinniest kid on the team, because I could always put the ball exactly where I wanted it.

This was just the same. Except instead of the ball, it was me. And if I missed the shot, I would die. We would *both* die.

And then Alicia moved into position, and before I could think any further, I leaped.

There's no sound in space, but I knew that Cayce and Kane were yelling their heads off at me for being a stupid damn selfless idiot. Alicia too, probably. I know I was, in my head.

137

But I was committed now.

Amazingly, I seemed to be on target, heading straight toward Alicia. To make that leap from a rotating platform, compensating for all the vectors, was either a brilliant feat of intuition or sheerest luck. Probably both. If we survived, I would tell everyone that I'd run the numbers in my head and never had any doubt.

Alicia's suited form grew and grew, still tumbling rapidly end-over-end. Her eyes each time she came around to face me showed a mix of fear for both our lives, disapproval at my idiocy, and hope that my stupid risk would pay off. At least, that was what I thought I saw in them.

And then I ran into her, with an impact that knocked the air out of my lungs and rattled my head in my helmet. I held her tight, pressing my faceplate against hers. "Are you okay?" I yelled.

"You fucking *idiot!*" she yelled back. I took that as a yes.

I pulled out Alicia's waist tether and began tying her to myself, belly to belly, each looking over the other's shoulder. I wanted us both to be in a position to observe and take action, no matter how we tumbled. Working together, we managed it without losing hold of the blanket.

Our tumble was now slower than Alicia's original spin had been, with the addition of my mass and the blanket's, but we were still turning pretty fast. And with the additional momentum from my leap, we were moving away from the vault even faster than Alicia had been.

I wadded up the blanket behind Alicia's back. I had to hope its mass, with a good hard shove, would provide enough delta V to reverse our course. I would only get one shot. And I had to do it while facing away from my target.

You can do this, I told myself.

I didn't believe me.

We were turning every three and a half seconds. As the vault passed my view, I counted *one* chimpanzee, *two* chim—and then *pushed*, hard, flinging the blanket away at what I desperately hoped was the exact correct moment and the exact correct direction.

Our tumble changed. We were now spinning longitudinally instead of end-over-end, and it took me a moment to reorient myself.

There was the Ring ... and there was the vault, with Kane and Cayce attached. It was frighteningly far away.

Our rotation took the vault out of my sight. Then it came back. It was closer. And each turn brought it closer still.

Thank you, inexorable laws of physics!

After a few rotations, I had some idea how long it would take us to reach the vault. It was a little under three minutes.

And the client's ship would be picking up the vault in—the chronometer on my suit's wrist was just visible—two minutes and thirty-eight seconds.

It was going to be close.

Very close indeed.

Alicia's tether was keeping us together, and I didn't want to mess with that. I pulled the tether at my own waist out to its end and held the weighted hook in my hand, ready to throw it in case of a near miss.

Two minutes passed, with the vault growing nearer and nearer. It seemed like a very, very long time.

And, though it was hard to tell with everything spinning, it looked like we were not, in fact, going to hit the vault. Too much to ask for, I supposed. But we might very well pass within ten meters.

I clutched the hook in my trembling hand.

Cayce had already rearranged himself to face away from the vault, lower body still firmly attached to it, both hands open and ready to catch my thrown hook.

I held my breath, waiting for a moment when Cayce and I were facing each other as we both spun.

So hard to judge. Were we close enough already? Were we getting closer or farther away? How far was ten meters, exactly?

Was this it? Should I wait for a better opportunity?

And then Cayce gave a sharp hand gesture: *now*.

I didn't think. I reacted. I hurled the hook at him with all my strength.

The hook wobbled gently as it sailed through the vacuum, the tether snaking after it ...

... and it flew right past Cayce's reaching hand ...

... but then Kane caught it!

Immediately, he reeled us in with all the considerable strength of his arms, jerking us around like a fish on a line.

My helmet clanged against the vault with an impact that left me dizzy.

I felt hands looping tether around my suit's hard upper torso.

And then came a hum, which quickly rose to an earsplitting screech—the grapple's intense magnetic field pushing sound directly into my earphones, despite the disabled radio—and a sudden, massive rush of acceleration that crushed me against the vault and pressed my helmet ring chokingly against my throat.

I blacked out.

I came to in a strange airlock. The light was harsh and bright, the air that struck my cheeks and chin as I removed my helmet was icy, and the harsh hum and rattle in my ears told me we were inside a ship that had sacrificed every last vestige of comfort and safety for speed.

I squinted against the glaring light and shook my head in an attempt to shake off the effects of the several severe blows I'd suffered in the last six minutes. It didn't help much; my head throbbed like a big painful heart.

Jesus, had it been only six minutes? It had felt like a lifetime.

Then a hand landed on my shoulder and whipped me around, which didn't help my headache at all. It was Alicia, and she was pissed. "You fucking *idiot!*" she yelled in my face. "You were already safe! We could have *both* died!"

Cayce came up from behind her. "The Cannibal Club doesn't leave anyone behind," he stated with calm deliberation.

"Strange would have!" Alicia screamed at him.

And she was right.

Strange *would* have left her behind, I realized. Even back when he and Alicia had loved each other, he would never have risked his own life the way I just had. Not when the odds were that terrible. He would never have let his heart overcome his head like that.

"Wait," Alicia said to Cayce, interrupting my thoughts. "I'm sorry. I'm … a little twitchy right now, for some inexplicable reason."

She drew in a shuddering breath and turned to me. "I should have said … I should have said thank you. Thank you for saving my life."

"You're welcome," I said.

And then a high, frenzied voice started shouting at me in rapid Vietnamese: "Who the fuck are you and what are you doing in my ship?"

"Bitch, please," I said to the captain. "We just pulled off the heist of the century for your boss. The least you can do is offer us a ride."

I didn't literally say "bitch, please." I addressed her in Vietnamese as *em*—little sister—even though she was older than me and a captain to boot. That deliberate snub brought her up short, just as I wanted, and stopped her incoherent screaming. Really, I'd hope for better from a high-speed independent transport operator. Especially for the rates I suspected the client was paying.

"I wasn't hired for this!" she sputtered back, addressing me as *mày*, which was really rude but at least gender-neutral. I gave her a point for that. "I *never* carry passengers!"

"I'm not a passenger," I replied smoothly, using my preferred pronoun *bạn*—friend. It's gender-neutral and maybe a little too friendly for most social situations, just like me. "Just treat us as part of the cargo. Take us wherever you were going, drop us off, and we'll be fine."

"What, you like eating vacuum?" she snapped. But she used *bạn*, and I knew I'd slipped inside her defenses.

"Not too fond of it," I admitted. "But if you can refill our air tanks and get us wherever we're going in four hours, I guess we can just hang on outside. If that's what it takes."

"Hunh," she snorted, and stared at me a while, sizing me up. Riding on the outside of a ship this fast at full skip was hazardous but not inherently fatal. Personally, I wasn't really looking forward to any more risk to life and limb today, but my offer demonstrated insouciance, bravery, and willingness to negotiate.

"Oh, all right," she conceded eventually. "You can stay inside. Just don't breathe too much."

I smiled, made a lip-zipping gesture, and bowed respectfully. "Captain." Addressing her by her title was the "proper" level of formality and restored a cordial, businesslike relationship.

"You can hang out in the galley until we reach the exchange point," she said, continuing to address me as *bạn*. I nodded politely, accepting the offer. "It'll be about six hours." She turned away, presumably heading back to the cockpit, but paused at the hatch. "I don't have any spare clothes you could use, but the bathroom can fab you some towels."

"Your servant," I replied, bowing.

I returned my attention to the others, who awaited expectantly the results of my negotiations with our host. None of them spoke Vietnamese. "She's generously allowed us to remain within the ship until we reach the rendezvous point for the handoff of the Scroll," I explained, "and offered towels to clothe our sweaty bodies. That's all. But it really is about the best we could realistically expect, under the circumstances."

"Well, we're still breathing, anyway," Alicia summarized. Cayce, unusually subdued for him, just nodded assent.

Kane's eyes narrowed. "She's solo?"

I looked around. "Ship this size, this fast, doing this kind of job? Yeah, she's solo."

"We could take her."

"But we won't," Cayce said. "Not only would it piss off the client—and whoever they are, it's plainly someone with government-level resources—but it wouldn't be polite."

Kane didn't seem completely mollified, but he went along with it.

We used the bathroom, one at a time, to strip off our suits and whatever sweat-soaked clothing we'd been wearing underneath. An hour later, we were lounging in the ship's tiny galley, wrapped in freshly printed towels. If we'd been under thrust, there wouldn't have been enough floor space for the four of us, but in free fall, it was merely snug. "Reminds me of Vesta," Alicia said to me, sipping from a bulb of tea, and there was more than a little melancholy in her voice. I nodded, feeling some of those same feelings myself.

When I'd first joined up with Alicia and Strange, they'd been a couple for a year or two, running small cons and the occasional heist. They had invited me in for a jewelry store job—I didn't really have the chops yet, but through luck and bravado, we got away with it—and we'd worked so well together that we decided to make it a gang. And a threesome, for a little while, but it didn't stick. I was the one who first called us the Cannibal Club, which was originally a name I'd had in mind for a band. If the two of them had been musically rather than criminally inclined, we might have had a very different life.

In those days, we'd been dirt-poor, spinning fast and close around the gravity well called Poverty, with the occasional influx of cash from successful jobs barely keeping us in orbit. But as we'd gained in experience, contacts, and reputation, the Club had grown and stabilized, with first Max and then Shweta accreting on to form a core of five. We added Kane for a job that required extra muscle, and he'd stuck around. Then Damien had come along, and things got complicated. First he'd formed a triad with Alicia and Strange, then Strange spun out of that and into a rebound thing with Shweta, and then came the Orca Job … and that was the end of it.

But our current situation—theoretically or potentially rich as Croesus, but in current fact reduced to nothing more than our stolen emergency suits, some borrowed towels, and whatever tiny stash of personal possessions we'd been able to bring with us—felt very much like the days when there had been four of us holed up in a storage container on the Vesta docks, living small and dreaming big, with Cayce and Kane as younger versions of Strange and Max.

Younger? No, wait, Kane was about the same age now as Strange, Alicia, and I had been then. Shit. Where does the time go?

And Cayce … he was a lot younger now than we'd been then, but it was easy to forget that. There was something old and cold behind those young eyes.

"When we get to the rendezvous," Cayce said, breaking into my reverie, "we're going to need passage to somewhere we can rest up and marshal our forces for the next step. And we'll need at least a down payment from your client."

"I'll see what I can do," I said, and left the galley to knock on the control room door where our captain was hiding from her unwanted guests.

I couldn't get the captain to give us access to comms, but she did promise to pass a message to her contact, and when we arrived at the rendezvous point, there were two ships waiting ... an ugly, very nondescript cargo hauler that displayed more than the usual complement of high-powered weaponry as it took the vault aboard, and something that looked like a private yacht.

The yacht was for us, of course, and the getaway ship's captain didn't even say goodbye as we sealed ourselves back into our stinking emergency suits and made our way across the vacuum to it. She did at least let us fill up our oxygen tanks before we left, so that was something.

The yacht, I noticed as we approached, was astonishingly anonymous. It lacked the usual flag-of-registry decals on its skip vanes, which were only a convention, but it also didn't display any visible registration numbers ... and that was a pretty serious, not to mention obvious, regulatory no-no. Even the chandler's plaque on the airlock door—you know, that little thing with the ship's name, final assembly date and place, and an inspirational quote?—was missing, and I've *never* before seen a ship, no matter how scruffy or illegal, without one of those.

It was the same inside. Scrupulously clean, impressively well-ordered, and completely anonymous. There wasn't even any written language to hint at the ship's origin ... all the visible signage was limited to international standard symbols. The crew, too, were disciplined, orderly, and clad in neat dark-blue jumpsuits utterly lacking in identifying information other than a three-digit number above the breast pocket.

But even though they addressed us in accentless machine-assisted English, they were all Vietnamese, which kind of gave the game away. Government, for sure.

I wasn't sure how I felt about that. I mean, I had suspected, of course. No one but a major player could have offered such ironclad guarantees of safety after the job was done. But the money had been so good, the job itself so tempting ... I chose to overlook the client for the opportunity to stick Nguyen Van Thu in the eye and make a fortune in the process. But now that the mask had slipped, and it was clear we'd done this job for an Earth government ... well, my heritage was Vietnamese, but my citizenship was Outer Belt.

At least Earth and the Outer Belt weren't at war. Currently.

I spoke to the one who seemed to be in charge. None of them had introduced themselves by name or title, but you could always tell. He was a solid, stolid guy whose brush-cut hair was speckled with gray, and his number was 053. "I'm sorry for the inconvenience," I said—in English for the benefit of my companions—"but thank you for meeting us here. We'll need conveyance to an open port—"

"Ceres," Cayce interrupted, and I gave him a glare. During our discussions on the way here, he had been insistent that Ceres be our next stop. We would be able to lose ourselves in the crowd, I must admit, and it would be an excellent place to rest up and reequip ourselves, but it would also be crawling with people who knew our faces and didn't exactly have our best interests at heart.

"An open port," I repeated firmly. "Perhaps Cassowary Station. And I hope that it will not be too forward if I request a cash advance on our agreed-upon payment. Due to circumstances beyond our control, we find ourselves in a rather"—I gestured to our emergency-suited selves and lack of any baggage—"reduced condition."

053's eyes flicked from me to Cayce, sizing up the situation, then his jaw firmed and he gave me a curt nod. "We will take you to Ceres." I felt a flare of annoyance at that, though I kept it off my face. How dare this … *minion*, listen to a *kid* like Cayce, instead of me, the one who'd put the deal together? But Ceres *was* an open port, and I supposed he might have his own reasons to prefer it as a destination. "I will consult my superiors about the advance. In the meantime, you may avail yourselves of the facilities of this vehicle." He gestured to two of his subordinates, who stiffened to attention—their bodies perfectly aligned in free fall, further evidence that they were regular military—and then ushered us to the yacht's passenger quarters.

There were two staterooms, each with sleeping nets for two. A quick silent negotiation, conducted in shrugs and glances, sorted me and Alicia into one, Cayce and Kane in the other.

It was the first time Alicia and I had been alone together and not otherwise occupied since … well, since before the Orca Job. But after we got undressed, we found that all we wanted to do was hold each other and cry. It had been a very, very long day. We drifted off to sleep like that, snuggled together in one sleeping net.

Some time later, Alicia woke me, and that was delicious. Afterward, we held each other, the sweat cooling on our bodies in the breath of the recycled air, and talked.

"So," I said. "Cayce. Being around him must be … complicated."

"It is," she admitted.

"If he's sixteen, Strange must have been involved with his mom at the same time as you. Did you know her?"

She shook her head. "Cayce said he was born on Io, and when I first met Strange, he had just come from there. I think he must have left Cayce's mom, whoever she was, before Cayce was born. I don't think he even knew she was pregnant."

I considered this intelligence. "What do you see when you look in his face?"

"He looks a *lot* like his dad did when we first met." A small smile crept onto her face.

"He does." I smirked. "I've seen how you look at his ass."

"He's *sixteen!*" she insisted, shocked, but I noted that she didn't deny having checked him out. Then she blew out a long breath. "I never really stopped loving Strange, even after he broke up with me and Damien. And then, after Damien died … well, I blamed Strange, of course—"

"We all did."

"—but I couldn't hate him. There was a lot of blame to go around, and seeing him did remind me of Damien, in all the good as well as the bad ways. I needed him. And he needed me too. We both were mourning Damien, each in our own way."

I thought about those days after Orca. The anger and the sadness and the recriminations had driven me away as soon as we'd reached port. Alicia had stuck around for a couple of months after that, and in some ways, I admired her for her persistence. But eventually, the Club had disintegrated completely, and stayed that way for ten years.

And now here we were.

We held each other, each awash in memory, and slept again.

After we all woke up, we rendezvoused in the lounge, relaxing in freshly fabbed jumpsuits with mangosteens, butter cookies, and strong hot tea. Bliss. Alicia and I did not hold hands, did not even sit together, but I saw understanding in Cayce's eyes. Kane, of course, was oblivious.

"So," I said. "They tried to kill us. We survived."

"Let's eat," said Alicia, raising her squeeze bulb in salute.

We munched and sipped in companionable silence for a time until Cayce, humorless as his dad ever was, called us back to order. "Once we hit Ceres," he said, "the first order of business is to get our hands on a shuttle. We'll need something small, fast, and untraceable for the next phase of my plan."

"Whoa." I held up both hands. "*Your* plan? And why Ceres, specifically?"

Cayce straightened in response to my challenge, probably trying to look older. He was actually a bit taller than me, the little rat. "My plan to break Strange out of Cronos as quickly as possible. Which, even ignoring the fact that you all owe him your lives and careers several times over, is your best shot at preventing Aquila from extracting information from him that will lead them straight to *you*."

Yes, I owed Strange. We all did. But I didn't like being railroaded, especially not by someone half my age. "So what's at Ceres?" I fumed.

"Shweta. The next member of the renewed Cannibal Club."

The conversation stopped dead for a long moment, all of us staring at Cayce in incredulity. It was Kane who broke the silence, saying what we were all thinking: "You can't be serious."

"We need her," Cayce said, shrugging, as though the question were ridiculous.

Alicia's brow furrowed with skepticism. "Isn't she ... kind of busy right now?"

Shweta had been the Cannibal Club's diplomat, persuader, and mouthpiece as well as being auntie to all of us. So it wasn't a complete surprise that when the Club broke up, she'd gone straight ... straight into government service. She'd changed her name, of course—Shweta, the name we'd known her by during her time with the Club, wasn't her real name either—but we all recognized her face in the news. Over the years, using personal relationships, strategic bargains, and almost certainly blackmail, she'd risen through the ranks to the position of Secretary of Transportation for the Inner Belt Coalition.

Cayce acknowledged the truth of Alicia's statement with an eye roll and spread hands. "Of course. But I've heard through ... back channels, that she isn't happy in her current position. And with what I have to offer her, I'm pretty certain I can get her to join us."

"And what's that?" I asked, obviously enough.

Cayce grinned like a cat. "The fastest ship in the System."

Kane and Alicia seemed puzzled at that, but I knew exactly what he was referring to. "You mean the *Malakbel*? She already has it!"

Cayce's grin widened into a genuine smile, the first one I could recall seeing on that young face. "Exactly. But she's just an administrator now ... with our help, she could be an independent operator. Along with the rest of the Club, of course. There's no limit to what we could do with a ship like that. But she needs us to steal it, and we need her to make it possible."

The Malakbel project—named after a messenger of the gods in one of the old Earth pantheons—was a massive Coalition project to develop a Quantum IV skip-drive, which promised effective speeds ten or twelve times faster than anything possible with current technology. The project was years behind schedule and billions over budget, of course, but according to the rumor mill, the most recent prototype ships were actually starting to deliver on the promise.

Cayce's statement didn't reduce Alicia's skepticism. "Seems overly ambitious," she said. "Even assuming we can get her to go along with the job, which I doubt, why do we need something like that? We could have a perfectly respectable career without it. And stealing something *that* big is not only an enormous risk, it would paste a gigantic target on our backs."

Cayce's grin didn't diminish. "I have a plan to mitigate the risk and let all of us get away clean—even Shweta. And we need the ship—this ship in particular—because … well, because of some-thing I haven't told you yet."

Another pause. Kane, again, broke the silence. "Well?"

Cayce took a breath, and his face resumed its usual seriousness. "My dad is being held on Cronos Station, like I said. But there are lots of stations called Cronos, and he's not on the one that's in a po-lar orbit around Saturn. That's an incorrect assumption Kane made."

"Which you didn't correct!" Kane spat. Cayce at least had the decency to look abashed.

"So where is it really?" I asked.

"In the Kuiper Belt," Cayce replied with studied calm. My eyes widened at that—so did everyone else's—but he kept talking into the astonished silence. "Which is why we need a really fast ship, if we're going to break Dad out before he spills the beans."

The Kuiper Belt was the outermost settled region of the System, and that was only if you were exceedingly generous in your defini-tion of "settled." It stretched from 30 to 50 AUs from the Sun—that was six to ten times as far out as Jupiter—and had a total population of less than a million. Which, given the volume involved, worked out to an effective population density of zero. The largest bodies in the Kuiper Belt were iceballs like Pluto and Eris, and the only signifi-cant resource they had was water, which could be had much more cheaply in the Inner Belt. And to get there from the Outer Belt with any normal commercial ship would take most of a year … each way.

Kane crossed his arms on his chest. "Why the *fuck* would anyone put a prison station that far out?"

"To keep it secret. To reduce the chance of escape to zero. And … it's more than just a prison station."

"How do they even service the damn thing?" Kane persisted.

"The Malakbel project, secretive as it is, is only the *public* face of Quantum IV skip drive development. Cronos has a small fleet of very fast ships. But the latest Malakbel prototype, the *Malakbel VII*, is … well, it's a quantum leap beyond even those. So that's the one we have to steal."

If all this was true—and given the curtain of lies and half-truths Cayce had just pulled partway back, I was extremely dubi-ous about anything else he said—it had very serious implications.

"So Cronos is part of a secret project that's even more secret than Malakbel," I said, speaking very precisely and looking him straight in the eye. "Which implies even more money and power than the Coalition government. And you're proposing to take us right into the heart of it?"

"Yes," Cayce replied. "For Strange."

We all stared uncomfortably at each other for a while—Kane huffing with anger, Alicia distraught, and me with a feeling of cold indignation in my chest. "You," I said to Cayce, "have been a very naughty boy. You need to go to your room and let the adults talk this out."

Outrage at my words warred in his face with acknowledgment that he had, indeed, seriously overstepped some bounds. Finally he took in a breath through his nose, pursed his lips hard, nodded curtly, and pushed himself out of the lounge and into the stateroom he shared with Kane. The door closed behind him, leaving the three of us alone.

There was a lot of screaming then.

Given our previous conversation, I wasn't too surprised that Alicia was the one arguing most strenuously that we should cut the kid some slack. It was for Strange, after all, she argued, and it was true that we all owed Strange our lives several times over. She admitted that Cayce had lied to us, but she felt that he was doing the best he could with what he had and she respected that some information had to be kept close to the chest.

Kane, for his part, was almost too angry to speak, and was often reduced to spluttering and waving his hands. He owed Strange more than any of the rest of us—he'd been an impoverished dock rat when Strange had taken him under his wing and into the Club—which made him both intensely loyal to Strange and furiously disappointed by Cayce's lies. He would be just as happy to punt Cayce out the airlock right now and split the proceeds from the Emperor's Scroll three ways.

And as for me … I was of two minds. Yes, Cayce had lied to us, but that actually wasn't a deal-breaker for me. The Cannibal Club had been tighter than family when we'd been together, but it's true that there's no honor among thieves. We hadn't told each other everything even back then, and despite his parentage, Cayce hadn't ever been a member of the Club. So I didn't completely trust him, but on the other hand, a few lies were just part of doing business. I certainly hadn't shared every single thing *I* knew. And the job itself … it was an enormous risk, yes, but my fingers itched to get ahold of that prototype ship—not just for the drive, but for all the sweet *sweet* tech that would certainly come along with it.

"I don't care if you're banging the kid," Kane said to Alicia, which made her gawp like a fish, "but you can't just think with your pussy! We can't trust him!"

"If you had any brains at all outside the end of your dick," Alicia growled back, "you'd know that there's such a thing as non-sexual affection. And respect! Okay, yes, the kid hasn't been a hundred percent straight with us. But his heart's in the right place, and he's got his dad's brains. I'd follow him to the edge of the System."

"Literally." I folded my arms on my chest and breathed slowly, trying to lower the temperature of the discussion. Screaming at each other wasn't going to get us to the bottom of anything. "Look, I respect the kid's skills too. I *want* to believe in him. But can he really pull this off, even if we can get Shweta? This job makes stealing the Emperor's Scroll look like just the first act in a cheap drama."

Alicia calmed down a little, following my lead. "It's a stretch, I'll grant," she said. "But once we pull this off … with a fast ship, and Strange back, we can tackle any job we like."

"Big plans just blow up big," Kane snapped. "We got lucky back at the Ring … we should just take what we've got and split."

"What, and break up this happy family?" I spread my hands in an encompassing gesture. I wasn't quite convinced yet, but I was prepared to hear Alicia out.

Alicia faced Kane with an expression combining annoyance with indulgence, as though he were a small child rather than a dangerous full-grown man. "You're missing the big picture." She tapped off points on her fingers. "One: we wouldn't be where we are now without Cayce."

Kane snorted at that. "Riding in someone else's ship without even the clothes on our backs?"

Alicia glared back. "Free, independent, and filthy rich! Or we will be, once Tai's client pays off." She looked to me, and I nodded in acknowledgment. "Two: Cayce has a plan to put the Club back together—*including* Strange—and set us up for a long and successful career. And three: how far do you think you can get without him?"

That took Kane aback. "Huh?"

"Thunderbolt, Aquila, and Turvallis are all looking for us. Cayce has stayed one step ahead of them for … I don't know how long, but at least as long as any of us have known him, and he's kept us out of their hands too. If you take the money and run, do *you* have the skills to evade them forever?"

"Hell yeah!" But Kane's bravado was plainly covering uncertainty, and Alicia could see it as well as I could.

"You can believe that if you like. But if I were a betting woman, I'd put my money on Cayce over you any day." She looked at me. "And for all your smarts, you know he's better at the long game than you are. Than any of us is. Even at his age."

"Not as good as Shweta," I replied, but I knew she was right.

"Possibly. That's why we need her. And I trust that Cayce can get her."

Kane just snarled incoherently and turned his back, but I stroked my chin, thinking hard. Cayce had been useful back at the Ring, no doubt, but he was a scorpion and the rest of us might just be his frogs. Did I really want to throw in my lot with a kid who, whatever his skills, however preternaturally composed he might be, still set my teeth on edge in a way I couldn't quite articulate?

On the other hand … the prospect of stealing the fastest ship in the System right out from under the Inner Belt Coalition's nose gladdened this Outer Belter's heart. And the job itself, working with Alicia and maybe Shweta—and, yes, even annoying Kane—promised to be more fun and excitement than I'd seen in years on my own.

"I'm in," I said to Alicia, extending my hand. She took it. "You, me, and Cayce. We get Shweta, we get the ship, we get Strange, we set ourselves up for a highly profitable life of crime." I cast my glance over to Kane. "How about you?"

Kane's back was still turned, but he had that situational awareness thing and I knew he knew I was looking at him. And I also knew that, orphan dock rat that he still was, he treasured his independence but desperately craved family. I could practically see him tremble with the tension between the two.

Finally, with a frustrated growl, he spun to face us—a neat freefall maneuver despite his anger—and pointed hard at me. "You're just going to get us all killed!"

"I note you said 'us,'" I observed mildly, but I couldn't keep a grin off my face.

And with that, he deflated, the anger whooshing out of him like a suit with a fingertip meteoroid puncture, leaving the frightened, lonely child behind. "Yeah," he admitted with a head-shaking, self-disbelieving grin. "I can't quit the Club. You asshole."

"Wouldn't be the same without you," Alicia said.

"Yeah," I admitted. "You asshole."

Despite our continuing differences, we presented a united front when we invited Cayce back to the lounge. Alicia spoke for the three of us. "Okay," she said, "we're in. But isn't what you're proposing now a little … ambitious?"

"It's the only way to save Strange," he replied, trying to project confidence … though he was clearly shaken by our near-rebellion.

Alicia glanced at me, and I picked up the conversational ball. "You're going to have to be a little more forthcoming, then," I said. "What's the plan?"

"It'll be half-con, half-heist," he replied, gaining confidence as he shifted into an explaining-his-brilliant-plan mode. "Shweta can get us in, but we'll have to shoot our way out. I've already put some of the pieces in motion, but it will need all our skills." He looked to Kane. "There *will* be screaming and threats of violence, I assure you."

"I can get into that," Kane admitted.

"Once we have the ship, we can get to Cronos and get away. But while we're there … I know what the situation was a few months ago, but it may have changed. We'll have to improvise. But I have confidence in the Cannibal Club."

"Back up," Alicia said. "How can we possibly get away with the ship? It's kind of conspicuous."

"So is Shweta. But I have a plan to get away clean with both of them ..."

Once we hit Ceres, my very first stop was Saville Row, home of the Inner Belt's trendiest boutiques. "Surely you don't expect me to meet with the Secretary of Transportation in *this*?" I'd asked Cayce, gesturing to my ugly, scratchy printed jumpsuit. I dumped it into the recycler as I entered the changing room in the very first shop.

I drifted out of there in a long burgundy coat with gold braid epaulets and frog closures, tall black boots in the softest suede, a form-fitting fawn-colored body suit that accentuated my curves, and a broad-brimmed hat with a ludicrous purple feather. Two more complete outfits and a selection of accessories would be delivered to our hotel. I felt much more myself.

The money had been waiting in our anonymous drop when we arrived at Ceres, as promised, along with clearances that made the customs agent gasp and wave us through without another word— and Ceres customs had seen *everything*. Even though the numbered jumpsuits on the nameless yacht had been brusque with us, even rude, I gave them a big tip as thanks to their bosses. Feeling flush, we'd checked into the second-nicest hotel in the South Dock neighborhood and then had happily run off in separate directions. The yacht had been comfortable enough, but the quarters had been rather tight.

When I returned to our suite after a full day's shopping, I found my new outfits already racked in my closet, with my other purchases— technological trinkets from a variety of sources, some of them even legal—neatly arrayed on the shelves below. A quick inspection of the parcels verified that the security seals on each had not been broken, which was against hotel policy but very much according to my wishes. The valet would definitely be receiving her second payment.

Once I'd checked my purchases and freshened up, I returned to the suite's common room to find Kane tearing open his own purchases like a rich kid during Tet. The smells of gun oil and explosives stung my nose, but his joy was infectious. Alicia's shopping bags bore the logos of legitimate pharmaceutical companies and high-end chocolatiers, and her new two-piece outfit was boringly practical—comfortable, festooned with pockets, and completely lacking in any trim or fringe that might catch on something during a heist—but it was, at least, from one of the more respectable designers and not one of the cheap knockoffs she'd favored in the past.

Cayce was still in his room, where he'd been when we left, and still had his nose pressed to his screen. But dozens of freshly delivered parcels floated around him, and he'd changed from the ugly jumpsuit he'd arrived in to faded Ganymede blues. It was, in some ways, the most characterless outfit possible, but it was perfectly tailored to his slim form, and in it, he could blend into the background in almost any situation. I had to admit that it suited him.

"All right," Cayce said, stowing his screen in its charging station. "I've made contact with Shweta and set up a rendezvous. I'm meeting her tomorrow morning."

"What about the rest of us?" Alicia asked, rather taken aback.

Cayce paused, realizing he'd overstepped his authority again. "The more people, the more risk. But if you want to come along, you'd be welcome."

Despite his acquiescence, I still didn't like his attitude. "We are in this job together," I said, "or we aren't. You said it would need all our skills, so it's everyone or none."

Cayce was stung by that but tried to cover it up with a shrug. "Have it your way. I'll book a table for five."

The jitney dropped us off at a tiny out-of-the-way barbecue joint called the Smoke Ranch. "Never heard of it," Kane remarked dismissively when he saw the sign. "We should have gone to the Cayuse." Barbecue was Ceres's signature dish, the product of its famed zero-gravity cattle ranches, and Kane considered himself a connoisseur of the stuff.

"Shweta says it's a hidden gem," Cayce replied. "But we really aren't here for the meat."

The ribs were good, I'll grant you that, and we had plenty of time to savor them while we were waiting. "Are you sure she's coming?" Alicia asked, wiping her hands after a second helping.

"It's not like her to be this late," Cayce said, drumming his fingers on the table's edge.

Another half an hour went by. Then another half-hour. The staff were eyeing us hard—it was a small place and we'd been occupying one of the few tables for a ridiculously long time, even granted that we kept ordering. But, amazingly, Kane's impatience won out over his love for the ribs.

"That's it!" he spat, pushing himself away from his place and rising into the air above his seat. Though the restaurant had an Earth-style decor, the gravity was little more than a vague suggestion of downward pressure. "I'm not going to take this kind of kiss-off from anyone, not even Shweta!"

And then one of the other customers—a small round person who'd been sipping tea in a corner booth the whole time—cleared their throat. "You'd think someone who prides himself on situational awareness as much as you do, Kane, would notice a dear old friend."

Shweta.

I stared aghast—appalled at myself for failing to recognize her, and even more so for failing to notice that we were being quietly surveilled the whole time. But then, disappearing into the background was one of Shweta's many special skills.

We'd all seen her on the news during her rise to her current position, but in person, it was easier to see that she was ten years older than the last time we'd been in one place. We all were, of course, but she was showing her age more than the rest of us. The face that had been round and maternal before had gone jowly, the hair that had been glossy black was now salt-and-pepper. She had always had a full figure but was even more zaftig now. It suited her, I thought. But her black eyes hadn't changed … they were still full of life and intelligence and warmth. She was more a grandmother than an auntie now, but she still looked like someone you could trust.

Which was, of course, another one of her special skills.

"Apologies, Shweta," Cayce said, extending his hand and drifting over to her. "I'm Cayce. I'm very pleased to meet you; my father told me so much about you in our limited time together."

"Pleased to meet you," she said in a neutral tone, accepting his hand but withholding judgment. She was much less reserved with the rest of us, greeting Kane like a long-lost nephew, Alicia like a sister, and me with the same affable banter we'd always shared. "Nice to see you in one piece," she said, smiling. "You never could stay away from the organized criminal element."

"I did!" I protested. "I didn't pull a single job for the gangs in my whole time on the Ring!"

"Then why did you have to slip off the Ring through the back door? A back door which, from what I hear, you had to create with high explosives?"

"Um." I had to look down. "It was a case of artistic differences."

"Oh?" She folded her generous arms on her equally generous bosom and regarded me with a small expectant smile. The others looked on with curiosity. This was a story I hadn't shared with them.

"I was hired to provide the music and sound for a wedding," I explained. "It was a *big* wedding, okay? Social event of the season. I *killed* myself getting everything just right … and then I had to go and play the groom's worst enemy's favorite song." I looked up, still sheepish. "Well, okay, I kind of knew what I was doing. I knew that both families were high in the Ring's crime hierarchy. I knew whose favorite song it was. But the groom had been an asshole to me all during the run-up to the big night, and I thought I could get away with tweaking his nose." I shrugged. "Well, I couldn't. But I did manage to stay clear of them for months. I really didn't think they'd *still* be watching for me at the terminal."

Shweta shook her head and held out her arms for an embrace, which I gladly accepted, shaking my own head at my stupidity. It felt so *good* to be enfolded in those soft, warm arms! "If you'd been there," I said, "you would have talked me out of it."

"I know," she said, and kissed the top of my head.

We ordered drinks and desserts and settled back down at the same table; the staff now seemed perfectly content to let us remain. "They know me here," Shweta explained. "And I'd already told them that I was prepared to wait until I was good and sure you were here on your own initiative and hadn't been followed." She nodded to Kane.

"Your … outburst, was so characteristic of you that I could be certain you weren't under any outside pressure."

"Thanks, I think," Kane muttered. I smirked behind my margarita bulb.

Cayce didn't waste any time getting to the meat of the matter. So to speak. "Is your situation the same as it was the last time you wrote to Strange?" he asked Shweta. This wasn't something he'd mentioned to us previously, which annoyed but didn't surprise me.

"It is," Shweta said. "Or perhaps even a bit worse." She looked around and leaned in just fractionally, prompting the rest of us to lean in as well. It didn't make surveillance any less likely, but it emphasized the importance and confidentiality of what she was about to say. "I won't say I haven't enjoyed my time in the corridors of power. But every privilege has its price, and that's a price I'm no longer willing to keep paying." Kane started to speak up, but Alicia shushed him with a touch on his wrist. This was Shweta's story to tell.

"The Malakbel project," Shweta continued, "has been very close to my heart for my entire time in government. I've supported it, sometimes at considerable political cost, over many other priorities because of the benefits it offers to every citizen of the Coalition. This technology promises not only a far higher maximum skip but greatly improved energy efficiency—and hence lower cost—even at conventional skip levels. The drive may also be cheaper and simpler to manufacture. This will improve quality of life and provide economic benefits to all levels of society." She sighed. "But nothing in government is ever simple or straightforward, especially not when there is as much money involved as there is here. In order to obtain funding, I've had to make … arrangements, with certain corporate interests. This has given them leverage over not only the Malakbel project—leverage which they have not been shy in exploiting—but also over me personally." She laid a pudgy hand on her breast. "I would like to say that I would never, ever do anything illegal or immoral merely to protect my own position and personal safety. I would *like* to say it. But, unfortunately, I cannot." She bowed her head, eyes closed. "I must confess I have benefited from these arrangements, sometimes quite handsomely. But the things I have been asked to do and to support … they are no longer tolerable." She looked around the table, her dark eyes seeming to bore into each of our souls. "I want out."

"You could've just quit," Kane growled, and Alicia shushed him.

Shweta grinned ruefully. "The kind of games I've been playing, one cannot merely cash in one's chips and leave the table. Accidents befall those who make the attempt." She tapped her temple with her forefinger. "Certain information cannot be allowed to become public."

"So Shweta and my father," Cayce continued smoothly, "worked out a plan to get her out of her current position and safely into a new life. A plan which, incidentally, delivers the *Malakbel VII* prototype into our hands and makes Strange's rescue possible."

"When did he do this?" I asked, "and why didn't you mention it to us before now?"

"It was about two months before he got hauled off to Cronos," Cayce replied, dodging the second half of my question. "He sent the plan to me from there, and I negotiated the remaining details with Shweta after that. But we couldn't proceed without the whole Club." He was looking specifically at me, the most recent one to rejoin, as he said it, but then his eyes flicked to Alicia. "The *whole* Club."

"You mean Miyuki," Alicia said. It was an accusation.

Cayce didn't flinch. "Do you have someone else in mind?"

"She's just a *kid!*"

"She's twenty-nine." He smiled slightly. "She was older at Orca than I am now."

"You're … unique. And she's str—" She stopped herself with an ironic snort. "Let's just say that she's had a hard life."

"We all have. That's what made us who we are. That's what made us the Cannibal Club."

Alicia's brow furrowed in concentration, or perhaps consternation. "After … after Orca, when I promised I'd take care of her father, and failed, I felt responsible for her. I took her under my wing and got her to someplace safe. And I've kept in touch since. She's … she's never quite settled down, to be honest. I think she has it in her to be a great pilot. But I never even *considered* bringing her into the Club. She deserves better."

"We all deserve better than we've gotten," Shweta said. "But no one is going to just hand it to us—the only way to get it is to work for it. You know this."

"Dad told me all about Damien," Cayce said, his brown eyes warm and fixed with open sincerity on Alicia. "How skip piloting was the only thing that kept him sane. Doesn't Miyuki deserve the same opportunity?"

"Piloting *killed* Damien," Alicia said, but she whispered it low, almost to herself.

"He died doing the thing he loved," Cayce continued. "Saving the ones he loved. You. All of us. Miyuki too. And you remember how she rose to the occasion ... after."

The table got very quiet then. I recalled our escape from Orca: Kane and Strange shouting at each other, Alicia sobbing, Miyuki's eyes peering firmly ahead and her skinny little hands so steady on the controls. It was like Damien was guiding her from beyond the grave. And she was smiling fiercely. I'd never seen her smile like that, before or after that moment. "What's she doing with her life now?" I asked.

"Homeless," Alicia said. "Drifting. In and out of therapy. I've tried to help out when I can, but ..."

Shweta reached across the table and took Alicia's hand with motherly affection. "Some people are born to pilot. Damien was one of them. Miyuki is another. Yes, there is risk in the life we lead. But all careers carry risk, and she deserves to fulfill her destiny."

Alicia's expression was half convinced, half defeated. "Okay, I'll ask her. But I'm not going to cajole or persuade. The choice has to be *hers*."

"I would never ask for anything else," said Cayce. And it seemed to me as though he truly meant it. Which wasn't, I reflected, something that I would have expected from Strange in a similar situation.

The kid might be annoying, but he was starting to grow on me.

We went over the plan then. It was audacious and had a lot of moving parts and would require a *lot* of prep—weeks or months of work, and the expenditure of a frighteningly high percentage of our take from the Emperor's Scroll—but eventually we all agreed that it could work … as long as we had a damn good skip pilot.

First things first. Cayce would procure us a short-range shuttle, with appropriately obscured paperwork; Shweta would arrange to have it dropped just outside of Malakbel Station's detector range; Kane would begin acquiring explosives and other necessary hardware; and I would accompany Alicia to help recruit Miyuki.

"Why do I have to go with Alicia?" I asked Cayce privately, after Shweta had left the Smoke Ranch and the rest of us were gathering our things to return to our suite. "Don't you need me working with Shweta to prepare for the Malakbel Station break-in?"

"Alicia's carrying a lot of guilt," he said, "even today. She thinks that if she'd done something differently at Orca, she could have saved both Hiroshi and Damien, and she's transferred that sense of responsibility to Miyuki. I'm afraid that she'll try to persuade Miyuki *not* to come with us, for her safety. Maybe not even consciously. So I need you to keep an eye on her. You can work with Shweta after we get our pilot."

"Okay," I said.

But I wasn't a hundred percent sure I *was* okay with that.

As it turned out, though, I wound up spending most of a week working with Shweta anyway, while Alicia tried to track Miyuki down. Despite the fact that they had kept in touch over the years, Miyuki didn't always answer messages immediately and her physical location was uncertain.

Shweta wasn't meeting with us in person, of course; she slipped me detailed plans and technical specs for Malakbel Station via a secure blind drop. "I'm glad we're trustworthy," I remarked to Cayce as I scrolled through the gigs of data I'd just received. "I'd hate to think that this top-secret Inner Belt Coalition information might fall into the wrong hands."

Cayce pointed out, not unreasonably, that I was an Outer Belt citizen and he had been born in the Jupiter Union—though his current citizenship, if any, was unclear. In point of fact, the only member of the Club whose Inner Belt Coalition citizenship was beyond question was Shweta, who was certainly engaged in active treason against the government of which she was a senior official.

"It's the principle of the thing," I continued, opening one of the specs. Malakbel was using Monoceros as their sensor platform, I noted, and I grinned at the discovery. Monoceros was a high-security platform, and under most circumstances was a tough nut to crack. But Monoceros was built on the JACOB resource management system, and the underground had recently found a vulnerability in JACOB which wasn't yet publicly known. I might have days, weeks, or years before that hole was patched and the patch made its way to Malakbel. I made a note of the opportunity and kept looking.

Two days later, Alicia tapped on my door. "I just got a message back from Miyuki," she said.

"Oh?" I removed my earphones—Alicia rolled her eyes at the thumping music that emerged, but it helped me concentrate—and rubbed my aching eyes. The information I'd received from Shweta was invaluable, but actually making sense of it and turning that into a concrete plan of attack was still a daunting, time-consuming task. "Where is she?"

"Pallas." I winced at that. Pallas was well out of the plane of the ecliptic at this time of its year. "But she's maybe thinking of leaving soon."

"So we have to go there right now?"

"Yeah."

I took one last look at my screen and folded it up. "Well, then. Let's go."

The one good thing about Miyuki being at Pallas was that it was one of the bigger rocks and there were plenty of commercial transport options to there from here. I'd been afraid we'd have to charter a ship to reach Miyuki, which would have been expensive—Cayce's shuttle and Kane's munitions were eating an even bigger percentage of our cash than we'd expected—and unavoidably conspicuous. It wasn't surprising, though, that she was hanging out on a big rock if she was living rough; the smaller stations didn't offer as many places for an unwaged breather to hide out, or as much crowd to lose oneself in.

I changed into a subdued traveling outfit—a subtle red-on-black paisley coverall with maroon neosilk collar and cuffs—and packed a bag with a few coordinating pieces that could be assembled into a variety of looks. But if the trip went longer than a couple of weeks, I'd have to acquire more. So sad.

After saying our goodbyes to Cayce and Kane, and sending a coded message to Shweta, Alicia and I made our way to the docks with one small bag each. "Feels like old times, doesn't it?" I remarked, mindful of the dozens of ears sharing the transit car with us.

"Yeah," she replied, but her smile was a bit wistful. I couldn't blame her for that. I shared her memories of similar rides with Strange and Damien and Max, all of us holding hands and hugging in various permutations at various times, and out of that original core group, only the two of us were left. Still, if everything went right on this trip, we'd soon be six, and that would put us on the way to a full house of seven. It would be a different seven than it had been at Orca, of course, but somehow that number felt balanced and right.

We booked passage on a fast skip freighter with a half-dozen passenger berths and settled in for the journey to Pallas. It wasn't luxurious, especially by comparison with our recent digs at Ceres, but we'd both had worse before.

The freighter had twin pilots, pale skittish brothers named Shmuel and Shimon. They looked alike, sounded alike, and dressed alike, but Shmuel had a full head of hair and was clean-shaven, while Shimon was bald with a wiry black beard. I kept thinking that one day they would both show up bald and clean-shaven just to mess with us.

Piloting ability has a genetic component, though the mechanisms were still poorly understood. But it wasn't uncommon for both members of a pair of twins to have it, and in many such cases, they worked as these two did, trading off twelve-hour shifts to keep the ship going at full skip around the clock. This trade-off would get us to our destination much quicker, and pilots who could do it earned top dollar.

Damien had once said to me that changing off with another skip pilot was like sharing a vac suit. "Every time you put it on," he'd said, "you have to adjust all the joints and fittings, and you smell the other person's stink for the first hour." This was why most pilots worked alone, but apparently for twins, it wasn't as bad.

I talked with Shimon, the bald one, one day at breakfast. "If you had a choice," I asked him, "would you rather be doing something other than skip piloting?"

He gave the question serious consideration. "It's kind of a shitty life," he admitted. "You have a ton of responsibility but not a lot of authority. You have to spend just about every waking hour either working or hustling for another job. But the *flying* ..." He fluttered his fingers, making his hands soar over the table, an ethereal grin on his face.

My expression told him I didn't quite get it, and he backed up a bit. "Look," he said, "it's like this. Here in normal space"—he gestured around the galley—"you have to play by the rules or you get punished. Laws, morals, physics, whatever. It's predictable. It's stifling. But in the skip ... sometimes you have to twitch *here* to make a fling *there*, sometimes that same twitch sends you backward. It's moment-by-moment. It's a dance without music. Machines can't do it, not really. Most people can't do it. But me and Shmu, we've got the whatever-it-takes. In here." He tapped his forehead. "We *can* do it, and so we kind of *have* to."

"So what would you have done if you'd been born before the skip?"

"I'd be dead or institutionalized." He didn't hesitate, just stated it as fact. "Before the skip, people like me"—again he tapped his head—"got burned as witches, or became mass murderers, or cut their own heads off with an axe." I quirked a skeptical eyebrow at that one. "No, really, it's possible. If you really, *really* need to, you can do it."

"Who really, *really* needs to cut their own head off with an axe?"

"Me. If I didn't have the skip."

We arrived at Pallas at a ridiculous hour, half-awake after just a few hours' sleep. But the twins kicked us out of our berths as soon as we docked, without even a goodbye. Not big on tact, those two.

Even near the docks, which ran twenty-four seven, most of the coffee shops were shut. We finally found one that was open and had a space for two.

"Anything?" I asked Alicia, blearily. The coffee was terrible.

Alicia checked her pocket comm for the fiftieth time since we'd left the ship. "Nothing." It had been three days since we'd last heard from Miyuki, and she'd never responded to repeated requests to set a rendezvous. I was beginning to be seriously concerned that this whole trip would be a bust, leaving us without a pilot. And then Alicia's comm vibrated. "No, wait! This is her." She frowned as her eyes flicked across the incoming message. "She's sorry she's been so incommunicado. She's been having a really tough time focusing. And she got kicked out of the place she'd been staying."

"So where is she now?"

"Hang on … green sector, she says. Ell-forty-one-kay-seven."

I looked up the coordinates. "We can be there in half an hour. Tell her to hang tight."

"I'll tell her." She looked at me over her comm. "No promises."

Green sector coordinate L41K7 turned out to be located in what Pallas called a "park." Most people understand a park to be a recreational zone, open to the public, offering open space, plants, and a view of the sky. Pallas being Pallas, the most low-rent of the major rocks, the open space was a hemispherical volume maybe fifty meters across, the plants a lawn of tough hybrid grass and a few clumps of ferns, and the sky view a three-meter window at the apex of the dome which, at the moment, showed little more than distant Jupiter. But the park was, indeed, open to the public, and we found Miyuki at a drinking fountain.

Drinking fountains in public parks were among the very few places in the whole of Pallas where one could obtain potable water for no charge. This one was very deliberately designed as a brief, minimal refreshment for people taking advantage of the open space to do free-form exercise, and not for what Miyuki was doing: filling a water bottle to take away with her. Each press of the activation button made the nozzle release a one-second squirt, then shut off for ten seconds. She'd obviously been at it for some time; the bottle was half full.

I recognized her immediately, though she was now a nearly thirty-year-old woman rather than the just-past-teenager she'd been the last time I saw her. She was still slim to the point of wiry, still had the same coiled energy, still had the same black hair and smooth round face. Her outfit reinforced the idea that she was doing the best she could with extremely limited resources. Very practical pants and top, plenty of pockets, dark neutral colors that mostly hid the wear and grime at the elbows, knees, and cuffs. Cheap plastic free-fall shoes. A torn seam at the shoulder was tidily but inexpertly repaired with thread that didn't quite match.

Her attention was fixated on the bottle, to the extent that she completely failed to notice us approaching, even as we came well into earshot and repeatedly addressed her by name. Finally, tentatively, Alicia reached out and touched her shoulder.

The girl jerked like a line-caught fish and whirled to face us, startled panic clear in her eyes.

"Miyuki!" Alicia said, in the sort of placating tone you might use with a small, frightened animal. "It's me, Alicia! And Tai! You remember us?"

"If you're thirsty," I said, "we could buy you a drink." But I didn't move any closer. Part of me was afraid of spooking her; part of me wanted to keep out of her reach. Her fingernails, I noted, were ragged and filthy.

"Alicia?" Miyuki said, as though the word had a vaguely familiar flavor that she couldn't quite place. Then she swallowed, blinked, repeated "Alicia!" with genuine glee, and flung herself into Alicia's arms, clinging like a drowning monkey. She made a quiet keening noise something halfway between a squee of delight and a frightened whimper.

Alicia hugged her back, fiercely, burying her face in the girl's tangled hair. "It'll be all right, baby," she whispered over and over. "It'll be all right."

Miyuki's eyes opened, looking at me over Alicia's shoulder. They were wide and bright and red-rimmed and seemed to bore into me like a couple of mining lasers. "It will be all right," she said to me, very precisely.

It sounded almost like a threat.

We took her to a homey little place near the park for a proper lunch of fried noodles with plenty of vegetables and protein. I half expected her to tear into it with fingers and teeth, but she floated quite primly in her free-fall seat straps and ate her meal with chopsticks like a civilized person, albeit with considerable rapidity. But she also kept her worn and filthy rucksack pinned to the floor under one foot at all times—that thing wasn't going *anywhere* without her knowledge.

Once she'd settled down from her initial reaction—"I'm sorry I startled like that, I have issues with focus"—she seemed almost normal, conversing intelligently and in complete sentences. But she could also move with startling rapidity from dreamy distraction to frightening intensity. The overall impression she gave was of a rather flighty intellectual, perhaps a painter or poet—the kind of person who might completely forget to attend the presentation ceremony for a major award they'd won.

"I have a lead on a new place to stay," she said. "They're willing to forego the rent if I clean the other tenants' spaces. But I have to get bonded before I can do that, and—"

"You don't need to do that," Alicia interrupted. Her fingers trembled, and I felt that it wasn't just the Parkinson's but a barely restrained desire to reach out and take Miyuki's hand. "You can come back to Ceres with us. We have plenty of space, and you're welcome to stay as long as you like."

"Thank you. It's just that I'm ... I'm not ... I couldn't possibly repay you." She took another chopstick full and chewed. "This is delicious, thank you."

"You wouldn't owe us anything," Alicia insisted. "We're your friends."

"It's more what *we* can offer *you*," I said, ignoring Alicia's glare.

Miyuki's eyes snapped to me, bright and inquisitive and fearful. I felt as though everything else in the restaurant vanished. "Oh?"

167

"We can offer you … a chance to fly skip again," I continued. "The newest, fastest, and best ship in the whole system." Alicia's hand gripped my wrist hard but I shook it off.

Miyuki's eyes released me and she curled into herself, fixing her attention on her plate. "I don't fly anymore."

"Why not?" I asked, just as Alicia said, "You don't have to do anything you don't want to do."

"I don't fly because I don't deserve it. I've let so many people down. I'm small and weak and worthless."

"You are *not* weak," Alicia insisted, and now she did reach out and take Miyuki's hands. The girl twitched at the initial contact but didn't pull away completely. "You are. *So. Strong.* You saved us all, when the universe seemed stacked against us. And you have survived all the years since then, all by yourself, without help."

"You've helped me …"

"Only when you would let me! Which wasn't often!"

"And you *do* deserve to fly," I said. "You have a natural talent that can't be bought or taught or implanted. Machines can't do it. Most people can't do it. But *you* can do it. The universe gave you this gift when you were born, and you deserve to open it and play with it." Alicia was glaring again, but I noticed she didn't take any action to shut me up. "I remember your face when you flew us out of Orca Station. I want to help you get that smile back."

She smiled again then, but it was just a wistful echo of the fierce ecstatic grin I remembered. Then even that smile faded. "No one would trust *me* with a skip ship."

I felt Alicia's touch on my wrist and we exchanged a long glance. She seemed uncertain. I nodded fractionally … and then she nodded back and turned to Miyuki. "*We* trust you," she said. "The whole Cannibal Club. Tai and I wouldn't be here if we didn't."

"We've trusted you with our lives before," I said. "And we'll do it again. If you let us."

Miyuki seemed to fold in on herself then. Her eyes closed, she hunched forward in her straps, and that strange keening noise sounded from somewhere back in her throat. But a moment later, she straightened. She still seemed subdued and unsure, but once again, she was more flighty intellectual than trapped animal. I felt whipsawed. "All right," she said. "But I have a few things I need to take care of before I leave Pallas. See you back here in an hour."

"We'll come wi—" I began, but Alicia interrupted with, "All right, see you then."

Miyuki hugged Alicia and shook my hand—her fingers cool and dry and surprisingly soft under the filth—before she left with her rucksack.

"Why did you just let her go like that?" I challenged Alicia as soon as Miyuki was out of sight. "We might never see her again!"

"We have to show we trust her, Tai," she said, "or she'll never trust us."

We found passage on a passenger vessel heading back to Ceres. It wasn't quite as fast as the freighter we'd taken to Pallas, but we weren't in as much of a hurry. And the accommodations were better, though still far from luxurious.

We wound up booking what they called a "suite," which consisted of a "living room" a little larger than an average cabin, with two fold-out sleeping racks; a separate "bedchamber" with a sleeping alcove; and—hallelujah—a private bathroom. We offered the bedchamber to Miyuki, of course, but she said she'd rather share the main room with Alicia.

I was happy to have my privacy, frankly. Miyuki was a good kid who had plainly done the best she could to maintain her independence and sanity in very difficult circumstances, but she'd been a little strange when she was a child and was even stranger now. Most of the time, she seemed fine—quiet, polite, maybe a little dreamy—but a couple of times a day, sometimes for no visible reason, she would either fold into a catatonic whimpering ball or lash out in sudden fear or anger. Once, another passenger bumped her by accident and she slapped the coffee bulb out of his hands, sending hot coffee flying everywhere. That incident took a lot of apologies and promises of future good behavior to paper over. Another time we passed by an observation port and she suddenly went rigid—staring, unblinking and unresponsive. We towed her back to our room until she calmed down. "Too much space," was all she said when she came back to herself.

After that incident, Alicia and I had a tense whispered conversation while Miyuki was taking a shower. "Can we really count on her?" I asked. "Or will she freak out in the middle of the job?"

Alicia blew out a long breath, giving the question serious consideration. "We're in an unsettled situation right now," she said. "Once we get her into the Club and give her some stability, I think she'll calm down."

"The Cannibal Club? Stability?" I snorted. "Have you noticed what we do for a living?"

Alicia's mouth quirked in an ironic smile. "True. But it's still better than her situation in the last few years." Her face turned serious then. "I'm … I'm glad you said that about offering her a chance to fly again. I was afraid it would be too much, too fast, but it's clear that only the promise of a ship got her to go along with us."

"Thank you. And from what I got from talking with the pilots on our last ship, I think that getting her hands on the controls might actually help her mental health considerably."

"I hope so." Her brow furrowed. "But we can't know for sure until we try it."

"And that'll be in the middle of the job." We looked at each other, worried, uncertain. "We're betting a lot on this kid."

"And she's betting *everything* on us." She took my hand. I felt her trembling, and again I didn't think it was entirely the Parkinson's. "We owe her a lot, Tai. We owe her a chance, and a life. We broke her, and we're the only ones who can fix her."

And then the shower stopped running and we had to shut up. But I gave Alicia a quick, definitive nod. "Okay," I whispered.

I hoped we were right.

Despite what Alicia said about travel being an unstable situation, I thought that Miyuki found our presence calming, and she seemed a lot more grounded and focused by the time we moved into final approach at Ceres.

"This might be the first time in ten years," I mused to Alicia, "that she's been with people who care for her, who aren't going to run away, and who don't want anything from her."

"Well, we *do* want something from her."

I winced at the uncomfortable truth. "This is different. We want to help her achieve her full potential."

"Do we? Or are we just telling ourselves that because we have no other prospects for finding the pilot we so desperately need?"

"We're doing the right thing." I said it because I needed to hear it. "Yes, we need her. But we know her—well, *you* know her—and we owe her, and no one else is going to give her what *she* needs. It's a mutually beneficial situation."

"Right up until we all get shot by Coalition authorities for trying to steal their ship."

"At least we'll be together till the end."

Cayce, Kane, and—to my surprise—even Shweta met us at the dock when we returned to Ceres. Though even I would probably not have recognized Shweta without the context of the others. She wasn't in disguise, exactly, but she was wearing green-tinted glasses, and she'd rearranged her clothes and hair and stance to the point that she no longer read as herself, despite being a public figure. I remember studying her during some of the Cannibal Club's longer cons, trying to figure out exactly how she did it ... and I never did.

But Miyuki recognized her right off, somehow, embracing her like a grandmother she hadn't seen in ten years. Which wasn't too far from the truth. Kane got a less effusive greeting, though still more enthusiastic than the handshake I'd gotten ... which irked me a bit, but I reflected that they were much closer in age, and also in life experience. As for Cayce ...

Cayce and Miyuki regarded each other like a couple of fighting cocks squaring off. "I don't know you," she said, flatly stating the obvious as she sometimes did.

"My dad knew you," he said. "Not well. But he told me he respected your abilities." He tilted his head as though inspecting her. I expected his next utterance to be a technical question challenging her piloting abilities, or a judgment on her conformation and gait, but instead, he paused, visibly collected himself, and then reached out his arms with a genuine smile. "I'm happy to meet you."

She hesitated, then embraced him, tentatively at first. I saw his arms tighten warmly around her shoulders and he whispered into her ear. It was plainly meant only for her, and if I'd been floating even half a meter farther away, I probably wouldn't have been able to make it out at all.

"Welcome to the family," was what he said.

And then she hugged him back, and at the sight of that, all of us moved in for a big group hug.

It wasn't that unusual a sight at the Ceres docks, especially when a passenger vessel had just pulled in.

But it might have been a first for the Cannibal Club.

Shweta stuck around for dinner, which was held in our thoroughly debugged rented quarters—Cayce was a surprisingly competent cook, though not particularly creative—and we took the opportunity to suss out a few details on the upcoming job as well as to feel our way as a group toward some kind of relationship with our newest member.

We hadn't gotten much past small talk when Kane asked her, point-blank, "How's your reaction time?" This made me wince. Yes, it would be critical for the job, but it's not exactly the sort of thing one asks on a first date.

Miyuki's reply puzzled me. "Pass the salt," she said. "Hard."

Kane was at the far end of the table, a good three meters away. The salt was close to his right hand. Immediately he snatched it up and flung it at Miyuki's head.

I didn't have time to do more than gasp before it came to a halt—between Miyuki's palms, right in front of her face. She'd moved faster than I could follow. "Thank you," she said, and set the salt down. Its magnetic base clacked loudly against the table in the sudden silence. "Does that answer your question?"

"It does," Kane acknowledged. "It does indeed."

That exchange, awkward as it was, did break the ice. We learned about what Miyuki had been up to in the past ten years—it was a difficult, unsettled life with a lot of gaps, but there were moments of humor in her story as well—and we updated her on our current situation. She was particularly interested in Shweta's story.

Shweta swirled her wine contemplatively in its bulb before replying. "From where you sit," she said to Miyuki, "it may seem that I have everything. Food, air, living space, independence, power. But what power I hold is so entangled in the hands of others that nothing is possible without extensive negotiations. And though I live in what must seem to you incomprehensible luxury, all of it—even my life itself—could be blown away by a shift in the political winds." She took a sip. "The uncertainty is part of the appeal of the game, I must admit. But after six years, the entertainment has palled … and the number of players and the favors owed to each grow without limit. So I have decided to retire from the game. And, with your help"—she gestured with her wine bulb around the table—"I will do so in style."

Cayce raised his own bulb, which held carrot juice. "As long as everyone follows the plan." Then, after a moment's pause, "That you and … and Dad worked out."

Shweta gave him an odd look then. "I would not have been able to do it without your father. I do hope we will not be too late to rescue him from his imprisonment."

"Yes." Cayce sipped his carrot juice. "All the more reason we need to focus our attention on the task at hand."

And on that rather awkward note, we did. There were a lot of details to work out.

Two months later, Alicia and I, in the guise of union negotiators Amanda Gaskell and Thuy Vu, approached Malakbel Station aboard an official Coalition courier vessel from Ceres.

The vessel was a hundred percent legit. Our documentation was also legit, or at least had been issued by the appropriate government authorities, though the identities it presented were fictional. We'd come in the front door at Ceres, arriving at the offices of the Coalition Transportation Department's Special Projects Division at the express invitation of the Secretary of Transportation herself, and had been processed through far more than the usual amount of administrative rigamarole before being ushered onto a shuttle departing for a destination which did not officially exist.

Honestly, it was a lot more cloak-and-dagger than our usual. I mean, yes, the Cannibal Club usually spent its time sneaking around back entrances and operating under false identities, but the amount of codespeak and bafflegab involved in reaching the top-secret Malakbel facility via sanctioned channels made our illegal work seem straightforward by comparison. In fact, the unauthorized and illegal shuttle on which Cayce, Kane, and Miyuki were even now making their way to the same destination had simply been dropped off nearby from an anonymous cargo vessel with no paperwork whatsoever.

From the outside, Malakbel Station looked very little different from any other Inner Belt shipyard. The station itself, a fat doughnut three hundred meters in diameter bristling with antennas, even bore the usual identifying codes on its hull, making it look perfectly ordinary ... but I knew that any attempt to track those codes would lead to a series of ratholes ending in an impenetrable bureaucratic void. And the clutter of partially assembled ships clinging to the doughnut or floating nearby were nearly indistinguishable from run-of-the-mill long-haul vessels ... if anything, perhaps a little junkier. A knowledgeable skip engineer—which I was not, but I'd been told what to look for—might notice that some of the ships' skip vanes were a trifle longer and thicker than usual, but even that was mere camouflage—a foamed plastic shell hiding their radically new configuration.

"I'll be back for you tomorrow," the courier's pilot remarked conversationally after we'd docked. She'd been silent for most of the trip out, not too surprising given the hush-hush nature of the whole project, but didn't otherwise seem antisocial ... or, at least, no more so than any other skip pilot. "Unless you'd like me to wait here to catch you when the Secretary kicks you out of her office? I don't know how you wangled this inspection visit, but she *isn't* going to budge on the contract terms. She'll send you packing."

"Even a secret project owes its workers a fair shake," Alicia said.

"Don't forget," I continued, directing my full attention to the pilot herself, "we're here representing *you*."

"Well, I wish you luck," the pilot said, and shook our hands.

Shweta had been deadly serious as she'd handed us each a fat data stick at the beginning of our training. "This isn't your usual bluff game," she'd cautioned. "You are going to have to *be* union negotiators. You have to know contract law. You have to understand the technology, to the extent anyone does. And you have to *care* about the workers." She'd meant it, too. The data sticks had been full to the brim with gigs and gigs of training materials, and she'd followed them up with many long teleconferences in which she drilled us on their contents until our brains were about running out of our ears.

I unbuckled and stood up—the ship had taken on the station's Inner Belt standard one-third gee as we'd docked, of course—and fetched Alicia's walker from where it had been stowed. It wouldn't have been in character for a union negotiator to afford an exoskeleton. She nodded thanks as she took it and snapped it open, all methodical and matter-of-fact. This was part of the act, of course, but she did an excellent job of hiding her frustration, and she managed to lever herself to a vertical position without my help. I played my part by hanging back nonchalantly as she preceded me out of the courier.

We made our way down the access tunnel to a chill reception area, where a clerk with a secure tablet scanned our credentials and quizzed us on the reasons for our visit. This had all been established over comms prior to our arrival, of course; the point of the interrogation was to have a human being assess our authenticity. People have an intuitive sense for these things that no amount of encryption and authentication can replace—as witnessed by the fact that we, hardened criminals though we were, had completely authentic credentials—but people also had their vulnerabilities. Neither Alicia nor I was in Shweta's league in exploiting those vulnerabilities, but with Shweta's training and our confidence in the solidity of our documentation, we managed to pass this test as we had the previous ones. We were in.

Shweta didn't meet us at the antechamber. This *was* a snub, but quite deliberately planned; it would actually make her subsequent acceptance of us more believable. The biggest challenge for me was not to look too confident. I knew the route—had memorized the whole station plan—but I needed to feign both ignorance and trepidation as we were led through the halls toward the Secretary's office.

No, I tell a lie. The trepidation was real. But I needed to channel it in a slightly different direction.

We were ushered into the inner sanctum. Two undersecretaries and a clerk were also present. "This visit is unnecessary," the Secretary said as she rose from her seat, came out in front of her desk, leaned her butt against it, and crossed her arms on her ample chest.

Hello to you too, bitch, I thought. Just to stay in character.

"Madam Secretary," Alicia said. Her contained annoyance was very good—would totally have fooled me—and I suspected she too was channeling her frustration with the walker in a slightly different direction. "We would really rather not be here ourselves, but your department's intransigence has left us no choice."

And so it began: a carefully prepared performance for a live audience of three plus anyone who might happen to be watching the security cameras now or reviewing the logs later. It wasn't a memorized script; Shweta had made it clear that a certain level of improvisation was absolutely necessary for the appearance of spontaneity. But all three of us had our roles: Shweta, the accused, bored and annoyed by this unwanted intrusion; me, the good cop; Alicia, the bad cop.

The nominal subject of the meeting was real. The staff *were* being overworked, and in fact, this was one of the things that had convinced Shweta that she needed to get out of the project. But the *appearance* of tough negotiation was the point of the exercise, and to this end, she had provided us with only the information the union might plausibly have. When she brought up certain counterarguments, we were genuinely surprised, and had to think on our feet and sometimes refer to our notes for our responses. But, thanks to our training and, dare I say, my exceptional acting skills, we did manage to win several critical concessions. The outcome of the meeting may have been preordained, but still, at the end of five thirsty hours, I felt seriously proud of the small but important victories we'd won. And they were real—the concessions were, in fact, signed and logged into the station's procedural manuals. If we managed to get away clean, they might even stick around afterward.

At the end of the meeting, Shweta again came out from behind her desk—now littered with coffee cups and dirty dishes—but this time, she did shake my hand, and Alicia's. "You drive a hard bargain," she said, with a very small hint of admiration. I was impressed anew by her stagecraft and noted with pleasure that one of the undersecretaries nodded in agreement.

We made small talk with the undersecretaries and clerk as we packed up our cases. Their attitude toward us was exactly what we'd hoped for. "I've never seen anyone bring her around like that before," the clerk admitted.

"Well, the facts were on our side," Alicia replied modestly. They were, too.

"I believe your courier will be returning for you tomorrow?" Shweta asked after a few more pleasantries had been exchanged. We acknowledged that this was the case. "Ah. I'm afraid your quarters are not yet ready." The undersecretaries exchanged a glance at this, which told me that no quarters had in fact been requested. Like the courier pilot, they had expected us to be thrown out of the office almost immediately. "In the meantime, may I offer you a tour of the facility?"

"We would be delighted," I replied. My heart began to race, and I lightly pressed my elbow against my side to verify that my small and specialized tool kit was still there in its hidden pocket.

The second undersecretary, the one with the shorter hair, did the honors, leading us down to the outermost level—Alicia bore the increased gravity with reasonably good cheer—where we were treated to a fascinating tour of the machine shops, laboratories, and simulators where the workers whose interests we represented performed their highly technical and occasionally dangerous tasks. Well, it *would* have been fascinating, except for the fact that we already knew everything we were shown and several top-secret details we were not, and the fact that the entire tour was just an excuse to get us to …

"Is that a toilet?" Alicia asked, pointing to a door plainly marked TOILET. "I could really use one."

"Me too," I said.

The undersecretary frowned, the space between her eyebrows puckering just slightly. "This is a secure area. I'm not supposed to leave you unsupervised."

"How much trouble could we get into in there?" I asked, opening the door. It was a single-seat facility.

"Please?" Alicia pleaded, pressing her knees together and putting a pained expression on her face. I thought she was overplaying it a bit.

The undersecretary sighed and rolled her eyes. "Oh, all right."

Alicia clattered into the room, leaving the walker outside, and closed the door behind herself. I engaged the undersecretary in conversation as buckles rattled and water tinkled behind the door.

The rattling and tinkling was a high-definition audio recording, covering the sound of Alicia opening the access panel in the wall of this specific toilet and cracking the security seal on the junction box behind it. She'd practiced dozens of times on an identical box, to the point that we were all confident that she could do it despite the tremor in her hands, but even so, I found my mouth bone-dry and my own hands threatening to shake. I tried to hide my nervousness as a full bladder, but without overplaying it as much as Alicia had.

"This is taking a long time," the undersecretary said.

"She's got mobility issues." I gestured to the walker.

That mollified her a bit, but inside I was thinking *come on, come on.*

And then came the sound of the sink—that wasn't part of the recording, I knew—and the door opened. "Sorry," Alicia said. But her eyes showed triumph.

"Excuse me," I said, and pushed past her before the undersecretary could speak, or notice the open access panel on the wall behind her.

I slipped my tool kit from its hidden pocket and triggered my own audio—it was a recording of me actually going to the bathroom, for verisimilitude. Every splash and tinkle marked a time point in my process, counting off the forty-seven seconds we'd budgeted for the operation.

Flip open the lid on the signal box, which Alicia had cracked for me. Tease out the diagnostic connector. Attach the injector, a custom and quite illegal little device. Watch with bated breath as the light on the injector flashed yellow, yellow, yellow ... and then green, indicating the device had located its target on the network. Press the button to unleash the payload. The green light flickered for a moment as the payload transferred itself, then blinked three times as a confirmation before going dark. Job done. Disconnect the injector, stow the connector, reseal the signal box, close the access panel. Breathe.

Oh, and wash my hands. I'm not a barbarian.

"Sorry for the interruption," I said as I exited, checking my fly. "Now where were we?"

We continued our tour as the payload—a carefully crafted retrovirus which would first insinuate itself into the station's security software, then use it as a trusted platform to strike at lower-level systems before erasing itself—did its work. It was during these few minutes, I think, that I turned in the best performance of the whole operation, as I feigned interest in the tour while inside, I was desperately wondering how my creation was faring in the electric flickering dark of Malakbel Station's secure network.

I've been a software creator, one way and another—amateur and professional, legitimate and illicit—for most of my adult life, and the damn stuff still manages to surprise me every single time. So many moving parts, so many unknowns … honestly, it's a marvel every time it works as designed. So I was just as surprised as anyone else when the alarm sounded—an urgent tone accompanied by a gently pulsing red light. "What's happening?" I said, trying to channel my excited anticipation into an expression of confused apprehension.

"I don't know," the undersecretary admitted, "but we need to get to our assigned shelters right away. You'll have to come with me."

We rattled down the corridor at the maximum speed of Alicia's walker, being passed in both directions by people whose expressions indicated nothing more than annoyance at the interruption. "I'm sure it's some kind of drill or false alarm," the undersecretary said. "We'll get you out of here and on your way shortly."

"Is this a frequent occurrence, then?" Alicia asked.

The undersecretary's silence was all the answer we needed.

The shelter was crowded with people by the time we arrived, and felt even more so after the door was closed and dogged. The air soon grew hot and stuffy, and noisy with confused conversation. These things were designed for meteor punctures and solar storms, which could sometimes last for days, but most of the time, they were just wasted space so they were not made any larger than absolutely necessary. And this one had three additional people—us and an electrical tech who'd been unfortunate enough to be working in an office nearby—which made it even more tightly packed.

Alicia and I exchanged glances as the conversation swirled around us. No one in this shelter knew anything, but that didn't stop them from speculating.

We weren't much better off ourselves.

According to our plan, what was happening outside was this: as soon as my virus took down the station's external detector net—which could be determined from outside by the cessation of active radar pings—the shuttle containing Cayce, Kane, and Miyuki would have broken from its parking orbit outside detector range and swooped in to dock with the *Malakbel VII*'s aft port. I couldn't be certain how long the detectors would stay down, so the shuttle had to move fast and accurately—and this was just the *first* step in the plan that depended completely on Miyuki's piloting skills. Once the shuttle docked, it would then be up to Cayce and Kane to seize control of the prototype.

The detectors going down, although unexpected, would not have justified an all-hands shelter call in and of itself. The alarms we'd heard almost certainly indicated that the incoming shuttle had been noticed somehow. But from where Alicia and I sat, we couldn't tell whether it had been detected—and perhaps destroyed—on its way in, or whether it had docked successfully and initiated the second phase of the incursion. Even if everything went according to plan, it could be anything from minutes to hours before …

The intercom next to the shelter door chimed, and the clerk in charge of this shelter—she'd been reasonably effective at getting everyone settled, moving through the checklists with brusque efficiency—pressed through the crowd to answer it. It was all done with physical buttons and hard wires, very low-tech, very reliable. I couldn't have hacked it. "Shelter Twelve," she said into the grille.

The voice on the other end was unfamiliar. "Central Command here. Are the union negotiators there? Ms. Gaskell and Mx. Vu?"

All eyes immediately turned to us. "They are."

"Station Security is on their way to you. Please turn the negotiators over to them when they arrive, then reseal the shelter. Everyone else is to remain in place until further notice."

"Acknowledged."

Alicia and I were immediately peppered with questions, to which our answers of "we have no idea either" were partly unfeigned. Security? This hadn't been the plan. Shweta herself was supposed to come and get us; this would increase our legitimacy in the eyes of the other station personnel. But still, plans sometimes had to change, and it wasn't entirely unreasonable for her to send Security to fetch us.

But this also might be a sign that the plan had gone horribly wrong.

Alicia's hands trembled white-knuckled on the grips of her walker. It wasn't completely out of character, but as for myself, I tried to push my anxiety down. I wanted both to reinforce my persona as an unflappable negotiator and to keep myself centered for whatever came next.

Which was that the shelter door was unsealed from outside, revealing four Security personnel in full vacuum armor, carrying rifles. I was no weapons expert, but they looked like the kind of thing that could put a hole in a hull or a person with equal ease. My nervousness about the situation immediately ratcheted up several notches. "Where are you taking us?" I asked. "And why?"

"I'm afraid I'm not at liberty to say, Mx.," replied the one with the most stripes on their upper arm. The suit's tinted helmet reduced their face and voice to an impersonal cipher. "Please come with us."

They didn't exactly threaten us, but they were armed and it was clear they wouldn't take no for an answer. But though they moved us along at a fairly rapid clip—two ahead of us and two behind— they were polite to Alicia and respected her limitations. If anything, it was me who was the one who kept having to slow down for her. Whatever we were moving toward, I wanted to get it over with.

The six of us, four in armor, were a tight fit in the lift. We took it all the way down to the bottom, a dizzying ride—feeling lighter on our feet as the cab descended, then suddenly heavier as we stopped at the station's rim, while Coriolis force pressed us to the left—and the doors opened to the chill, clatter, harsh light, and greasy smells of the dock level.

We made our way down the long, visibly curved deck to dock seventeen, where the *Malakbel VII* had her berth. And there, thank goodness, stood Shweta—surrounded by armed guards, but clearly under their protection rather than under arrest.

Of course, there was still the possibility she'd sold us out.

"Thank you for coming," Shweta said. "I'm sorry for the security escort, but I'm afraid we have a … situation." She indicated the dozens of other milling people around her, a gesture which subtly incorporated the hand signs *trouble* and *explain later*. I nodded my acceptance of both the overt and covert messages. "I'm hoping your demonstrated negotiation skills will be of use."

"What seems to be the problem?" Alicia replied.

"A small personnel shuttle, origin unknown, somehow managed to slip through our detector net and dock with the *Malakbel VII* prototype." She pointed down the docking tunnel leading to the ship's forward port—she was docked nose-in to the station—which was crowded with armed guards, almost all facing down the tunnel toward the ship. "At least two intruders, heavily armed and claiming to possess explosives, forced their way through the aft lock and compelled those aboard to evacuate. One of our people was slow to comply and was struck in the head with a rifle butt, but not seriously injured."

Kane, you asshole, I thought reproachfully. "Have they issued any demands?"

"They have demanded fifty million Ceres dollars." We didn't actually care about, or expect to get, the money—that was just to show everyone that we were serious. "They say that if we do not comply, they will destroy the ship, likely doing very serious damage to the station in the process."

"I see." Alicia blew out a breath. "Do we have eyes on the situation?"

Shweta shook her head. "They seem to know what they are doing. Onboard cameras and microphones have been disabled, and they've covered the windows. We have limited audio intelligence from what resonates through the hull, but that hasn't been very informative."

All of this was pretty much according to plan. "So you want us to negotiate," I said. "For real, or are we just stalling for time?"

She literally rolled her eyes at that. "Stalling for time, of course. We don't negotiate with terrorists." But the last two fingers of her left hand were crossed, meaning *under surveillance, can't talk*. So I couldn't take her words at face value.

"How much time do we need?"

"Not much." Her mouth smiled in satisfaction, but her eyes didn't.

I closed my eyes and took a breath, assessing the situation both in character and as myself. Something had gone wrong—something that moved up the timeline of the plan considerably, which explained why she'd sent Security for us rather than taking the time to fetch us herself, and something that she couldn't talk about in front of her staff. She didn't know exactly how much time we had, or she would have said so. And she didn't feel she could even communicate with hand signs—a possibility we'd been prepared for. There would be many cameras focused on this developing situation, and it was vital to our plans that Shweta maintain complete deniability no matter how carefully the records were examined afterward.

"Well," I said, opening my eyes. "Then let's begin immediately."

Initial attempts to communicate with the terrorists by radio had received only a brusque response in a synthetic voice: "Come to the front door where we can see you. No guns."

Shweta, Alicia, and I made our way down the docking tunnel with our hands in plain sight, unarmed except for Alicia's walker. As soon as we came within view of the ship's forward port camera, the attached speaker crackled to life. "Stop right there," came the same artificial voice. "Who's the gimp and the queer?"

I bridled at the slurs. It was supposed to be Cayce at the keyboard, but this sounded more like Kane. "They are negotiators," Shweta replied evenly.

"We are only here to help," I continued. "We want to find a way for everyone to get what they want and nobody to get hurt."

"As rapidly as possible," Shweta put in. Which was amazingly unsubtle for her. Whatever was happening, we really needed to pick up the pace.

Not for the first time I wished we had some form of back channel to the team inside the ship. But even the most sophisticated encrypted in-ear comms still had to use a radio signal, and any RF activity between the terrorists and the negotiators would inevitably be noticed.

"All right," replied the voice. "But those other goons need to clear out now." Cayce, or perhaps Kane, had plainly understood Shweta's message. We hadn't planned to remove the security personnel from the site until later in the negotiations.

And, indeed, they protested their removal firmly, as Shweta had told us they would if we tried to push them out before establishing a trust relationship. But Shweta played the Coalition Department Secretary card—a very powerful card, but one we knew she couldn't play too frequently without raising suspicions—and made them back all the way up to the station side of the tunnel's inner lock door.

Pushing the foot soldiers back made the next step easier, but doing so this early created an enormous risk. Without their own eyes on the situation, Station Security would almost certainly get nervous and start taking independent action. Those actions would be out of our sight and only somewhat predictable, which tightened our timeline still further.

"Tell them the ship's external guns are live and under our control," came the voice, and Shweta repeated the information into her wrist comm. Hopefully, this would make Security hesitate to attempt to take the ship from outside.

This, too, was a card we hadn't intended to play until later, and indeed at this time it might be a bluff. According to the original timeline, right now, Cayce would be negotiating, Kane would be placing the explosives, and Miyuki would be taking control of the ship's systems, using passwords provided by Shweta and tools provided by me. We were reasonably confident she'd be up to the task, but how quickly she could accomplish it was an open question.

I considered my next step carefully. We needed to provoke a confrontation, and fast—but not too fast, and without seeming to do so.

Then the artificial voice spoke again. "I don't trust the gimp," it said. "That frame thing she's got could be anything. I want her to clear out."

That was when I realized it was Cayce, not Kane, at the keyboard. *Damn, kid,* I thought, *you really do have your dad's brain.* "Don't give me that shit," said Shweta with what appeared to be genuine anger.

184

"We came here in good faith and I expect the same in return." She moved in close, staring up at the door camera, gesturing to me and Alicia to follow. "These negotiators have my trust and I expect them to be treated with respect."

"What, you think we signed the disability rights compact?" came the synthetic reply. "That bullshit? Who holds the cards here, sweetheart?"

"I do," Shweta spat back, and raised her wrist comm toward her mouth.

Suddenly the airlock door snapped open, its motors whining at double speed thanks to a software hack I'd provided. Two figures in black vacuum suits, with tinted faceplates and armed with nasty-looking guns, burst out and hustled all three of us inside. I heard the door snap shut behind us as I fell on my ass.

The two suited figures were Cayce and Kane, of course. Cayce handed me a welding gun as soon as I was on my feet; I took it from him and began welding the outer lock door shut.

"What is the meaning of this?" Shweta yelled, as her hands signaled *ears on the hull*.

"Good faith my ass!" came the synthetic voice from Cayce's suit, at top volume. Then he pushed back his faceplate. "*What's the rush?*" he whispered. Armored suit gloves made clear signing difficult.

"I demand you release us immediately!" Shweta replied, while signing *Coalition ships nearby. Heading this way now.*

"Shit!" Kane said aloud, earning him stares from everyone else. But he didn't notice—he was already gone, vanished through the inner lock door.

"*How long do we have?*" Cayce whispered, even as his fingers rattled on the suit's left forearm keyboard. "We're doubling our demands! One hundred million Ceres dollars!"

"If you don't release us within half an hour, I won't be responsible for the consequences!"

Now Cayce said "Shit!" as well, though he only mouthed it. Then he slapped his leg, hard, with his space-gauntleted hand. Shweta, taking her cue, shrieked like she'd been smacked in the face, and

Alicia and I did our parts by gasping and cursing respectively. "Now sit down and shut up!" said the synthetic voice.

We all looked at each other. Now we knew our timeline ... and Shweta's staff knew too, and knew that we knew. The good news was that they would probably not take any overt action for the next half hour. I finished my welding job—not very tidy, but it would do—and set the gun down.

Can we run? Shweta signed, then slipped off her shoes. Alicia and I followed suit.

"*Not yet,*" Cayce whispered back as we all padded silently into the body of the ship. Alicia abandoned the walker, leaning heavily on Shweta's arm; Cayce's suited feet were rubber-soled. "*Miyuki's having some trouble getting in, and we're still locked into the dock.*"

That was all the information we needed. I dashed toward the control room amidships, while Shweta helped Alicia to the ladder that led to the lower deck. "*I'll go help Kane,*" Cayce said, fingers tapping on his keyboard as he exited aft.

Breaking through the ship's security systems was something I could do a lot faster than Miyuki. And overriding the bolts that physically restrained the ship to the station—something that, on the original schedule, Cayce was supposed to have taken care of before pulling us aboard—was fundamentally a lock-picking exercise, albeit at a very large scale, and even with Alicia's limitations, there was no one better to tackle that job now.

Even though I had memorized the ship's plans and run through it in virtual many times, this was the first time I'd been aboard in person. There was no question it was a prototype—the walls were mostly open panels, with pipes and conduits secured for safety but not aesthetics, and every surface was scuffed and discolored. There was a smell of solvents and ozone, and the air hummed with an unfamiliar sound that must be the new skip drive.

"*What's the situation?*" I whispered, as loud as I dared, as I entered the control center. Miyuki didn't know Cannibal Club sign.

Miyuki swiveled in the pilot's chair, its padded bulk making her look even tinier and her face showing alarm. "It's taking forever!" she wailed, waving to her left, where a little box I'd built myself was patched into the skip drive's diagnostic port. Four of seven lights showed green.

I held a finger to my lips. *"How long has it been running?"* I whispered. *"Half an hour?"* she whispered back, following my lead.

I grunted and shook my head. Even with my skills and Shweta's inside knowledge, some parts of the crack had to be brute-forced. *"This can't be hurried. It'll be another hour and a half at least."* I waved a hand at her panicked expression. *"We'll cope. Is everything else on track?"*

"I can't get into the guns!" she replied. *"The password isn't working."*

I moved up next to her and scanned the instruments. The guns were offline, as she'd said, but most other systems were unlocked ... no, wait, the maneuvering thrusters showed yellow. We'd really need those, and soon.

Just then, Shweta arrived. *Help Miyuki with the guns,* I signed. *I'll work on the thrusters.*

I pulled up a keyboard and started running diagnostics to figure out why the thrusters were offline. We had control, but they just weren't working. *"How did those Coalition ships get here so fast?"* I whispered to Shweta as my fingers worked.

"Attack squadron happened to be on maneuvers nearby," she replied. I glared at her and she shrugged elaborately. *"I'm just the Secretary of Transportation,"* she whispered. *"Defense doesn't tell me anything."*

Just then a loud *clack* echoed through the ship. Alicia had freed the bolts. Now all we needed was thrusters. *"Come on,"* I whispered to no one in particular, or maybe myself, or maybe the balky prototype ship. *"Come on, come on, come on ..."*

There it was. Overpressure alarm on the port fore thruster cluster. *"Can we fly with that?"* I asked Miyuki, pointing at it.

"For a while ..." She sounded dubious.

"Good enough." I punched the override, and the light turned green. *"Now get us out of dock."*

Miyuki's hand darted out, her finger resting for a moment on the clear-for-maneuvers alarm control. She looked a query at Shweta, who nodded. I agreed; the rest of the Club needed the warning, and keeping quiet wouldn't help us much.

Miyuki keyed the control, and the alarm's distinctive tone echoed through the ship. Shweta held up five fingers, then four, then three—counting down the seconds we would allow Cayce, Kane, and Alicia to brace themselves—while she belted herself into the navigator's seat. I scrambled to the engineer's station and did likewise.

Two fingers, one … then Shweta pointed hard at Miyuki.

Miyuki pulled back on the joysticks.

With a boom of thrusters and a scrape of metal on metal, the ship slid backward out of dock, then suddenly dropped with a descending-elevator sensation as it disconnected from the rotating station. That sensation quickly faded to ordinary free fall, then was replaced by a twisting upward jerk as Miyuki spun us out of dock.

Screens lit up with outside views as the maneuvering cameras came online. Vac-suited figures tumbled from the docking port we'd just cleared, blown out by escaping air, but the visible puff of fog that surrounded them was small and faded fast. It was clearly only the air that had been in the docking tunnel—the inner door had been closed or had snapped closed in time.

Was it just the part of me that was still playing the part of a union negotiator that hoped that no one had been hurt by our precipitous departure? No, really, none of me wanted to see anyone hurt. But if push came to shove, the Cannibal Club would have to come first.

Now that we were disconnected from the station, we could speak freely. Shweta keyed the annunciator. "Is everyone all right?" she asked, her voice echoing through the corridors. Alicia, Kane, and finally Cayce checked in safe over the intercom. I'd have to get our private comms up and running as quickly as I could … once we were safely away.

"Can we lose the shuttle?" Miyuki asked, her hands firm on the joysticks and her eyes flicking from screen to screen. She seemed like a new person—alive, awake, aware, and in control. "Feels like I've got a sloth clinging to my ass here."

"All cleared out," Kane replied. "Dump it!"

But Cayce immediately countermanded that. "Wait until we're clear of the station. Hundred klicks at least. Don't want to kill anyone by accident."

A tense silence followed, as the station receded—fast, but not as fast as I would have liked to see—in the maneuvering camera views.

Shuttle pods and construction bots were scrambling to follow us, but our abrupt undock had caught them by surprise and we had a lot more delta V to play with. Then the range finder counted up past a hundred.

"Pull that!" Miyuki called to me, pointing to a red-bordered lever marked AFT DOCK EMRG JETT. I flipped back the safety and pulled it. A harsh klaxon sounded three times, followed by a *bang* and a jerk. Even I could feel the ship's handling improve.

In the aft camera view, the shuttle tumbled away, then vanished in a blinding, silent flash. When the camera's eye cleared, there was nothing more to be seen than glittering fragments.

I hated to see such a sweet machine—half a million Ceres dollars worth of painstakingly acquired hardware—sacrificed. But keeping it with us would kill our maneuverability, and leaving it behind to be inspected at leisure carried too much risk of exposure. Also, the detonation showed that we were not bluffing about having explosives.

There was a tense moment as the debris cloud caught up with us, but apart from a few disquieting bangs on the hull, we got away clean. Kane had done a good job with the scuttling charges. With luck, the second set of explosives—over a tonne of them—would also work as expected.

But my breath of relief was only half out of my mouth when another alarm sounded. It was the long-range detector, and the screen showed a distressingly large group of targets approaching rapidly from the west. They were tightly clumped, but as their vectors extrapolated themselves, it became clear that they were diverging as they approached.

"They're moving to englobe us," Miyuki said.

"How soon?" I said, even as Shweta asked, "Can they stop us?"

Miyuki's eyes flicked to a side screen. "Sixty-seven minutes, and yes." She turned to face Shweta. "Those are combat vessels. They can outmaneuver us and easily beat our top speed in normal space. Once they surround us, we'll only have two options: stop and be boarded, or risk a high-speed collision and mutual destruction."

"But we can beat them on skip," Alicia said, entering the control center. She looked extremely relieved to be maneuvering in the fractional gravity provided by our thrusters rather than the station's one-third gee.

"Not yet," I replied, pointing to my little box, which still had only four of seven lights showing green. "We won't get control of the drive for another hour and a half. At least."

"An hour and a half," said Shweta, "is definitely more than sixty-seven minutes."

SEVEN

The Orca Job, Part Four

The Cannibal Club—Ten Years Ago

Damien and Strange stared each other down, neither giving any ground. The rest of us hung transfixed. We couldn't leave without Damien; he wouldn't leave without Alicia.

And then the proximity alarm wailed.

"Shit!" Damien screamed. "Not *now!*"

Confusion reigned for a moment until we all understood what Damien had immediately realized: the alarm indicated the close approach of an Aquila ship. It was armed and had the drop on us, and we were still hard-docked to the station.

If we'd undocked a few minutes ago, we might have managed to slip away, but now it was too late for that. We'd have to surrender or fight our way out.

No one but Damien could do that. And we all knew it.

Damien scrambled to the pilot's seat and strapped in, cinching the straps down hard. "You," he said, pointing to all of us, "are going to go in there and take care of Allie." He ended with his finger leveled between Strange's eyes.

"She might already be dead," Strange countered without emotion.

"If that's the case ... what happens to me, and to you, doesn't matter to me." Damien took his hands off the joysticks, holding them up as though in helpless surrender, but his eyes on Strange's were hard. "Your call."

Strange might have been able to call Damien's bluff ... but it was Miyuki, the client's strange kid, who broke the stalemate. "I'm going back for my dad!" she cried, and dashed from the compartment. She'd been closest to the hatch and got away before we could stop her.

"Damn it," Strange said, then fetched his gun belt from its compartment. "Get rid of that ship," he told Damien, strapping it on, "and come back for us ASAP. We'll save Alicia if we can."

"All I can ask," Damien replied, and put his hands back on the joysticks. "Now move."

We moved.

But on his way out, Kane pulled the Jeroboam from its rack on the wall, grinning like a fiend.

Back inside the station, we found wailing alarms and blinking red lights above every hatch. Tai's leech might still be running on the cargo hall's cameras, removing us from the occupants' view, but even if it was that, it wouldn't help us much. We checked our weapons and moved forward, with Kane and Strange in the lead. Tai was nearly in a panic but Shweta placed a reassuring hand on their shoulder. They knew it was manipulative but welcomed the touch anyway.

Behind us, we heard and felt *Contessa* undock, her thrusters rumbling against the station's hull as Damien pulled away without regard to propriety or regulations. We were on our own now, with no escape route unless and until he came back for us.

Strange was first through the stairway door, easing his way cautiously in with pistols drawn. The lights were on full now, alarms echoing down the stairwell ... and then came the slamming rattle of gunfire. Strange got off two shots as he withdrew.

We all looked at each other. Strange pointed at Kane, in, and up; then at himself, in, and up; then at Tai and Shweta, in, and up. We all nodded understanding.

Kane raised the Jeroboam and chambered two heavy rounds with a metallic *snack snack* sound and a determined grin. They had a strong chance of holing the hull, but at this point, that was the least of our worries. He exchanged glances with the rest of us, then slammed the door open with his shoulder, rolled into the shelter of the ascending stair, then fired both rounds upward with a pair of thunderous booms. *Snack snack* again, then two more booms. Screams of pain pierced the ringing silence that followed.

Strange leaped through the still-open door and up the first flight of steps to the landing, flattening himself against the far wall. Leaning carefully out into view, he spotted movement and fired three shots upward. Screams and curses followed, and footsteps, then a slamming door.

There was a tense moment full of the smell of gun smoke and the sound of alarms, but from above, there came no further sound other than the creaks and rattles of a recently damaged stairway. The stairwell was ours.

Strange gestured firmly upward, then charged up the stairs. Shweta and Tai followed, with Kane right behind.

The Jeroboam had blown big holes through the stairs ... and through two of the Aquilas, who lay motionless on the middle-level landing. Blood dripped slowly down through the ragged gaps in the stairs, falling in Coriolis curves to splat on the wall below. More blood, smeared on the floor, showed where a third and possibly fourth had dragged themselves through the door there. There was no indication anyone had headed up to the upper level ... and no proof they had not.

Quick gestures separated us into two parties: Strange and Tai continuing to the upper level, Kane and Shweta taking the middle level.

It wouldn't be easy. We were four, they were eight, and we had to assume they had cameras everywhere.

We didn't have a choice.

Kane bashed through the stairwell door into the hall we'd vacated not very long before, rolling to a crouch and swiveling the Jeroboam from one side to the other. But the hallway was empty. Blood smears on the floor—seeming to change color from red to white in the blinking red alarm light—led to the second door on the right.

Kane handed one of his pistols to Shweta. She accepted it as though she'd been handed a dead rat—but a rat that might keep her alive in a pinch. She checked the action and moved forward, keeping close behind Kane with one eye over her shoulder.

As they passed the first door, the room where the firefight had occurred, Kane indicated the door with his eyes and Shweta shook her head. She would bet her life that the Aquilas wouldn't hole up in a room full of blood, smoke, and dead bodies. They continued at a silent near-run to the second door. Even if there were cameras, and the people inside knew they were coming, speed and stealth could still be valuable.

Kane kicked the door in, earning a yelp from his right as the door slammed into the person who'd been hiding behind it. Idiot. Kane fired one Jeroboam round through the door even as he ducked, rolling below the shots that came from the left and ahead, then came up in a crouch and fired left, taking out a second defender. *Snack snack* … but before he could fire, Shweta stepped into view and coolly took out the remaining shooter—whose attention was focused on Kane—with a shot to the head.

Kane ducked under a desk while Shweta plastered herself against the corridor wall outside the room, the shock of the pistol still tingling in the heel of her right hand. Kane listened hard, trying to hear past his ringing ears and the howling alarms, but heard nothing other than a few moans and gurgles from the dying defenders. He cautiously eased his eyes above desk level.

No movement from behind the shattered door. The second Aquila he'd shot was slumped against a wall spattered with her blood and brains. The one Shweta had shot lay still on the floor. And two more sat in chairs, eyes wide, hands raised and trembling. Kane stood and leveled the Jeroboam at them, then hissed for Shweta.

Shweta came in, grabbed some cables from a desktop, and approached the two living Aquilas. Both were injured—they must have been the ones who had dragged themselves from the stairwell—but one was only bleeding from the upper arm and had been attempting to stanch the other's nasty-looking head wound.

She tied them together, with the less-injured one's hand positioned to continue to apply pressure to the more-injured one's head. There was some risk they'd extract themselves, but it would take time, and this affair would be over soon one way or another.

"Where are the rest of you?" she asked conversationally, but the one with the head wound just spat at her. She shrugged and gagged both of them. It had been worth a try.

Having secured the two living Aquilas and determined that the remaining three were indeed dead, we searched the room—and found Miyuki tied up in a closet. "They caught me in the stairwell," she admitted shamefacedly, but Shweta told her not to feel too bad about it. Kane, meanwhile, searched the rest of the level, finding it unoccupied.

There had been ten Aquilas. Two dead in the stairwell, three dead and two captured here. Where were the other three?

Strange hurtled up the stairs three at a time, both guns drawn. Tai followed as rapidly as they could, breath ragged in their throat, the pistol Strange had handed them before taking off jouncing awkwardly in their Aquila uniform pocket. They were gasping by the time they caught up with him at the door to the upper level.

Strange waited impatiently there, pressed against the wall beside the door, feeling very vulnerable. If the Aquilas had cameras in the stairwell, which they almost certainly did, bullets might come ripping through that wall at any moment. As soon as Tai's head appeared above the edge of the landing, Strange stepped out, fired three shots through the door, and kicked it open.

Empty corridor. No movement but rotating red lights, no sound except blaring alarms.

We'd never been on this level before, but Strange consulted his memory palace. The construction diagrams for this general station type showed the control center at the forward end of the upper level, and the convergence of heavy power and data conduits there made it unlikely that Orca had changed that. Any Aquilas on this level would most likely be holed up there, where they'd have maximum access to camera feeds, communications, life support control, and other resources.

Of course, they might also have placed defenders elsewhere.

Boom. Boom. Bang. Two shots from the Jeroboam and one smaller round echoed up the stairwell. That might be good news. Might not.

Strange moved at a silent lope down the corridor, visually scanning ahead and back as well as to both sides. Whenever he spotted a camera, he killed it with a bullet in its eye; whenever he passed a door, he fired a couple of rounds through it. Tai scrambled after him as fast as they could, feeling exposed and useless.

As they reached the control room door, Strange killed the three cameras he could see, then immediately leaped to the opposite side of the door, pulling Tai with him. A moment later, heavy shots came through the wall where he'd just been standing.

Strange let out a loud groan, letting it trail off with an authentic-sounding gurgle, then reloaded while waiting for a reaction to his apparent death. Tai trembled beside him, mouth open to silence their breathing.

An eternity—half a minute or more—passed before the latch snicked and the door eased open … gently, almost inaudibly.

Almost. But Strange had his ear pressed to the wall.

A pistol barrel emerged slowly from the narrow opening. There would be an eye behind it. Strange squeezed himself against the wall, pressing Tai back beside him. Silently he holstered his own right-hand gun.

The barrel scanned toward them, then away.

Then Strange grabbed it hard and pulled.

Whoever was holding the gun yelped and pulled the trigger. The gun jerked in Strange's hand, hot as lightning. He held on, despite the pain, and kept pulling. A hand emerged into view, and Strange chopped down viciously on its wrist with the pistol he still held in his own left hand.

Another yelp, and the shooter let go. In a single motion, Strange threw the gun down the corridor and swiveled his own pistol to fire twice through the opening.

A shriek and a thud. He'd gotten lucky.

Strange drew his right-hand pistol and fired both guns repeatedly through the opening, a wide spread, high and low. Then he threw himself at the door and through it, rolling up to a crouch with both pistols raised.

The room was dark, illuminated only by screens and indicators. Three standing figures, two to the left and one to the right. The one on the right was raising a heavy antipersonnel weapon, probably the one that had put three slugs through the wall. Strange dropped him with a round between the eyes.

"Don't shoot." The voice from the left was loud enough to penetrate the ringing in Strange's ears, but remarkably composed.

Something in the stranger's voice prompted Strange to comply, at least for the moment. He waited, both pistols aimed at the voice, for his eyes to adjust to the darkness. The right-hand gun was an empty threat; two rounds remained in the left.

The stranger was big, muscular, female, wearing an Aquila uniform with command stripes on the shoulders. Broad nose, tight asymmetrical dreadlocks.

She held Alicia in a headlock with a pistol pressed to her temple.

And suddenly Strange realized why he'd complied.

"Hello, Lee," he said. "It's been a long time."

Alicia's eyes widened in surprise. Strange raised one eyebrow, trying to send her the message "nice to see you're alive, sorry about the situation, it's more complicated than it looks, Damien's okay, don't worry, we'll get you out of this." It was a lot to ask from an eyebrow, but his hands were full.

Tai, meanwhile, crept into the room, assessed the situation, and remained in the doorway with the pistol and three-quarters of their attention pointed outward. No telling who might be on their way.

The commander's stance loosened just slightly. She still held Alicia firmly with the gun to her head, but her attitude toward Strange was suddenly not quite so hostile. Or, Strange realized, perhaps "differently hostile" was a better descriptor. "It *has* been a while, Strange," she said. "Six years and a bit. How've you been?"

Strange didn't relax one iota, keeping both guns firmly trained on the commander's head. "Oh, you know, the usual," he commented in a casual voice. "Doing crimes, fencing loot, running from the law. You?"

She shrugged. "I keep busy." A head tilt indicated the command center. "They put me in charge, can you believe it?"

"You've come up in the world."

The commander snorted. "Got to pay the bills."

And then a tremendous crash interrupted, a hammer blow of a sound that smacked everyone in the gut and deafened us momentarily and painfully. As our ears cleared we heard new, frantic alarms and a rushing roar of air.

A softball-sized hole, edges glowing orange but rapidly cooling to black, had appeared in the ceiling. A matching hole, much more ragged, had appeared in the floor. A strong wind blew toward the ceiling hole as the room's atmosphere tried to equalize pressure with the infinite vacuum outside.

The smell of hot metal was everywhere.

"Truce?" Alicia hollered into the roar.

"Truce," the commander—Lee—replied, releasing her.

Strange waited until Lee's pistol had returned to its holster before lowering his own weapons. He took a moment to reload before moving to assist Lee and Alicia with the patch.

"When we get out of this," Lee said to Strange as she ripped open the hull-patch kit, "I'm going to kill you for holing my station."

"We don't have a rail gun," Strange replied, pulling the largest patch from the kit. "Must be one of yours."

"Still your fault."

The largest patch wasn't big enough. Lee pulled out the two next largest, and she and Strange worked to glue the three patches together into a single patch big and strong enough to cover the hole. Alicia worked at the hole, clearing fragments and strands of melted hull material from the edges to assure a clean seal.

Tai, meanwhile, ducked inside as the door closed and sealed itself. Moving to the nearest control panel, they called up a station status chart. They'd never run a station like this, but ship and station control software suites weren't that different. "We're holed through all three decks!" they called.

"Get someone on the exit wound!" Lee yelled back. She was busy with the epoxy.

It took Tai a minute to find the intercom. They muted the alarms, then called into the roaring silence, "Hey everyone! I don't care who! There's a big hole in the hull in … deck one, compartment seven! Put your guns down and fix it, or we're all dead!"

"Where the fuck is that?" came an immediate reply. Kane's voice.

"Lower level. Cargo compartments. Remember those? Door number seven." Tai turned to Lee. "Can you unlock the cargo compartment doors from here?"

"God damn it!" Lee yelled as the makeshift patch pulled apart, one of its smaller parts vanishing into the hole with a leathery *flumph*. "Here, you try!" She shoved the remaining pieces of patch at Strange, climbed down from the console she'd been standing on, ran to Tai's station, and keyed in a passcode. "There, you've got full authorization."

"Thanks."

"You won't get away with this," Lee muttered as she returned to the hole.

Tai gave a sardonic air-kiss to Lee's retreating back, unlocked every door in the cargo area, then called up the status display again. The station had taken some structural damage, a quarter or more of the electrical and data circuits were flashing red, and water spewed from a broken pipe somewhere on the middle level. But if we could patch both of the hull holes, we would probably survive. For a while, anyway.

One of the remaining security cameras showed Kane, Shweta, and Miyuki—oh good, they'd found her—charging down a corridor with two hull-patch kits. But then they passed out of view. Between Kane and Strange's bullets and Tai's own earlier hack, Tai had very limited visibility. "Let me know where you are!" Tai called through the intercom. "I can't see you."

"Just heading downstairs now," Shweta replied.

The next few minutes passed in raucous chaos as the two teams worked to patch the giant rents in the hull, with Tai passing messages between them and doing what they could to shut down damaged systems. The last thing they needed now was an electrical fire. But eventually there came a lull—both holes were at least temporarily patched, the worst interior damage under control—and Tai had a spare moment to check on the progress of the battle raging outside the hull.

There was no sign of one. Neither ship appeared on close-range or medium-range scan. What?

Tai touched a control that displayed previous nav data, scrolling rapidly back through time.

And suddenly a sphere of particles appeared, fading in from oblivion and shrinking down to a single point. A ship. A ship that had been utterly obliterated.

A moment later, a second sphere appeared and coalesced into another ship.

Tai's heart felt like it had stopped. Frozen.

The two ships whizzed around each other in high-speed reverse motion, like a pair of electrons in chaotic orbit around an invisible nucleus.

Tai's numb finger finally slipped from the scroll control, and the display switched to forward motion at normal speed. Two little blips on the screen dodged and pirouetted, exchanging fire, thrusting at each other and dodging collision at the last moment. It had been a brilliant battle.

But it didn't matter.

The blips were just the ghosts of two dead ships.

"Uh, people?" Tai said … or tried to say. Their mouth was dry and almost no sound had come out. They cleared their throat and tried again. "Uh, you all need to see this."

We all heard the note of despair in their voice, and despite the urgency of the situation we all left the still-hissing hole to come over and watch the screen.

We were all watching the replay when the first ship exploded. It had been the Aquila ship; probably a lucky shot to the ship's fusion plant. But not so lucky as all that, really—the expanding debris cloud was still deadly thick when it reached *Contessa* a moment later.

Damien probably had been dead from multiple impacts and explosive decompression for two minutes or more before *Contessa's* own plant had gone up.

Two expanding spheres of tiny blips slowly faded on the screen.

"I don't understand," Alicia said, her voice shaky. She understood, but her brain refused to accept what her eyes had seen.

"They're gone," Tai said, laying a hand atop Alicia's, which gripped the console edge with a white-knuckled grip. "They're gone. Both ships were destroyed."

Alicia blinked. "But when is Damien coming back?"

Instead of responding, Tai just stood, turned, and embraced her. Alicia squeezed back painfully tight. Strange reached out one awkward hand to rest on her shoulder. Lee stood silent, stunned, as enveloped in silent grief as the rest of us.

Then the tears started.

Eventually we got everything sorted out on the station, to the extent that was possible. Both holes were patched reasonably securely, all station systems were operational or cleanly shut down, and the surviving Aquilas were confined to their quarters. Exhausted and stunned, we were all moving like zombies. The recriminations and arguments and slamming of doors and angry departures and declarations of unending enmity didn't come until later.

Lee took her confinement with surprising grace. "I know when I'm beat," she'd said as Kane closed the door behind her. And when Strange called her a few hours later with his proposal, she took it very well.

"If we're still here when your people arrive," he said to Lee over the intercom, "it's going to be a firefight. Lots more people are going to get killed. Quite likely including you."

Lee's face on the little intercom screen showed more fear and horror than Strange had expected. He'd known her to be a pretty tough cookie. "I can't let that happen."

"Why not?" he asked, sensing an opportunity for leverage.

Lee took a shuddering breath, let it out. "I'm a mom. I'm all he's got." She gritted her teeth. "He's six … years … old."

Strange blinked, doing the math. It wasn't difficult. "Mine."

"Yeah. He's got my eyes and your nose."

"Shit." Another blink. "I'm sorry."

"Not your fault. Well, not the nose anyway."

Strange was glad none of the other Club members were in on this call. He had the leverage he'd hoped for, but sometimes leverage runs both ways. "Okay, so neither of us wants you to die. So here's my proposal. You have an escape ship docked here. Give us the codes, kill the trackers, and we'll get away. We took out most of the cameras that would have seen you cooperating with us, and if I know you, you can certainly wipe the remaining records before your people arrive." When she didn't immediately respond, he added, "I can have Kane beat you up so you can plausibly claim we left you no choice."

She glared at him. "I'll pass on that, thanks."

A pause. "What's his name? The kid."

"Cayce."

"Bad enough he never had a father. You don't want to leave him without a mother as well."

Another glare. "You're so fucking thoughtful."

Strange shrugged. "Your call."

She thought a while longer, then shook her head with a sigh. "All right," she said. "I'll do it."

"Thank you." And, to his surprise, Strange found it was sincere. "I'm … I'm sorry I left. You were good for me."

"I can't really say the same for you. But you left me with some-one amazing."

"I hope I get to meet him someday."

Lee's eyes met Strange's hard through the tiny, low-res screen. "I truly hope you don't."

EIGHT

The Cronos Job, Part One

Shweta—Present Day

"**A**n hour and a half," I said, "is definitely more than sixty-seven minutes."

Everyone looked at me.

"They won't shoot, at least," I said after a moment. "They don't want to risk the ship, or the hostages." Miyuki's face showed confusion. "Tai, Alicia, and I being the hostages in question," I clarified.

Cayce and Kane arrived then. Their faceplates were flipped back, their faces slick with sweat from the work they'd just done: dragging a tonne of explosives and other materials out of the shuttle in full station gravity.

"They're demanding we surrender," Cayce said, pointing to his ear. He'd routed all external communications to his suit.

"I did manage to take control of the guns," I said, "but that won't be enough to make a difference against a whole attack squadron."

Cayce shook his head. "How long until they arrive?"

"Sixty-six minutes now," Miyuki replied, consulting the side screen.

Cayce took that in stride. "How long after that until they have an englobement that's too tight for you to slip through at maximum skip?"

Miyuki ran a few calculations on her nav screen. "Maybe another half an hour after they arrive. Depends on how long our fade tail is." She was referring to the time the ship spent partially in normal space as it was transitioning to its first skip—which was an unknown factor with this prototype drive. "And how aggressive they're prepared to be as they move in."

"They'll be pretty damn aggressive." Cayce looked at Tai. "Can we get control of the drive in time?"

They glanced at the box, where only four of the seven lights showed green. It hadn't changed since we'd arrived in the control room. "I wouldn't bet my life on it."

Cayce paused, his eyes unfocusing for what felt like a very long time. Then he blinked and returned his attention to the room. "I have an idea. But you aren't going to like it."

Cayce's plan, insane as it was, was better than anything else we could think of, so we immediately put it in motion. Tai and Miyuki stayed in the control center, working together on taking control of the ship. Alicia, more maneuverable than she'd been on the station but still physically weak, bustled around the ship, making sure everything was properly dogged down. Even a stray bolt could hole the hull or disable the drive if it landed in the wrong place during sudden acceleration. And I went to the aft lock and started suiting up.

I *hate* vac suits—the confinement, the pinching, the *smell*—but even more than the suit, I hate going outside. Spaceships have hulls for a reason; people were not meant to ride on the outside of them. Outer space is so very *big*, and every bit of it is trying to kill you.

At least it was my own suit, which had come in on the shuttle with Cayce, Kane, and Miyuki. Adjusting one of the ship's suits to myself would have taken up just about all the time we had. Once I got myself all sealed in and inspected, we decompressed the lock and set to work.

The second set of explosives consisted of four long metal boxes, three hundred kilos each. We also had a set of brackets which Cayce had designed and Tai had printed on the ship's fabricator. They looked rough and fragile and improvised, but Cayce assured me they would do the job.

I hoped he was right. We'd have only one shot at it.

It fell to Kane and me to shove the boxes out the door and maneuver them to their positions on the outer hull. Cayce followed with the brackets; his nimble little fingers would do better than mine at placing and fastening them. Damn him.

Despite the desperate speed of our flight from the pursuing squadron, the exterior of the ship was as peaceful as ever. No rush of air, no whizzing bullets, no jerky evasive maneuvers … just dark and silent space, with the Coalition squadron invisible behind us. We were still in extreme danger, of course; at this speed, the tiniest rock or bit of space junk could kill any of us without warning. And the ship's acceleration meant that the boxes, whose inertia made them a bear to handle even in absolute free fall, were made even more awkward by an apparent weight of some tens of kilos in the aft direction.

That weight made the first box slip easily out of the lock. Too easily. It picked up speed as it traveled backward, and Kane and I had to strain hard, grunting from the effort, just to stop it from falling away aft. Which had been the original idea, of course, but circumstances had changed. Reversing that motion, and hauling the heavy box up the length of the ship, was even more work, and soon my eyes were half-blinded and stinging from sweat.

Cayce met us at the first position and fixed the box in place with the first bracket. I paused only a moment, gasping and panting, before returning to the lock with Kane for the second box. Cayce remained behind to attach the remaining brackets.

We only had half an hour to get all four boxes in place, but it felt like an eternity … a Sisyphean effort of hauling, hauling, hauling the bulky, balky boxes up a never-ending hull, one hand cramping from its unending grip on the box's handle while the other scrabbled for purchase on the hull. Then the pull, the brace of one foot on some protruding vent or antenna, and the reach for another half-meter.

I wasn't used to this level of physical exertion, and soon I was trembling, gasping, and soaked with perspiration. I kept shaking the sweat out of my eyes, and even so I was half-blinded by the floating droplets in my helmet. But I kept working. What choice did we have?

The last box was the worst. With only minutes left on the timer, Kane and I were both exhausted, irritable, and error-prone. At one point my foot slipped, and the box and I went sliding backward—panicked, dizzy, grabbing for anything—only to stop short with a curse from Kane as he caught the weight of me and the box. I hung there from one arm for what seemed like forever before I managed to grab a protruding camera and haul myself and the heavy box back under control. Finally, with an assist from Cayce, we got it into position and fastened it to its brackets.

Even my weight of only a couple of kilos felt like a tonne as I hauled myself up into the aft lock. I was the last one in and the door slid shut behind me; I lay panting on it as the lock repressurized.

"They're here," Cayce said as I pulled my helmet off, droplets of sweat shimmering around me and falling slowly to the aft wall. "Already moving to englobe." His fingers tapped on his keyboard, and through his helmet speakers, I heard the synthetic voice say, "Back off now or we will destroy the ship. This is not a bluff."

Kane wiped his eyes. His hair was lank with sweat. "Think they might back off?"

Cayce replied with a cynical grin that belied his age. "Not a chance." He turned toward the interior hatch. "Let's go see how Tai is doing with the drive."

"Do we have control of the drive?" Cayce asked Tai as we entered the control room.

"Not yet." Six out of the seven lights on the little box were now green, I noticed, but the seventh was blinking yellow. That didn't look good.

"How much longer?"

"I don't know!" Tai snapped.

"Miyuki," Cayce continued, "extrapolate their courses and map out an exit path for us. Assume zero percent fade tail. We don't want to risk clipping one of them on the way out." That would be … very bad.

Miyuki sat frozen, hands clutching the joysticks and staring straight ahead at the nav screen.

"Miyuki?" Alicia said, moving to put a hand on her shoulder.

Miyuki didn't move. "There's maybe a hole but it's getting smaller fast," she rattled off in a fast monotone. "And even if we can squeeze through it, they'll track us."

"They won't be able to track us," Cayce said in his statement-of-fact voice.

Kane snorted. "There won't be enough left of us *to* track." He had been the most skeptical of Cayce's plan, though once we'd all agreed to it, he'd worked as hard as any of us to make it happen.

Alicia silenced him with a glare, then returned her attention to Miyuki, holding her shoulders firmly and leaning in to speak low and calm in her ear. "We have a plan," she reassured her. "We're going to get away. But we need you to fly the ship. Okay?"

Miyuki twitched all over, then settled herself in the seat, flexing her hands on the joysticks. "Fly the ship," she repeated. "Fly the ship."

"You can do it." Alicia gave her shoulders another squeeze.

The next few minutes passed in tense silence, broken only by the increasingly frequent ping of the proximity alarm as the Coalition ships closed in around us. All we could do was watch Tai as they pounded the keyboard in increasing frustration.

Suddenly Tai spat out a Vietnamese curse. "It's the goddamn admin password!" they shouted. "How could that be wrong?" They turned to me. "The administrator password was one of the things *you* gave us. The hack used it to get access in the first place. How could it fail *now*?"

"Shit!" I said. "I just changed it a few minutes ago, so we could access the guns!"

Mingled anger and relief ran across Tai's face. "Key it in!" they said.

A keyboard appeared on my station, and I typed the new password. A moment later, the last light turned green, followed swiftly by dozens of other indicators on the drive control panel. A rising hum thrummed through the ship as the drive came online. "We're in!"

Cayce tightened his shoulder straps and turned to Miyuki. "Do you have a course?"

"Maybe." She still had a death grip on the joysticks but she wasn't frozen the way she had been. "It's going to be very tight."

"Lock it in and get ready to execute." Cayce turned to Kane. "Ready with the trigger?"

Kane, already strapped in hard, held the detonator control in his lap, the trigger button already uncapped and both thumbs resting on it. "Ready."

We all looked at each other. This might be goodbye.

No one said anything. Wishing good luck was bad luck.

"On three, then," Cayce said. "One. Two."

We all held our breath.

"Three."

Then everything happened at once.

An enormous crashing *bang* sounded from all sides.

The whole ship rattled like dice in a cup.

Every screen went white.

A dozen different klaxons went off.

Miyuki screamed.

And my eyes and ears twisted in my skull—the sensation of transitioning to skip, though far stronger and … *weirder* than I'd ever felt before.

I think I might have blacked out for a minute there.

The original plan, of course, had been to wait until everything was unlocked and ready for our escape before the "hostages" were taken aboard. We would then move away from the station, drop the explosives behind us, and detonate them just as we entered skip. But this depended on getting far enough away from the station that they wouldn't have sufficient parallax to detect that the explosion that apparently destroyed the ship had actually taken place between the ship and the station.

Being nearly englobed by Coalition craft meant that we had to mount the explosives on the hull, with standoff brackets to give us a chance of avoiding real destruction while we skipped away at the moment of detonation. But it was only a chance … the explosives, packed with carefully chosen space junk, had not been designed for this.

I awoke to flickering darkness and the smell of smoke. Not good.

Harsh white emergency lighting snapped on, revealing everyone still strapped in and no one screaming or visibly bleeding. The atmosphere was hazy and full of floating junk, half the screens and indicators were dead, and the drive was silent.

"Tai!" Cayce shouted, and I realized he'd been shouting their name for a while. "How's the ship?"

"Drive's fine," they said. "It ran the course Miyuki set, then shut itself off. Atmo shows a little pressure drop, not too serious. No structural alarms."

"Where are we?" I asked.

Miyuki consulted her instruments. "We're ... thirty-one hundred klicks from where we started." She turned to face me, still shaking, but with an elated grin plastered across her face. "In eight seconds. From a standing start."

That was half again faster than the best we could have done in *Contessa*, and she'd been no slouch.

Cayce didn't take any time to be impressed. "Any sign of pursuit?"

I had to help Miyuki with that. "The Coalition craft aren't moving out of the blast area," I reported after a minute. "No indication they're looking for us."

"I'm seeing a few active pings," Tai added, "but we should be out of their range."

We all worked together for the next few hours getting the ship back into shape after her very rough shakedown cruise. Despite Alicia's efforts, she hadn't been completely secured for a hard run, and some of the cabinets had spilled their contents into the air. The explosion and acceleration had shaken a few hull plates loose, but Cayce and Kane managed to patch the holes without having to go outside. Miyuki and Tai got most of the detectors and other ship systems back online, apart from a few antennas and cameras on the outer hull that had been completely destroyed, and Alicia and I worked to complete our takeover of the ship and assess our status in the outside world.

"They've found the salt," Alicia reported. We were all in the galley, sucking on coffee bulbs, sweaty and stinking and exhausted and very happy to be alive. The ship was under way at full skip, heading for a friendly and very private port. "And it looks like they're buying it."

The boxes of explosives and space junk had been carefully salted with actual pieces of *Malakbel VII*—that was one of the things

209

Cayce and Kane had been scrambling to do while Alicia, Tai, and I had been standing outside the lock—and some biological samples from me and the other "hostages," all to lend verisimilitude to the ship's destruction. There were also a few samples from friends of ours, people to whom evidence that they had been blown up in a failed ship hijacking might be beneficial.

"Condolences on your death, Madam Secretary," Cayce said to me.

I inclined my head in acknowledgment. "I was getting tired of being her anyway."

"Have they really bought it, do you think," Cayce continued, "or is it just what they're telling the public?"

"My ability to access secure comms while dead is somewhat limited," I remarked drily, "but as near as I can tell they have swallowed the bait completely. And there's no sign of any nibbles on our real trail."

"So we got away clean?" Kane grunted.

"Looks like it, yeah," Alicia said, nodding.

"Congratulations, people," Cayce said. "We are now the owners of the fastest ship in the System."

We all looked around at each other, smug and astonished in varying degrees.

"What are we going to call it?" I asked. "I have always hated the name Malakbel. It's impossible to spell or pronounce."

After a brief, considering silence, Alicia spoke up. "We should name it for Damien."

"That would be too weird," Kane protested. And he had a point … but something about the suggestion felt very right. Damien was the one who had saved us all at Orca Station … the one who had very deliberately sacrificed himself. He couldn't be here with us today, but he deserved some kind of recognition.

"I didn't mean we should name it *Damien*," Alicia protested. "But it should be something that reminds us of him."

"Zephyr," Cayce said without hesitation. "Zephyr Sedgwick-Foxley." And it was perfect.

Zephyr had been Damien's greatest love after Alicia. And to name the fastest ship in the System after a turtle—excuse me, a *tortoise*—was just the sort of joke that Damien would appreciate. "It is a good name," I said.

"I hereby christen thee *Zephyr*," Alicia said, and tapped her coffee bulb against the nearest stanchion. It wasn't much of a christening, but it would have to do for now.

"*Zephyr!*" we all chorused, and drank.

"So …" I said then, "I guess the Cannibal Club is back in business."

"I guess we are," said Alicia.

Tai grinned. "It's good to be back."

And it *was* good to be back.

This last day had been tense, hectic, terrifying, and full of drama … and it had felt *so* wonderful to be doing it with my old friends. My partners. My more-than-family. I had missed that camaraderie more than I had realized.

"To the Cannibal Club," we all said, and drank.

Nine weeks later, I was sitting with Cayce in our rented rooms, sharing a pot of tea. "I *hate* this place," I said.

Cayce raised his own tea bulb in ironic acknowledgment, gesturing around at exposed wiring, vents clogged with dust, and pipes shimmering with condensation. It stank of rust and mildew. "And this is the best suite in the house."

I had felt caged at Malakbel, but it had been a *golden* cage, and I certainly missed the luxuries I'd had as Madam Secretary. This place … well, as pirate sanctuaries go, and I'd experienced quite a few of them in my years with the Cannibal Club, it wasn't the worst. But not by much. "Well, at least we'll be out of here soon." That brought a fractional flicker of Cayce's left eyelid, and I knew there was trouble. He could hide his lies from everyone else, but not me. His father had had the same tell. "Oh no. What is it now?"

"Water. We need at least eight tonnes more, and Laurent is being a dick about the price."

"Water?!" I did not quite shout the word, but I did slam my tea bulb down on the table between us hard enough that a few drops wobbled out of the nozzle. Ironically enough. "We are in the fucking rings of Saturn. We are *surrounded* by water."

Cayce waved in the general direction of the outer hull. There weren't any windows here, not even a screen simulating an outside view. "Filthy slush full of tholins and God knows what else. You wouldn't want to drink it, and the drive is even pickier."

I knew this, and he knew I knew it. "I know this," I said aloud, just to call him out explicitly for lecturing someone who was more than old enough to be his mother. "If Laurent is being that much of a dick, we can mine it and refine it ourselves. The ship has the capability."

He shook his head. "We don't have the time."

"Then why are we sitting here and not already on our way?"

"I can wear him down on the price faster than we could mine our own ice." He paused. "I'm pretty sure. And it reduces our chance of getting caught."

He had a point. I sighed and sucked down the last drops of tea. Cold and bitter though it was, it was the last of the good stuff I'd brought with me from Malakbel and I wasn't going to let it go to waste. "How soon?"

"Tomorrow. Day after at the latest."

I tapped the empty tea bulb on the table ... then remembered that no one was coming to refill it. I snarled and flung it at the recycler; the air current caught it and snatched it into the chute with a gulping whoosh. "It'll have to do, I guess."

"At least we have fresh vegetables here. Once we're underway, it'll be nothing but the frozen and dried stuff."

I snorted. What he said was true, to an extent, but the local produce was pathetic—just a few courgettes and marrows, and outrageously expensive. "What does a kid like you know about fresh vegetables?"

"My dad taught me to appreciate the finer things." Smoothly delivered, but again accompanied by that little eyelid flicker. This time I didn't call him on it, just noted it for later.

It was the latest item in a very long list.

"I'm going out," I said, and pushed away from the table.

"Don't go too far."

I just gave him the hairy eyeball. There wasn't very far to go.

"Laurent's Place" was what everyone called it—a pirate refuge, trading post, and chandlery camouflaged as just another anonymous ice rock in the rings of Saturn. The big refit bay at the center of the rock, currently almost completely filled by *Zephyr*, was its largest enclosed space; the biggest space under atmosphere was "The Walk," a high-ceilinged twisting corridor about as long as a football pitch, lined with shops, bars, restaurants, and inns. All of them nominally independent, but actually firmly under Laurent's thumb. Which meant high prices and limited selection, but at least it kept everyone honest ... if by "honest" you meant "won't sell you out to the authorities."

But though Laurent was a greedy asshole, he treated everyone equally and never welshed on a deal once you'd agreed to his usurious prices. He'd refitted *Zephyr* exactly as we'd specified, and, somewhat to my surprise, had even stayed out of the top-secret parts of the drive as we'd requested. The lack of the bang-and-scream we would have heard if any of my traps had been triggered reassured me of that.

It wasn't so much that I wanted to keep the Malakbel drive tech out of the hands of the other powers—though there was some of that, as I *was* still an Inner Belter at heart despite everything—as that I wanted to keep its existence and capabilities a Cannibal Club secret as long as possible. That was one reason we'd selected Laurent over competitors who might have done the same work quicker and for less money. Once he was bought, he *stayed* bought.

The same couldn't be said for Laurent's other customers, though, and as I moved through the ragged crowd, I kept my head down and a sharp ear out for any evidence that one of them might be planning some mischief. As long as we were pinned down here with the ship half-disassembled, we were vulnerable, and between the theft of the *Malakbel VII* and the various prices on our heads from previous jobs, there was a lot of temptation swirling around.

It isn't that hard to be seen as no one—it's a lot easier than passing as someone specific. There are things the human brain and eye and ear trigger on to distinguish one person from another, and a few subtle tricks are sufficient to eliminate those triggers. I had read all the literature, and had done a lot of what you might call applied research, and I was very good at it. No one who might have been whispering with their neighbor about taking down the Cannibal

Club for a fat payout would know that one of them was sipping weak beer at the next bar stool.

But, as it happened, this day there was nothing of concern to us happening along The Walk. I heard plenty of gossip about possible big opportunities for the right sort of people, which I filed away for later, and certainly several choice items which would have been of great interest to Madam Secretary. But Madam Secretary was dead, alas, and it was with a mingled sense of relief and grief that I let those bits of information go.

I ended my rounds at a little coffee shop, and paused for a moment to consider what I'd learned. Most of it about Cayce.

There was no question he was lying about some important things. He lied all the time. Everyone does, in this business and everywhere else; my own existence is a net of fabrications so dense I sometimes have trouble keeping track of which bits of my history actually happened. But Cayce's lies ran deeper than most.

He was a good liar. He was *very* good, for a sixteen-year-old kid, and that in itself was worrisome. For a time I'd considered the possibility that his age was a lie as well. But I'd been watching him closely for a couple of months now, and unless there was some novel rejuvenation treatment I hadn't heard about, he really was only sixteen. His clear smooth skin—how I envied it!—and the pattern of fat, muscle, and tendon beneath it were things only a teenager could have. But he *moved* like someone with substantial martial arts training, and his patterns of thought and the things he knew were equally out of character.

I'd questioned him about it, indirectly, and he acknowledged that he was unusually competent for his age. "I am my father's child," he'd said with a shrug, chalking it up to genetics and training. But according to his own story he'd spent at most a couple of years with Strange, and that wasn't enough for him to have learned everything he knew. Or was it? He *was* a very quick study, I'll grant him that.

All in all, though … it didn't quite add up. It didn't add up to what he said about himself, certainly, but it also didn't add up to anything else. Not yet. So I'd continued to gather information, and had kept my suspicions to myself.

214

But very soon, perhaps in just a day or two, we'd be on our way to Cronos—all cooped up together in a not particularly large or reliable ship, heading out to a place that was vast and empty even by the extremely low standards of the Outer Belt. We'd *have* to trust each other then.

Everyone lies. And Cayce, for all his deceptions large and small, had repeatedly demonstrated his trustworthiness on important matters directly relevant to the Club, and to me. But I had to consider the possibility that we were nearing the endgame of a very long con.

It was time to share my suspicions.

I started with Kane. He had never been my favorite—impulsive and immature at best, a hotheaded idiot at worse—but he'd known Cayce longest of all of us and he had a certain level of animal cunning when it came to sizing other people up. As soon as he came back from his latest expedition—while the rest of us waited for *Zephyr* to be refitted he was running errands for Cayce, flitting across the Belt and back—I volunteered to be his sparring partner for a session, which basically meant me holding his punching bag for him. I've never been one for physical violence, though I do pride myself on my marksmanship.

"Cayce can be kind of an asshole," Kane acknowledged even as he gave the bag three swift blows with both hands and one foot, pushing the bag and myself back against the padded wall behind us. I adjusted the bag for another assault; Kane wasn't even breathing hard as he spun on his axis and smacked it again with the other foot. "But he's never let me down."

"What about at Amalthea?" I asked, bracing the bag with my shoulder. "He left you hanging there."

"I was pretty pissed off at that, yeah." Kane slammed the bag dead center with both feet—half knocking the breath out of me—which pushed him away from me. But he bounced off the far wall with his hands, propelling himself back to hit the bag again with his feet at what felt like chin and groin. "But that was just a comms snafu. If we'd gotten the message, we would have known he was coming back for us. And, in the end, we got away with the money."

He shrugged, then shot out a solid blow with his fist which landed on the side of the bag's head area, sending me and the bag spinning lengthwise. "That sucked. Set me up again."

I caught myself on the wall behind me, stopping the spin, and maneuvered the bag back between me and Kane. I felt a little safer that way. "He *said* it was a comms snafu. It could just as well be that he decided to dump you, then came back when whatever he'd planned for an escape didn't pan out."

Kane's fist shot out again, this time landing square on where the bag's nose would have been. I really felt the blow, which sent me and the bag rotating slowly end-over-end. "Better. One more time." As I moved the bag back into position, he continued, "You think too much. I prefer to take people at face value." Once again his fist lashed out, and this time I felt the heavy, stiff bag fold around the impact. The bag and I slammed against the wall behind us with no spin at all. Every erg of energy had gone into damage, none into rotation. "That's the way to do it. The straightforward approach. Fuck subtlety."

"The straightforward approach only works if your opponent is straightforward with you." My back was still against the wall. Without warning, I pushed hard with my feet, sending the bag's lower end hurtling toward Kane's groin.

I don't know how he did it, but Kane slapped the heavy bag away before it impacted, leaving me panting with nothing at all between us. "It works for me," he said, and his hand shot out.

I flinched. But then I realized he was only extending it for a handshake. "Thanks for your help," he said.

I took his hand, with my own trembling a little. "Thank you," I replied, "for your insights."

Alicia was next. I accompanied her to the clinic—well, the quarters of a doctor who'd lost her license but retained access to the very best drugs, which was the best Laurent had to offer—where she would be picking up several bottles of Serenizine, a powerful anti-tremor med. It had some nasty potential side effects, was horrifically expensive even through official channels and even more so here, and she and I had spent many late nights discussing whether or not to spend a substantial portion of our budget on it.

After handing over the first half of the money, in cash, we had to wait for the doctor to return with the pills. After running a quick scan for electronic surveillance, I took advantage of the lull to speak with Alicia in private. "You've known Cayce longer than I have," I said, as we floated side by side in the doctor's tidy bed-sit. "How much do you trust him?"

"With my life," was her immediate and very sincere reply. The fervor of her response took me aback—she was usually more reserved.

"But you have to agree that there's something not quite right about him."

"He is ... odd," she admitted. "But Strange is odd too, and we all trusted him." She gave me a sisterly smirk. "Some of us more than others."

I looked away from Alicia's gaze. It was true that both of us had been intimate with Strange; in my case it had been a rebound relationship after he'd broken up with her and Damien. It hadn't lasted. "Strange earned that trust," I said. "Cayce is an unknown quantity."

"It's true he hasn't always been forthcoming ..."

"He's outright lied to us!" I snapped.

"I'm not sure I agree with that assessment." She gazed off into the past. "He's ... shaved the truth, maybe. But, given his upbringing, I can understand if he feels he needs to play his cards close to his chest."

"But shouldn't we all be on the same side here?"

Now Alicia's eyes met mine, hard. "Have *you* been completely, one hundred percent, honest with us?"

I hadn't, but I didn't let my gaze drop. "We all have secrets."

"We do. And if he has more than he's let on ... well, I trust his judgement. In the months I've known him, he's gotten all of us out of more scrapes than I can count."

"How many of those scrapes did he get you *into*?"

A quirk of the corner of her mouth acknowledged my point. "Still ... I owe him, and more to the point, I owe Strange. I'd never forgive myself if I didn't at least try to help get him out of ... whatever it is he's gotten himself into this time."

"Despite everything?" I said. I knew she bore Strange some ill will for the way he broke up with her and Damien, and blamed him for Damien's death.

"Despite everything." She was dead serious, and fully committed. "And if that means trusting Cayce a little further than I really should ... well, that's my choice."

"We're in this together. Your choices could impact all of us."

"Yours too. Are you in? Really in? Can we trust *you*?"

Now I felt myself on the defensive. I relaxed my shoulders and put on my best motherly expression. "Of course you can trust me, dear."

The doctor returned with the pills just then, so we had to put that discussion on hold. But I think we both knew where we stood.

Tai was harder to pin down. I finally had to volunteer to suit up—have I mentioned how much I hate vac suits?—to accompany them on a final inspection tour of the refit.

After checking out the new gun emplacements, external cameras, long-range antennas, and black conductive-foam coating, we finished up floating below the ship's "chin" looking up at the giant skull and crossbones embossed on the lower forward hull. It was black on black, not garish white as Kane had wanted, but it was still pretty unsubtle.

"Don't you think it's a bit much?" I asked on our encrypted suit-to-suit channel.

"Damien would have wanted it this way," Tai replied. "And why not? It's not as though we'll ever be able to dock at Ceres in *this*."

"True enough." Despite the superficial changes in the ship's visual and radar silhouettes Laurent had made at our direction, the Inner Belt authorities would be looking deeper, and the former *Malakbel VII*'s identity couldn't be completely disguised without impairing her drive's capabilities. So, as long as we flew in her—and I hoped that would be a good long time—we'd be outlaws. "How do you feel about that? I know you had a pretty cushy life at Ngo Quyen Ring before Cayce showed up."

"I did," they admitted. "But it was my own fault I had to leave on short notice. Cayce just provided the means, motive, and opportunity to do so."

"Are you *sure* about that?" I asked. "It might not be coincidence that the family you pissed off managed to track you down at about the same time Cayce showed up."

"What are you suggesting?" Tai's voice revealed sudden suspicion, perhaps of my motivations rather than Cayce's.

"Cayce knew that, of all of us, you were the least likely to want to abandon your comfortable situation and hare off to the Kuiper Belt to help rescue Strange. Might he have put a few words in the right ear to help push you off the Ring?"

It was hard to read Tai's expression through their vac suit visor. "Anything's possible, I suppose. Do you have any evidence of this?"

"I've only been asking around for a little while," I replied noncommittally.

"So no."

"Not hard evidence, no. But still, the timing is suspicious."

"Y… eah," Tai drawled, seeming to give the point serious consideration. "But even if Cayce accelerated the situation—and I'm not saying he did—it still might have come to a head any time. I messed up at the wedding, I admit it. And Cayce made it possible for us to pull off a big, big job together that none of us could have managed solo. I call that a win."

"Fair enough," I replied, sensing that I wasn't going to get any further with this line of attack. "But please do keep in mind … we don't really know him. We know that he isn't sharing everything he knows, and sometimes shades the truth. All I can say is … Cayce is playing his cards close to his chest, and if you have your own ace in the hole, you might want to hang onto it."

"I understand," they replied. "And I appreciate you sharing your concerns."

And I knew that was the best I was going to get.

Eventually Cayce and Laurent settled on a price for the last eight tonnes of water, we moved our things from our guest suite back onto *Zephyr*, and the six of us—me, Cayce, Kane, Alicia, Tai, and Miyuki—gathered in *Zephyr*'s control center, prepared to depart for Cronos. I hadn't bothered sharing my suspicions with Miyuki; she was too erratic for me to read well, and she had no more reason to trust me than she did Cayce. I considered her a bit of a wild card in whatever might come next.

We floated in a circle, but somehow Cayce was at the head of it. "I haven't known you very long, really," he said, "but thanks to what my dad told me about you all, I already feel that you're closer than family. I hope the same is true for you. We've come a long way together already, and we have a lot farther to go, but I'm sure we're up to the challenge." He took a breath and looked around, meeting each pair of eyes in turn. "Look, I know I'm just a kid, and you're the freaking Cannibal Club. You should be telling *me* what to do. But this is *Strange* we're talking about. He's my *dad*. He matters more to me than anything, and I know he's important to you too. And even if his life has no cash value"—Kane scoffed aloud at that, and I wondered what he might have heard about a bounty on Strange's head—"it's not just his life on the line. Rescuing him is part and parcel of rescuing ourselves." Tai nodded sagely. "But, all that being said, I know this is a big, big ask. If any of you want out, just say the word. As far as I'm concerned, you can walk out of here right now with your share of the remaining loot—no regrets, no recriminations, and no apologies necessary. But once we launch from here, we are all in it up to the hilt. So … is everybody in?"

That offer was a complete surprise to me, and I could see in everyone else's face that it was to them as well. It was a generous offer, too; we'd spent a lot of the Emperor's Scroll money on the refit, but there was still more than enough left that a sixth of it would pay for a long and very comfortable life off the grid.

I thought that Kane might push back. Being the one whose parents had abandoned him, and the one least prepared to survive on his own, he was the most committed to keeping the Club together no matter what. But even he nodded slowly, seemingly accepting the fairness of the offer and perhaps even considering taking it up himself. Alicia just looked around the circle, expressionless. Tai pursed their lips in consideration. Miyuki waited expectantly for everyone else to declare. And me?

I didn't trust Cayce. I knew I didn't know as much about him as I would like, and I wasn't sure how much I liked what I did know. But

I didn't trust *anyone* completely—not even myself, some days—and, whatever Cayce's faults, he had a brilliant mind and had master-minded some jobs in the past year that no one else, perhaps not even Strange, could have pulled off.

If nothing else, life with Cayce would not be boring.

"I'm in," I said. And just like a pressure vessel giving way after the first crack, everyone else chimed in almost at once. Tai was the last, and not by much.

"Thank you," Cayce said. "Thank you for your trust, for your strength and skills, and for your commitment." He looked around at us, his face radiating happiness, confidence, and determination. Then he grinned—his teenage self coming to the fore. "Let's roll."

We rolled. Each of us took our station: Miyuki as pilot, me as navigator, Tai as engineer, Alicia as communications officer, and Kane and Cayce in two of the three passenger seats.

This was an engineering prototype, not a combat vessel, and lacked specialized stations for a commander and a weapons officer. Laurent had rigged up a weapons control panel for Kane, in the starboard pas-senger seat, to control the newly installed offensive and defensive sys-tems. And as for Cayce, though his seat was all the way at the aft end of the compartment and didn't have any kind of specialized equipment—indeed, was the least well protected in case of disaster—somehow he managed to dominate the space from there. "All set?" he asked.

We each acknowledged that we were, in our anarchic and unmil-itary way, and without further ado, Alicia contacted station control to open the refit bay doors.

It was Laurent himself who replied, a surprising courtesy. "Bon voyage, *Zephyr*," he called, and the doors slid open. Dislodged ice crys-tals glittered, startlingly bright, in the blackness between the doors as they slid back, and I realized it was the first sunlight I'd seen in weeks.

"Here we go," said Miyuki, and nudged the joysticks forward. Thrusters fired aft, a low rumbling hiss, and *Zephyr* slipped smoothly out of the bay.

I checked my navigational displays carefully as we slid into the dense ice field that hid Laurent's Place from outside observers. A path through the floating ice rocks, carefully plotted to appear random, was kept clear by drones and marked with low-power beacons whose intermittent schedule of pings had been programmed into *Zephyr*'s computers by Laurent's technicians.

Anyone else would have used autopilot to navigate out along that twisting, constantly shifting path. Not Miyuki. With one eye on the short-range nav display, the other on the forward real-time view, and a steady hand on the joysticks, she guided us forward at what felt to me like a reckless pace. But the proximity alarms never triggered once.

Miyuki was an extremely odd duck. I still couldn't read her, which bothered me. But she was a very, very good pilot—maybe even better than Damien. I was glad she was on our side.

"We'll be in the open in ten minutes," I announced, watching the long-range nav display. "No sign of anyone waiting for us."

Kane's weapons console, I noted, was live and ready to fire on anyone who dared to poke their nose in our business. "I'd advise against pulling that trigger," I murmured to him, "unless absolutely necessary. No sense attracting attention with gunfire if we might slip by instead."

"Okay, okay," he muttered back, theatrically raising his hands from the controls and spreading the fingers wide.

Cayce, I noted out of the corner of my eye, was taking this all in silently ... no doubt filing it away in that memory palace of his. It was a trick he'd revealed to me that he shared with his father—a mental organizational technique that I'd always envied, but never been able to duplicate.

"Still clear," I announced as we passed the last beacon. Kane, beside me, snorted in disappointment, but apart from an inward smile, I let it pass.

"No scent of any signals," Alicia confirmed.

And then we were out of the path and out of the ice field, skimming along the surface of Saturn's F ring. "Ooh," said Tai, and I echoed their sentiment—cynical and well-traveled though I might be, even I was not immune to beauty.

The ring curved away ahead of us, chaotic swarms of ice particles in the near field of vision melding together with distance into impossibly precise ellipses, a fairy road glittering white against the utter blackness of space beyond. Saturn loomed huge on our port side, milky bands of pale butterscotch and café au lait swirling together like an exotic cocktail, the motion of the gases just barely perceptible. Three moons were in view, two merely bright points but a third—Titan, I thought—showing a visible disc.

Laurent's Place had been on Saturn's night side when we'd arrived, so this was our first exposure to this particular view. We all soaked it in, staring in silence at one of the solar system's most spectacular panoramas.

Once we were well clear of the ring's deadly ice particles, Miyuki triggered the skip and our stately pavane along the ring sped up to a brisk trot. There was no feeling of acceleration, and no stutter whatsoever—the Malakbel tech used a skip frequency comfortably faster than human senses could perceive—but the mildly nauseating feeling of entering skip was no more intense than usual. The plan was to keep to conventional skip speeds until we were well away from Saturn and the ever-curious antennas in its neighborhood.

"How's she handling?" Cayce asked Miyuki.

"Like a dream," she replied, and she did indeed sound a little dreamy, perhaps even a bit stoned. I looked at her askance, but the rapturous expression on her face didn't reach her eyes, which continued to flick across the displays with unyielding attention, or her hands, still firm and steady on the joysticks.

"Drive's running smooth," Tai put in, helpfully translating the flood of numbers and diagrams on their displays into plain English.

To be frank, I was a bit annoyed that Tai, who'd had only a couple of months' experience with the Malakbel drive—and not much more than that with skip drives in general—could read that gibberish better than I could. I'd been in charge of the program, and in theory, I should be as familiar with the readouts as Tai, but in reality, I'd always left those details to the technicians.

But really, it didn't matter. We were together again, we had a fast ship and a plan, and we were on our way to rescue a friend.

Even with the Malakbel drive, the Kuiper belt was still a *long* way off. It would take us six weeks to get there.

It was an awkward six weeks.

Yes, we'd once been closer than family. Well, except for Cayce and Miyuki. And Kane had been fairly new to the Club at the end. And it had been ten years since that family had been shattered, with plenty of blame to go around. And there had been a lot of water under the bridge since then. A *lot*. So we all had a lot of catching up to do, and grievances to be aired, and reconciliation to be attempted. Not to mention that, for all the time we'd spent together back during the Club's active days, we'd never been so confined in such a small space for so long.

There was also sex in the mix, just to make things interesting.

I don't do girls. I consider this a failing, but there you have it. And I wasn't interested in Cayce because of the age difference, nor Kane because of the intelligence differencFFe. Which left Tai, and Tai was definitely interested. Tai was always interested in everyone. So we gave it a try, but it wasn't really satisfactory for either of us, so we went back to just being friends.

Tai and Alicia also hooked up, resuming a long-standing on-and-off relationship. Kane did a terrible job of hiding his jealousy at that, but we all knew he'd had an unrequited crush on Alicia forever and we just pretended not to notice. Kane did spend some time with Tai as a sparring partner, and possibly more ... I didn't really want to know.

I saw Miyuki approach Tai at least once, but Tai—bless their shiny black heart—turned her gently down. She was too young and too emotionally unstable. I think she was hurt by the rejection, but Alicia helped her through it and their relationship, already quite strong, deepened.

Alicia had always been the most emotionally sensitive of us. I could read people better, of course, and manipulate them, but Alicia was genuinely nice. Sometimes I envied that.

And then there was Cayce, a fascinating study. Only sixteen, so off limits sexually even for a bunch of hardened reprobates like us— yes, even Tai, though I could tell they were tempted—and much too smart to get involved in such a problematic relationship. But he had a sixteen-year-old boy's gonads and the struggle between his brain and his cock was sometimes painfully amusing to watch. He might plausibly have hooked up with Miyuki—the age difference between them was something that many cultures would have overlooked—but he could see as well as I could that it would be harmful to her. So both of them spent a lot of time masturbating.

The cabin walls were quite thin.

Apart from all that, we all had work to do to prepare for the upcoming job. We didn't have engineering diagrams of Cronos Station, but Cayce had spent time there and had drawn quite detailed plans from his memory palace, which we all tried to commit to memory. The plans included many details that I would not have expected a child to be able to access, which raised my respect for him another notch ... as well as my suspicions.

Tai spent most of their time between assignations working on some kind of software hack—"two different hacks, actually," they told me once—monopolizing the long-range comms antenna and spending a lot of time wandering the halls and swearing loudly. This was, I remembered well from ten years ago, how they approached problem solving, and I learned to ignore the noise. At least they were using earphones rather than inflicting their waka-waka music on the rest of us.

Kane trained incessantly, strength training and stretching and yoga and tai chi and virtual target practice and lots and lots of sparring with Cayce and occasionally Tai. Once Tai showed up with a black eye, and Kane was *so* apologetic for a week. It was adorable. I spent time in the gym too—we all did, we would be dealing with one-third gee at Cronos—but Kane was *always* there, straining silently against three or four times my maximum load. And yet somehow he remained thin as a rail, all wires and cables under the skin.

Alicia also spent a lot of time in the gym, working hard to retain as much strength and coordination as she could. It was painful to me to see how much she worked, and how much it *hurt*, for so little result, but even when the tears floated out from her clenched-shut eyes, she never complained. She also spent hours picking locks that she'd fabbed from plans that Cayce had downloaded from somewhere. It was frustrating to her how difficult she was finding them—they would have been trivial during her Cannibal Club days—but she said that with the Serenizine, they were at least possible. Sometimes she worked together with Kane to tackle projects that her hands simply weren't up to, which was good for both of them.

I also saw her clenching and massaging her hands when she thought no one was looking. This was worrisome, but, as she was taking pains to conceal it, I decided not to bring it up just yet.

Miyuki practiced incessantly with simulations, familiarizing herself with the ship's systems until they were practically an extension of her slim fingers. Once we passed the orbit of Uranus, well away from most observation, we all strapped in once a day so she could practice those maneuvers for real. The combination of stony concentration and near-orgasmic pleasure on her face during those exercises was frankly terrifying.

As for myself, I worked at memorizing the amazingly detailed org charts that Cayce had drawn from his memory palace. They were as much as a couple of years out-of-date, he warned, but there wasn't a lot of turnover at a station so distant from civilization. Knowing those names and relationships, and discussing with Cayce the personalities of the key players, could save our lives if we had to bluff or con our way through a tricky passage.

And Cayce? Cayce was everywhere—sparring hard with Kane; conferring with Tai day and night about the hack and other technical things; strategizing locks and doors with Alicia; poring over navigational plots with Miyuki; and spending hours with me discussing the staff of Cronos Station. I wasn't sure he ever slept.

He really was his father's child. His voice, his face, his mannerisms, were so very familiar that sometimes, late at night, I nearly forgot who I was talking to. We fell into conversational rhythms that I'd shared with Strange, and once in a moment of weakness, I actually started to flirt with him. He immediately called me on it, the little rat, and I wondered if he'd maneuvered me into it for a lark.

There was one thing that bothered me in the org charts: a big ugly hole in the position of Director of Security. Cayce tried to wave it away, saying, "The director was removed from his post right around the time I left. I don't know who replaced him." But his very best nonchalant act—and it was very good—only served to point out just how significant that lacuna was.

So six weeks passed—six weeks of fucking and swearing and sweating and strategizing, all cooped up together in a tiny box speeding through millions of kilometers of pure emptiness. And then we arrived at Cronos Station.

"We came all this way for *this*?" Kane groused as the first ragged images started to come through on the forward display.

Cronos Station did not, indeed, look like anything special. It was a conventional "wedding ring" design—a doughnut six decks thick, but only a three-quarter circle, the gap being filled by the ugly, heavy lump of the fusion plant. It was a compromise between a full ring and the "Thor's hammer" design, having the structural stability and materials efficiency of the full ring but keeping the power plant isolated from the living quarters for safety and spin balance. This sort of thing was typical for stations where solar power was inadequate, and given how far we were from the sun, it wasn't at all surprising to find it here.

We were coasting, and had been coasting for almost a full day, with the drive, all active detectors, and some other ship systems shut down. We wanted to be absolutely sure they wouldn't see us coming. But now that the station was in visual range, it was time to begin our attack.

"Got it," said Tai, centering a crosshair on the station's image in one of Kane's displays. But though Tai was using Kane's weapons station, the payload that deployed when Tai pressed the button was not a missile but a virus.

"Security at Cronos is so tight it makes Malakbel look like a candy dish sitting out on a counter," Tai had explained to me once. "There's absolutely no way I can hack its systems from outside, which is why we'll have to physically break into the station's computer core to finish the job. But to do that, we'll have to get to the station, avoiding their navigational scanners. Fortunately I am very good at my job." They'd breathed on their already-perfect nails and buffed them on a maroon velvet lapel. "Navigational scanners, by their very nature, have to have external antennas. And where a signal can get in, *I* can get in."

We couldn't hide completely in open space; there was no such thing as true stealth tech, despite decades of attempts. But the virus Tai was now transmitting via an ultra-low-power steganographic signal—don't ask me what that meant—would, over the course of many hours, infect the station's navigational systems and remap *Zephyr*'s radar profile to a harmless bit of drifting rock. Combine that with our blacker-than-black foam coating, which would minimize the chance of visual detection, and we could sneak right up to the hull … as long as we were very, *very* careful.

Once we were in, the plan was this: first, make our way to the computer core where the evidence against us, including anything they'd already gotten from Strange, was stored. Kane and Alicia would get us in, and Tai would plant a virus to wipe the data. Next, make our way to the brig and break Strange out. Cayce admitted that he wasn't sure what we'd find there. We would talk our way in if we could, or cut through a back wall with the torch if we couldn't, or failing that, take him by force. Kane, naturally, was hoping for the third option. Then we would return to *Zephyr* and escape at full Quantum IV skip.

None of this would have been possible without Cayce's detailed knowledge of the station's systems. Which, again, was not something a child should have been able to discover. All he would say in explanation was, "Nobody suspected me. I had the run of the place." Which was just plausible enough, but still left me suspicious.

The crosshairs on Tai's display changed from yellow to white. "Signal locked," they said. "Now we wait."

Closer and closer we drifted, and I, for one, became increasingly anxious. I ameliorated my stage fright by checking and rechecking my equipment and quizzing myself on my knowledge of station systems and staff. Kane, I knew from the repeated irregular thuds that echoed throughout the ship, was taking out his anxiety on a punching bag; Tai and Alicia were nowhere to be seen, but probably together somewhere. Cayce was holed up in his cabin, probably strategizing. Miyuki didn't budge from the pilot's console.

Finally Tai and Alicia emerged from hiding, with Tai looking as coiffed as ever but having exchanged their brocade and lace for a dark insulated coverall the same as the rest of us. No, not quite the same—unlike the rest, Tai's coverall had black velvet piping on the shoulder seams. "The virus should be in place by now," they said, and it was clear to me that they were papering over uncertainty with bravado. "Miyuki, you're on."

Miyuki cracked her knuckles and positioned her hands on the joysticks. "Everyone strapped in?" she said, grinning over her shoulder at the rest of us. This was, I realized, *fun* for her.

Everyone signaled that they were properly secured for maneuvers. I, for one, clutched at the straps across my chest with white-knuckled fervor. Soon we'd either land or be blown to bits, but either way the nervous waiting would be over.

"Here we go." Miyuki gently nudged the joysticks forward, and with a low huff from the thrusters, we began moving toward the station.

Closer and closer we drew, the station repeatedly filling the display and then pulling back to a lower magnification level. Detail increased. Soon we could see shadows shifting on the surface as the station rotated. We all held our breath, hoping to avoid detection and fearing a sudden transmission—or missile—from the station. Finally, the display reached its minimum magnification and the screen filled with a closer and closer view of the ship's hull, whizzing past with its one-third gee rotation. I half expected to see a startled pair of eyes in one of the windows that flashed by.

What we were about to attempt was, if we were lucky, the most frightening five seconds of the whole job, and would not have been possible without Miyuki's freakish piloting skill. "This is something they can't possibly predict," Cayce had explained to us. "We're going to land on the *roof*."

If you've grown up in gravity that might sound trivial. But the "roof" of a wedding-ring station is the inside surface of a rapidly rotating cylinder, studded with antennas and crisscrossed by structural members. Landing a ship *Zephyr's* size on a specific spot in the middle of all that was something that only an insane pilot would attempt, and only an insanely good pilot could achieve.

We knew we had the one. We were hoping we had the other.

"Maneuvers in five ..." said Miyuki. "Four ... three ... two ... one." The ship yawed to the left and pitched up her nose, to match the angle of our intended landing spot, while forward acceleration drove us into our seats.

On the navigational display, the rapidly rotating station's surface slowed, slowed, then vanished from the screen as we crossed past its upper edge. "Hang on!" Miyuki said, then cranked the joysticks hard.

The ship flipped, twisted, shot forward, shoved down, then came to a halt with a gentle thud. My stomach took a moment to catch up with the rest of me.

"Locked on," Miyuki said.

Now that we'd locked on, the clock was ticking. We didn't know how long we had until our intrusion was detected, so we had to move fast. This was something we'd rehearsed again and again, and we proceeded without unnecessary chatter.

A fusillade of clicks and rattles as we undid our seat straps was followed by a series of gentle thuds as our soft-soled feet hit the deck in one-third gee. Snap, snap as Tai unfolded Alicia's walker—a new walker, ultra-lightweight, sintered-carbon-fiber frame with low-friction bearings. Shuffles and mutters as we unshipped our equipment and made our way down to the ventral lock, which Laurent had equipped with a limpet airlock for this job.

Alicia might have been able to afford an exoskeleton with the Emperor's Scroll money, but no one at Laurent's Place had the necessary expertise to build and fit one. If we survived this job, it would be one of the first things on our shopping list.

Cayce was the first one through the lock, after checking the air pressure on the other side. He jumped down into the limpet, a cramped space two meters square by one meter high, and felt the seal all the way around the base with his gloved fingers. Thick black goo filled any gaps between the base of the limpet and the station's hull; no air was escaping. But both hull and limpet were space-cold, steaming gently, and we needed to be careful not to touch them with bare skin. Cayce gave a thumbs-up and hopped up out of the space, making room for Kane to take his place. Once Kane was down, Alicia and Tai handed him the oxyacetylene torch and its bulky cylinders of gas. He slipped goggles over his eyes and ignited the torch; the acrid stink of burning metal immediately filled the space.

This was one of the riskier phases of the operation. We couldn't help but make a lot of noise and throw off a lot of heat. But this spot had been very carefully selected.

The station had been built in an Inner Belt shipyard in eight separate sections, then hauled out to the Kuiper Belt by automated tugs. It must have taken years to get here. Each section was independent, firewalled from the others for safety; they were connected to each other only via one main corridor on each deck, paralleled by power and signal cables, water pipes, and air ducts, all of which could be cut off by heavy doors in case of emergency. The space between sections was pressurized, but was otherwise unused, unheated, and mostly unoccupied.

Mostly.

The station's designers had equipped the inter-section spaces with cameras, motion sensors, fire sensors ... all the stuff you'd expect in a secure facility, which should have made what we were about to do a lot more difficult. But Cayce knew something that the original designers hadn't, which the station's crew had discovered in the years after its construction.

Rats.

The common rat, *rattus norvegicus*, was among the species that had accompanied *homo sapiens* into space. Given access to air, food, and water—and the rat's definition of "access" was extremely aggressive—they were perfectly capable of surviving and even thriving anywhere that humans could live. So well had they adapted to the cold, darkness, and low gravity of environments like the spaces between sections of Cronos Station that they grew to quite large sizes, and were almost impossible to eradicate. And they loved to nibble on wiring.

So the inter-section spaces were not nearly so well monitored as the station's designers had intended, with the majority of the sensors nonfunctional and most of the rest being offline due to the constant false alarms triggered by the busy, furry bodies of the station's most unwanted inhabitants.

Most unwanted except for us, that is. Though not unwanted *by* us. Because, thanks to the rats, as long as we didn't make too much noise or set off any fires, we could move through the spaces between sections with near impunity.

Kane finished cutting through the hull and carefully lifted out the circular plug he'd just created. A draft blew from the hole, smelling of rust and mildew and rat droppings, and just fractionally warmer than the near-space-cold air in the limpet dock.

Tai shone a light down the hole. Nothing at all was visible, but the sound—a deep echoing whoosh of moving air—made it plain that the space between sections went very far down indeed. It was seventeen meters to the lower hull, more than enough of a fall to kill you even at one-third gee.

"Time to saddle up," Kane said, and started putting on his harness.

I really didn't feel ready for this part, although I'd rehearsed it thoroughly. I triple-checked my buckles and descender, switched on my headlamp, and tossed my cable into the hole. Then, as soon as Tai had disappeared below, I sat on the edge, took a deep breath, and pushed off. Kane had cut the hole just big enough for me to slip easily through.

I would much rather have had Kane go all the way down, cut through the section wall, then return to *Zephyr* to lower each of us one by one, but that would have taken way too much time. So Kane went first, with the torch; Tai came next, with the gas tanks dangling below themselves; I followed Tai; and Alicia and Cayce came last, with Alicia dangling below Cayce. Miyuki would remain aboard *Zephyr* as our getaway driver.

I let myself fall a short distance before squeezing the descender, to make sure I was clear of the opening before Alicia came after me. But I squeezed too hard and brought myself up with a jerk that drove the air out of my lungs with an "oof" and pinched my butt painfully. *Steady, steady,* I told myself, and gently relaxed my grip on the descender.

We descended in silence for some minutes, the intermittent *zizz zizz* of our descenders and the creak of cables the only sound. The blackness of the inter-section space was fitfully illuminated by five headlamps, rotating like searchlights as we spun slowly down.

The first few meters were a broad empty space between the upper curves of the section four and five pressure vessels, but soon we descended to the tighter space between section walls. There was only about a meter between the walls, and both sides were festooned with pipes, cables, ducts, and structural members, a random forest of *stuff* that meant that in places, we had to squeeze through, or find another route, while in others we faced a sheer drop of some meters. The tight quarters were why we weren't wearing vac suits, which might otherwise have been a useful precaution.

Cold though the space was—my breath fogged white in the light of my headlamp—I soon felt overheated in my insulated coverall. It was hard work, managing the descender for the drops and clambering between pipes and filthy ducts in the tight places, all the while making sure not to foul my cable. Soon my arms and legs were burning from the effort and I had to keep wiping sweat from my brow, trying not to touch my eyes with my grimy gloves.

We each picked our own path down through the thicket of infrastructure. It was quicker than moving single file, but I soon felt myself isolated, with the flicker of the others' headlamps only intermittently visible through the struts and cables. I moved in a circle of illuminated, grimy ducts and walls, surrounded by echoing darkness. An occasional clank or grunt was the only sound, other than the continuous distant hum of station systems.

And then something skittered across my downward-reaching foot.

"Aah!" I shrieked—not my finest moment—and snatched the foot back. Looking downward, I saw a gray, sleek body and two shining discs of eyes staring momentarily back at me before the rat slipped away. It had to be over a meter long, if you included the tail.

"Are you okay?" Cayce said. His voice was just barely at a conversational level, but in the chill silence of the space between walls, it carried well enough.

"I'm fine," I replied, but the tremor in my voice belied the statement. I swallowed, took a moment to breathe and let my hammering heart slow, then repeated, "I'm fine." It came out more convincingly this time. "Just a rat."

We all waited where we were for a moment, concerned that my shriek might have alerted the station to our presence. But soon, I heard Kane begin descending again—he was already well below me—and I steeled myself to do the same.

Eventually, we all met up at deck five, the next-to-lowest level, where we unhooked from our cables, tied them off for our return, and began picking our way horizontally to the stretch of wall Cayce had identified as our next target. First, we came to the inter-section corridors, which required us to clamber up, squeeze through the narrow space between the ceiling of the deck five and floor of deck four corridors, and clamber down on the other side.

This was all done without safety lines, and I was frankly terrified … though, the fear of getting stuck was, for me, even greater than the fear of falling. I really would have been happier if we'd been doing this at one-quarter gee, but at least it wasn't full Earth gravity. It was worse for Alicia, though; she was gasping and nearly weeping from the effort of hauling her uncooperative body along. Cayce and I both helped her as much as we could; Tai and Kane had their hands full with the torch.

Once we made our way back down to deck level on the far side of the corridor, we measured off three meters from the wall, locating a panel fairly clear of pipes and cables. "This will have to do," Cayce said, and he and Kane began assembling the torch. The other three of us backed away, finding places where we could rest for a moment away from spitting sparks.

This was another risky step—one of the riskiest. In addition to the inevitable noise and heat the torch produced, we had only an approximate idea of what lay on the other side of the wall we were cutting through. We had to be prepared to find a squadron of armed security waiting for us. I had a story ready for that eventuality, though it was very much a last-ditch effort and unlikely to succeed.

But Kane made short work of it—the section wall was considerably thinner than the outer hull—and when he gently lifted out the cut-away chunk of wall, all we saw on the other side was a dark storage room. Best possible outcome. I breathed out a sigh of relief, but we still had many, many steps before we'd be in the clear.

We paused for a moment in the storage room to shuck off our insulated coveralls, revealing sweaty business casuals. Cronos Station didn't use uniforms much, Cayce had explained—there was no need for that kind of security at a station so isolated—so we'd selected outfits that would blend in with the sort of technical and clerical people who made up the bulk of the station's staff. Even the unit where Strange was imprisoned was business casual. Tai had been disgusted at the unfashionable short-sleeves-and-slacks outfit we'd forced them into, but despite its cheap fabrics and the fact that it had just come out from under a sweaty coverall, Tai still somehow managed to look sharper in it than any of the rest of us.

I checked everyone over before opening the door, correcting Kane on how he wore his collar. The station was a pretty small community, so if we were intercepted, we would not be able to pass as locals for long, but dressing the part would make it possible for us to avoid immediately raising suspicion if we were spotted on security cameras.

After taking one last look at my own very conventional skirtsuit, brushing my hair, and wiping my face, I eased the door open a crack. The corridor outside was silent and only dimly illuminated, and the clock on the wall showed 02:35 Inner Belt Standard Time. Middle of the night.

We crept out into the corridor, keeping the torch on its cart and Alicia on her walker as quiet as possible; both of them were equipped with the softest, smoothest-running wheels we could find. The torch looked suspicious, no question about that, but we would need it to cut Strange out of his cell. Before we could do that, though, we had to break into the station's computer core and wipe the primary database. That would cover our escape and prevent them from tracking us down afterward.

I took the lead, in case we had to talk our way past anyone, but in the short distance between the storage room and the computer core, we didn't encounter any station personnel.

So far, so good.

The computer core door was our next challenge, an imposing physically secure hatch. Cutting through it with the torch would be quick, but too obvious, so this step was up to Alicia and Kane. Tai had argued that they could hack past the lock quicker than Kane and Alicia could pick it, but Cayce and the rest of us had disagreed. And it wasn't just out of pity, either—it was respect for their skills, repeatedly demonstrated on her practice locks aboard *Zephyr*.

Alicia wheeled up to the door and painstakingly lowered herself to her knees while Kane rolled out her tool kit on the floor. He paused then, looking down at the array of tools as though he'd never seen them before.

"Just like we practiced," she prompted him.

Kane sighed and picked up a little pry bar. Working quickly and fairly deftly, with only a little direction from Alicia, he pried off the escutcheon of the lock panel, exposing a confusing mess of electronics. "Shit," he whispered.

"There," she said, pointing.

He placed the pry bar where she'd indicated and levered the electronics package out, revealing the lock mechanism behind it. "Got it," he said. With greater confidence, he selected two small screwdrivers, gently teased open the lock mechanism, then pulled back the bolt with a satisfying click. We all sighed happily at the sound.

Kane, Tai and Cayce immediately slipped inside while Alicia reassembled the lock, leaving no evidence we'd ever come this way. This part was something she could do herself, as it required more in the way of knowledge and observation than dexterity and strength.

I squeezed Alicia's shoulder as I helped her stand. She placed her hand on mine and squeezed back, with a small but triumphant smile. I'm sure she would have been happier if she'd been able to crack the lock herself, but as far as I was concerned, educating Kane was an even bigger triumph.

Alicia and I wheeled inside—the wall was more than half a meter thick—and gently closed the door behind us. It locked with a definitive click, but this door was designed to keep people out, not in; there was a simple handle for egress.

The computer core itself was disappointing. I'd envisioned some kind of vast dark space with electronic signals flashing across it like contained lightning, but what we actually found was racks and racks of square beige boxes, a steady hum of fans, and a mess of cables. There weren't even any flickering lights or spinning tapes, just one steady white light on each box. Boring.

Tai immediately moved to a beige box that looked exactly like the others, only a little bigger, and pulled down the front of it. Behind that panel was a standard screen and the usual collection of inputs; Tai pulled a data stick from their sleeve pocket and inserted it into the appropriate socket. A display immediately appeared, showing a progress bar rapidly growing from zero toward one hundred percent. Tai smirked.

And then a klaxon started howling, the lights went red, and a loud *clack* sounded behind us.

"Well, shit," Tai said.

Cayce immediately pulled a pistol from his pocket. "Kane!" he called, and drew a hand across his eyes, an unsubtle sign meaning *blind them*. The two of them fired repeatedly, the noise of the guns horribly loud even over the already deafening klaxon, and all over the room, little boxes with lenses and microphones disappeared in a burst of fragments. We had hoped to be able to slip away, leaving no physical evidence of our intrusion, but the time for subtlety was gone.

Cayce's last bullet took out the klaxon, which continued a pathetic little *mrf mrf mrf* even after its speaker was punctured. *Cameras?* he signed, and we all looked around. No one saw any, and Tai pulled out a small instrument and declared that we were free of microphones as well. "And this room is thermally insulated," they added, "so they're not going to be able to hear us through the walls."

Cayce stepped to the screen where Tai's data stick had been downloading, which now displayed a lock icon. He tapped the screen, but it didn't react at all. "Did it finish?" he asked Tai.

"Don't know, sorry."

"Shit."

That was when I knew we were in trouble. Cayce almost *never* swore.

"We're locked in," said Alicia from the door. That explained the loud *clack* we'd heard.

"Can you break us out?" I asked.

Alicia shook her head. "Lock mechanism's on the outside."

"And there's only one door," Cayce continued, quashing all hope.

Alicia pulled out her pocket comm. "Miyuki!" she called. "We're caught! Save yourself!"

"What?" came the immediate response.

The situation was moving almost too fast for me to keep up, but Alicia was right. We were certainly in deep shit, but if Miyuki got away right now, with *Zephyr*'s capabilities, she had a good chance of a permanent escape. Her reputation wasn't entangled with the rest of ours, and with the proceeds from the sale of the ship, she could have a very comfortable life. "She's right!" I called. "Run!"

"I'm sorry!" Miyuki replied, but behind her, we could all hear the sounds of the skip drive spinning up. "Good luck!" A moment later, the signal cut off.

"So, we're trapped," Tai said, "and our getaway ship just left without us. Now what?"

"Let's level the playing field," said Kane. He ignited the torch and used it to weld the door shut. We couldn't get out anyway, but now no one would be able to burst in on us without warning.

Just then a polite little buzzer sounded, along with a blinking light from a small display panel next to the door. A smashed camera sat just above it.

We all looked at each other. "Answer it," Cayce said to me. No one disagreed, so I did.

The display lit up.

It was Strange.

Ten years older. Buzz cut hair. Clean shaven. A large and fairly fresh scar on the chin. But definitely Strange.

He was wearing a Cronos Station security uniform. With commander's pips, no less.

"Hello Cannibal Club!" he said. "What a pleasant surprise to see you again after all these years. I spotted Kane, Alicia, Tai, and Shweta before you so rudely shot my cameras out. And my dear son Cayce, of course. Welcome to Cronos Station."

Cayce's hand shot out and slapped the intercom to darkness and silence. "I can explain."

I pulled out my pistol, stepped up to Cayce, and pointed it right between his eyes. "All right," I said. "Explain. But don't try to bullshit a bullshitter."

Cayce took a breath, let it out. "Yes," he said, "I've lied to you. But only when I knew you wouldn't possibly believe the truth. So I'm going to come absolutely one hundred percent clean now. I know you have no reason to believe me, but I swear it's all true. All I ask is that you hear me out."

And he began to speak.

NINE

The Desk Job

Strange—Two Years Ago

"You're going to have to do something about the boy," I said.

"He's your *son*," Lee replied.

I leaned back in my chair, clomping my booted feet on the desk. This had only been my office for a few months—Director of Security, me, can you believe it?—and I was still getting used to having a desk of my own. Not to mention a third instead of a quarter gee. "He's been your son a lot longer than he's been mine. He listens to you. Not me."

"He's been your son since he was conceived, asshole. And he might listen to you if you listened to him. I mean, really listened."

I put my feet down, leaned forward, steepled my fingers. I knew she hated that. "I've tried listening, but there's not much for me to hear. He doesn't agree with the goals of the Project. That's all."

Lee took in a breath, but decided not to say what was on her mind. I could see it cross her face. She thought a moment, then came out with a different tack. "He's only fourteen. He'll understand when he's older. I probably wouldn't have understood myself, when I was his age. But now that I'm getting old and infirm myself ..." She

240

worked her shoulder, which I knew was giving her a touch of pain and stiffness. She was only two years older than me, but forty-five was plenty old enough to start hearing the swish of the grim reaper's scythe behind her. Which was the whole point of the Project, after all.

I recognized this tactic as a play for my sympathies and deflected it. "Look, it doesn't matter why he's doing it—these destructive little stunts of his are getting out of hand. I've tried talking to him, but he just stares at me through that mop of hair and won't listen. If you can't get through to him, I'm going to have to deal with him as Director of Security instead of as his dad. And once that hat goes on, I can't play favorites. He'll be punished just the same as any other member of staff."

Lee blinked. "He's not a member of staff! He's just a *kid!*"

I shrugged. "Technically, everyone on the station is staff. Remember, it was your choice to bring him with you out here. Most of the other parents left their kids back home."

"Most of the others aren't single parents. Or they have family. I've been solo since I was a teenager." I knew this, and she knew I knew it. She was still attempting to play on my sympathies. "I wasn't going to let go of the only family I've ever had."

Pointedly implied, though not explicitly stated, was that I wasn't family. Which had been true for years, I had to admit. But now circumstances had brought us together again, and I was doing my best to be the partner and parent I'd never been during the first thirteen years of Cayce's life. "All right," I sighed. "I'll talk to him."

"That's all I can ask." She kissed me lightly on the cheek. "See you tonight."

After my afternoon rounds, I signed out and made my way down to the break room where Cayce liked to hang out after school. There was a games table there where he liked to play 3-D Go with his friend Stef, a person about his own age who was one of the test-subject volunteers.

I found Cayce there, but just sipping a soda, not engaged in a game. "Hey, scamp," I said, and recognized immediately from his reaction that this term now struck him as babyish. I filed that detail away in my memory palace; I wouldn't make that particular mistake again. But there were an infinite number of other mistakes to be made in parenting a fourteen-year-old. "Sorry. Hey, can we talk?"

He glared at me with one eye, the other hidden behind his long black hair. "Can I stop you?"

I wondered if I'd given adults that look when I was his age. Probably. He was so much like me in every other way. The resemblance to my old photos was frightening. "If you really don't want to talk right now, I can leave you to … whatever it was you were doing. But it's important."

He sighed theatrically, slumped in his chair, and slurped at his soda. "Okay, fine. Stef stood me up anyway. Talk."

I sat on the other side of his small table. Part of me wanted to mirror his posture, but I'd noticed that he was already catching on to that tactic and would consider it manipulative. Which it was. Another part of me wanted to lean forward in an intimidating way, but I recognized that it would be counterproductive. So I tried to sit naturally, but that wasn't easy. "It's about the stink bombs."

"Bomb. Singular."

"I admit we only caught you planting the one. But three others of the same type have gone off in the past month, all of them in places you could have had access to."

"Copycats." A little bit of a smirk accompanied the statement. We were playing a game of catch-me-if-you-can, all right. "Trying to get me in trouble."

"I don't think you need any help with that." I paused, collected myself, started again. "What do you think you're accomplishing?"

He took a big slurp of his soda, ending with an obnoxious gurgle. "Sand in the gears."

"The Project is too big to stop that way. If you keep trying, those gears are just going to grind you up."

"It'd be worth it." He looked at me with both eyes this time, and I'd rarely seen so much intensity in them.

"Are you really willing to risk your *life*?" I asked. "Why? Does it matter *that much* to you if the Project goes forward or not?"

"Don't you understand, Strange?" He never called me "dad." "It's the rich eating the poor! Almost literally!"

242

"We've talked about this before. Once the Project is complete and the tech is perfected, it will be made available to ..."

"Wah wah wah," he interrupted, making yakking-mouth motions with his hands. "You and I both know that this tech will always be kept for the ultra-ultra. Unless and until there's something even better, and then *that* will be kept for the ultra-ultra. If everyone is immortal, nobody's better than anyone else, and the rich can't stand that. Not to mention the solar-system-wide resource collapse that would result from widespread immortality."

"Who put *that* notion in your head?"

A sly smirk. "*System Impact Assessment, Revision 6.2.*"

I felt a brief hot snap of anger, and immediately chilled it down. "That document is secret. You will tell me where and how you obtained it, immediately."

"No I will not." He matched my chilly intonation exactly, the little shit. "I have secrets too, Strange."

I wanted to yell at him to go to his room. Instead, I took a breath, settled into a more comfortable position, and tried to address him like a peer. "Your mother and I have both committed ourselves to the Project, for the good of humanity. You should too. The problems you refer to will be resolved eventually."

"That's bullshit. You're both here for the money! And as far as that good-of-humanity crap goes, you're both here because you're afraid of your own mortality!"

That stung. Not only because it was true—he seemed to share my talent for sussing out people's secret motivations and getting under their skin—but because I realized he was mirroring my posture. "You are treading on thin ice, young man," I said, straightening. "This Project is too big and too important for you to get in its way—or in mine. If you persist in your nasty little pranks, I'll have no choice but to punish you as an adult."

"Well then, I guess I'll have to upgrade my childish little pranks to something more grown-up."

I sensed a line had just been crossed. But I wasn't sure which of us had crossed it. "What do you mean by that?"

"I guess we'll both have to find out." And he leaped up and ran away.

◆ ◆ ◆

I could have run after him. I could have called for a security officer to catch him. I could have told his mother.

I did none of those things.

Instead, I sat and considered what he had said.

It was true that I was afraid of death. Who isn't? And, as Lee had said earlier, it's easier to ignore that fear when you're fourteen than when you're forty-three. It was also true that I was here for the money. But it was more complicated than that.

It had taken me years to puzzle out the data I'd downloaded from the noteboard on Orca—to figure out that the Blue Diamond lab we'd come to raid had been converted to a different anti-aging technology, one that was still in its infancy. Scenting big money in the air—the name Terce implied this project was very close to the top of the org chart—I tracked the project across the solar system to a top-secret facility in the Kuiper Belt. That had taken more years, and the hardest part had simply been getting out here. My surprise appearance in the project director's office was just a theatrical flourish to make them take me seriously.

I arrived with a stash of data I wasn't supposed to have, about a project that wasn't supposed to exist, planning on blackmail. But as I talked with the project director, I discovered two things I hadn't expected: that I was actually excited about the project, and that Lee was part of it. And my ability to waltz into the inner sanctum of a top-secret project a million kilometers from anywhere got me an offer to head up security for the whole project.

Would I have agreed to join the project if Lee hadn't been there, if I hadn't been at an emotionally vulnerable moment, if I weren't looking at the back side of forty, if the money hadn't been so damn good? Maybe not. But all of that together was enough to make me take the offer and settle down.

But Cayce had come with the package, and that was a complication I had no experience with.

I told Lee I'd talked with Cayce and left it at that. But I also set up a background process to track his movements and alert me of any suspicious activity.

That process gave me a ping just three days later. He was in the main lab—a place he had no business being. But before I could do more than take note of the fact, I got an urgent call on my pocket comm. It was the main lab. "Get down here right away. Your son is here, and he has a bomb."

It was a real bomb. I could *smell* the explosives. He wore it strapped to his chest like a baby, the detonator was plainly visible, and he held the trigger in his hand with his thumb on the button. He was shaking with anger, so much so that I worried he would push the button by accident.

"Okay," I said, "you've made your point. Now let's disarm this thing and we can talk this over like civilized people."

"*Civilized* people," he spat, "wouldn't be doing this project in the first place. You're going to stop this atrocity right now, or I'll blow up the whole lab." He walked closer to the prototype—a room-sized machine surrounding two uncomfortable-looking chairs, each equipped with straps and electrodes.

"That won't make a difference, son. We can always rebuild." I took a step toward him, holding out one hand in what I hoped was a non-threatening manner. I really wished Shweta were here.

Cayce stepped back, raising the trigger in a clenched fist. "It'll slow you down, anyway! And maybe, just maybe, it'll make a few people here reconsider what they're doing."

His eyes were wide and white. He was right on the edge. I gestured behind me to my lieutenants, a predefined signal; they backed slowly away, closing the door behind themselves. All other personnel had already been evacuated from the section for their safety—including, at my firm insistence, Lee. "All right, son, it's just you and me now."

"I'm not your *son!*" he shouted. "Not in any way that matters! You're just my … sperm donor!"

That stung, but I let it pass. "Let go of that trigger." I said it as gently and as firmly as I could.

"If I let go, it'll go off. If I push the button, it'll go off. The only way you get out of here with your prototype intact is to convince me you'll never use it."

"That doesn't really make a lot of sense." I relaxed my stance and lowered my voice. "Come on, Cayce, this is just a disagreement. There's no need to get violent."

"I'm not the one who started the violence!" he shouted. "You killed Stef!"

"What?" But I immediately understood what had happened. Stef was a test subject. "Stef's fine," I temporized. "I saw them in the corridor just an hour ago."

He shook the fist with the trigger at me. "That's ... not ... *Stef!*" he shouted, tears in his eyes and voice ragged. "They didn't even *recognize* me!"

The situation was perilously close to getting out of hand, but it could still be defused. I smiled encouragingly and opened my arms wide. "Come here. We can talk. We can work together, find some kind of compromise."

His face showed fear and anger and determination and suspicion, but he took a step toward me. Then another.

I waited patiently.

Two more steps, and then he was in my arms. He was trembling with rage, but I hugged him as sincerely as I could. "It's going to be all right," I said.

"Goodbye, dad," he said into my shoulder.

And then the bomb went off.

I awoke to pain and smoke and pain and fire and pain and howling alarms. And pain.

I was lying on my back about three meters from where we'd been standing. My chest and stomach were a mass of blood and char. I smelled burnt hair. In fact, my beard was still on fire. I slapped it out—the burning pain in my hands was just one note in a symphony of agony.

My ears were ringing almost loud enough to drown out the blare of alarms. Blood was running out of me into a spreading pool. Every move felt like something was tearing inside. I felt myself growing weaker by the moment.

Why was I even alive? The bomb had been big enough to destroy the entire lab. But as I hauled myself to a sitting position, looking around at flaming chaos, I saw Cayce's body and I understood what had happened.

The bomb was only half-detonated. A charred crater had been blown out of the side of it—the right side, where the detonator had been inserted—but the rest was intact. Cayce, too, seemed intact, but wasn't moving.

The irregular, incomplete blast had also failed to destroy the prototype behind Cayce, but had nonetheless done considerable damage. A big chunk of the ceiling had fallen down, blocking the door with flaming debris. No one was getting in or out that way any time soon.

I crawled over to where Cayce had landed, slumped against the base of the prototype he'd tried to destroy. He didn't react to me tapping his face or calling his name, but his pulse was steady.

Unlike mine; my heartbeat felt fast and thin, hummingbird-like. I tried to take my own pulse but my fingertips had gone numb. I felt cold and faint.

I'm dying. The thought came unbidden, unwanted, unavoidable, undeniable.

And ... unacceptable.

But there was an alternative.

It wasn't easy to haul Cayce up into the second chair and put the electrodes on his head. I didn't have much left after that; I could barely manage to crawl into the first chair, and my cold and trembling fingers failed several times to fit my own electrodes. My vision was going black around the edges.

I flailed my hand around blindly until I hit the actuator.

There was a flare of light and sound and flavors, like static in all my senses at once.

I stopped being.

TEN

The Cronos Job, Part Two

Cayce—Present Day

"I woke up in the second chair."

By now the rest of the Cannibal Club was just staring, open-mouthed. Shweta had let the hand holding the pistol drop to her side. Behind me the intercom continued to blink and buzz. Strange must have decided to call back while I was telling my story. His story?

Our story.

I kept talking. "I felt … words can't really convey just how weird I felt. It was like my body was a vac suit that didn't fit. I tried to sit up and just fell on the floor. I couldn't make my limbs work, and my vision was all wonky."

"The first thing I did when I got myself sort of under control was to check out … my body. Strange's body. It was so weird to see the mole on the wrong cheek. I still *thought* I was Strange, but when I touched my own face, I *felt* Cayce's smooth cheeks. Cayce's nose under my fingers. Cayce's fingers. I knew that if I looked in a mirror, I'd see brown eyes, not blue."

Shweta, the queen of being able to disguise herself as others, gasped, horrified by the implications.

I had to continue the story. "I was alive, and yet I was looking down at my own body—my *original* body. I couldn't find a pulse. There was blood everywhere. The lab was still on fire, and the door was still blocked. The smoke was getting thick, and I was coughing like crazy. So I left ... the body there and took an escape pod."

Launching the pod had been easy—just slam the door and pull the big red lever. Disabling its location beacon had been a lot harder. Cayce—the original Cayce—couldn't have done it. Probably wouldn't have done it, even if he'd had the knowledge. But as I was tumbling away from the station I realized that in this body—my son's teenage form—I'd have a really, really hard time explaining myself. All anyone would believe is I had just killed the director of security while attempting to destroy the prototype. My staff might just shoot first and not ask questions at all.

So I ripped out the beacon and triggered the emergency skip. The autopilot wasn't fast, but it would get me to safety before my air and water ran out. By the same token, I had plenty of time along the way to rejigger the course so I wouldn't actually wind up where they would be waiting for me.

"In the escape pod I had a lot of time to think," I said aloud, then paused. "I had always been selfish. My last act in my original body had been to save myself—not save my son." I grimaced. "I can't take that back."

The chief reaction in the room was horror. I couldn't blame them.

The intercom was still insistently buzzing and I gestured to it. "I have no idea how Strange—the original Strange—isn't dead. I didn't find a pulse when I left the body." I knew he wouldn't wait too much longer for an answer, so I picked up the pace. "Long story short, going through this procedure—living in my son's body—I started to change. The horror of what I had done sank into even my selfish soul. I realized that Cayce had been right all along." I hesitated, hoping the Club would understand. "I decided to pick up where he'd left off. To destroy the Cronos Project, for good this time. And I knew I'd need all of *you* to do it." I looked around at them—at those faces I'd known for so long, and yet had only technically met for the first time in the last year. They looked back with expressions of disbelief, anger, suspicion, and astonishment. I kept talking. "So I told you what I had to, to get your wholehearted cooperation. My plan was to come back here, destroy the database and the prototype, then 'discover' that Strange was dead and get away. I had no idea he'd survived."

"You killed your own *son*," Alicia said. Flat. In shock. And not wrong. "You wiped his mind. You're a monster."

"I was *dying*," I responded. Not defensively—at least I tried not to sound defensive—but as a statement of fact. "I wasn't thinking straight. And I thought … okay, I hoped against hope, despite what I knew about the process, that Cayce would … that he and I would coexist somehow." I tapped my temple. "But there's no sign of him in here. He's gone." I sighed. "I'm never going to forgive myself for it, but I don't want anyone else to be … *eliminated* like he was. Which is why I decided that I needed to come back here and stop the project."

"Maybe there *is* still some of him in there with you," said Tai. They pointed to their head.

I shook my head. "It's not here." I tapped my forehead. "It's here." I slapped my heart. "I'm more like Cayce now because, physically, I *am* him. Hormones, brain structures, enteric neurons, I don't know. But when I think about some of the things I did when I was Strange … I get a gut reaction of horror and shame."

I looked around at the other Club members. I knew that they had just had a *lot* of new information dumped on them and it would take them some time to integrate it and decide whether to believe me or Strange—the original Strange, who had never experienced the impact of continuing on in his own son's body. Who had never found his humanity in the process. But I knew what a dick he was— how much of a dick I used to be—and I couldn't afford to wait for them to process and make a decision.

So I forced the issue.

I slapped the button under the intercom. Strange's face appeared immediately. "I've told them the truth," I said, seizing the conversational high ground. "About how you sold out to Aquila. About how and why I tried to destroy the project. And about how you put me in the machine and tried to replace my mind with yours." I chose my words carefully. Strange had no way to know whether or not the transfer had succeeded, whether or not some fragment of Cayce had survived, or how I'd changed since we'd parted. If he continued to think of me as Cayce—just a punk kid, not his intellectual equal— he might underestimate me at a critical juncture.

"*Sold out* is such a loaded phrase," he said, looking me right in the eye. I reminded myself that he couldn't see me. At least, I was *pretty* sure we'd shot out all the cameras. "I came here with blackmail in mind, but an unexpected opportunity presented itself and I took it." He shrugged. "Any of you would have done the same. Wouldn't you, Kane? Tai? Shweta?"

My heart hammered and I slowed my breathing to try bring it under control. Of *course* Strange would use what he knew about the others to manipulate them to his side. It was what he'd—what I'd—always done, and he was very good at it. I could see them giving his words serious consideration. "It doesn't matter why you joined the project *initially*," I shot back. "Once you were on board, once you realized exactly what the project was and what the consequences would be, you became complicit. You could have fought the project from inside, like I did. Instead you bought into it."

"You're young, Cayce," Strange replied. "When you're as old as I am, you will have a different perspective on the value of life."

I didn't mention that I *was* as old as him. "What about the lives of the young people whose bodies are 'repurposed' so that older, richer people can keep living? People like Stef?"

Strange shook his head. "Stef was a volunteer. A stepping stone. Once the project is fully operational, we'll be using cloned bodies. Mindless."

"That's what the plan says," I said, "but it'll never actually happen. It's not economically viable." This was only a suspicion on my part, but Strange suspected it as well. I knew this—I'd *been* him. "Healthy warm bodies are cheap and easy to obtain, if you don't give a shit about where they come from."

I wasn't arguing with Strange, not really. I knew exactly how long and how hard he'd been working to convince himself that the Project was a righteous cause, and I wasn't going to change his mind in the next ten minutes. What I was really doing was trying to get him to show his hand so the Club would side with me.

251

Was I being just as manipulative of them as Strange was?

"Look, this doesn't matter right now," Strange said, taking control of the conversation. "Our immediate problem is that you've been caught red-handed." He placed a slight stress on the word *our*, which certainly didn't escape Shweta's notice, or Alicia's. "I may be head of security here, but you've left me little room to maneuver." He folded his hands on the desk before him and leaned in toward the camera. "If you surrender, I can keep you alive. If you don't …" He held up his hands in a show of helpless uncertainty. "Once you're in custody, I can try to negotiate your release. Or perhaps I can find a way to engineer your escape. But if you don't surrender *right now*, I can't be held responsible for what happens next."

Strange was a very good liar, but as everyone eventually learns, you can't fool yourself. *If we surrender*, I signed to the Club, *we die.*

But which of us would they believe?

I looked around. Kane was the most straightforward; he'd come in with me, and would stick with that unless and until he sensed advantage in changing sides. Alicia wanted everyone to get along, but her face suggested she was currently more sympathetic to me than Strange. Tai always knew which side their bread was buttered on … and Strange seemed to hold all the power in this situation. I'd have to show, somehow, that wasn't really the case. And Shweta, who had been suspicious of me all along—hell, she'd pulled a gun on me just a minute ago—would be the toughest nut to crack. She and Strange had a *lot* of history together and it was clear from her body language that she would choose him over me in a heartbeat. But if I could get her on my side, Tai and Alicia would come along.

I decided that it was time to reveal an uncomfortable truth. "It's odd that you would help Shweta like you did, though," I said to Strange, "if you didn't intend us to wind up here." Everyone looked quizzically at me for the apparent non sequitur.

Strange's face didn't show surprise, outwardly, but I saw his mind working. "There are factors of which you are unaware," he said, an excellent dodge.

Shweta's eyes showed that she, too, was thinking fast. "Your idea about fogging the detector net was brilliant. Couldn't have pulled it off without that. Where did that come from?"

"It was suggested by something you said," he replied. "I forget what, exactly." Another excellent dodge.

"I see," Shweta said noncommittally, then, "Give us a minute to talk this over." She cut him off before he could protest.

"We'll be lucky if he gives us a whole minute," I said.

Shweta looked hard at me. "So it was *you* who helped me plan my escape from the Malakbel Project. Why did you pretend to be Strange then, if the rest of the time you were pretending to be Cayce with us?" she asked.

I smiled. Despite her anger, I could tell she was hooked. Now I had to reel her in. "If unknown teenager Cayce had come to you out of the blue with a plan to steal the fastest ship in the system, you wouldn't have given him the time of day. Even if I could have convinced you I was Strange's kid. I had to approach you as Strange, then hand off to Cayce."

"And why keep that lie to yourself until now?"

"You were suspicious enough of me already. I needed to wait until our relationship was on firmer footing."

She tilted back her head and looked down her nose at me. "And *now* is that time?" But there was a little grin on her face and I knew I'd landed her.

I shrugged. "No time like the present."

She blew out a breath. "All right. We'll deal with that later. But for now, I'm with you. God help me."

We looked at each other, then around at the Club. Kane seemed a little confused by recent events, but he seemed amenable, and the rest—especially Alicia, thank god—were in as well. "So," I said, summarizing the situation, "we're trapped, the whole station knows we're here, we've lost our getaway ship, and as soon as Strange gets tired of waiting, he will pull the fire alarm."

Everyone knew what that meant. We were sealed into the computer core, and if the fire suppression system were triggered, it would replace all the oxygen in the room with an inert gas. Which would also knock us out in short order. Whether or not we woke up after that would depend on how long Strange decided to wait before flushing the room with fresh air. And if I knew him—and I knew him *very* well—he would wait just long enough to be sure we were all dead while retaining plausible deniability that he had done so.

Tai was the first to recover the power of speech. "So what are we going to do?"

"I have a plan."

The plan depended on outsmarting someone who knew all of us intimately, especially me. So we had to act against type as much as possible.

Which is why I had Kane negotiate for us, rather than Shweta.

Kane was a perfect negotiator. He wouldn't let anything slip, because we hadn't told him what we were doing and he wasn't going to figure it out on his own. All he needed to do was buy us a little time.

"Yeah, uh, hi," he said to the intercom. "So … I guess you're in charge here now?"

Strange didn't hesitate. "Yes. And I'm holding all the cards. I know who you are, I know why you're here, I know all your tricks. You can surrender, unconditionally, right now, or you can die. Your choice."

I was ninety-five percent sure that surrender wouldn't actually save us. The five percent was if Lee was in the room with him and overrode him, but I was confident he'd have shut her out if at all possible. I just gestured *keep talking* to Kane and kept working.

"So … what do you do here, exactly?"

"Head of security." He snorted. "I suppose you might call me a black hat, but I don't like labels. That being said, I'm not exactly a white hat either, and you know I don't make idle threats. So are you going to open that door right now, or are you going to make us cut our way through and take the bodies out later?"

"We, uh, we can't open the door," Kane replied. "It's kind of welded shut." Which was true, but not the best negotiating tactic. I cursed under my breath and cut off another length of tubing, passing it to Shweta. Tai, meanwhile, continued typing furiously on their tablet.

Strange gave a little half-chuckle. "You do realize that reduces my options to one?" he said.

"What?" Kane said.

And then I came up from behind and put a plastic bag over his head.

A moment later came a roaring rush, and a dense white fog flooded out of vents at the top and bottom of each wall panel. I barely got my own bag over my head in time.

The flow of gas from the oxyacetylene torch's oxygen cylinder was harsh and chill and tasted of metal and oil. It wasn't exactly Inner Belt Standard Breathing Mix—it was pure oxygen, more or less, except for the industrial contaminants and metal slivers. Even the connector on the cylinder was deliberately incompatible with those on suits, because you *really* didn't want to be breathing this stuff. But it was better for us than the fire suppressant gas.

I felt the hose slipping from the laughably bad seal I'd improvised, and took one last cold dizzying breath as it fell hissing away. It took everything I had not to cough that last lungful of oxygen away, but I held it … held it … held it … then blew it out and ripped the bag from my head.

The fog had already mostly dissipated. Tai, Shweta, and Kane still clutched the bags around their necks. Alicia's bag had fallen off and she lay still on the floor. I found the cut-off hose end that had fallen out of my bag, still hissing weakly, and took as much of a breath from it as I could as I brought it over to her. There wasn't much pressure left but I held it under her nose, still holding my own breath, until the last trickle of gas faded away.

The room fell silent then, save for the slow drip of condensation from the vents where the cold gas had spewed. We all held our breaths as long as we could, until first Kane and then Shweta and finally I coughed out what we'd been holding and started breathing what was in the room. Which was non-toxic, but decidedly lacking in oxygen, and we were all soon gasping like fish.

The oxy cylinder had bought us just a minute or two. Would it be enough? *Plausible deniability*, I kept thinking over and over as I coughed and choked and the darkness began creeping into the edges of my vision.

And then came another roaring rush as pure air, chill enough to come with its own burst of fog, came out of the same vents. We all rushed to the vents—except Alicia, I had to drag her—and gulped it down eagerly.

255

Alicia came to a minute later, gasping and choking. Thank god.

"Okay," I hacked out, my voice a rough rattle. "We've got maybe ten, fifteen minutes until they cut through that door. Kane? Tai? How's our timing?"

Kane checked his wrist. "First signal's going to arrive in about three minutes. The next one at seven. Then ten, sixteen, twenty, and twenty-one." I nodded.

Tai was already busy on their tablet, which they'd kept working on right up until the fire alarm went off and had pulled out again as soon as they'd been able to breathe. "Almost ready ..."

"Pull the trigger on that as soon as you can," I told Tai, then joined Shweta, who was helping Alicia to sit up and cough the last of the crap out of her lungs.

The intercom, I noted, wasn't blinking. Strange must be certain we were dead, or willing to wait until they could cut through the door. He might be arguing with Lee already, or maybe she was still in the dark. But that argument would come, and soon.

But before we could take advantage of that, we had to bullshit a bullshitter. Big time.

Cayce had been a fool—a young, innocent fool. The Cronos Project wasn't some amateur operation that could be stopped by blowing up one piece of equipment. Nor would simply exposing the project work. The people behind it were too entrenched, and had too much power, for public pressure to do anything but drive them a little deeper underground. No, Cronos had to be thoroughly destroyed, smashed so hard that it couldn't recover. It was a massive project, governmental in scale, and the information needed to continue development in case of disaster was backed up in a dozen places, half of them safely offsite.

So my plan to take the project down—the plan I'd begun formulating in the escape pod, and had continued to refine over the following months and years—started with the backups.

While the rest of us had been supervising the refit of *Zephyr* at Laurent's Place, Kane had been flitting hither and yon across the Belt like the Time Bomb Fairy, setting explosives on all the offsite backup locations. His task was made easier by the fact that the project directors, not trusting this top-secret data to any of the commercial backup services, had placed most of the backups on unoccupied and uncharted rocks. It was security by obscurity, but as the coordinates were firmly stored in Strange's memory palace—and thus mine—it was a simple matter of rigging them all to blow. Only one of the backups was at an attended facility, an Aquila Corp data store, and in that case, it had been sufficient to plant the bomb nearby. Kane had taken real pleasure in building that big one.

The timers were all set to go off at staggered times so that the news of their destruction, crawling across the System at the speed of light, would all reach Cronos Station at about the same time—right after Tai's virus had finished corrupting the main database and the onsite backups.

There was the small problem that we didn't know whether the virus had completed loading before we were locked out. But that wouldn't matter if we didn't survive for the next half hour or so.

Reinforcing that concern, a harsh buzzing whine suddenly started at the door. Hull saw, sounded like. Which was good, from our perspective—it wouldn't go quite as fast as a torch. Still, they'd be through in ten or twelve minutes at most. "Tai?" I asked. "How's it going?"

"Just a sec more … okay!" With a flourish, they pressed a control on the tablet. "Done!"

Nothing visible happened.

We all looked at each other. The saw kept sawing. Alicia kept coughing. Kane kept loading his guns.

"Is it working?" Shweta asked.

Tai peered at the tablet. "It's working. I'm sure of it. Maybe they haven't noticed yet …"

And then came yelling from outside, and the saw stuttered to a halt.

The yelling continued, but even without the noise of the saw, we couldn't make out what they were saying. There was a lot of it though—sounded like a pretty intense argument—and it ended with a clearly audible curse, a clatter of equipment, and the sound of running boots.

Then silence.

And then the roaring rumble of a ship thrusting hard away from the dock in clear violation of normal safe operating procedures.

"I think it worked," I said. I must confess it came out a little smug.

The key to our survival was the hack Tai had perpetrated to get us safely onto the station's roof—a virus whose purpose was to make the station's nav system see *Zephyr* as a random space rock. Knowing that the signals from the destroyed backup sites were just about to arrive, Tai had tweaked the hack to add several more random space rocks to the nav system's model of the solar system. Each of these rocks seemed to appear out of nowhere just before striking and eliminating one of the backups … and one more, far larger than the others, had also just appeared out of nowhere, heading toward Cronos Station itself.

There was no such thing as stealth in space, not really. But when your backups started getting destroyed in a coordinated fashion—and multiple sources confirmed that they were indeed gone—and the evidence was that they were being eliminated by rocks that weren't there a minute ago, it was less impossible that the rocks were somehow hidden from view until they appeared than that they had teleported or manifested out of the vacuum. And when one of those rocks was barreling toward you, massive and unstoppable and just an hour or two away, it might seem prudent to evacuate first and figure out how this happened later.

Yes, it had been a desperate gamble. But I had the advantage of knowing Strange, and his relationship with the Cronos management, intimately. I knew that his combination of smarts and caution, combined with the very limited time I'd given him to react, would lead him to take the action I wanted.

So now we were alone on the station, or very nearly so. We'd have an hour or two until they figured out that the giant rock tumbling toward Cronos Station was nothing more than a phantom and came back, pissed and loaded for bear. That might just be enough time for us to finish the job we came here to do. No, scratch that—it *had* to be.

But first we had to get out of the computer core we'd welded ourselves into.

We had, of course, used up all the oxygen we'd brought for the torch. But an air-acetylene mixture does burn, just not as hot as oxy-acetylene ... and we didn't have to cut through any walls, just break the rather hasty weld Kane had made to seal the door. It took him less than five minutes to undo his own previous work.

We emerged to an untidy scene, with the hull saw and its accoutrements lying around where they'd been abandoned in haste. I'd hoped that there might also be some spare guns or ammunition, but, alas, the evacuation hadn't been *that* hasty.

The blinking word EVACUATE dominated every visible display, along with a map with moving arrows directing to the nearest available escape pod. But we wouldn't be following those. "I need another secure terminal," Tai said to me. "This one's hard-locked."

Dusty portions of my memory palace, rooms I hadn't accessed since I was Strange, rotated into place. "Nearest one is in the main lab." I pointed. "Next section, two decks up."

"We stick together," Shweta said, and her tone brooked no argument. "I'm not letting you out of my sight."

"I support this plan." I had reasons of my own to keep the Club together.

We moved out with me in the lead—I was the only one who knew where we were going—and Kane watching behind. We couldn't be certain we were completely alone on the station, though as we moved through empty corridors, it became easier and easier to believe that we were.

We paused in the corridor outside the main lab, checking cautiously in all directions before entering. It was an obvious place for any remaining station personnel to be hanging out. But it seemed our ruse had worked, and every last Cronos staffer had evacuated.

The passcode I had for the door was over three years old, but I wasn't too surprised to find that it still worked. I smiled grimly, remembering how the project director had pushed back against my own earlier attempts to enforce frequent changes. But as the door swished open, revealing the lab inside—it looked just about the same as it had before I'd blown it up—I felt the smile fade.

I had a lot of memories about this place.

As Strange it had been the core of my job and the seat of my hopes for the Project. It was also the place where I'd been blown up by my own child. As Cayce, or whatever I was now, it was the place I'd been reborn, in fire and smoke and blood and confusion. And it was where Cayce, the original Cayce, had ceased existing. In some ways I'd died here—twice. And now I was back, to kill it for good.

Alicia was right behind me, and I turned to help her when one of her walker wheels got stuck in the door track. But then there came a siren.

I looked up to see the emergency blast door coming down.

I pulled Alicia inside just as the door slammed shut, followed by the clank of latches. Shit. I rolled to my feet and pulled out my pistol in one motion.

"So predictable," said Strange. He had two pistols of his own, coolly trained on me and on Alicia. I knew immediately that if either of us made a move, both would die.

"Aren't you worried about the incoming rock?" I said, trying and failing to match his cool.

"Not once I knew *you* were still here. Oh, it was a very good ruse, and obviously one months in the planning. Convincing enough that I let the Director evacuate everyone else, in fact. But something about it bothered me, and so I stayed behind long enough to check the security cameras … and when I saw you emerge from the computer core, I knew you'd be heading here. I've already alerted the escaping staff. They'll be back in an hour or less." He shook his head sadly, though his eyes didn't move from mine. "It's over, Cayce. You aren't going to stop the project."

"That's where you're wrong," I said. "Even if you kill us all now, we've *already* stopped the project."

He chuckled at that, the bastard. "That's where *you're* wrong. Oh, yes, I know you've destroyed most of our backups. Very clever. But you didn't get *all* of them, and as for the main system … I'm afraid

Tai's hack wasn't quite quick enough. The data there is still very much intact. You've lost."

You can't lie to yourself, and he was lying about the backups. We'd gotten every one. But the main system was indeed still intact.

"So why don't you just shoot me now?" I asked. I knew the answer, but asking the question would stall for time and would help to mislead him about just how well I understood him.

"Curiosity," he said, as I'd known he would. And though neither gun wavered, his attention fixed more firmly on me. "When I woke up in the infirmary—you *did* kill me in the lab, technically, but the techs got to me just in time and the Cronos Project has some amazing doctors on staff—and found you gone, I had no idea whether the transfer had gone through or not. Of course, I didn't tell my superiors that I'd used the machine. But now that we've met, I can tell from your behavior that the transfer was at least partially successful." His finger tightened just slightly on that trigger. "So who *are* you?"

And then there was a clank, and the blast door came rushing up.

Strange immediately fired through the opening—one shot from each pistol—and I took advantage of the distraction to dive and roll to my right, fetching up behind a sturdy console. Alicia, I noted, had also dropped to the floor and was crawling away in the opposite direction. I unshipped my own pistol and fired blindly toward Strange to provide her some cover.

With Alicia stuck inside, Strange hadn't expected anyone outside to be able to open the door. He didn't know Kane had been taking lockpicking lessons.

A tense silence followed, punctuated by scuffling feet—Strange was on the move, but I couldn't tell exactly where—and the hissing spitting sound of something electrical that had been pierced by a bullet. I saw Alicia reach another console like mine and pull herself behind it. No sound from outside the now-open door.

I scuttled to the far end of my console and peered out, exposing just one eye and the muzzle of my pistol. I couldn't see Strange, but if I were him, I would have taken the high ground: the observation console. It sat atop a raised dais at the far end of the room, with its back to a wall, and from there, he would not only have clear sight-lines to all corners of the lab, but he could control much of the equipment.

Without hesitation, I leaped from behind my console to the next one to the right. Strange's pistol barked once—the shot came from behind the observation console, as I'd expected—but he missed. I couldn't count on that.

We both knew I would poke my head out to see if I had a better shot at him from my new vantage. But would I emerge from the same side, the opposite side, or the top? I decided to accept that whatever I came up with, he would also predict. Instead I crawled silently *away* from him, keeping the console between myself and him, to a place where I could get a view through the door.

Kane, Tai, and Shweta were crouched in the corridor, just around the doorway corner. Kane immediately noticed my movement and raised his pistol, but just as quickly realized who I was and lowered it, tapping the other two and pointing to me. *Situation?* Shweta signed to me.

I summarized the situation, indicating Strange and Alicia's positions by pointing. *You three come in*, I signed. *I'll cover. Tai, to me. Kane, Shweta, to Alicia.* All three acknowledged the plan.

I checked and reloaded my pistol, then took a breath.

I couldn't outthink Strange. Couldn't surprise him, either. Anything I might do, he'd anticipate subconsciously. And trying to factor this in would just lead to a pointless cycle of indecision.

So I closed my eyes and picked up an empty shell casing from the floor. It was still warm. I turned it over and over in my hand, eyes still closed. Then opened my hand and looked.

The casing pointed left.

I leaped in the indicated direction—back to my first console, which wouldn't have been my first choice, which was the whole point of the exercise—firing at Strange's position as I went. A moment later the other three came charging through the door, Kane in the lead, all three firing at Strange as they ducked right and left respectively.

It almost worked.

Kane's curse was audible even over the fusillade of gunfire. I saw a spray of blood from his leg and he collapsed on his face in the middle of the floor. Sitting duck.

"Strange!" Tai yelled even as they landed beside me. "Don't shoot! *I love you!*"

That completely-out-of-the-black declaration stunned *everyone* momentarily—except Kane, bless every unromantic bone in his body, who managed to drag himself over to where Shweta could pull him the rest of the way out of danger. Strange recovered and fired twice … but a moment too late.

I stared at Tai. *Really?* I mouthed, aghast.

Tai blinked at me. *No*, they signed, with a sidewise sneer indicating just how ridiculous they found the concept.

I looked across the doorway, where Alicia was tying an improvised bandage over Kane's leg wound. Looked like the outer left thigh, just above the knee. Not life threatening but it would greatly reduce his mobility. Shweta gave us a cautious thumbs-up, which might indicate that the situation was under control or that she approved of Tai's tactic. Maybe both. It had been exactly the sort of thing she would do.

Now what? Strange had the high ground and the home field advantage, and furthermore his cavalry was less than an hour away. To our credit, we had him pinned down and outnumbered, though Kane was injured.

We *had* to destroy the last copy of the project data, and in less than an hour.

"There's the secure terminal," I whispered to Tai, pointing. It was near the lab's far wall, and I couldn't see any route from here to there that wasn't horribly exposed to Strange's position at the observation console.

Neither could Tai. "Is there another one?"

I consulted my memory palace, shook my head. "Not anywhere nearby. Is there any other way to wipe the main system? It's the very last copy of the project data."

Tai's lips pursed for a long time. "Not that I can think of."

And then I heard a whir and hum of electric motors. I recognized the sound immediately and ducked, dragging Tai down with me.

A huge metallic claw came whooshing through the space Tai's head had just vacated.

"What the *fuck*?" Tai shouted, even as the claw came back for a second pass. I grabbed them by the shoulders and took us both into a diving roll across the room's open center, hoping that with

Strange's hands busy on the material-handling system's controls, he wouldn't be able to fire while we were exposed.

The hope paid off, and we managed to squeeze under another console, out of the claw's reach, without a shot being fired. We were four or five meters closer to the secure terminal. But the material-handling system, on its overhead tracks, could reach nearly anywhere in the lab, and it had a lift capacity of over seven tonnes. A high-pitched ascending whine from above ended in a horrific crunch as the claw closed on our console, peppering Tai and I with fragments as it crushed the console and wrenched it from the floor.

Tai and I scrambled away, still heading toward the terminal. This time we heard shots from the dais—Strange must have figured out how to do two things at once. But a fusillade of bullets responded from behind us, as Shweta, Kane, and Alicia fired on Strange's revealed position.

In the chaos, I took the opportunity to poke my head up very briefly. I didn't know exactly where I'd landed and I figured Strange wouldn't know either.

There he was. Crouched behind the observation console, as I'd figured. Bullet holes pocked its forward surface, but the console was packed with equipment and the odds of a bullet going through with enough velocity to do serious harm were slim. He could almost certainly hold out back there until his staff returned.

From here, I had a shot at him, but before I could raise my pistol he noticed me and whipped his own in my direction. I fired as I ducked, but it was nothing but a wild hope. A moment later, the claw smashed down on the position I'd just vacated, spattering my face with bits of shattered flooring. I crab-scrambled away, but it followed, smashing chairs and equipment racks aside as it came.

And then something smacked into my side, shoving me out of the oncoming claw's path and into the far wall. Then the claw slammed against its stop. I was just beyond its reach.

The "something" was Shweta. "Thanks," I panted, as we hugged the wall. The claw's servos whined for a moment as it tried to reach us, but Strange knew the system's limitations and gave up quickly. I grabbed Shweta and we scrambled behind a server rack, just as bullets rang against the wall where we'd been. "How's Kane?" I asked.

"He'll live, but he's not going anywhere. He can shoot from there, though." She gestured. Kane and Alicia, near the door, could keep Strange pinned down and do at least a little good when the defenders returned. It was something.

I considered the situation. "Strange will perceive me as the biggest threat," I said. "But he also knows that he has to keep Tai out of the secure terminal." I looked over to where Tai was huddled under a console, unable to move toward the terminal without coming into Strange's line of fire. "We need a distraction."

But before I could formulate a plan, Alicia screamed, "*Cayce!*" Immediately, I flattened myself on the floor, hearing bullets *pang* off the wall above me. Strange must have shifted to a position from which he could see me. I slither-crawled forward, as fast and as low as I could, while shots and ricochets sounded all around me, ending up crammed under Tai's console with them. Shweta was safe under a table nearby, closer to Strange's position. Alicia and Kane were still where they had been. Kane was reloading.

I heard the whir of motors, which told me two things: Strange had returned to the material-handling system control panel, and our covering console was about to be removed. "Kane!" I shouted. "Target the claw's tracks!"

Kane's rifle shifted upward and he hammered the ceiling with a couple dozen rounds. A moment later, there came a crunch, followed by a keening whine. Sounded like the claw had hit the damaged section of track and gotten stuck, as I'd hoped.

Strange wouldn't waste time trying to get it unstuck. "Move!" I told Tai, and we moved, scrambling toward the secure terminal. But I paused in the shelter of the first heavy piece of equipment we came to, holding Tai back—just as Strange's bullets slammed into the floor right ahead of my nose. Kane's rifle clattered back at Strange, silencing his pistol for the moment.

I looked around, making sure that everyone was safe for the moment, then closed my eyes and visualized the room. Strange had been at the handling system controls a moment ago. Kane's covering fire would have driven him to his right, from which position he'd be able to pin me and Tai down completely, with a clear view to both sides of us. And he'd be out of Kane's line of fire. Stalemate.

But … if Kane was out of Strange's line of fire, Alicia was out of Strange's.

"I saw you hack the main system back in the computer core," I whispered to Tai. "You just stuck that data stick into the socket. Is that all that needs to happen?"

"Yeah. But we're not getting there anytime soon."

"No, we aren't. But …"

I outlined my plan to Tai via whispers and to the others via sign. Alicia hesitated for a long moment before acknowledging her part in it. I couldn't blame her.

On my signal, I signed. Everyone indicated their readiness and I counted down on my fingers. *Five. Four. Three. Two. One.* "Go!" I shouted.

Kane immediately leaned out and started pummeling Strange's position with bullets. Meanwhile, I leaped toward the secure terminal, my right hand reaching out for it … but I held onto the leg of my console with my left hand, which stopped me in mid-leap. I felt a sharp pain in my shoulder from the sudden stop, but it worked: Strange's bullets peppered the spot where I would have landed if I'd kept going. I yanked myself back under the console before he could react.

I pulled myself upright and looked around. Alicia held up the data stick triumphantly! Tai had tossed it to her across the intervening space while Kane and I had distracted Strange. She and Kane exchanged a glance, then she began dragging herself across the floor toward the secure terminal. If I was correct about Strange's position, she would remain out of his sight until she had almost reached it.

And if I was wrong, she was a sitting duck.

Slowly, painfully, Alicia crept toward the terminal.

I had to know where Strange was. Despite the ringing in my ears, I thought I heard him shifting to his right. From there, he'd have a better shot at me … and he'd be able to see Alicia. "Strange!" I called. "What's your end game?"

No response. Didn't expect one, really. But the sounds of movement ceased. Or was he just moving more cautiously?

"The project is *over*, Strange. I've salted the networks with copies of what I know. If I die, it becomes public knowledge."

"Don't bullshit a bullshitter," Strange replied. I cursed inwardly. Can't lie to yourself. But at least I could be sure, from the direction of his voice, that he couldn't see Alicia ... and as long as I kept him talking, he was unlikely to hear her.

"This game isn't over yet," I called back.

"Not quite yet, but in about forty-five minutes, you'll be very badly outnumbered. And once we've eliminated you, we'll be back to the status quo ante."

"I can understand why you want to kill me," I asked—still stalling for time, as Alicia kept creeping toward the terminal—"since I'm the one who almost killed you. But why the rest of the Club?"

"I'm sorry, but they know too much. I can't risk compromising the project."

Now Tai spoke up. That was okay, Strange already knew exactly where both of us were. "We know too much about *you*, you mean," they said. "We know you sold out to Aquila, and we know you *killed your own son*. You put him in that machine there and pushed the button to replace his mind with yours."

"I was *dying*," he responded, exactly as I had. It came out sounding pretty damn defensive. "I wasn't thinking straight. And I hoped that Cayce and I would ... coexist, somehow."

"You *wanted* to hope," I replied. "But you knew better."

No response. No, wait, not *no* response. A slight scuff of shoe on flooring. Definitely moving to the right.

Alicia had reached the terminal and was pulling herself up onto the chair. In moments, she'd be in a position to insert the data stick in the socket ... and Strange would have a clear shot at her.

"Dammit, Strange!" I yelled. Standing up. Making myself visible to him. Saving Alicia. Stopping the project. Whatever the cost. "Take responsibility for your actions, for once in your fucking life!"

Strange raised his pistol. His eyes locked on mine. And then I saw the calculation in them, swift as lightning. I've had people tell me how disquieting it can be to see that, but I'd never before witnessed it for myself.

He turned the gun away from me, toward the secure terminal.

Toward Alicia.

Sitting duck.

"Alicia!" I screamed.

Strange pulled the trigger.

And then Shweta leaped up from the base of the dais, where she'd silently crept as Strange and I were talking, and clobbered him over the head with a big crescent wrench.

I don't remember making my way across the space between me and Alicia. I just found myself there, catching her as she fell away from the terminal.

The terminal which was spiderwebbed from the bullet that had pierced the screen.

The bullet that had just missed Alicia's head.

"I didn't make it," she sobbed. "He shot it before I could …"

I shushed her, looking over to where Shweta was none-too-gently fastening the unconscious and bleeding Strange's hands behind him with sticky-strips.

"Nice shot!" Kane called to Shweta. "Didn't think you had it in you!"

Shweta snorted and gave the sticky-strip one last vindictive tug. "Fuck subtlety."

I brought Alicia's walker from where she'd left it near the door, and we gathered together in the open center of the room. Oil dripped from the dead material-handling claw. Strange lay unconscious at Shweta's feet, but she still held a gun on him.

"That could have gone better," said Kane. He was vertical, at least, but leaning heavily on a length of dexion strut as an improvised crutch. He didn't let the pain show in his face, but he wouldn't be much good if it came to a fight.

I nodded in acknowledgement. "But we have the station to ourselves for the next"—I checked my watch—"thirty-five minutes or so."

Tai shook their head. "We need to leave *now*. As it is, we'll have a hard time slipping past the returning escape craft."

"You can do what you like," I said, "but I'm not leaving until I've destroyed the last copy of the project data. And I have a way in mind to do that *and* give us cover for our escape."

They all looked at me. I took a deep breath.

"We have to blow the station's fusion plant."

After the shouting slowed down a little, I walked over to a wall display that still showed a station map with moving arrows pointing the way to the nearest escape pod. Almost all of the pod locations were just open circles now, but there were a few blinking green dots remaining, indicating available pods. "The plant is here," I said, tapping the jewel in the station's "wedding ring" design. "We can be there in ten minutes." I glanced at Kane, then at Alicia. "Maybe fifteen. But it won't take very long to rig it to blow, and there's an escape pod right here." I tapped a green dot just past the fusion plant control room. "Once the plant starts overheating, the station will send out a warning signal that will make all those incoming pods turn right around. Between that and the radio noise from the blast, we'll have no trouble slipping away. And I can jigger the autopilot to get us somewhere safe. I've done it before."

The shouting started again, and I could understand why. We were all spaceborn, after all, and the idea of blowing up a perfectly good station—especially the one on which we were currently standing, with no escape craft currently in hand—was a bit of a hard sell. But I would not be moved. Destroying the Cronos Project was the one thing I'd had as my life goal since leaving this place two years ago, and I was willing to risk *everything* else to get it. So no one else's child would go through what mine had.

Kane was the first to come around, but he'd always been a fan of explosions. Shweta was next. She had a long-standing hatred for Earth-based corporations in general and Aquila in particular, and the massive blow this would deal to them was an opportunity she couldn't pass up. Once they came over to my side Alicia joined them, and finally even Tai had to admit it was our best chance at finishing the job we had come here to do. Even if I'd lied to them all at first about what exactly that job was.

"So we are all agreed then?" I asked, looking around.

"Yeah," Kane snarled. "But what about *this* one?" He gave the unconscious Strange a kick. "I vote we shoot him now and dump the body out an airlock."

My reaction to that was ... complex, but I shook my head. "No. Not even him."

Shweta cocked her head at me. "He killed *his own son*."

"And I *was* him when he did it." I looked her in the eye. "People are complicated. Strange more than most. No, we take him with. Keep him tied up, deal with him later. Agreed?"

If nothing else, we all agreed we didn't have time to argue about it. But they made me be the one to haul Strange's unconscious body, which made me even slower than Kane and Alicia as we made our way down empty corridors, still illuminated by blinking EVACU-ATE signs, to the fusion plant control room.

Fusion control was one of the places where the entry passcode *was* changed frequently, and it was a long random sequence of digits, impossible to guess. But between Strange's memory palace, Tai's hacking abilities, Alicia's skills, and Kane's hands, we managed to get past the lock. Shweta kept her gun pressed to the still-unconscious Strange's head in the ultimate diplomatic maneuver.

The heavy door slid open to reveal a small control room whose walls were covered with dedicated meters and monitors. There were even physical knobs and levers for the most critical controls. No "glass cockpit" here—fusion control was simple, basic, and robust, hard to get wrong and impossible to hack. Which was why the door was so secure.

There was no reason for Strange to have known how to operate the fusion plant. But, Strange being Strange, he'd finagled a copy of the manual—hardcopy, of course—from one of the operators and had memorized it. Never can tell when something like that might come in handy.

In some ways, I had a lot of respect for my previous self. But his priorities … well, mine were different now.

I turned to Shweta, standing outside the open door. There was really only room for one person in the control room. "May I borrow that?" I asked, referring to the large wrench she had used to knock Strange out, which she had tucked in her belt as a souvenir. She handed it to me. "Thank you," I said, politely.

And then I twisted every feed knob all the way to the right and every damper all the way to the left, using the wrench to smash each one into a worthless, abstract tangle. It was very satisfying.

Alarms began to sound almost immediately. I ignored them, and there was no one in the office behind us—which would under ordinary circumstances have been staffed 24/7—to hear them and rush over to stop me. By the time I'd smashed the last knob, the noise was deafening. "Thank you for the use of your wrench," I yelled in Shweta's ear, politely.

Just to make sure, I scrambled the passcode before closing the door. I had to confirm three times that I had recorded the new code … but the confirmation process didn't verify that my eyes had been open. *No* one, not even me, was getting back into that room any time soon.

I brushed my hands together as the door slid closed behind me. "Now let's get out of here," I said, and shouldered Strange's body.

The EVACUATE signs weren't actually blinking any faster or brighter than they had before, but they seemed to have gained a new urgency. We certainly made the best possible time to the number eight escape pod cluster.

Tai, in the lead, reached the cluster first, and came hurrying back to me as I was dragging Strange around the last corner. "We have a problem," they said, and there wasn't a single gram of flippancy in their voice, which told me it was extremely serious.

I glanced at Strange—still out cold, wrists still firmly sticky-stripped—and dropped him unceremoniously. We hurried back to the cluster.

We had a problem.

It was extremely serious.

The reason there was still one pod left in this cluster, unlike any of the others nearby, was that this pod had been under maintenance. An entire segment of its hull was missing—presumably taken back to the shop for repairs. The gap where it had been was over a meter square, way too big to patch. As soon as the pod lock's outer door opened, anyone inside the pod would be breathing vacuum.

"Well, shit," Kane said as he hobbled up.

Shweta's eyes were cold as she turned to me. "What's plan B?"

The evacuation map on the wall wasn't pretty. I tapped the nearest green dot. "At least ten minutes away," I said. "At a dead run."

"Assuming there's really a pod there," Tai snapped.

"True," I admitted. I stared at the map, comparing it with my memory palace. Looking for shortcuts. Ducts. Chutes. Ladders. Anything.

Alicia looked dubious at the prospect of a dead run. "And how long do we have?"

I shrugged, still staring at the map. "There's no timer on this bomb. It blows when it blows. Maybe an hour, maybe half an hour? But we need to be well away from here when it does, if we want to survive." I shook my head. "There's nothing nearer. We'll need to patch this one."

"Where's the nearest workshop?" Tai said, already moving toward the door. "We'll need … hull patch, plastic sheeting, adhesives, I don't know what."

"Fusion control. Back the way we came."

"On it." Tai left the room … and then suddenly came flying back through the door, crashing into Alicia, sending the two of them and Alicia's walker clattering to the floor.

"What?" Shweta shouted, reaching for her gun … and then something smashed into her jaw. She too collapsed in a heap.

It was Strange—swinging Shweta's wrench, which she must have left near the door. His hands were scraped raw, covered with blood, like the hands of someone who was going to get out of those sticky-strips no matter how much damage it did.

Kane drew his pistol and fired, but Strange dove below the shot, sliding on his belly across the floor, scooping up Shweta's dropped pistol as he came. He got off one shot as he rolled to a stop. Kane shouted "Agh!" and fell.

Strange came up in a crouch with the gun leveled firmly at me. "Drop it," he panted.

I dropped my pistol. I knew for a fact that if I didn't, I wouldn't live another moment.

"Now put them in the pod."

Part of me wanted to drag the process out, just to keep Strange busy until the fusion plant blew. But part of me wanted to move fast, hoping against hope that I'd find a way out of this situation with enough time left to escape. I still wanted to live, damn it.

The part that wanted to move fast also had the encouragement of Strange and his pistol. It won.

Kane had a long furrow along the side of his head, streaming with blood, but he was still alive and groaning. Tai, too, was still alive, but unconscious, as was Shweta, who probably had a broken jaw. Alicia was merely stunned, but once Strange grabbed Tai's pistol and backed into the far corner, he had the drop on both of us. Again. Damn him.

Strange had me sticky-strip everyone at elbows, wrists, knees, and ankles, then drag them into the pod. Alicia didn't go quietly. "You little *shit!*" she screamed at Strange. "You *meant* something to me!"

"And you meant something to me," he admitted, though neither his voice nor his pistol wavered. "You all did. But I'm afraid Tai was right—you all know too much about me. I've sacrificed a lot to achieve my current position, and if I were to leave you alive and free that would jeopardize it too much."

Alicia struggled and shouted obscenities, but Strange had us both under the gun. He made me carry her into the pod and fasten her sticky-stripped wrists to a cargo tie-down, making sure he could see that the work was done to his satisfaction. I did the same to the others, unconscious though they were.

Strange and I stared at each other for a moment after that, both of us clearly thinking the same thing and both coming to the same conclusion: if Strange tried to hold the gun on me and tie my wrists at the same time, I would probably escape. So he just pressed the pistol to the base of my skull and physically forced me into the pod, then slammed the door behind me. I immediately tried the latch, but by the time I could turn around and get my hands on it, he had already wedged the wrench into the handle's outside arm. I pushed and rattled it anyway, but that did as little good as I'd expected.

I pressed my cheek against the little round window in the pod door. "You've still lost!" I shouted, my breath fogging the plastic. At this point, it was just a middle finger from the grave.

"Oh, I know you've rigged the fusion plant to blow," he said. "But I can still eject the core and save the station. And first I'm going to kill *you*, you snot-nosed by-blow." He strolled to the control console opposite, dramatically hovering his finger over the red LAUNCH button. "I wish I'd never met your mother."

Then there came a *bang*.

Two lifetimes of training kicked in: I blew out my breath and clenched my eyes shut against the sudden decompression. I wasn't sure what I could do in the minute or two of consciousness I'd have, but I wasn't going to go out without a fight.

But the decompression didn't come.

It took a moment for the realization to penetrate my brain. Once it did, I took in the breath I'd just expelled—it was one of the sweetest breaths I'd ever taken—and opened my eyes.

Through the little window I couldn't see much, just the control console with the blinking red LAUNCH button. No sign of Strange, no indication what had happened to him.

And then Lee came into view, moving cautiously, gaze firmly down, shoulders set and arms straight. She was holding a gun two-handed, pointed toward the floor. She paused, apparently turning something over with her foot ... and then her face relaxed into a complicated expression of sadness, disappointment, anger, and maybe a few other things. She shook her head, just slightly, then looked to me. "Are you okay?" she asked.

"I'm okay ... mom," I said. I hoped she hadn't noticed the hesitation.

My own expression at that moment was probably pretty complicated too, no matter how good my control was. This was the first time I'd seen Lee in almost two years. I'd lived with her; I'd loved her, to some extent. She was the mother of my child—of *me*. Of this body anyway.

I would trust her with my life.

Hell, she'd just saved it.

And I had about two seconds to decide how I was going to play this.

Lee came over to the pod, pulled the wrench out of the handle, and opened the door. I fell out and landed in a heap on the floor. The events of the past few hours had hit me harder than I realized.

Strange lay on the floor near the console. His face was a mass of blood, two white staring eyes below a ragged hole in the forehead. Dead for sure, this time.

More complicated feelings. Very complicated. Even after two years of being Cayce, Strange's face was still *my* face at a very deep level, and seeing it destroyed was more than a little disturbing. And even now, even being who I was and knowing what I did, I could see his side of things. I couldn't deny that if I'd been in his position, I might have done exactly the same things. If nothing else—and egotistical though I knew the thought was—I regretted that I would never get another chance to face off with someone who was so much my equal in every way.

"So ..." It was Lee's voice. I turned my eyes away from Strange's ruined face to hers. She seemed ... remarkably unpleased to see me, given that it was the first time in two years and she had just saved my life. I couldn't fail to notice that she still held her pistol, safety off, though her finger extended along the trigger guard rather than resting on the trigger. "Where have you been all this time ... son?"

She'd noticed my hesitation.

"It's complicated," I said.

I couldn't lie to her.

"I'm not Cayce," I admitted. "Not really."

Sounds of movement from the pod. Alicia cried "No!"

Without taking her attention from me, Lee shoved the pod door closed with her hip and leaned against it, ignoring the noises that came from behind it. Her finger slipped quietly onto the trigger, though the pistol remained aimed at the floor. For the moment.

Then my pocket comm vibrated, which was really not something I'd been expecting. But Lee heard it, and the pistol came up to target my heart. "Hand it over." Moving slowly and non-threateningly, I pulled the comm from my pocket with two fingers and slid it across the floor to her. She picked it up and flung it away, still buzzing, into the corridor outside.

"So," she repeated. "You're not Cayce. Please explain."

I took a breath ... then I told her exactly who and what I was. That Cayce was gone, and that Strange had killed him and a copy of his mind—me—had taken over his body. I had more than enough details to convince her of the truth of what I said, especially given that she'd been working on the Cronos Project for years and knew what the general idea was—though she hadn't been privy to all the details that Strange had managed to ferret out.

"And if the Cronos Project is allowed to continue," I said, "the rich will keep on killing poor people and taking their bodies, just like Strange killed Cayce. Cayce didn't want that to happen. He'd seen it happen to his friend Stef, and he was willing to die to keep it from happening to anyone else. And after that … after I left here two years ago, I realized he was right. So I came back to stop it. And I'm still committed to that. To honor our son's last wish. Even if it costs me my life."

It all came rushing out. I didn't really think it through. But even as the words passed my lips, I realized they were one hundred percent true.

I didn't want to die. But I would if I had to.

Lee slid down the door until she was sitting on the floor, still keeping the pod shut with her weight and still keeping the pistol trained on me. "You keep talking about 'Strange' and 'Cayce,'" she observed. "But … who are *you?*"

I thought long and hard about that. "I … I'm *not* Cayce," I said at last. "This is his body"—I slapped my heart with my open palm—"but I don't remember *being* him. I *do* remember being Strange"—my eyes drifted from Lee's face to the body on the floor—"but I'm not him either. Not completely. Not anymore." I looked back at Lee. "And I remember *you.* I remember … living with you." I couldn't quite make myself say *loving.* "There's something of you in me, in this body's genetics. In *me.* I can see that—feel that—now. I don't know if biology is destiny, but I guess to some extent I'm the man Strange might have been if you'd been his biological mother."

The noises from the pod were getting louder. One or two of the others must be awake now. I thought they might have some pretty strong opinions about the situation, but Lee had the leverage—in both senses of the word—to keep the door shut if she wanted to, and she did. "He said you'd rigged the fusion plant to blow," she said to me, and now she aimed the pistol right between my eyes. "And he said he could eject the core and save the station. Can you do that?"

I considered the question carefully. "No," I said at last. "Strange might have been able to do it in time. Barely. If he'd started right away. But it's ten minutes later now, and he knew current passcodes that I'd have to guess, bypass, or hack my way around. Where's your ship?"

She shook her head. "When I realized Strange had stayed behind, I dumped everything so I could get back here quicker. Nobody's getting away in *that* pod."

"Pity."

"How long do we have?"

"Maybe twenty minutes. Tops."

"Pity. As you said." She contemplated my face for a long time. "You're *not* Cayce," she said at last. "A mother knows her son." Another long pause. "But you're right. *Cayce* was right. The project is … misguided. At best." She stretched out her legs and crossed her ankles, still keeping the gun leveled at me. "After you—after Cayce—left, Strange and I had a lot of arguments. A *lot* of arguments. Cayce's action opened my eyes to the consequences of the project, but in the end, Strange convinced me to stay on board. You know how persuasive he could be. But now …" Her eyes inclined toward Strange's body, though the pistol remained focused on me. She sighed. "There's been enough killing. It should end here." She looked back at me, and though the gun was still pointed in my direction, it relaxed somewhat. "The crew has gotten away. It's just you folks and me. And we're all going to stay here until everything goes boom."

I considered my options.

There weren't any.

It was … kind of a relief, actually.

"I just have one question," she continued. "Zephyr. The tortoise. Do you know where he is now? I could never get Strange to give me a straight answer."

"Ah. Well …. Yes. That." Zeph had been a gift from Lee to Strange during their brief intense affair. I remembered evading that question, when I'd been Strange, and I wasn't surprised Strange had continued to evade it after he and I had parted ways. But I saw no reason not to be honest now. "I'm afraid he died at Orca Station. He was on *Contessa* when she blew. But our new ship, the ship we came in on, is named after him. Fastest ship in the System."

"That's … that's good. Poetic, really."

Then this charming mother-son reunion, or whatever it was, was interrupted by a sudden and unexpected *clunk* from the vacant pod dock to my left. The sound of something locking on from outside. Lee's eyes met mine and we both surged to our feet and away from the hatch.

Then the door blew open, slamming against the wall beside it as a gust of air knocked both Lee and I back on our asses.

The blast of air was followed by the entrance of Miyuki, of all people, silhouetted against the clean white light from *Zephyr*'s forward lock.

She was holding a gun on Lee. It was one of Kane's. It was big. "Drop it, bitch!" she shouted.

Lee, still on her knees, set her pistol carefully down on the deck and raised her hands. I immediately scooped it up, stepping back and training it on Lee's heart from a good distance away. "Thank you," I said to Miyuki. "But please don't talk to my mother like that. And take the safety off." Miyuki grimaced with chagrin and flicked the safety off. It was a good thing Lee hadn't been able to see it from her angle. "Now open the pod and get the others out."

"Overpressuring the lock was very clever," I said to Miyuki as Kane and Tai carried the still-unconscious Shweta from the pod to *Zephyr*. I didn't take my eye off Lee, who sat on the floor with hands raised. "Your idea?"

Miyuki shook her head. "Tai's. And Kane told me where to find the gun and what to say."

I nodded. If Shweta had been awake, the scene might have run a little differently. "How did you know where to find us?"

"I told her," Alicia said, rising from her inspection of her walker. It had been smashed by the impact of Tai's body and would have to be remade. She leaned on the wall and started making her way toward *Zephyr*.

"I turned around when I got the distress signal," Miyuki explained, "and called all of you as soon as I got back in range." That must have been when my comm had buzzed. "I was just about ready to give up when Alicia finally answered."

Alicia grunted. "It took me a while to get Tai's comm out of their pocket with my foot, okay?" She stared at me. "Did you really have to tie us so tight?"

I shrugged. "Strange was watching me."

"Uh huh." She didn't seem convinced, but she had reached the lock and stepped inside *Zephyr*, assisted by Tai. I glanced at Miyuki and gestured to her to follow with my chin, then returned my full attention to Lee.

"So," I said, and in that moment I recognized how much my voice sounded like hers. "You want to join us in our life of crime? Never a dull moment."

Lee considered the offer, then shook her head sadly. "No. To see your face, day after day, knowing that my son is gone and that *you* killed him? I couldn't bear it."

I wasn't happy to hear that, but I nodded my understanding. "Can I offer you a lift to the rendezvous point, then? We can get there before anyone else and drop you in a suit. You won't have to wait more than a few hours."

She gazed at Strange's ruined face for a long while, then put out a hand and gently squeezed his blood-soaked shoulder before turning back to me. "All right," she said.

"Come *on!*" Kane's voice came from behind me.

"Coming," I called back, and helped Lee to her feet. "I'm sorry," I said to her, and I was as sincere in that as I ever have been about anything.

"I'm sorry too. Now let's go."

We went.

ELEVEN

The Next Job

The Cannibal Club—Present Day

We were six then, at the beginning. Though there were actually seven on board *Zephyr* when we departed Cronos Station.

As soon as Cayce and Lee came on board, Kane slammed the lock behind them and hollered "Go!" into the comm. Miyuki blew the seal unceremoniously and powered away on maximum thrusters.

"Radiation levels are already past critical!" Tai shouted from their station. "Skip now! Skip skip *skip!*"

"Not yet ..." Miyuki growled through gritted teeth. The station was massive enough to disrupt skip in its immediate vicinity.

Meanwhile, Cayce and Kane finished securing Shweta in the medical bay and scrambled to the control room, where Alicia and Lee had already strapped themselves in.

"Hang on ..." Miyuki said.

And then a bright light flared from half the screens, followed almost immediately by a rattle on the hull, as the station's power plant blew itself to smithereens. The rain of fragments rapidly accelerated from a patter to a storm ...

… and then dropped away to silence as *Zephyr* fled into the skip. Tai blew out a breath. "Too close."

A few bits of shrapnel rattled on the hull, drawn into the skip with us, as Tai pulled up an exterior view on the big screen. It was nothing but a huge flare of light, cut by a dark curve—a bit of the station's ring that happened to be between us and the exploding fusion plant. Even that vanished a moment later, dissolving into fragments and then vanishing completely.

The light of Cronos Station's death flared for a while longer, then dimmed to darkness. The screen compensated then, revealing a few ragged fragments still glowing red, but these too soon faded to black, vanishing behind us as they cooled and receded into the distance.

"Good thing we're so far out," said Tai to no one in particular. "That's going to be a traffic hazard for *years*."

We gathered in the galley a few hours later, after dropping Lee off at the rendezvous point and getting ourselves bandaged and cleaned up and fed. Kane had even managed a nap, after getting his head wound stitched up. Shweta was a little foggy from the pain meds, and with her teeth glued together—the jaw was indeed broken, though it wasn't bad enough to require surgery—she couldn't talk very well, but she used sign to get around that.

After we get to wherever we're going, Shweta signed, *do we stay together?* The question was directed to the Club as a whole, but she glared at Cayce as she signed it. "Can. We. Trusht. Him?" she enunciated carefully.

Tai crossed their arms on their chest. "That's a damn good question." They had changed into a black velvet captain's coat with epaulets and silver piping and four rows of buttons, which gave them confidence and an air of authority. They ticked off points on their fingers, looking at Cayce as they spoke. "You lied to all of us, repeatedly, including about the very basic question of *who you were*. You got us into a situation in which we all damn near got killed, and we wound up with nothing. And you *killed your own damn son!*"

Kane snorted. "We're none of us angels."

"It's complicated," Alicia said, which wasn't exactly a ringing defense.

Miyuki remained silent. It was hard for the rest of us to know what she was thinking. That would come along, in time … if we stayed together.

We all looked to Cayce, who seemed remarkably subdued—even uncertain, which was a rarity for him. Now that we knew who he really was, his previous confidence and capabilities made more sense. But now, with all pretense stripped away, we saw him as he was—an old and cynical soul in a young, vulnerable, and extremely conflicted body.

"That's all true," he said at last. "And I'm not going to try to defend my actions, or my lies. I did what I thought I needed to do. Some of that was just plain wrong, and I knew it at the time. But, going forward, I will work to make amends. Whether you choose to accept me on those terms is up to you." He looked around at all of us. "But before you decide … you need to understand exactly who you are dealing with. Who you are going to partner with, or not."

He closed his eyes, took in a breath, let it out slowly through his nose. "I remember being Strange, okay? I remember pushing the button to transfer my mind to Cayce's body. I knew what I was doing. I told myself that Cayce's consciousness might survive in some fashion, but I realize now that even then I was lying to myself." Cayce opened his eyes. "But although I remember pushing that button … I'm not the person who did it, not anymore. Certainly not physically"—he gestured down at his skinny sixteen-year-old body—"and no longer mentally. I *feel* different now. I didn't realize until I met Strange, and Lee, just *how* different I've become."

No one spoke. It was clear that Cayce was working something through as he talked, and we were willing to hear him out. He'd earned that much, at least.

"Is biology destiny? Or does mind trump matter? If you put a forty-three-year-old mind in a fourteen-year-old body, do those habits of mind outweigh the chemistry and structure of the new brain? I'm no scientist, but I read all the reports, and I think even the Cronos Project scientists didn't know for sure. They assumed the mind would win out—that's kind of the premise of the project— but having lived through the process, I think they were wrong." He looked around at the rest of us. "I don't remember being Cayce, at all, but I *feel* more like Cayce than Strange … I think. It's hard to tell from in here." He tapped his temple. "And I'm not sure exactly which parts are which, and I'm sure it will continue to change over time."

"So … can you trust me?" He shrugged. "All I can say is that I am who I am, whatever that is. Same as anyone, really. If the events of the last few months don't demonstrate to you that I can be trusted … well, you can drop me off somewhere and keep the ship. It really doesn't matter where. Hell, you can kick me out right here. Just leave me a suit. I'll find a way to survive, somehow."

We all considered the question. Even Cayce wondered what was the right thing to do. But as we looked around the circle, exchanging postures and glances rather than words, it became clear that we all knew where we stood.

We were the Cannibal Club. Closer than family, closer than lovers. Better than ever, in fact—we realized that in our years with Strange, he had kept us siloed, restricted to our specialties, while Cayce had encouraged us to cross-train and broaden out. And now we had the fastest ship in the Solar System.

It was Alicia who broke the silence. "Strange would never have offered to let us leave him behind," she said. "He would have found a way to manipulate us into keeping him around."

Kane snorted. "That's for damn sure." And Shweta grinned, though one side of her face didn't move because of the anesthetics.

Tai looked at Cayce a bit askance. "So if you aren't Strange, and you aren't Cayce, what do we call you?"

He blinked. "Well … I've been 'Cayce' for the past two years. I'm kind of used to it." He fell silent for a moment, then nodded sharply, and perhaps a tear glistened in the corner of one eye. "Yes," he said. "Call me Cayce. In his honor."

"Cayce," we all said—even Shweta slurred it—and it was like a christening.

"So …" said Kane, looking around and rubbing his hands. "Here we are again. Still. The Cannibal Club. Where do we go next?"

Cayce grinned fiercely. "I have a plan …"

Acknowledgements

David D. Levine—June 2023

Writers work alone, but a novel is a team effort. Here are some of the people who helped make this one possible.

My agent, Paul Lucas, who kept on believing. My publisher, Shahid Mahmud, and editor, Lezli Robyn, for turning the manuscript into a book.

Mary Robinette Kowal, for sharing her family home and a thousand other things. Laura Anne Gilman, for help figuring out how to grift a grifter and much else besides. Emily Chenoweth, for the "Write a Novel in Eight Weeks" class which was extremely helpful although it actually took me almost six years to finish the damn thing. Grá Linnea, for the Coastal Heaven novel workshop. Patrick Swenson, for the Rainforest Writers Village writing retreat. DongWon Song, who said that I should "one hundred thousand percent call it a space opera!"

Cecilia Tan, for transcontinental support and plot advice. Kathy Kitts, for insights about planetary science and related topics. Lee Godfrey and Marie Brennan, for help with zero-gee combat. Yuki

Saeki, for illustrations of the Cannibal Club. Erin Cashier, for insights on the publishing biz and setting expectations. Alan Smale, for recommending Arc Manor. Andrew McCollough and Loreen Heneghan, for critique at Coastal Heaven.

Mishell Baker and Isabel Yap, for a tweet thread about "post-trilogy syndrome" that made me cry. Deliah S. Dawson, for a tweet thread about villains that helped me understand who the villain of this book really was. Fonda Lee, Curtis Chen, Cat Rambo, Rebecca Roanhorse, Nisi Shawl, Alison Wilgus, Piper J. Drake, Malka Older, Kelly Robson, and others for hosting Zoom writing dates on the Airship Nebula.

Sara Mueller, Thorn Coyle, Sarah Gailey, Sandra Tayler, Alethea Kontis, K. Tempest Bradford, Shanna Germain, Monte Cook, Jennifer Willis, Amanda Clarke, Jennifer Linnea, Robin Catesby, Dave Molner, Rhiannon Marie Louve, Alberto Yáñez, Mark Ferrari, Shannon Page, Brenda Cooper, Miriam Zellnik, Myrlin Hermes, and Sam Dyche for writing dates and moral support.

And Alisa Wood-Walters, Amy Young-Leith, Lee Godfrey, and Cynthia Nalbach, who were there when I needed them.

◆ ◆ ◆